On the Lee Shore

On the Lee Shore

by

Philip K. Allan

ISBN-13: 978-1-946409-48-5(Paperback)
ISBN :13: 978-1-946409-49-2(e-book)
BISAC Subject Headings:

FIC014000FICTION / Historical
FIC032000FICTION / War & Military
FIC047000FICTION / Sea Stories

Editing: Chris Wozney
Cover Illustration by Christine Horner

Address all correspondence to:
Penmore Press LLC
920 N Javelina Pl
Tucson, AZ 85748

Dedication

To my Suzy Q

Acknowledgements

Like most authors, I rely on the support and help of those around me to help make my vision a reality. The books of the Alexander Clay series start with a passion for the Age of Sail. Mine first began to stir when I read the works of C S Forester as a child. Then, in my twenties, I graduated to the novels of Patrick O'Brian. That interest was given a little academic rigor when I studied the 18th century navy under Pat Crimmin as part of my history degree at London University.

Many years later, when I decided to leave a comfortable career in the motor industry to see if I could make it as a novelist, I received the unconditional support and cheerful encouragement of my darling wife and two wonderful daughters. I strive to make sure that my work is accessible for those without a detailed knowledge of the period, or a particular interest in the sea, and the crucible of my family is where I first test my work to see if I have hit the mark. I have also been helped by the input of my dear friend Peter Northen.

One of the most unexpected pleasures of my new career is to find that I have been drawn into a community of fellow authors, who offer generous support and encouragement to each other. When I needed help and advice the most, I received it from David Donachie, Bernard Cornwell, Marc Liebman, and in particular Alaric Bond, creator of the Fighting Sail series of books.

Finally my thanks go to the team at Penmore Press, Michael, Christine, Chris, Terri and Midori who work so hard to turn the world I have created into the book you hold in your hand.

List of Contents

Chapter 1
The Savage

The last gale of the winter had grown in fury all day. Long lines of slate-grey waves swept in from the open Atlantic to batter against the bow of His Majesty's frigate *Titan* as she struggled to hold her course in the Western Approaches to the Channel. Rain poured off her rigging in silver skeins and drummed down onto the tarpaulin hats of her crew as they huddled for what shelter they could find underneath the gangways. On the quarterdeck George Taylor, the *Titan*'s grey-haired first lieutenant, struggled across the steep pitch of the deck to where his captain stood, and saluted with one hand whilst clinging on to the mizzen shrouds with the other.

'What is it, Mr Taylor?' growled Captain Sheridan. Taylor bent his head close to make himself heard above the roar of the storm and the thunderous flapping from both men's oilskins as the wind tore at them. He was near enough to be able to smell the alcohol fumes on Sheridan's breath, in spite of the rushing air.

'I submit we need to take another reef in the foretopsail sir,' yelled the lieutenant. 'She is over burdened now that the wind has freshened.' The captain rolled his yellow eyes towards the foremast. He noted the way the ship struggled to shoulder her way through the heavy sea, and saw that the foretop yard was bent like a bow by the power of the wind.

'Very well, Mr Taylor,' said Sheridan. 'Do as you see fit.'

'Aye aye, sir,' replied Taylor. He touched his hat again to his captain and then made his way across the rain-soaked planking to the rail at the front of the quarterdeck. He wiped the spray from his face, cupped a hand against his mouth and yelled towards the forecastle. His order was soon picked up by the boatswain's mates, and their calls shrilled through the ship as they summoned the men on deck.

'All hands! All hands to take in sail!'

Soon a flood of seaman made their way up the shrouds. The gale howled through the rigging, making the soaked rope hum beneath their hands and feet. Once they were level with the foretop cross-trees they spread out to their places on the yard. They lay across the wooden spar and reached down to claw up the sodden canvas and secure it into place. In the strong wind their clothes ballooned and thrashed about like so much washing on a line. Taylor watched their efforts with concern, unaware that his captain had made his uncertain way forward to join him at the quarterdeck rail.

'You are wholly deficient in your management of the men, Mr Taylor,' said Captain Sheridan. 'Look at the leisurely fashion in which they go about their duties. They make sport of your kindly nature behind your back, you know. You must be firmer with the blackguards.'

'But the yard is wet and treacherous, sir,' protested the lieutenant. 'I submit the care they take is quite necessary in these conditions.' The captain ignored him and reached forward to take the speaking trumpet from its becket. It dropped with a clang to the deck, and a midshipman stooped to recover it. Sheridan tilted his head back into the storm, the rain running off his face, and bellowed up at the yard.

'You're all too damned slow!' he roared. 'Master at arms! I want the name of the last man off the yard. He shall have three dozen at the grating.'

The result of his threat on the lofty spar was electric. Men battled to complete the reef in the sail with no regard to those about them, and then flung themselves for the backstays. With almost all of his shipmates pouring down the rigging, the sailor at the extreme end of the yard realised he was going to be the last to come down. He pulled himself up onto the yardarm, took a few uncertain steps along the top of it and turned to jump across to the backstay. As he launched himself, Taylor saw one foot slip. For a moment the man was airborne, a silhouette against the grey sky, arms stretching out to catch the rope he would never reach. Then he turned through the air in a slow cartwheel as he fell, gathering speed like an avalanche till his descent was stopped by the iron-hard deck. No one moved to help him. Lieutenant Taylor saw the faces of the crew, blank with shock as they turned towards the quarterdeck. The captain swayed for a moment with the rain cascading from his oilskins and the speaking trumpet loose in his hand. Then he returned it to his mouth.

'Master at Arms!' he bellowed. 'Bring me the name of the second from last man off the yard instead.'

*****

'I am telling you, Mrs Walsh, it is quite in opposition to what is natural,' exclaimed Old Widow Fry. The stiff black bonnet that she had worn every day since the death of her husband quivered with the strength of her emotions. 'How can it be endured?' she continued. 'Never in life have I heard of such a thing. A blackamoor, attending the village schoolhouse alongside honest Christian children. My only comfort is that dear Mr Fry never lived to see the like.'

'You're so right,' agreed her neighbour. 'Why, I shudder to think of the savage cunning he might employ to corrupt those poor innocents behind the teacher's back.'

'I would not be surprised at all if presently those same children were to scorn the wearing of clothes and take to the woods with bones through their noses, you mark my words,' said the widow.

'Oh, don't I know it, Mrs Fry,' replied Mrs Walsh. 'And yet Mrs Clay seems to be such a decent, upstanding lady. I cannot conceive why she might allow that son of hers to return to the village with his Negro follower. He may be a naval captain now, but even so... ' Mrs Walsh dropped this last choice piece of gossip in with deceptive indifference.

'What!' spluttered the widow. 'Young Alexander Clay, a naval captain? Why, he is barely out of the schoolhouse himself.'

'In truth he is a little older than you suppose, Mrs Fry,' said her neighbour. 'Did he not first go to sea as a child, during the war with those wicked, rebellious Americans?'

'I suppose that might make him as much as eight or nine and twenty years now,' conceded Old Widow Fry. 'How did he come to be so senior a rank then?'

'Mrs Clay was saying that he has captured some manner of Spanish galleon, out in the Americas, or thereabouts. They made him a post captain on the spot for the deed,' said Mrs Walsh. Her companion sniffed at this.

'That may all be very fine,' she said, ' but that don't give him licence to overrun the village with half the savages he may have chanced upon during his travels. Why, we might all be murdered in our beds.'

'Very likely,' agreed Mrs Walsh. Her neighbour looked around her and dropped her voice.

'Or perhaps we shall suffer an even worse fate,' she muttered.

'Worse than being killed, Mrs Fry?' queried her fellow gossip. 'Whatever can you mean by that?' The widow beckoned her neighbour closer, till their trembling bonnets were almost touching.

'I hear that Negro men have certain appetites,' whispered the widow. Mrs Walsh shivered with delight.

'What manner of appetites?' she asked.

'Base appetites of a most impure lustfulness which they are wholly unable to control,' said Old Widow Fry. Her neighbour squeezed her eyes closed, all the better to envisage the horror of the prospect.

'Good morning, ladies,' said a deep voice from the path behind them. The neighbours' heads clashed together as they both spun round to find themselves face to face with the object of their concern. Mrs Walsh let out a shriek while the widow rubbed at the place where her friend's solid cranium had struck home.

'I hope I did not startle you,' added the sailor, his hand still holding up his hat. 'Are you unwell, Mrs Fry? Shall I help you to sit down?'

'No, no!' cried the widow. 'I shall be fine in a moment. Come no nearer, if you please.'

An awkward pause followed as the man, who had been hastening forward, stopped in confusion, while the two ladies seemed to be frozen with fear.

'Well, I will be on my way then,' said the man at last. 'Good day to you both.' Then he replaced his hat and, without showing any immediate signs of wanting to murder, or indeed ravish, either septuagenarian, he resumed his way towards the village school.

Able Sedgwick was certainly an imposing figure. He was a tall, pleasant looking young man. His face was handsome enough, with a solid jaw framed by short sideburns. He kept his black hair cut short, except at the nape of the neck, where the beginnings of a pigtail was tightly plaited and secured with a neat blue ribbon. His deep brown eyes looked out on the world with intelligence tinged with sadness. He was dressed in the high-waisted trousers and tight short blue jacket of a shore-going sailor, and the clothes suited his powerful frame well.

Regrettably that same powerful build made it difficult for him to squeeze into the tiny place allocated for him in the back row of the schoolroom when he arrived there. The bench he sat on had obviously been designed with a much smaller person in mind. His long legs protruded far beyond the narrow table that served as a desk, and the bench creaked a little when he shifted his considerable weight on it as he tried to get comfortable. When he was wedged into place, he was able to look around him. The room was small and bare, with a swept wooden floor and whitewashed walls. It had four rows of benches, each with one of the narrow tables before it. Pupils' places were indicated by wooden framed squares of slate and pieces of chalk. Behind where Sedgwick sat, the spring sunshine flooded into the room through a large, arched window that looked out onto the village green. At the front of the room hung a blackboard and a square of white canvas with the letters of the alphabet painted on it. There were ten other children in the room, the oldest of whom was just half the age of the sailor, and all of whom were staring round at him. He rummaged in his pocket for a moment, then turned to the little boy who sat next to him on the bench.

'Thomas, I nearly forgot,' he said. 'I have finished that beast I said how I would make for you.' He produced a small carved wooden animal and gave it a final polish on his sleeve before placing it on top of his neighbour's slate.

'Oh, thank you, Mr Sedgwick!' exclaimed the boy. He examined his gift with obvious pleasure. 'Is that truly what your proper oliphant looks like then?'

'I think so, although I ain't no authority on the subject,' explained the sailor. 'I've only seen one before in my life.'

'Really?' queried the boy. 'I thought how Africa was quite thick with oliphants.'

'Some parts may be,' conceded Sedgwick, 'but not where I come from. It were a while ago now that I saw him, when I was no older than you are now. My uncle and I found the remains in the forest near my village.' He tapped the back of the carving with his index finger. 'Best as I can remember, he looked like that.' Thomas picked the carved elephant up and made it walk across the desk a few times, watched with envy by his fellow pupils.

'Was your village very like Lower Staverton then, Mr Sedgwick?' he asked.

'No, not really,' answered the sailor. 'It were on the banks of a much larger river than the mill stream, for a start. Proper close to the sea and quite surrounded by forest.'

'Any lions?' asked Thomas, his eyes alight.

'No lions,' he replied. He noticed Thomas's look of disappointment and added quickly. 'But there was no end of leopards in the forest, which are quite the equal for your lion when it comes to ferocity.' The boy nodded at this, as if it confirmed a view he had long held.

'Did your village have a church spire as tall as ours?' he asked.

'No, for it had no church, or any manner of stone buildings for that matter,' replied Sedgwick.

'No church? What, not even a chapel?' queried the boy. 'How wonderful! My mother makes me go to church every Sunday without fail, and twice during the week. I wonder at you ever choosing to leave such a grand place?'

'Well now, it wasn't so much a matter of my leaving or no,' replied the sailor. 'It were all a bit complicated like. See, I was made to go by these men who came to my village.'

'Why would they have done such a wicked thing?'

'Have you heard tell of slavery at all, Thomas?' asked Sedgwick. The boy scratched one cheek with the trunk of the elephant.

'I think the parson may have talked of that Pharaoh in Egypt and the Israelites once?' he said at last. 'Would that answer?'

'Aye, I was taken just like that.'

'And brought here to go to school?'

'Ah... well not exactly... you see... oh dear. Ah, here comes the teacher at last.'

With a clatter of shifting furniture, the class all rose to their feet.

'Good morning Mr Guthridge!' chanted ten high little voices and one booming bass.

*****

'Your coxswain is making tolerably good progress with his letters, according to Mr Guthridge,' said Betsey Clay to her brother as they sat together in the parlour of Rosehill Cottage. Clay looked up from his newspaper and across the cluttered table at his younger sister. Their late father's calm grey eyes were the only obvious feature that the two siblings had in common. Where Alexander Clay was a tall, lean man with curly chestnut hair, his younger sister was petite and fair, just like their mother would have been at the same age.

'He is quite a remarkable man, to be sure,' he agreed. 'Particularly if you consider that he spent his formative years as a field slave in Barbados. I believe he must be in possession of a very determined character. That is abundantly clear from how readily he has taken to his duties as a sailor.'

'Is that what motivated you to bring him back to England with you, Alex?' she asked.

'He proved his worth repeatedly on my last commission,' he replied. 'But I confess that part of my motivation was also the knowledge that he can never truly be free while he remains in the Caribbean. As a run slave he was unable to take any shore leave because of the danger of recapture, so the poor man had to remain on board ship whenever we were in port. At least in England he can walk through the village to the school house without arousing suspicion.'

'Do you know what he told me his chief objective was in acquiring an education?' said Betsey.

'He is not motivated by a simple desire to improve himself?' asked Clay.

'I am sure he is, brother,' she replied. 'But his stated aim is that he wishes to set down his experiences as a slave with a view to producing a work that may assist the abolitionist movement. He was asking my advice on how he might arrange to have such a tract published.'

'Did he, by Jove! Well, you are very much the expert there, Betsey,' said Clay. 'How does your second novel progress?'

'Oh, very ill indeed,' she sighed. 'I am dabbling with a little poetry at present, but my publisher is most insistent that I return to composing prose. *The Choices of Miss Amelia Grey* has sold so well that he wishes me to produce a fresh work soon to place before my public. Which reminds me, I must ask you for some advice.'

'On writing romantic novels!' exclaimed Clay. 'I fear my experience is sadly deficient where matters of the heart are concerned.'

'What nonsense, Alex,' scoffed Betsey. 'This from the man who has won the heart of the lovely Miss Lydia Browning?'

'Now that is most uncertain,' he cautioned. 'Our understanding has never received the sanction of her guardian, and since she has departed to far Bengal, I have no idea when we shall chance to meet again. I have received no replies yet to any of my letters.'

'You will, my dear,' smiled his sister. 'She is my friend too, you know. But it was not your intimate knowledge of the fairer sex that I stand in need of. It was your experience of the sea. I must have mentioned to my publisher that you were a naval captain, and he has written to me seeking some advice on behalf of one of his other authors. Now, where did I put his note?' Betsey scrabbled through the various piles of paper that cluttered the surface of the table, and emerged with the letter.

'Here we are... yes, I have it... *one of my authors of poetry, Mr Wordsworth...*' she read.

'Wordsworth?' said Clay. 'That's a deuced appropriate name for a poet.'

'Yes, I suppose it is,' said Betsey. 'It had not really struck me before. He is a notorious radical, you know, but a very accomplished writer. Now, where was I? ... *one of my authors of poetry, Mr Wordsworth, has a particular acquaintance who is a fellow writer of some potential. His friend desires to compose a long narrative poem set onboard a ship, but has little direct experience in that quarter. In conversation he confessed that he had been seeking guidance on matters nautical. He struggles in particular with how best to describe the sea in all its variety of states. I recalled that when we last met you informed me that your brother was a captain in the Royal Navy and that he was recovering from his wounds at home...* etc. Might you be able to oblige him at all, Alex?'

'How best to describe the sea?' mused Clay, 'That is much harder than it has any right to be, for its colour and general appearance alters much, depending on conditions. It is chiefly a mirror for the weather and the sky. Blue of course, but then the blue of the deep ocean is quite different to the blue of the Caribbean. Green in home waters, and grey more often than not, and sometimes even silver. I recall one time on the *Agrius* when we were becalmed for two days and nights crossing the Atlantic. The sea was so still it was as a sheet of glass. The ship and ocean might have been from a painting, they were both so in want of animation.'

'Why Alex,' exclaimed Betsey. 'You are quite the poet yourself when you try. I rather approve of your painted ship upon its painted ocean – I shall pass that image on to Mr Wordsworth's friend.'

'Oh Alex, do make haste!' said Mrs Clay as she burst into the room.

'Whatever is the matter, Mother?' he asked, jumping up from his chair.

'There is a uniformed messenger at the door,' she gasped, clutching her mop cap to her breast. 'He has a letter for you that he will only pass into your hands.' Clay exchanged glances with his sister, and strode out of the room.

'Do you believe it to be orders from the Admiralty?' asked Betsey. Her mother nodded.

'I could tell from the black wax seal,' she said. 'And who else would use such an official person to bring a letter?'

'We have known that this day would come, Mother. It has been a joy to have Alex here with us for these several months, but we always knew that it was not forever.'

'But he almost died the last time he was away!' wailed Mrs Clay. 'That shoulder of his is still not right. I cannot begin to picture what I should do if I was to lose my dear boy.' Betsey rose up from her chair and came across the room to comfort her mother. A little while later Clay walked back into the room, reading the letter as he came.

'Is it orders, Alex?' asked his sister.

'Yes Betsey,' he replied. 'I am to present myself at the Admiralty as soon as may be convenient.'

'Oh, did it say "when convenient",' said his mother with relief. 'That doesn't sound too urgent. Does that mean you may stay with us a little longer then?'

'I am sorry, Mother, but no,' he replied. 'It is just a polite form of words used in such communications. It means straight away, whether it is convenient or not. I had best go and get changed into my uniform.'

*****

Sir Charles Middleton, baronet, Admiral of the Blue and senior Naval Lord at the Admiralty, looked up from his desk as his clerk open the door of his office and put his head around the frame.

'Captain Clay is here to see you, Sir Charles,' he said.

'Ah, capital,' said Middleton. 'Do show him in, Fox.' His clerk swung the door open and then stood to one side to let the officer enter. The naval lord sat back in his chair to study his visitor with care. The young naval captain who walked through was a tall man with a full head of curly hair and matching sideburns. His uniform hung well on his lean, athletic frame, and he regarded Sir Charles with steady grey eyes. He seems pale for a man who has returned from the Caribbean, thought the admiral, and he holds his left arm a little carefully, but otherwise he seems to have made a good recovery.

'Captain Clay, thank you for coming to see me so promptly,' he said in his gentle mid-Lothian burr. He rose to his feet and extended a hand across his large desk. 'I am delighted to make your acquaintance. Do please take a seat, I pray. May I offer you some refreshment perhaps?' Middleton rang a small hand bell on his desk and the clerk returned to the room.

'Some Madeira for the captain and myself, if you please, Fox,' he ordered over Clay's shoulder, before sitting down again himself.

'Do I find you in good health, captain?' he asked. 'Has your period of convalescence served to quite restore you?'

'Tolerably well, Sir Charles,' answered Clay. 'My shoulder is still painful on occasion, and my left arm is a little deficient. I can no longer raise it above my head, for example. I am told by my physician that it is doubtful if I ever will be able to do so again. It means that I will not be able to climb the rigging as I once could. But perhaps now that I am made post that shall not be too excessive a burden.'

'Yes, a musket ball in the shoulder is a most unwelcome visitor,' agreed the admiral. 'Have you considered the waters at Bath? Admiral Howe has very decided opinions on their restorative powers for any ailment. Indeed he can barely be persuaded to quit the place, even when he had command of the Channel Fleet and the French were out, what?' To be polite Clay joined in with his superior's laughter, until Sir Charles was serious once more.

'So you are ready to return to duty, I collect?' he asked, gazing across the top of his glass of Madeira at the young captain.

'I am, Sir Charles,' replied Clay.

'Good, I am delighted to hear it,' said Middleton. 'The fact is, captain, I have been very much looking forward to meeting you. I have always regarded Admiral Caldwell to be a man of singular discretion. So when he prefers a man to whom he has no apparent ties of blood or long acquaintance by promoting him twice within twelve months, even Naval Lords may be persuaded to take note. Your defeat of that Don ship of the line, the *San Felipe,* with such a wee ship as your sloop was a most creditable action, and shows you to be a man of some intelligence as well as dash.'

'That is very kind of you to say so, Sir Charles,' said Clay. 'It was not achieved purely by my efforts. I was assisted by Captain Parker and the *Agrius.*' He let himself enjoy the praise of such a senior admiral, while deep inside he wondered what unpleasant duty it was that he was being buttered up for.

'Even so, it is rare for a sloop and a frigate to best a ship of the line, I am sure you will agree?' said the admiral. 'The fact is that the service stands in some need of officers who display intelligence as well as pluck. We are beset from all sides by enemies, not all of whom lie on the far side of the Channel.'

'Whatever can you mean, Sir Charles?' asked Clay.

'I mean sedition, treason, mutiny,' said Middleton, his face grim. 'Hardly a day goes by when a fresh petition from one ship or another does not cross my desk here at the Admiralty. Some of them complain about inferior vittles, others speak of being denied shore leave, but their principal complaint is of low wages. Are you aware that an ordinary seaman has not seen an increase in his rate of pay since the time of the Stuarts?'

'Can that be right?' exclaimed his visitor. 'Why, that would have been over a century ago!'

'I assure you that it is,' continued the admiral. 'So you can well imagine that when we press a man off a merchant ship where he will have been enjoying three-fold as much as we shall pay him, and then we hold that paltry amount for months in arrears, it is small wonder that he is inclined to resent the change. You will not have witnessed the effect this can have, serving as you have on a foreign station in smaller vessels with plenty of opportunity for prize money. For the line of battle ships of the main fleet where there is little prospect of such rewards, want of pay breeds great resentment, and it is that sense of injustice that those who would do us wrong feed upon. United Irishmen, Democrats, Jacobins, or any other base ne'er-do-wells who wish their country ill.'

'But if you hold these demands for better pay are warranted, why not accede to their request, Sir Charles?' asked Clay. 'Would that not answer to cure the problem?'

'I am quite sensible that many of their claims are just, but where is the money to come from?' said the admiral, 'The Board have repeatedly recommended an increase in sailors' pay, but the government is in the grip such of a financial crisis, and the Admiralty is forever asking for more money. We have a constant need for new ships, better dockyards, more stores – I tell you, bottomless pits aren't in it. Then to add insult to injury the army had their pay increased not two years ago. I inform you of all this not to alarm you, captain, but so you are aware of the background to the duty I have in mind for you to perform.'

'I understand, Sir Charles, and what, pray, is that duty?' asked Clay.

'On Monday last I received yet another petition, this time from the crew of the *Titan*,' explained Middleton. 'She is a fine well-found 36-gun frigate that serves as part of Commodore Sir Edward Pellew's Inshore Squadron blockading the principal French naval base at Brest. She put into Plymouth last week for stores and water, since when her crew have refused to weigh anchor and return to their station. I have the document they sent me here. It takes the form of a round robin, of course, so we have no notion as to which of all these signatures are the leaders of this mischief, but as you will see it is of a rather different character to those

I mentioned before.'

Clay accepted the sheet of paper as it was passed across the desk by the admiral. It was large and rather grubby. Someone with a reasonable hand had written a block of text in the centre, while arranged in rings around the margin were over a hundred signatures. Most had signed with a simple 'X' with a notation underneath. *Thomas Rodgers, his mark* he read under one of the shakier letters. Clay turned the paper round so he could read the writing in the middle.

To their Right Honorable Lords of the Admiralty

Sirs, we the loyal crew of His Majesty's ship Titan *most respectfully petition to solicit your help in a grave matter. You should know that we suffer very severely under the ill usage we have received from that tyrant Captain Sheridan which is more than the spirits and hearts of true Britons can bear, for we are born free but now we are slaves. He has punished us most savagely without reason, stopped our allowance of liquor without just cause, and of late has committed crimes worse even than these. During a topsail gale in the Soundings he did unjustly threaten to flog the last man to come down from the foretop yard, causing John Worthy, Able Seaman, to fall to his death which we do all hold is murder.*

We are all resolved that we shall no longer serve under Captain Sheridan, and we humbly submit he be removed from his post and that he be made accountable for his many crimes. Until this should happen we will not weigh anchor nor obey any orders Captain Sheridan shall issue.

We are all loyal to His Majesty King George, but if any attempt is made to force us to yield we are prepared to resist, and if pressed shall raise the red flag of Mutiny and will sail for France to hand over our ship to the enemy.

Signed by all the loyal petitioners of the Titan

'So what do you make of it?' asked Middleton.

'Are any of these names known to be trouble makers, Sir Charles?' asked Clay.

'There is only one we suspect might be,' replied Middleton. 'Richard Sexton. You will find his name on the left hand side, one of the few who is able to sign in full. He was a petty officer until late last year when Captain Sheridan had him reduced to the ranks for drunkenness and insubordination. It would be strange if he did not bear some sort of grudge.'

'There do seem to be a lot of Irish names here, Sir Charles,' continued Clay, looking up from the petition. 'Is that significant?'

'The *Titan* was based in Ireland for some time, so that is perhaps not strange,' said the admiral. 'But that may be a factor. The government is having considerable trouble at present with this damned United Irishmen movement, and there has been rebellion afoot on that unfortunate island.

England's woe is Ireland's chance, as they would have it.'

'Well, Sir Charles, I should say that the principal text shows an author who knows his Thomas Payne,' said Clay. 'The part about being born free but now we are slaves might have come directly from the pages of *The Rights of Man*. But these demands do not seem to be of a radical nature, nor to fit into those disputes about pay and conditions you are wont to receive. I have no knowledge as to the character of Captain Sheridan, but the allegations of the crew appear to be concerned with insupportable treatment at his hands, and a particular allegation concerning the death of this John Worthy. If true I would say that they must warrant an investigation.'

'I see you are very much of my way of thinking,' said Middleton. 'I do know a little more about Captain Sheridan than you, and I find little difficulty in believing him to be capable of such actions. That said, he will never swing for murder, as this petition demands. He is far too well connected, and in any instance the allegation is not one that can stand legal scrutiny. It is not as if he pushed this unfortunate man to his death. He has only to say that his threat was just that, a threat, and that he had no intension of carrying it out. Almost any court will conclude that this John Worthy's fall was an accident.'

'So what do you intend to do, Sir Charles?' asked Clay.

'I shall relieve Captain Sheridan from his command, and I will replace him with a man I can trust to restore the *Titan* back to a state of order and discipline,' said Middleton. 'It is a task that will require intelligence, for I do not believe that simple force will answer, matters have advanced too far for that now. I also believe that you may well be that man, Captain Clay, and I would be very much obliged if you will take command of this unhappy ship. You can promise the crew that the Board will give them their investigation, but as I have explained it is most doubtful that it will succeed as they have requested. After some months of the proper leadership that I am confident you shall supply, I am sure that this whole matter will be forgot.'

'May I ask what will become of Captain Sheridan, Sir Charles?' asked Clay.

'He will not command another ship while I serve at the Admiralty, you may be sure of that,' said Middleton. 'I have enough problems with all these other petitions to worry over much about captains who do not understand the limits of their authority. In time I may find some duties for him to perform on shore. So am I to take it that you are minded to accept the appointment?'

'I am, Sir Charles,' said Clay. 'If we can resolve some of the particulars with regards to followers. Is there any news of my former ship the *Rush?* She was due to return from the Caribbean shortly.'

'Yes, I believe she docked at Portsmouth two days ago,' said the admiral. 'What did you have in mind?'

'It will help me exceedingly if there are at least some among the crew of the *Titan* who know my worth,' he explained. 'Naturally I will have my servants and my coxswain Sedgwick, but I would also like to have four sailors who have volunteered to follow me in the past. I would appreciate it if they could be transferred from the *Rush* to the *Titan*.'

'That would seem reasonable, assuming the current commander of the *Rush* has no objection,' said Middleton.

'Commander Sutton is my particular friend, Sir Charles, so I am sure he will agree,' said Clay.

'Yes, especially as I understand that it was you that recommended him for promotion, what?' smiled the admiral. 'What else do you believe you will need?'

'A reliable officer I can trust in charge of the *Titan*'s marines, if you please Sir Charles,' he said. 'In case matters turn ugly. May I have Lieutenant Thomas Macpherson as my marine commander? He served under me in the Caribbean and currently commands the detachment on board the *Rush*.'

'Let Fox have the names on your way out, captain, and I will see that he makes all the arrangements,' said Middleton, rising to his feet. 'If that is agreed, I will have your orders sent to you later today. Congratulations on your new command, Captain Clay, and the very best of luck. Be firm but fair with the men, show no fear, and I am sure all shall be resolved.'

Chapter 2
Lines

Lines and yet more lines, everywhere I look, thought Clay, as he stood by the rail at the front of the quarterdeck of His Majesty's frigate *Titan*. To his left was a solid line, the arrow-straight column of the main mast soaring upwards. The space all around him was full of the black lines of stays and shrouds, like the mesh of a cage against the grey overcast Plymouth sky. Then there were the softer hemp lines of the running rigging, attached at regular intervals along the quarterdeck rail next to him that rose up above his head like the parallel strings of an enormous harp waiting to be plucked.

There were lines of men too. The line of largely unknown officers he had been introduced to moments earlier when he arrived, a river of names that had flowed past him. Only the last of them provided any warmth to his welcome, and he had gripped Lieutenant Thomas Macpherson's hand with genuine pleasure. The Scotsman's bristling dark sideburns and erect figure had spoken to him of calm confidence, but he had gone now to resume his place beside the triple line of his marines that stood on the quarterdeck behind Clay, leaving him alone at the rail.

The main deck below him was packed with the members of the crew, arranged in their divisions. He could see no one familiar here at all, apart from the solid figure of Sedgwick who stood to one side at the bottom of the companion ladder. None of his sailor followers had joined the ship yet. He scanned the lines of men and saw a mixture of surly and resentful expressions. Some faces were full of anger, others were contemptuous, while most of the rest seemed to be simply indifferent. He felt fear knot in his stomach. I have never seen such a sullen crew, he thought. He could feel the hostility in their gaze like a force throbbing in the air as they stared up at him. He reached into the inside of his coat and drew his orders from his pocket. He paused for a moment to let the trembling in his hand still a little, and to make sure that his voice would hit the right note. He swallowed hard in the hope that he could lubricate a throat which was now suddenly dry, and then he started the formal process of taking command of the ship.

'Orders from the Lord Commissioners of the Admiralty, addressed to Captain Alexander Clay of His Majesty's Navy,' he bellowed. 'You are hereby requested and required, immediately upon receipt of these orders, to take command of His Majesty's ship *Titan*.' Clay read through the rest of the words that were his authority for his new position. He knew that once he had reached the end of the brief document, he would have legal authority over all the men gathered around him. And yet it was only a piece of paper, he thought, and would protect him as little as it had his predecessor.

By the time he reached the end of his commission, he had decided what he would do next. He turned towards his new first lieutenant.

'Mr Taylor, I shall now inspect the crew. Kindly accompany me, if you please.'

'Do you really think that is wise… ' began the lieutenant, before he saw the look of determination on Clay's face. 'Aye aye, sir,' he concluded.

Clay started with the marines. They all stood upright at attention, their immaculate red coats contrasting with the white pipe clay of their cross belts. He moved along the line of faces, each frozen into stillness and all staring past him at something high in the foremast. Which of you can I trust? wondered Clay, as he strode along the line and looked at each man in turn. None of you were much help to Captain Sheridan, but which of you were active in opposing him, and which just stood aside and did nothing?

'You have a fine body of men there, Mr Macpherson,' he said, as he reached the end of the line. The marine officer swept his sword out in salute.

'Aye, they shall be, once I have had the leisure to lick them into shape, sir,' he replied. Clay returned the salute, and then walked down the companion ladder and out onto the main deck.

The men's hostility was all around him now. He could sense the animal power of it as if he had stepped into the centre of a bear pit. He took his time as he advanced down each line. Suppressed rage, unhappiness, indifference, he could see it all on the faces of his new crew. Not one of them bore any trace of welcome. He studied each with care, held their gaze and searched for clues. Which of you led the mutiny against Sheridan, and which of you was just swept along by the tide of anger, he asked himself. Whom can I trust, and whom must I watch? He stopped at one sailor who had a large rip in his shirt.

'What is your name?' he asked.

'Prince, sir,' replied the man, after a pause. 'Ordinary seaman in the afterguard.'

'And why is your shirt in such a state?' he continued. He saw fear in the sailor's eyes.

'I just tore it on the pump, sir,' he stuttered. 'Earlier today, like.'

'As we have only now encountered each other, Prince, I shall let it pass on this occasion; but in future I will expect you to appear at divisions properly dressed,' he said. 'Mr Taylor, see that the purser issues Prince with a new shirt.'

Another line and another row of hostile faces. Clay had almost reached the end when at last there was a change. A man was smiling, the gesture as welcome to him then as rain in the desert.

'I know you,' said Clay, his eyes narrowing with the effort to remember the long forgotten name. 'Davis!' he said at last. 'Foretop man in the old *Marlborough*. You taught me how to long splice when I was just a nipper.'

'That's right, sir,' replied the man. 'And look at you now, a captain and all, beggin' your pardon, sir.'

'Good to have you on board, shipmate.' Clay held out his hand, delighted at the opportunity to make some connection with his new crew. Davis shook his hand, and Clay carried on the inspection. There was still hostility, but at least he could now see a spark of interest on a few of the faces.

At the start of the final division he came upon a sailor who stood with legs apart and tattooed arms folded. He was a tall man, almost as tall as Clay, heavily built with a thick brown pigtail and piercing blue eyes. He stared at his new captain with an air of complete contempt. Clay stopped and held his gaze for a long moment.

'What is your name?' he asked.

'Richard Sexton,' a pause, 'sir.'

'Mind your manners, Sexton,' muttered Taylor.

'Aye aye, sir,' said the seaman, not taking his eyes off Clay.

'Do your duty, Sexton,' he said, 'and you shall have nothing to fear from me. Do you understand?'

'Aye aye, sir,' repeated the sailor, with no less contempt than before.

Once Clay had returned to the quarterdeck, he stepped forward again and rested both hands on the rail, where the whole crew could see him.

'Men, I have seen your petition that you sent to the Admiralty,' he began. 'It was shown to me by Admiral Sir Charles Middleton himself, so you can be assured that it has been received at the highest level. Captain Sheridan has been relieved of his command, and I have been asked by Sir Charles to tell you that the allegations made in that petition will be investigated.' A murmur of talk rolled around the main deck till it was hushed into silence by the petty officers.

When it was quiet again, Clay continued.

'In your petition you stated that you were all loyal to the King, and I have seen that loyalty in your eyes today. Now it is time for you to make good on that pledge. This fine ship has skulked in Plymouth long enough. We must go and do our duty to our King and our Country, and to return to join the rest of Sir Edward Pellew's Inshore Squadron blockading Brest. We shall complete our stores today, and we weigh anchor tomorrow.' He turned away from the rail.

'Mr Taylor! Dismiss the men below, if you please,' he ordered.

*****

'What manner of salt pork is this that you're trying to palm me off with?' asked George Haywood, raising his face from the top of the hogshead. He had been sniffing with care along the seam between the wooden staves of the barrel, holding his nose close to the brine-soaked wood. 'I am not taking this trash. It has been in the barrel at least three year if it has been a day. Why, I can smell the corruption through the very wood.' The purser of the *Titan* wagged a warning finger in the direction of the Superintendent of the Plymouth Victualling Yard. 'You must hold I was new born yesterday, to play such a base trick on me. If you have some rotten provisions you need to move, go and find yourself a vessel with a fool for a purser. Kindly replace these with something fresher. I have a tide to catch, and much work to do to get all this lot stowed away onboard.'

Although he spoke of his impatience to get away, the

purser showed no immediate signs of hurry. He was stood on the quayside at Plymouth with his book of indents tucked under one arm and surrounded with various ship's stores. Haywood was a small, intense man with lank ginger hair that hung down around his bald crown. Years of work as a purser, poring over manifests in the gloom of too many ships' holds, had weakened his small hazel eyes so he now had to wear a pair of steel-framed glasses to read. But there was very little wrong with his sense of smell, either for finding rotten provisions or for detecting an opportunity to make some extra profit on the side.

'Now Mr Haywood,' smiled the superintendent. 'I would not go so far as to say that this pork is rotten, but I will own that the casks might be a little older than is regular. One of my clerks has made a grave error, and this batch has been quite overlooked. All very vexing I am sure you agree, and a black mark against my yard if the Victualling Board was to learn of it. We have know each other for many a long year, so I thought you might oblige me with a little assistance in the matter.'

'What did you have in mind?' asked the purser. The eyes that peered over the top of his glasses glittered with avarice.

'I am sure when these casks come to be opened, you will find that some of the flesh is like as not to be tolerable,' suggest the superintendent. 'Would you not agree?'

'Perhaps I might be persuaded of that,' said Haywood. 'What proportion of the flesh do you hold to still be sweet?' The superintendent stroked his chin for a moment.

'I doubt that more than an eighth will prove to be inedible. I might be prepared to give you a discount of such on each barrel for your trouble. Which I would pay you in coin, now. Naturally there would be no need for such a transaction to appear on any of your ship's indents.' The purser of the *Titan* laughed aloud.

'An eighth!' he scoffed. 'This meat is quite rotten, any fool can see that. I will take five eighths in coin and not a farthing less.'

'Five eighths!' protested the superintendent. 'I would as soon tip the meat into the Tamar for the fish to have and then see what I can get for the empty casks.'

'I did wonder why the fish hereabouts had such an ill savour,' said the purser.

'Come, Mr Haywood, it is not as if you and your fellow officers shall have to eat this pork in you wardroom! You can have it served up to those mutinous scum on that ship of yours. It will serve them back for their disloyalty to the King. I shall give you ten pounds if you will take the lot.'

'Fifteen,' snapped Haywood.

'Twelve!'

'Make that guineas, and we have a deal,' said the purser, spitting on his hand and holding it out.

*****

The *Titan* left Plymouth at high water the following morning, and headed out into the green waters of the Channel. A light wind blew from the west, and watery spring sunshine sparkled off the tops of the long Atlantic rollers as they swept past the stern windows of the ship. Clay watched them go from behind his desk in the great cabin.

On the Lee Shore

The room seemed enormous compared with his previous accommodation onboard the little sloop of war *Rush*. He had a choice of seven different windows through which to look at the sea, arranged in a sweep across the stern of the frigate, and if he should tire of the view through those, he had a further three lights in each quarter galley. The cabin's size was further emphasised by the lack of suitable cabin furniture to fill it with. Clay's desk and dining room table had fitted well in the little *Rush*, but were quite dwarfed in this space. Even the pair of massive eighteen pounder cannon that stood on each side of the cabin did little to fill the void. But if the cabin seemed empty, his desk was anything but. Piles of ship's books and various sheets of notes in the captain's spidery hand covered the surface, while more ledgers were laid out open on the floor in a half ring close around his chair. With a sigh Clay returned to his work, until he was disturbed by a knock at the cabin door.

'Enter!' he called across the room. 'Ah, Mr Taylor, do come in and take a seat, I pray. May I offer you some of this excellent coffee? Hart! Another cup for Lieutenant Taylor, if you please.' While the two men waited for his steward to bring the cup, Clay studied the first lieutenant of the *Titan*. He was a man of medium build with short, iron-grey hair, in his late-forties. His face was a kindly one, with crow's feet that fanned out from the corners of his warm brown eyes when he smiled. His skin had been weathered to a deep shade of brown from long years of sea service, and yet he is still only a lieutenant, thought Clay to himself.

'How many years seniority do you have in the Navy, Mr Taylor?' he asked.

'Three and twenty years in total, sir,' replied the lieutenant. 'Twenty of those as a lieutenant. I joined as a master's mate from the merchant service at the start of the American War, and passed for lieutenant a few years later.'

'That is a prodigious time to spend as a lieutenant,' exclaimed Clay. 'I collect you have not had much fortune in the matter of promotion, then?'

'No sir, not really,' said Taylor. 'In truth I have lacked the connections to have been preferred in the service, and have not been fortunate enough to gain promotion through success in battle. Between the wars I was unable to secure a post in the navy, what with so much of the fleet laid up in ordinary, so I returned to the merchant service. I was master of an east coast collier bringing coal from Newcastle to London, which may have served to hamper my prospects.'

'Perhaps it might,' said Clay, studying his new subordinate. But for a couple of bloody actions and a fair slice of luck, that could so easily be me, he thought. 'Well, we are at war now, Mr Taylor, and bound for the French coast. It would be strange indeed if there were not to be some opportunities for you to distinguish yourself presently.'

'I do hope so, sir,' he replied. 'The last action I saw was the Battle of the Saintes under Rodney back in eighty-two.'

'But this war has been going on for over four years!' exclaimed his captain. 'Has there really been no action at all in your time onboard the *Titan*?'

'Your predecessor was not, perhaps, what you might describe as an active commander, sir,' said Taylor, avoiding his new captain's gaze.

'So it would seem,' said Clay. 'But for us to succeed in battle we must first have a well found ship, with some trust and goodwill in existence between the quarterdeck and the crew. From what I have seen so far we stand wholly in want of such a relationship. Instead we have as surly a body of men as I have ever come across.'

'At least they are no longer in open revolt against their captain, sir,' said the lieutenant. 'That is progress of sorts.'

'Not in open revolt, Mr Taylor!' he repeated. 'Perhaps I should be pleased that the crew have at least permitted us to weigh anchor? We are still very far from being a happy ship, and I need your assistance in helping to change matters.'

'Yes, sir,' said the first lieutenant. 'What can I do to aid you, sir?'

'I would like to have the particulars of what transpired to make the men rebel in the first place?' asked Clay.

'By all means, sir,' began Taylor. 'Firstly you should understand that we had been part of the blockade of Brest for almost four months, right the way through the winter. As a part of the Inshore Squadron our role is stay close to the Brittany coast. It is a savage lee shore at the best of times, especially during foul weather. I cannot start to count the number of westerly gales we had to endure, each one trying its best to drive us onto the rocks. Conditions were very difficult on board, with long periods when the men had little opportunity to rest or to dry their clothes. Once we went for ten days together when it blew so hard the galley fire could not be lit to give anyone on board the comfort of a hot meal.'

'Trying conditions, I make no doubt,' said Clay, 'Still, wet clothes and storms are a sailor's lot. They are hardly occasion for a mutiny. Doubtless the other ships on blockade suffered the same?'

'I dare say they did, sir,' replied the first lieutenant. 'We'd had a deal of grumbling from the crew over the past few months, but then we had some fresh agitation driven by other matters. Some of the complaints were of a general character, principally about low pay, while some were more specific. For example, the men were very unhappy about the clothing that was being issued. Mr Haywood, our purser, had secured some slops that were of a rather deficient quality.'

'Had he?' said Clay. 'Was that why that sailor's shirt was torn yesterday? Prince, I think his name was.'

'Almost certainly, sir,' replied Taylor. 'And as the cost of the men's clothes are taken from their wages, you can understand their concerns.'

'So how did Captain Sheridan deal with all of this?'

'Very robustly indeed, sir,' replied the older man. 'He had all those that had complained punished, and matters seemed to die down for a time. It was when we left our station to return to Plymouth to resupply that matters truly became unpleasant. We were a day out from Plymouth in a gale and we sent the men aloft to reduce sail. The captain was unhappy with the manner in which the crew went about their duties, and declared that he would flog the last man off the yard. That made them work rather more briskly, and unfortunately one man did fall to his death.'

'Was that the John Worthy mentioned in the petition?' asked Clay.

'That's right, sir,' replied Taylor. 'It was a shame, for he was a good seaman. Captain Sheridan then declared that he would have the second from last man flogged in his stead.'

'You jest, surely?' exclaimed Clay.

'No sir, you will find it duly recorded in the punishment book,' said the lieutenant, pointing to the volume on the desk. 'Three dozen for O'Brien.' Clay found the entry and ran his finger along the line.

'It states "Insubordination" here as the reason for the flogging,' he said, looking up from the book.

'Yes sir. That is how Captain Sheridan had such ad hoc punishments recorded.'

'But Mr Taylor, are you not aware that the false recording of punishments is against every direction of the Admiralty?' said his captain. 'Did you not object to the practice?'

'Eh, not openly sir,' said the older man. 'I did not see it as my place, and Captain Sheridan could be most forceful when he felt his will was being opposed.'

'I make no doubt he was,' said Clay. 'We shall return to the punishment book presently. In the meantime please continue your account, Mr Taylor.'

'Once O'Brien had been flogged, and John Worthy had been committed to the sea, I regret to say that matters onboard began to turn very ugly, sir.'

'You don't say,' muttered Clay under his breath. After a pause Taylor continued.

'That night the men started to gather in groups. At first it was chiefly to talk and plot together, but then they took to rolling cannon balls along the lower deck. By this time most of the petty officers had joined with the men. The captain attempted to restore order, but the crew were now quite mutinous and addressed him in a most uncivil manner. He resolved to send in the marines, but that wouldn't answer either. Many of the soldiers joined with the mutineers, and the rest refused to stir. The men took control of the ship after that. There was little violence offered against the officers beyond some rough handling. Captain Sheridan was confined to his cabin, the officers were sent to the wardroom, all under guard, and the men took the ship into Plymouth without any direction from us.'

'Did you identify which of the hands may have acted as leaders of the disturbance?' asked Clay.

'Not really sir, no,' said the lieutenant. 'It was dark, and the men made sure that none could be singled out in that fashion. I suspect that Richard Sexton was one of the principal troublemakers, but I am sure he cannot have acted alone.'

'No, I am sure he did not,' said Clay, sipping at his coffee. 'So I collect you might describe Captain Sheridan as a brutal man?'

'It is not really my place to find fault, sir,' replied Taylor. 'He was certainly a very firm man, perhaps too firm when he had been drinking. But then he was also obliged to be. We have many Irish papists among the crew, and they are known for their rebelliousness.'

'There have been Irish sailors on every ship that I have ever served on, and most have performed their duty well, Mr Taylor,' said his captain. 'You need to look a little farther for the cause of this mutiny than that. You may not choose to describe Captain Sheridan as a Tartar, but I certainly shall. I can form no other opinion from my study of the ship's punishment book.' He returned to the open volume and leafed through the pages, stopping from time to time to read out entries at random.

'Spitting on the deck, a dozen lashes. Appearing on duty in inappropriate and slovenly dress, two dozen. Use of blasphemous language, a dozen and no grog for a week.' Clay shook his head at what he read. 'These are not offences that merit a flogging. A day with no grog perhaps, an hour spent cleaning the heads or pumping the bilges will answer very well in most ships. I would expect the first lieutenant to administer such sanctions, with no need to come to me.'

'I see, sir,' said the lieutenant. 'That was not Captain Sheridan's custom. He wanted to know of every infraction, however small. I sometimes wondered if he did not derive some pleasure from the process.' Clay glanced up from the punishment book with a look of distaste.

'Did he, by Jove,' said the new captain. 'That explains much. Well, I am in command now, and I want you to handle such minor matters. No more floggings for spitting, if you please. I am sure you can find enough unpleasant or tedious tasks about the ship for such malefactors to perform. Is that clear, Mr Taylor?'

'Aye aye, sir,' said Taylor.

'Good,' said Clay, pushing away the punishment book, and drawing another volume towards him. 'Now, I am puzzled by the gunner's return of powder and shot. God knows our official allocation for live firing practice is little enough, but we do not seem to have expended any at all.'

'Ah, yes,' said Taylor, stroking his chin. 'Captain Sheridan did not hold with live firing. He liked a trim looking ship. The recoil of the guns marks the deck most cruelly, and powder stains do so spoil the paintwork.'

'And how did he propose to beat an opponent should he chance upon one?' queried Clay.

'Oh, he always held that English pluck would answer for that,' said the lieutenant.

'Or even Irish pluck, perhaps?' said his captain. 'I have always found that it is the ship which can fire three broadsides every two minutes that will win most fights at sea, whether blessed by English courage or not. I want the hands to perform an hour of gunnery training every evening from now on, with the discharge of some live rounds to finish each session. Kindly put that in place too.'

'Aye aye, sir,' replied Mr Taylor.

'Also, can we not encourage the crew to play music, or sing and dance of an evening? For a ship with so many Irish onboard, the people seem to be very solemn when not on watch.'

'Ah, yes, sir. That was because Captain Sheridan disliked mus—' began Taylor, but he trailed to a halt when he caught sight of the steel in Clay's grey eyes. 'I... ah... well that was then. Shall I let it be known that the men are permitted to indulge in such practices again, sir?'

'If you please, Mr Taylor,' said Clay.

Chapter 3

The Ghost Ship

'What a miserable fecking ship,' moaned Sean O'Malley to his fellow volunteers from the *Rush*. 'I know we were after serving with Pipe again, but what's wrong with our new shipmates? Presbyterians on the Sabbath are livelier. And what makes it even worse is half of the buggers are Irish!' He plucked at his fiddle in anger and a loud note twanged across the crowded lower deck, causing other sailors to look around in surprise. O'Malley held up an apologetic hand. 'Sorry, lads, I didn't realise someone had fecking died. Will you be letting me know when the wake is, at all?'

'You're right there, Sean,' said his close friend Adam Trevan, his long blond pigtail bobbing with agitation. 'The captain has got himself a proper bad ship here. I hope he knows what he is about. There's a lad in the afterguard as is from the same part of Cornwall as me, and he was saying the last captain was as mean a bastard as ever walked. A devil by the name of Sheridan. Apparently he killed one of the crew, while he was pissed on bishop, and this lot all mutinied. Officers locked up. Marines disarmed; he reckons it was a proper rising an' all. I tell you, I love our Pipe dear as a brother, but I am thinking we should have stayed put on the *Rush*.'

'All a bit late now,' said Joshua Rosso, from the far side of the mess table. His more educated Bristol accent stood out among the oath-edged talk of his fellow mess mates. 'We are on our way to at least three months on patrol off the Brest roads, to judge by all of the supplies we took on board in Plymouth. Still, being based out of Plymouth must be a nice change for you, Adam. Did you get to see your wife while we were on leave?'

'That I most certainly did, Rosie,' said Trevan with a smile. 'I went back home and spent two whole days with my Molly. I would like to say it were good and restful, but after so long apart we had a deal of catching up to do, if you gets my drift. I've had more sleep getting in sail during a hurricane. It's right hard being apart an' all, but it's good to have someone at home who cares about me. Can you believe that what with us going to the Caribbean an' all it's been over a year since I was last home? Molly hasn't changed any, but our lad Sam's running all over the place like a proper little jack rabbit. Home comforts! You boys should try it sometime.'

'Ha!' scoffed O'Malley. 'Chance would be a fine thing, stuck here on the barky for months on end. Besides, the parting must be fecking cruel and all.'

'Aye, you have the truth of it there, Sean,' said the Cornishman. 'My Molls were proper clinging to me when I left. The lad's not so bad, but then seeing me for only two days after a year he barely gets who I am to him. I left her with the remains of our prize money from the *San Felipe*, and then I had to come away.'

'Bet that ain't the only thing he left her,' said O'Malley with a wink for Rosso, 'or has the quicksilver salve worked at last?' Rosso chuckled at this, his smile broadening further as he saw who the fourth volunteer from the *Rush* had with him.

'Look who that bastard of a Londoner has found, shipmates,' he said. O'Malley and Trevan turned on their stools to follow his gaze. Looming up behind them was the huge figure of Sam Evan, his six and half foot frame doubled up under the low deck, together with a familiar stocky figure.

'Here he is, boys,' said Evans. 'An' ain't he a sight for sore eyes.'

'You have no idea how good it is to see you all!' exclaimed Sedgwick. 'At last, some friendly faces.' He embraced each sailor in turn, before he joined them at the mess table.

'So tell us, what is happening, Able?' asked Rosso. 'Why is the atmosphere so bad on board this ship of yours?' The captain's coxswain looked around him first before he answered.

'Have you all heard about the mutiny?' he asked.

'Aye, but surely that is over now Pipe has taken charge?' said Trevan. 'It was this Tartar Sheridan the men rose up against, and he is long gone. The captain will give them little cause to grumble.'

'You would reckon so, Adam,' said Sedgwick. 'And some of the changes he has made are much liked, make no doubt, but there are plenty on board who want him to fail. One is named Richard Sexton, have you seen him? He's the big bastard with lots of tattoos and blue eyes like Adam here. He and his mates seem to have a taste for causing trouble now, and I doubt they are ready just to go back to their former places.'

'Well, I have seen that Sexton bloke hanging around with his muckers,' growled Evans, 'an' there ain't one of them I couldn't put down if it comes to a mill, easy as kiss my hand.'

'That may be so, Big Sam, but then there are all of these Irish sailors too,' began Sedgwick.

'What's wrong with the fecking Irish?' protested O'Malley. 'Jesus, Able! Most of my life I have had to take slights from the bastard English.'

'Steady there, Sean,' cautioned Trevan.

'Not you lot, obviously, but all the fecking rest of the buggers,' continued the furious Irishman. 'But let me tell you, matters are after reaching a strange pass when the Negros are pitching in too!' The others all laughed at this. After a pause Sedgwick gave his arm a reassuring pat.

'Most of the Irish on board are fine, Sean,' he explained, 'just regular jacks like us. But there are some who ain't. You must have seen them. Like them over at that mess table by the foremast. Do you mark them? Right strange, gloomy men who keep themselves apart. But then when you speak with them, they are truly hot in their inclinations. One had a long yarn with me the day I joined the barky. He wanted to know why I was fighting for the masters who had enslaved my fellow Africans. He said Ireland had been enslaved too. He even named himself a white Negro, and said how we should be on the same side by rights.'

'I am not one of them radicals myself, Able, but he does have a fecking point,' said O'Malley. 'Why are you fighting for the English?'

'I don't hold that it is the English I fight for,' said Sedgwick. 'I don't rightly know what the England you speak of is. If you mean the strange little village that the captain comes from, where the men cross the street as soon as they clock me, and the old ladies believe I live to kill them in their beds, then the answer is no. But perhaps I fight for other stuff. For the captain, of course, who took me into his ship in Barbados to save me from going back to the plantation and that bastard Haynes. I fight for the navy, who gave me back at least some of my freedom. And in truth I fight for you, my shipmates, and the first white men what showed me any kindness.' The men were quiet for a moment, surprised by the eloquence of their friend. Rosso put a friendly arm about Sedgwick's shoulders. O'Malley shifted on his bench awkwardly.

'Well, if yous is interested at all, I am not fighting for any of what Able was just after saying,' he muttered. 'It's the generous rate of fecking pay as keeps me loyal.' The others smiled at this, and Rosso turned back to Sedgwick.

'Some radicals that want a free Ireland and a few sea lawyers who wish they were on board the *Bounty* will not answer to start a mutiny, Able,' he said. 'You know how good a captain Pipe is. Didn't we all follow him here? He will win the rest of the crew over for sure, soon enough.'

'In time he will, Rosie, I make no doubt,' agreed the coxswain. 'But it is not just the hands that worry me. He has a poor set of Grunters too. The petty officers and the gunroom are sound enough, but the wardroom is very uncertain. The men say that Taylor, the first lieutenant, is weak. He never opposed Sheridan as he should have done. The man they call Beaky is Morton, the second lieutenant. He is an arrogant bastard who still smarts over Sheridan's removal, and Blake the third is a babe in arms. He will do whatever Beaky wants. Our Tom Macpherson, and perhaps Warwick the master, are the only grunters in the wardroom he can truly rely on.'

'Well, at least he can rely on us, if matters turn cruel,' said Evans.

'Can you play that fiddle, mate?' asked a young sailor who had stopped by their mess table. O'Malley looked him up and down before he replied.

'Can I play the fiddle?' he asked in disbelief. 'Aren't I after being the finest fiddler in all of Leinster? Sean O'Malley is the name, in case yous haven't heard of my playing on your side of the fecking water at all.' The sailor shook O'Malley's proffered hand.

'I am Pete Hobbs. Some of us top men fancy a hornpipe now that Old Man Taylor says we can if we wish. Would you come and play for us?'

'It would be a pleasure, shipmate,' said O'Malley, picking up his instrument. 'About time we had a bit of music on board this fecking ghost ship.'

*****

Several lanterns had been moved up into bow-end of the

lower deck, and in their flickering orange glow danced the graceful figures of the young sailors as they twirled and stepped in time to O'Malley's rapid playing. One of the Irish hands had produced a small drum to beat, and the two musicians sat and faced each other, the rattle of the drum syncopating with the cascade of notes that flowed from the fiddle. A dozen sailors had gathered to watch the dancing, and some had begun to keep time by stamping their bare feet on the deck. Richard Sexton watched the dancing with a frown, before turning back to his two companions.

'It will take more than a couple of fucking hornpipes to bring this ship to order,' he sneered.

'You're right there, Dick,' enthused Morris Page, a small, dark haired, intense man. 'Getting rid of that bastard Sheridan was just the start. This fight is not over yet, not by a long way. When do we rise up again?'

'Patience, Morris,' said Sexton. 'All in good time. He is a cunning one, this new captain, damn his eyes. Letting the hands have a sing and a dance, that's very deep, that is. Why, it costs him nothing to do, yet directly it begins to get some of the men on his side. An' all that talk of loyalty to the King when he joined, that hit the mark with a few of the more idiot hands. There is nothing like a bit of that rot to make a man forget the chains he wears. Where was the bleeding King when I got reduced to the ranks? All I did was sip a bit too much knock-me-down. And that bastard Sheridan, he was more pissed than I was when he sent me back before the mast.'

'Loyalty to the King,' scoffed Page. 'Our brothers in America have no need of any King. The French have got rid of theirs. What need do we have for one? The sooner we can replace the corrupt rule of the men of property with a true democracy, the better, I say. We must have annual parliaments, an open franchise and ballots in secret.'

'Easy there, Morris,' said Sexton. 'No one doubts your heart is in the right place, and I agree with what you hold – didn't I let you put some of that talk in the petition? But it will not answer with the major part of the men; they have no interest in all that radical talk. If we want them to rise, we need to keep our reasoning simple. Poor pay, cruel treatment, no proper shore leave, rotten vittles, that is the stuff they all care about.' He turned to the third person seated at the table, a redheaded sailor with pale green eyes. 'You've been right quiet, Shane Kenny, letting us do all the talking. What about your Irish sailors, can they be relied on?'

'It's like the rest of the fecking crew, Dick,' he said. 'Don't the Irish just love to talk all big about being free of the English an' all, but most of them are truly just after a quiet life. There are maybe a dozen committed rebels I can call on, but the others will need something to get their anger up. Like last time, when Sheridan flogged that poor bastard O'Brien for being second to last off the yard. Now that served to get them proper mad with rage. But it's like you was after saying, your new man seems to be much too cunning to make that sort of easy mistake.'

'So when will it be our time?' urged Page. Sexton looked around him with care. Most of the sailors at the nearby tables were either chatting amongst themselves or watching the dancing.

'Soon, lads,' he whispered. 'I have heard that the whole

Channel Fleet is ready to rise up in mutiny. It will be over a demand for better pay, and that will be our chance.'

'The whole fecking fleet!' gasped Kenny. 'How the hell do you know that?'

'You got to trust me on this, but I have a way of corresponding with like minded jacks on most of the other ships. Don't go asking me how. The less folk as know about it, the better. But we all need to be ready when our moment comes. Patience, brothers. We must bide our time for now and wait for matters to align in our favour. Then, the moment something shall happen on board that we can rally the men over, we can make our move.'

'What do you plan to do about the Lobsters?' asked Page. 'They did little to stop us last time, but since that new Scottish Grunter came, he has a proper grip on them. I have tried to talk with the ones that helped us, but they're not in the mood to listen any. It's right hard for men with clasp knives to take on soldiers with muskets, however just their cause.' Sexton tapped his nose with the index finger of one hand.

'You're right, Morris, but I have a plan for that. You know Stephenson, the armourer's mate? He used to be a locksmith. When the last mutiny ended I had to give the Grunters back all the keys we took off them. Only before I did, I got him to make me a copy of the one to the arms chest. Have no fear on that score, it will not just be clasp knives we will have next time. I reckon even the Lobsters will be a bit more willing to see reason when it's us as have muskets too.'

'That's very good, Dick,' smiled Kenny. 'With proper

weapons we only need a few committed rebels. Just enough to boss the others, like.' Page nodded his agreement at this. He looked past the Irishman to where Sedgwick still sat chatting with Evans, Rosso and Trevan.

'We need to watch those new volunteers too,' he muttered. 'They might be trouble. They look as if they know how to handle themselves, especially that big bastard.'

'It's funny you mentioning him,' said Sexton. 'I have a strange feeling about that one. He seems familiar somehow. I wonder where I might have seen him before?'

Chapter 4

The Inshore Squadron

Captain Alexander Clay clambered down the side of the *Titan* in his full dress uniform and sat next to Sedgwick in the stern of the barge. He had settled himself in place, with his best cocked hat on his lap, and his sword held upright between his legs, before he noticed what the crew were wearing. Each of them had on a white shirt with seams lined in dark green ribbon. Their white duck trousers were clean and neat, and on every head was a matching straw hat, decorated with a further band of green ribbon.

'Push off there in the bow,' ordered Sedgwick, from beneath his own straw hat. 'Give way all!' The men started to swing their oars in unison and the barge gathered pace as it swept away from the tall side of the frigate.

'I must say I do approve of the way the crew are dressed, Sedgwick,' said Clay. 'Is this your doing?'

'Yes, sir,' replied his coxswain. 'The oars are now painted in green and white too. I have some way to go before I have the barge as I wants it, mind. I need to find a shipmate with a good steady hand to add '*Titan*' in white paint on our hat bands, and I shall ask the boatswain to repaint the hull of the barge to match the oars.'

'Good idea,' agreed Clay. 'The men do look very smart. What gave you the idea?'

'Watch your stroke, Rodgers!' barked Sedgwick, before returning his attention to his captain. 'Do you recall how back in Bridgetown the admiral and all the grand captains had barge crews dressed up fancy, sir. I thought that we should do the same, now you are made post. Beggin' your pardon, sir, if I speak out of turn, but I also hold this new ship of ours needs a bit more pride in itself. It is but a small matter, but perhaps having a smart barge crew shall help, if you don't mind me saying so.'

Clay looked back at the *Titan* and thought about what his coxswain had said. Her long black hull was almost a hundred and seventy feet long from her gilded stern to the bulging, muscular figure of the Titan that glared out at the world from under her bowsprit. The length of the ship was emphasised by the broad stripe of yellow that ran along the line of her gun deck. It spoke to Clay of her power and strength. Behind that layer of paint were her thick oak sides, and the row of heavy eighteen-pounder guns, big enough to overwhelm any foe she might meet below a ship of the line in size. Above her hull her enormous masts soared a hundred and fifty feet into the grey sky. From there her wide yards reached out far on either side. She was a fast ship too, he thought; speed and power, a potent combination. Nothing that she could not beat in battle would be able to catch her.

'You are quite correct, Sedgwick,' said Clay. 'We do have

the benefit of a magnificent ship. Any right thinking seaman should be proud to serve upon her.'

'Starboard side, sir?' asked Sedgwick, gesturing towards their destination. Clay looked back towards where the *Indefatigable* lay hove-to ahead of them. A commodore's broad pennant flapped languidly out from the top of her mainmast, showing her to be the flagship of the squadron. She was an even larger frigate than the *Titan*, with twenty-four-pounder cannon for her main armament.

'If you please, Sedgwick,' he answered. His hand drifted up to adjust his best neck cloth of thick china silk. Coming aboard on the starboard side was the right thing to do for his first visit to his new commander, but Clay was a shy enough man to still be nervous at the ceremony this would involve him in.

In the stern sheets of the barge Sedgwick leant forward in his seat. His eyes flickered backwards and forwards across the narrowing gap between the boat and the ship's side.

'Boat ahoy!' came a hail from the *Indefatigable*.

'*Titan*,' shouted Sedgwick, without taking his eyes off his approach.

'Easy all!' he ordered. 'In oars! Clap on in the bow there!' The boat slid ever closer to the black wall of oak and came to a halt next to the bottom of the ladder of slats built into the frigate's side. The bottom few steps were treacherous with olive green weed, but two braided lines of hemp hung down either side of the entry ladder to act as hand rails. Clay settled his hat in place on his head, stood up in the barge and hitched his sword around behind him so it would be out of the way of his feet. The boat rose and fell a good three feet in the swell, despite the best efforts of the crew to hold her steady. Clay waited for the top of the rise and jumped for the ship's side. One foot slipped a little, but he managed to scramble up clear of the treacherous lower steps. His coxswain watched his climb anxiously from below, wondering if he would be able to pull himself up with his injured shoulder. As his captain's head reached the level of the *Indefatigable*'s main deck, Sedgwick heard the first squeal of the boatswain's pipes.

'Present arms!' yelled an unseen lieutenant of marines, and Clay disappeared from view.

While Sedgwick watched his ascent up the side of the frigate he caught sight of a tiny movement out of the corner of his eye. It was as if something small had been dropped down into the boat from above them. He glanced towards where the movement had come from, just in time to see the slither of a gap under a port lid close. He looked round at his barge crew. All the men were able to meet his enquiring gaze except one. Now then, he thought, was it just the way that the folds of linen hung, or did Rodgers in the bow of the boat seem to have something concealed under his shirt?

*****

'Welcome aboard, Captain Clay,' said Sir Edward Pellew, with a voice thickened by his slight Cornish accent. He stepped forward to greet his visitor and gripped his hand with a strong handshake. He was an athletic looking man with thinning, sandy coloured hair that had just started to grey over his temples. The pale blue eyes that regarded those of his new subordinate were thoughtful, almost questioning. 'Do please follow me below.'

The great cabin of the *Indefatigable* was decorated with a degree of sumptuousness that Clay had last seen at sea on board an East Indiaman. The duck egg blue bulkheads were lined with gilt-framed paintings of Pellew's wife and children. Thick Persian carpets covered the deck beneath his feet, while the light from the silver lanterns that swung above his head was reflected from deep within the gloss of the polished cherry wood furniture.

'Just over six minutes, in case you were wondering,' said his host, smiling at the surprise in his guest's eyes as he ushered him across to his chair. 'It is a little longer than the cabin of a man of war should take to be cleared for action, but I have been tolerably fortunate in the matter of prize money, so I feel able to surround myself in a little luxury. How long does your cabin on the *Titan* take to clear?'

'Nothing like as long, Sir Edward,' laughed Clay, thinking about the few Spartan possessions he had in his quarters.

'And yet you too have been blessed with some prize money of late, I believe?' asked the commodore. 'The capture of that Spanish ship of the line last year was quite the talk of the navy, I recall. Why, I received my knighthood for a much less notable victory.'

'You are very kind to mention it, Sir Edward,' said Clay, as he accepted a crystal glass of sherry from the tray held out to him by Pellew's steward. 'I fear it has been rather eclipsed now by your victory over a French seventy-four during the winter.'

'Ah yes,' smiled the commodore. 'But while the *Amazon* and ourselves received some honour from our victory, we gained no other reward. Regrettably we drove the *Droits de l'Homme* to her doom on the rocks. Still, I am pleased to have another fighting captain in the squadron. Your predecessor was anything but. Confusion to the French!' Clay joined in the toast, and the steward refilled the glasses.

'Now, captain,' said Pellew, 'tell me if you have succeeded in suppressing all this mutinous nonsense on board your ship?'

'To a certain extent, Sir Edward,' replied Clay. 'The crew are at least now obedient to their officers, but the *Titan* is far from being a happy ship. If I can be frank with you, the men yet smart over their treatment at the hands of Captain Sheridan.'

'I did try to warn him that he was all together too thorough with his people,' said Pellew, shaking his head. 'There is such discontent in the navy at present that it takes very little to provoke the men. I had a petition from my own crew only this week demanding an increase in their pay.'

'Sir Charles Middleton at the Admiralty told me that he is obliged to consider such demands almost every day,' said Clay.

'Quite,' said the commodore. 'But at least I have the comfort of knowing that if the French should come out my people will still fight. Will yours, captain?'

'I have an officer I trust in charge of my marines now, Sir Edward, and I have put in place some other changes that I hope will answer. So yes, I believe they will.' Clay met

Pellew's eyes confidently enough. After a moment, the Cornishman continued.

'Very well, Captain. Then welcome to your new role as one of the guard dogs of the fleet. We number five hounds in total. In addition to our two ships there are the *Argo*, the *Concord* and the *Phoebe*.'

'And our role is to guard the approaches to Brest, I collect?' said Clay.

'Sounds simple, don't it?' said Pellew. He turned in his chair to point out of the stern window of the frigate. 'Over yonder is Brittany and the principal French naval base at Brest. The Channel Fleet keep safely out at sea if it is calm, or run to the shelter of Torbay if it blows above a cap full of wind. They can do that because they are certain that my Inshore Squadron will keep watch over the Frogs, and will tell them the moment they come out.'

'That seems clear enough, sir,' replied Clay. Pellew fixed his new subordinate with his pale eyes once more.

'Our duty is clear, but that don't make it easy,' he said. 'Because regrettably we are on the most savage of lee shores. There are hidden rocks and wicked reefs too numerous to count. Riptides and sea currents the like of which you never dreamed possible. Our station is to spend our days and nights close amongst such hazards. You will have need of unwearied diligence, Captain Clay. Most days the wind blows from the west, constantly pushing us towards the shore. Yet when the wind is elsewhere, we have little prospect of rest, for that is when the weather will serve to bring the French out.'

'Do they come out often, Sir Edward?' asked Clay.

'Annoyingly they do,' said Pellew. 'It is seldom the whole fleet that emerges to challenge us. Chiefly we must watch out for a swift frigate or a little squadron, slipping out to sea on a dark night. They come out to prey on our commerce, or to rush supplies out to one of their colonies or to their rebel friends in Ireland. And their warships are only a part of our problem. There is also a lively coastal trade that we must try and disrupt. With Brittany so poorly served with roads and rivers, almost all of the French fleet's supplies must needs come to them by sea.'

'And there was I congratulating myself that regaining some control over my ship from mutineers was to be my chief trial, Sir Edward,' exclaimed Clay. His new commander laughed at that.

'Do not worry overly, captain,' said Pellew, favouring his new subordinate with a smile. 'I have become melancholy by being over long on this damned coast. We do have compensations, you know. Unlike the ships of the Channel Fleet, we at least have the prospect of prize money. There are no end of coasters trying to bring supplies into Brest, if you can contrive a way to come at them.'

'I am pleased to hear it, Sir Edward,' said Clay. 'Perhaps the prospect will serve to reconcile my crew to their duties.'

'Let us hope that it does,' said the commodore. 'And swiftly too. I have your orders here. You shall be relieving the *Phoebe* outside the entrance to Brest itself. Look into that port whenever wind and tide serve. Report back to me what you find, attack any French ships that may come your way, and above all keep clear of the rocks! Achieve that much, and you will have done your duty.'

*****

Second Lieutenant Edmund Morton of His Majesty's frigate *Titan* was a thin man of twenty-four, with brown hair and eyes. His face had a haughty, aristocratic look to it, enhanced by his prominent hook nose. He was known aboard for the shortness of his temper, so it came as little surprise to his brother officers when he barged through the wardroom door and threw his hat in the general direction of his servant.

'Good God!' he exclaimed. 'The damned hands have taken to *singing* now, as if all that infernal dancing weren't enough. It really is becoming insupportable. Captain Sheridan would never have permitted such behaviour when he was in command.' He thumped down into a vacant chair at the table that ran the length of the cabin and glared around him.

'Were his views of a puritan character when it came to the hands enjoying themselves off duty, then?' asked Macpherson, looking up from the game of cards he was playing with Henry Warwick, the *Titan*'s quietly spoken ship's master.

'No, sir,' replied Morton. 'I would not describe him as a Puritan. He had no objection to the men seeking to divert themselves, provided they did so *quietly*.'

'You were well acquainted with Captain Sheridan then, I collect?' asked the marine.

'Exceedingly well,' said the lieutenant. 'The Sheridan and

Morton estates are in the same part of Wiltshire. Together they have supplied officers to serve the Crown for generations. Captain Sheridan was my godfather, don't you know?'

'Was he now?' said the marine. 'I didn't realise. You must have found the change in command rather vexing then?'

'Bloody ridiculous if you asked me,' snorted Morton. 'We can't have the damned hands deciding who shall command which ship! Where in all damnation will that sort of Jacobin nonsense take us? I cannot imagine what the Admiralty were thinking.'

Warwick placed his cards face down on the wardroom table and joined the conversation, just as the frigate went over onto the other tack. A mass of creaks and groans from the timbers all around them served to mask what he had said.

'What was that, Warwick?' bellowed Morton, cupping a hand around one ear. 'Do speak up, man.'

'I was asking you what you would have done if you were in the Admiralty's position, Edmund?' repeated Warwick, rather more loudly.

'Why, I would most certainly have been firmer with these damned mutineers,' said Morton. 'I should have ranged up next to the *Titan* with a loyal ship of decidedly superior firepower, and then boarded with a decent sized body of marines. String up the ringleaders and flog the rest. That would have ended matters in pretty short order.'

'Hmm, I am not sure that would have answered,' said Warwick. 'The men were resolved to slip anchor and sail for

France at the first hint of trouble, with we officers locked away down here.'

'I am inclined to agree with our worthy master,' said Macpherson. 'I am not acquainted with your godfather, Edmund, but whatever his failings may have been, a want of firmness does not seem to have been among them. When I took command of my marines they were so in sympathy with the plight of the crew that they were not to be relied on at all. I am still not sure that they would oppose a rising even now, if I gave the order.'

'But don't you see how the land now lies?' exclaimed Morton. 'The men believe that they have won! Are we to expect them to mutiny afresh whenever they are required to perform some service they are disinclined to do? If you ask me this is what comes when you allow those of the middling sort to become officers. They don't have a proper feel for it, not like those of us born to the role. Until the start of the war, Taylor was the master of a *collier* for the love of God, and I have never heard of Captain Clay's people at all.'

'Let me reassure you on that point, Edmund,' said Macpherson. 'While Captain Clay's origins may be humble, he is quite the best commander I have ever served under. In time the hands will come to realise that, and then I believe we shall have no further talk of mutiny.'

*****

'Hart, this pie is really quite excellent,' enthused Clay to his steward as he had his lunch in the great cabin of the *Titan*. 'The quality of your fare seems much improved of late.'

'Why thank you, sir,' said Hart. 'I have changed my manner of cooking since I last served your honour. I believe I may have over reached myself in the past, when I was trying to produce them fancy made Frog dishes what Lloyd used to do for Captain Follett. Fact is they never did come out quite right, did they, sir?'

'No, Hart, they did not,' said his captain, relief evident on his face. 'So where do you find your inspiration now?'

'For that pie there, sir?' said the steward. 'Why, I followed the directions that my mother gave me, she being renowned for her made dishes.'

'Did you, by Jove,' said Clay. 'Well, it is a very fine pie. Come in!' This last comment was directed towards the cabin door.

'Mr Morton's compliments, sir,' said the burly midshipman who came in. 'The tide will ebb in the next hour, and La Feels... Less Fillets... eh, that reef you wanted to be told about is in sight, dead ahead.'

'Do you mean Les Fillettes, Mr Butler?' asked his captain.

'Yes, sir, that's the one,' said the relieved midshipman.

'You do not have any facility with the French tongue, I collect?'

'French, sir?' queried Butler. 'I can't say as I do. There has never been much call for it in the gunroom.'

'I appreciate that these French names can be vexing, but you must oblige me and at least learn the names of the principal reefs. This is a very dangerous coast. It matters little on a calm day such as we have now, but when the weather is less kind I shall need all my officers to be able to report on what they see with precision. Is that clear, Mr Butler?'

'Aye aye, sir,' said the teenager, a worried frown appearing between his eyes.

'Very well, please tell Mr Morton I shall come on deck directly.'

When Clay walked out onto the quarterdeck, the *Titan* was deep within the Iroise Channel. She slid along under easy sail down the centre of a wide inlet that cut deep into the coastline of Brittany. Danger was wrapped all around the ship. The green fields of France came to an abrupt end in steep cliffs where the land tumbled down into the waters of the channel. He could see rocks littering the coast, while nearer at hand broken lines of reefs were marked by the occasional black-toothed rock proud of the swirling white foam all about them. At regular intervals gun batteries studded the coast, revealing themselves to the frigate with the occasional puff of smoke, followed by a line of water spouts rising up off the calm water as a ranging shot skipped across the sea. None of them endangered the ship, but they served to remind Clay how careful they must be so close to the enemy shore. Ahead the inlet narrowed down into the Goulet, the deep water channel that led through to the Rade de Brest, where the enemy fleet would be at anchor. Right in the middle of the Goulet was a further wash of white water that spat periodically into the air, showing him where another dangerous reef lay.

'Les Fillettes,' mused Clay as he gazed at the rocks through his telescope. 'What a strange name for a reef upon which hundreds of sailors must have perished over the years.'

'It means the Little Girls, sir,' said Morton, standing next to his captain.

'I know what it means, Mr Morton,' said Clay. 'I was speculating why rocks with such an evil reputation should have been given such an innocent name.'

'Your pardon, sir,' replied the lieutenant. 'My mistake. I imagined that with your background you might not have had the benefit of a French tutor. Your late father was a village curate, was he not?'

'No, he was a parson, actually,' said Clay. 'Am I to understand that you did have the benefit of such an education?'

'Oh yes, naturally I did, sir,' replied Morton. 'In my family it is considered to be a necessary accomplishment for a gentleman.' Clay looked at his second lieutenant with a frown as Morton lingered a moment on the word 'gentleman'.

'I am delighted to hear it, Mr Morton,' said Clay. 'I believe you shall be able to oblige me by helping some of the junior officers.'

'In what particular, sir?' asked the lieutenant.

'I have just now discovered that the navy has been rather less thoughtful than the Morton family when it comes to the education of our young gentlemen. It seems that they are quite unable to say these difficult French names in any intelligible manner. Perhaps you could give them the benefit of your knowledge of the language by holding some lessons for the gunroom?'

'What! Surely that cannot be necessary, sir,' protested the lieutenant, quite aghast at the prospect.

'Oh it is absolutely necessary,' said Clay. 'It will serve to enhance the education of my ship's officers beyond measure. For some in the French language, and for others it will provide a useful lesson in the perils of looking down on those one holds to be inferior.' He held the young lieutenant's gaze for a long moment.

'Aye aye, sir,' he said at last, his face flushed and red. The pair of large gun batteries that guarded each side of the mouth of the Goulet both opened up at that moment, their huge forty-two pounder balls throwing up a mass of tall splashes from the sea in front of the *Titan,* returning both officers' attention to where the ship was.

'Close enough, Mr Morton,' ordered Clay. 'Bring her into the wind, if you please. Now, Mr Butler, and you too, Mr Russell, I want you to take these spy glasses and go aloft up different masts. You are to count all the shipping you can see. Take your time, now. I want to know how many warships are in the Rade de Brest, what sort they are, and if they have their upper masts and yards set up. Make your observations separately, then consult on deck and agree what you have seen.'

'Aye aye, sir,' both midshipman replied, and scampered off to climb the fore and main masts.

'Keep her steady into the wind, damn you eyes,' yelled Morton at the quartermaster.

'Aye aye, sir,' said the man at the wheel, and Morton spun

away to pace up and down the quarterdeck.

'You can go fuck yourself, Beaky,' the helmsman muttered to his fellow quartermaster. 'No cause to get arsy just because Pipe as brought you down a peg or two.'

While he waited for the two midshipmen to report back, Clay returned to his survey of the coastline around him. It seemed strange to be so close to the main French fleet and yet to be safe. The Iroise Channel had been crowded with costal craft all headed towards Brest when they had first stood in, but like fish before a shark they had run from the big frigate as she swept forward. He could see the boats on either side of him, some huddled under the guns of the various batteries, others lying safe behind the numerous reefs.

'There is a fortune in prize money all around us, sir,' remarked Taylor, as he came to stand beside him. 'All so close, and yet vexingly out of reach.'

'Is the channel always this crowded, Mr Taylor?' asked Clay.

'It can be when the tide is as it is,' explained the lieutenant. 'The Goulet is sufficiently narrow that the sea races through it. If it is running out, as it has begun to do now, all these craft can get backed up, waiting for the next tide to bear them in.'

'That will not be until tonight,' mused his captain. 'I wonder where all of these coasters will go to wait?'

'Berthaume Bay over there, sir,' replied Taylor, pointing to the south of them. 'It has good holding ground to anchor, is well protected from a westerly gale, and is conveniently close to the mouth of the Goulet for when the tide turns. Regrettably the entrance is also covered by several tolerably large French batteries. When I was in the merchant service during the peace, I used it several times.' Clay turned his telescope that way and examined the bay. It already contained several coasters, with more entering as he looked.

'Is that a town I can see at the bottom of the bay?' he asked.

'Oh aye, that will be Camaret, sir,' the lieutenant replied. 'It is more of a village really, but it does have a number of taverns. I have rowed to shore there for a mug of cider a few times while waiting for my tide.'

'You would need the wind in the south or east to bring any prizes out,' said Clay to himself. He tapped his closed spy glass in the palm of one hand. His first lieutenant looked at him.

'You are surely not thinking of cutting out anything from under those batteries, sir,' he protested.

'Not today, Mr Taylor,' said his captain, still deep in thought. 'No, not today. The wind will not serve.' He looked up as the two midshipman came along the gangway. 'Ah, here come our intrepid young spies. Mr Butler, Mr Russell, what have you to tell me?'

'We counted nineteen ships of the line, sir,' said Butler. 'All were two deckers. Five of them have their yards crossed. Then we saw a further ten frigates, four of those have yards in place, and perhaps twenty smaller vessels, brigs, sloops and the like.'

'Well done to you both,' said Clay. 'Mr Taylor, have these

gentlemen's observations entered into the log, if you please, and then let us make our way back out to sea. When we have sight of the *Indefatigable* please signal a full report on the French fleet to the commodore.'

*****

When the watch was changed at eight bells the following day, the ship exploded into a mass of activity. The men below came boiling up the ladder ways from the lower deck under the urgings of their petty officers in a torrent of humanity. Henry Warwick, the new officer of the watch, strode out of the wardroom, buttoning up his master's blue coat and adjusting his hat as he came. The junior officers that were to assist him ran up from the gunroom, and throughout the ship men dispersed to their stations. The forecastle men ran to the bow, the waisters to the main deck, the lookouts clambered up to the lofty royal yard, the afterguard congregated on the quarterdeck, and the quartermasters took their place at the wheel. Then the flow of men reversed as those who had been relieved by the new arrivals went below for food and some rest.

In all the confusion, nobody noticed Sedgwick down on the lower deck as he took Thomas Rodgers by the arm and drew him into the relative privacy of the space between the captain's pantry and the boatswain's locker.

'Afternoon, Able,' said Rodgers. 'Good to be coming off watch for a bit of a breather, like.'

'Afternoon, Tom,' replied Sedgwick. 'You're right there, shipmate. Mind you, being in the barge crew does mean we have a lot less grind than most. You must enjoy the privileges you get from crewing for the captain? I know I do.'

'Yeah, course I does,' said the oarsman. 'There ain't no problem is there, Able, mate?'

'I am not sure,' said the coxswain. 'Can you think of anything that might be a problem?'

'No, can't say as I can,' replied Rodgers, his eyes shifting away from the remorseless gaze of his questioner.

'Because I think that if you was to try a bit harder, something might occur to you, Tom.' Sedgwick stroked his chin for a moment. 'See, the captain's barge is my boat, and I say who is in the crew or not, and I like my crew to be loyal. Loyal to me, as well as to the captain. Are you loyal, Tom?'

'Sure I am, Able,' said Rodgers. 'You can count on me, mate.'

'Now, that is very good to hear. So you won't have a problem telling me what it was that you were slipped when we was alongside the old *Indy*?'

'W... w... what you talking about?' stuttered Rodgers.

'Oh dear, that is a shame,' said the coxswain. 'So all that talk just now about how I could count on you was so much gammon. Pity, mate. I will need you to give me your hat back and all that green ribbon needs to be taken out of your shirt. Middle of the dog watch will be fine for you to return it. And I will let Mr Taylor know you need to be reallocated to other duties. Not to worry, I have plenty of men who will jump to take your place in the boat.' He turned away to leave, but was stopped by a hand on his arm.

'Hang on there, Able, mate,' said Rodgers. 'There is no

need to do anything hasty like.' He pulled him back behind the bulkhead and then peered around the corner to check they were not being overheard. 'Look, if I let's you know, you must keep it quiet,' he hissed. 'He would bloody kill me if he knew I was telling you.'

'I have never grassed on a shipmate yet, Tom,' said Sedgwick. 'I just need to know what is going on in my boat. What was it that was passed down to you? Some baccy? A bit of booze was it?'

'Nothing like that, Able, I promise,' said Rodgers. 'It was only a letter. I collect them for Sexton.'

'A letter for Sexton?' mussed Sedgwick. 'That is very interesting. And what did this letter say?'

'Well how should I know?' protested the bargeman. 'I can't bleeding read.'

'No, I don't suppose you can,' said the coxswain. 'Alright. If I let you keep your seat in the boat, here is what is going to happen. You still take the letters just like now, but you pass them to me first, before they get delivered to Sexton.'

'You've got to promise me that no word of this will get to him,' said Rodgers. 'You don't know him like what I do. He's as mean a bastard as they come.'

'Then stop helping him,' said Sedgwick. 'But alright, I'll see you get them back before he realizes anything's up. So are we good Tom?' The bargeman let out a sigh.

'Alright, I'll do it.'

Chapter 5
Bertheaume Bay

Two days later the *Titan* sailed back along the Iroise channel and out to sea once more, after another successful reconnaissance of Brest harbour. A breeze from the south was blowing across the calm water, pushing the frigate along and making the gentle waves sparkle in the sunlight. Clay could feel the spring sunshine on the back of his dark blue coat as he stood with his telescope and examined the north shore of the channel. The warmth helped to ease the ache in his wounded shoulder, so that today he could hold his spyglass up to his eye for a little longer than was usual. The coastline that slipped by was thronged once more with costal traffic, huddled in clumps beneath the batteries and waiting for the frigate to pass before they could resume their journey towards Brest. Just opposite he could see a large, heavily laden brig that lay deep on her reflection.

'She will be snug in Bertheaume Bay tonight, waiting for the tide to turn, you mark my words, sir,' said the first lieutenant from the rail beside him. 'If she is carrying an ounce less than two hundred tons of cargo, all of it military stores, my name isn't George Taylor. A prize court would condemn her in a flash.' He stared with longing across at the brig, and as if to emphasise how unobtainable she was, the battery protecting her tried a ranging shot. A cloud of dirty smoke appeared, together with a mass of tiny white specs. Clay had just decided that they must be disturbed sea birds flying up from the cliff below the gun battery when the shot landed a comfortable few hundred yards from the ship's side.

'*Indefatigable* in sight, sir,' reported Warwick, touching his hat in salute. Clay took his eye from his telescope and looked at the ship's master. He was a small man, middle aged, with brown hair and eyes. He was also very quietly spoken, which meant that Clay had to take a moment to recall what it was that he had said.

'Thank you, Mr Warwick,' he replied. 'Please have the commodore signalled. *Titan* to flag. One additional enemy ship of the line present over last report.'

'Aye aye, sir,' replied the master.

'When the signal has been sent, would you be kind enough to join myself and Mr Taylor on the starboard rail, and can you bring your chart with you.'

'It seems strange for a sea officer to be so quiet in his discourse,' remarked Clay to his first lieutenant. 'After so many years in direct competition with ship board noise and gales of wind I would have expected him to speak with greater volume. My sister and mother always protest at how loud I am for the first few weeks after I am newly returned ashore. Has Mr Warwick always spoken thus?'

'Always, sir,' replied Taylor. 'In the wardroom we have

the tiller just above our heads, and when the sea is running I confess I struggle to comprehend one word in six. It is a shame, for he is a most accomplished channel pilot whose opinions on navigation are well worth attending to.'

When Warwick returned to join his captain and first lieutenant, the *Titan* was level with Point de St Mathieu at the entrance to the channel. Now the coast swung away from them to be replaced by a group of rocky little islands that disappeared in a ragged line towards the north west. In among them Clay could make out one of the other frigates of the Inshore Squadron.

'That will be the *Concord,* sir,' explained Taylor. 'She guards the northern passage from Brest that runs towards Ushant and the Channel beyond.'

'Thank you, Mr Taylor,' said Clay. 'Now Mr Warwick, can you show me... good gracious, what has happened to your chart?'

'My apologies, sir,' said the master. 'I leant it to Mr Morton this morning, and he stood a little close to Nancy, our wardroom goat. Fortunately she has only consumed the one corner, and it don't signify excessively, being a portion of the land. I shall repair it directly we are finished here.'

'Please see that you do,' said Clay, trying his best to keep a straight face. 'I had thought that we might profit by this fine weather for you to identify some of the more perilous reefs for me. Where, for example, is the Vieux Moines?'

'If you direct your gaze towards the headland, do you see a cluster of dome shaped black rocks, sir? They are perhaps two cables out from the land.'

'Yes, I see them,' said the captain. 'What does it mean then, Vieux Moines?'

'Apparently the name means old monks,' explained Warwick. 'I imagine that the rocks are meant to be the tops of their shaved heads and the white water splashing about them is their hair. When the sea is tolerably lively they can indeed look like that.'

'Well I never,' said Clay. 'I daresay they do. And where is that wicked Black Stones Reef that I have heard about?'

'We shall pass it soon on this course, sir,' said the master. 'If you look a point off the starboard bow, do you see a long line of troubled water? That is Black Stones. It is set down in the French, Pierres Noir on the chart. That can be a very nasty spot, sir, particularly at high water when most of the rocks are under the surface.' Clay turned his glass to follow the line of the master's arm.

'A very long reef indeed,' he said. 'Why, it must be at least four, maybe five cables long. Are those fishing boats I can see, working right in amongst the rocks?'

'Very likely, sir,' said Warwick. 'These reefs are full of lobster. In good weather the boats will be out checking their pots, whether we are present or not. They know that nobody makes war on fishermen.'

'What did you just say, Mr Warwick?' asked Clay, looking round at the master.

'Eh, I believe I said that nobody makes war on fishermen,' he repeated.

'Yes, that is quite correct, they don't,' said Clay, his voice far away. He shut his telescope with a snap, and looked up at the commissioning pennant that flapped at the masthead. The wind was still blowing from the south.

'The tide will be running out from the Goulet de Brest until about, what, eleven tonight, Mr Warwick?' he asked.

'Eleven twenty, sir,' corrected the master.

'Good, and the moon sets about an hour earlier,' said Clay to himself. He looked once more towards the reef.

'Tell me, is there any good holding ground near to the Pierres Noir where we might anchor till sunset? Somewhere close to those fishing boats?' he asked.

'Yes sir, the bottom on this side of the reef is of good firm sand. I would not want to anchor there in a blow, but in these conditions we should be quite safe.'

'Capital, that will do passing well,' said Clay. 'Kindly sail the ship over there, if you please. Mr Taylor, we shall drop anchor where Mr Warwick directs, and then can you have the men exercised at the guns. We are still a long way from the three broadsides in two minutes I talked of when I first took command. Let Mr Morton take charge of the gun drill, and then you and Mr Warwick can join me in my cabin. All this talk of fishing has given me an idea.'

*****

The gun drill was over, and late afternoon was moving towards early evening. In the great cabin of the frigate, Clay sat at his dining table with Warwick's damaged chart spread out on it, and the sheaf of notes he had put together in front of him. Grouped around the table were Taylor, Morton and Warwick.

'Now, gentlemen, here is the plan,' he began. 'Just before sunset Mr Taylor in the pinnace and Mr Morton in the launch will row across to the Pierres Noir. You will each surprise and capture a fishing boat and return with it here to the ship. Timing is key, gentlemen. I want the sun setting in the west to blind any French observer on the Point St Mathieu to what we are about. It is essential that the French are unaware that we have taken possession of these boats.'

'I understand the order, sir,' said Morton. 'But why are we to capture these fishing boats in the first place? I had understood that we were not to make war on fishermen?'

'We are not capturing them, Mr Morton, only borrowing them,' explained the captain. 'The crews can stay confined on board till we have no further use for their vessels. They shall be sprats to catch us a mackerel. When we have them in our possession, we will fill each with a boarding party of thirty seamen and twenty marines, concealed below decks. Mr Taylor will take the first boat and Mr Morton the second.'

'What is to be our target, sir?' asked Taylor.

'You will sail down the Iroise Channel, seemingly bound for Brest to land your catch,' said Clay. 'There will be plenty of moonlight for you to navigate by, and Mr Warwick will pilot the lead boat. When you reach the Goulet the tide will still be running against you, so it will be quite natural for you to wait in Bertheaume Bay. Right in amongst all the other shipping gathered there.'

'But what will stop the French batteries that guard that bay from opening fire on us, sir? asked Warwick.

'On French fishing boats waiting for the tide to turn?'

queried the captain. 'I very much doubt that they will, Mr Warwick. As has been said repeatedly, nobody makes war on fishermen.' Clay looked around the table in his cabin to see if there were any other questions. When there were none he continued.

'When the moon sets at ten thirty, that will be your chance,' he said. 'Attack and capture what you can. If that big brig Mr Taylor and I saw earlier is to hand, make that your chief object. The wind is in the south, which will serve for you to bring her out. Once you have your prize or prizes you can return the fishing boats to their owners.'

'I suppose we are to do all this as stealthily as possible, sir,' asked Morton, 'so as not to alert the batteries?'

'Certainly on your way into the bay, Mr Morton,' said his captain, 'but once the action starts you must do quite the reverse. Plenty of noise in the dark, if you please. You must let the French know there is a fox among the hens. I want you to panic the other vessels into flight. That will cover your escape, for the French batteries will have no idea which ships to fire upon. You can pose as another startled vessel making your escape, and in all the confusion it would be strange if you will not be able to slip away.'

'Which only leaves us the challenge of sailing any prize back up the Iroise Channel in the dark, sir' said Taylor.

'The *Titan* will remain at anchor here, displaying three red lights in a row from the masthead. That will give you a good reliable mark to steer by, Mr Taylor.'

*****

'For the love of God, will you move your fat arse up, Sam,' moaned the voice of O'Malley from somewhere in the dark of the fishing boat's hold. 'I am right on the fecking edge.'

'I can't make any more room, Sean,' protested Evans. 'I got Adam's cutlass sticking in me bleeding leg.'

'It ain't my cutlass, Sam, said Trevan's voice from the other side of the boat. 'I am over here.'

'It might be mine, mate,' said the voice of Rosso, apparently from somewhere under Evans' arm. 'Sorry.'

'Christ, I hate the smell of fish,' muttered the big Londoner. 'It's like Billingsgate in August down here.'

Just above their heads the hatchway of the fishing boat slid open and a stream of moonlight silvered the upturned faces of the forty-odd sailors and marines that packed the hold. The shape of Midshipman Butler loomed over them, his bulky frame silhouetted by stars.

'Hold your noise down there,' he hissed. 'We are about to pass one of the French gun batteries. Absolute silence, you men.'

'Aye aye, sir,' replied Evans. 'Any chance you can leave that there hatch open? We're all fit to pass out down here.'

Butler disappeared, leaving the hatch ajar. A little cool night breeze came through it to help disperse the worst of the smell of fish.

'Absolute silence, is it? Easy for him to fecking say,' muttered O'Malley, giving Evans a savage dig in the ribs. 'He ain't the one with one buttock being torn from the other.' He wiped at some of the glitter of fish scales that sparkled on his arm and settled down as comfortably as he could on the little slither of upturned fish box that was not occupied by Rosso or the huge Londoner.

‘Qui va la?’ came a challenge from some distance away. Someone on deck gave a reply, and the boat sailed on.

‘Who was that talking in Frog?’ whispered Evans.

‘That’s Duplain, foretop man,’ muttered one of the marines. ‘He’s from Jersey, and can jabber like a proper Frenchy.’

More hails came down through the open hatch to the men who waited in the hold. Some seemed distant, others frighteningly close from either left or right as the boat crept deeper into the bay, and each time Duplain replied. They felt the boat swing up into the wind and then a rattling roar sounded from forward as the anchor was dropped. Evans rose to his feet and extended himself upwards till his head emerged proud of the deck. From his six foot six inch frame he peeped around him.

‘Get out of sight, Evans,’ hissed Lieutenant Taylor’s voice, and the Londoner ducked back down into the hold.

‘What did you see, Sam?’ asked O’Malley, now settled in place on the fish box.

‘Bay is right full of boats and ships,’ replied Evans, looking around for somewhere to sit. ‘There must be at least twenty, including a proper big one that we are moored close to.’

‘That will be the brig Pipe was after us capturing,’ said O’Malley. The others all looked at him in surprise. ‘What you all staring at?’

‘How do you know what the bleeding captain wants us to

do?' asked Evans.

'Oh, that's easy enough,' said the Irishman. 'Isn't Hart one of my mates, and wasn't he serving the fecking coffee in the cabin earlier when Pipe was telling the Grunters the plan?' O'Malley taped his moonlit nose with a single silver finger. 'If yous wants to know what is going on aboard, share your baccy with the captain's steward once in a while, fellers.'

A few minutes later it went dark again at the hatch as the shadow of Lieutenant Taylor loomed over them.

'Only another half hour or so till the moon sets, lads, then we will get you all up on deck,' he said. 'Haven't you got anywhere to sit, Evans?'

'Eh, not any more, sir,' replied the Londoner, glaring down at O'Malley.

'Oh, just make yourself as comfortable as you are able,' continued Taylor. 'When the order comes to deploy I shall require the marines to go to the stern with Lieutenant Macpherson; the rest of you will be with me in the waist. Till then hold tight, and keep the noise down.'

'Isn't that Grunters all over?' asked a gruff voice opposite O'Malley. 'We are required to suffer down here while they lord it up on deck.' The man leant forward into the moonlight and first hawked and then spat onto the floor of the hold. He was a tall man, with arms that were heavy with tattoos. Once he had cleared the phlegm from his mouth he held out his hand to the Irishman.

'Richard Sexton,' he said. 'Formally captain of the afterguard, now just an able seaman.'

'Sean O'Malley, forecastle man,' said the Irishman, taking

his hand. 'That's tough on you, feller. I heard it was the last captain as had you disrated. Drunkenness, wasn't it?'

'That's right,' said Sexton, 'but I got the old bastard back good an' proper, don't you worry on that score.' A number of the seaman around him rumbled their approval.

'Tell me, Sean,' he continued. 'Are you one of the lads that volunteered to join the ship?'

'Sure I was, along with Evans and Rosso here, and Trevan over there. We been with Pipe a while, and always done fine in the matter of fecking prize money, like.'

'That's good,' said Sexton. 'Cause Sheridan was such a useless arse we never got a sniff of any lucre. So you having been with Pipe an' all, have you shipped with the new Grunter in charge of the Lobsters? This Macpherson bloke?'

'Sure I have,' said the Irishman. 'He was in charge of the Lobsters on our last barky – the old *Rush*.'

'Is he any good?'

'Is Macpherson any good?' exclaimed O'Malley. 'I doubt if there's a better Grunter in the whole fecking Royal Marines. He saved our lives when we was on shore in St Lucia last year. We were serving these guns trying to batter down a fortress wall when all manner of Frog soldiers came sneaking out. I am telling you there was hundreds of them. We were up to our shanks in shite till Macpherson showed up and saw the feckers off with a bare forty of his Lobsters. He is as game as they come, that one.'

'Is that right?' said a thoughtful Sexton. 'That is very reassuring, my friend. Thank you for that, Sean.'

*****

It was dark now in Bertheaume Bay. The moon had set behind the sea cliffs and hills of Brittany and left the night sky to those stars that were not veiled behind wisps of cloud. From the dark bowl of the shore around them the occasional light from croft or cottage winked in the night, while at the southern end of the bay light spilt out across the water from the fishing village of Camaret. On either side of the entrance of the bay, where the dark shore touched the star-filled sky, were two blocks of something more solid. The stone walls and straight lines of the twin shore batteries that guarded the entrance.

Lieutenant Taylor looked away from the batteries and back into the boat. Running his way back through the cross fire of those guns was a problem for the future. First he had to capture the brig. She was just beside the fishing boat, perhaps sixty yards downwind of them. Her twin masts towered up above the other vessels in the bay. They lay dotted across the water, perhaps twenty or thirty little coasters and luggers. All of them swung and bobbed at anchor, waiting for the tide to turn. He returned his attention to the brig, the main prize tonight. He could tell that her crew were alert. The sound of their noisy talk drifted across the water to him. Alert, but perhaps not expecting any attack, he decided as a burst of laughter rang out. He looked down on to the deck of the fishing boat. The marines and sailors lay in a packed line along the portside gunwale, out of sight but ready. Lieutenant Taylor looked over the side and tried to gauge the state of the tide. He spat onto the surface of the sea and watched the globule of saliva. It lay still on the surface. Good, he thought, it is slack water at last.

'Mr Butler,' he hissed, 'signal to the other boat to attack.'

'Aye aye, sir,' replied the midshipman.

'Let slip the anchor in the bow there,' he whispered.

He heard a splash from the front of the fishing boat, and they began to drift with the wind down towards the brig. Looking across at the other fishing boat he could see that Morton too was now adrift. Closer and closer they came, the boat starting to rotate like a top on the calm water as her bow turned towards the southerly breeze.

'Mr Butler, take a couple of hands and get some oars deployed on the starboard side,' he ordered. 'I want us to strike her broadside on.'

'Aye, aye, sir,' replied Butler. Taylor resumed his watch on the growing dark mass ahead. When they had drifted half of the way towards their target, the noise of the crew's conversation stopped. There was a pause, and then a hail was shouted out into the night.

'Make a suitable reply, Duplain,' he said. The Jersey man started to talk, but his flow was interrupted by an angry shout, followed by the flash and bang as a musket was fired from the brig. A bullet whined past Taylor's head.

'They have guessed what we are about, sir,' replied the foretop man, a little unnecessarily.

From all around Taylor came cries of alarm as the crews on the other boats realised something was amiss in the anchorage. He tried to ignore the commotion and just concentrate on the large ship that was their target. From onboard he heard the blast of a whistle and the stamp and rush of the crew being summoned to man her side. A little later came the sound of someone clanging the brig's bell continuously in warning. Two further muskets flashed in the night.

'Mr Macpherson!' he shouted. 'Kindly ready your men to give the French a volley just before we board.'

'Aye aye, sir,' came the Scotsman's reply, his voice harsh and tense. 'On your feet, men, and form a two deep line there.'

'Come on,' urged Taylor, as the gap between the fishing boat and the ship's side inched narrower. He glanced across at the second fishing boat, to check that it too was approaching the brig. More muskets flashed in the night, and one of the marines gave a cry as he crashed down.

'Close up there!' said the voice of Macpherson. 'Marines, fix bayonets!'

Another musket flashed orange, and in the brief moment of light Taylor saw the side of the brig, lined with the faces of her crew and the glint of the weapons they held. She was close enough now, he decided.

'On your feet, men!' he barked. 'Now with the grappling irons!' From the each end of the fishing boat two lines flew out through the air. They caught high in the rigging, and as they were hauled inboard the strip of water between the gunwale of the fishing boat and the side of thc ship vanished.

'Marines, take aim!' yelled Macpherson, drawing his sword in a flash of silver under the stars. 'Fire!' The crash of the volley and the bang as the boat struck home came almost together.

'Up and at them, lads!' yelled Taylor, drawing his own sword and jumping up into the main chains of the brig. With a ragged cheer the other sailors and marines followed him up the side, and they were soon locked in a struggle with the French defenders. Cutlasses clashed and sparked as they struck together, pistols and muskets banged out, and the marines thrust with their needle-sharp bayonets to clear the way onto the deck. A second thump and cheer from near to the stern of the brig announced the arrival of the other boat.

In the bow of the fishing boat Evans had finished hauling in on the grappling line and now looked about him for somewhere to make it fast. His fighting lust was up, and he longed to join the battle. He ran his hand along the unfamiliar gunwale of the boat until he felt the rounded end of a cleat in the dark. He secured the line around it, reached down to pick up his boarding axe and turned towards the fight. Another musket went off in the dark, and the flash of light froze the scene in front of him. It highlighted the struggling mass of sailors and marines he expected to see, slowly forcing themselves onto the deck of the French ship against the fierce resistance of its crew, but he also saw something unexpected. In that moment he saw that he was not the only man left on board the fishing boat. In the waist of the vessel he could make out the figure of Richard Sexton, crouched down behind the boat's winch. One arm was held out like a finger sign as he took aim with his pistol. The gun was pointing at Lieutenant Macpherson's back as he led on his marines.

'Oh no you fucking don't!' yelled Evans, his cry lost

amongst the clash of battle. He threw his axe over arm, and the handle clattered flat against Sexton's back, knocking him forwards. He sprang back up and turned in surprise, saw the big Londoner racing across the deck towards him and swung his pistol round. Evans struck his arm to one side and the pistol went off as the two men crashed down onto the deck. They scrabbled together, Evans trying to keep free of Sexton, where he could use his longer reach to land solid blows, while the smaller man sought to grapple with one hand while he tried to reach the clasp knife in his belt with the other. The Londoner ducked back to avoid a vicious head butt and brought his fist crashing down onto Sexton's jaw. He followed up with a huge blow into his opponent's body and felt him go limp as the wind was knocked out of him. He rose to his feet, picked up his boarding axe and stood over the prone figure, yelling down at him.

'You're going to fucking hang for this,' he shouted. 'I saw you try and kill Macpherson, you piece of shit!'

'Wait Evans,' gasped Sexton, pushing himself up. 'You don't want to do that.'

'No, you're wrong,' said the Londoner. 'I really do want to see you swing for this.'

'Aye, I bet you do,' said Sexton. 'But that's not what is going to happen. See, I know who you are. I was sure I had seen you before when you first joined, but I just couldn't place you. And then we did gun drill this afternoon. It was right hot work, what with all that sun. Soon as I saw you with your shirt stripped off, it all came back to me. You're the prize fighter who knocked down Southwark Jack back in ninety-five.'

'Yeah, I bleeding did,' snarled Evans, raising the axe. 'And he was a damn sight tougher than you are.'

'That's right,' smiled Sexton, picking himself back up. 'Only I was in the know about that mill. You was supposed to take a fall, not win, weren't you? There was a bloody fortune lost that night, and there are no end of angry traps that are still after you Sam, my boy. I know many of them, all good mates of mine. Be a real shame if I told them where to go a looking for you now.'

'You wouldn't dare!' said Evans. Sexton laughed at him.

'Come off it, Sam. You don't really think I ain't got the balls to do it? You do know I have led a mutiny on a King's ship? Compared with that, telling a few mates where they can find you is of very little note. I wouldn't be so sure as to what a desperate man is capable of, if I was you.'

'Maybe I am desperate too,' shouted Evans, raising the axe again. 'Maybe I'll kill you now.'

'In front of all these people?' said Sexton, pointing at the fight still raging yards from them. 'It'll be you that'll swing for murder.' He patted the ex-prize fighter on the side of his face. 'Vexing, ain't it? Still, this is how it shall be. You keep your trap shut about what you saw me do tonight, and I might be persuaded to hold my peace a little longer. Now, we had best join in this fight, else we will both be hanged from the same yardarm for cowardice.'

Chapter 6
Alone

'So how the deuce did you contrive to get the brig out from under the French noses?' asked Pellew, laying down his knife and fork, the food on his plate ignored for now.

'The chief part of the vessels in the bay were all cutting their cables in panic and heading out to sea, Sir Edward,' explained Clay. 'Some ended that night on the rocks, others fell on board each other, and in all the confusion Lieutenant Taylor was able to sail the brig out through the middle of them all. The French batteries barely fired a shot for fear of striking their own commerce.'

'Sounds like the scramble at the start of the St Leger! How simply splendid!' laughed Captain Warburton, the commander of the *Concord* and the other guest seated at the dinner table in the *Indefatigable*'s great cabin.

'He performed well then, your first lieutenant? said the commodore. 'Strange that Captain Sheridan never had occasion to bring his name before me.'

'Hardly, Sir Edward,' said Warburton. 'Sheridan would

never have attempted such a coup.' He turned back towards the captain of the *Titan*. 'Do you consider it to be a ruse that you might take advantage of again?'

'That will be rather less easy now,' said Clay. 'When we stood in to reconnoitre Brest yesterday I observed that the French have now stationed one of their larger frigates in Bertheaume Bay, doubtless to deter any further attacks.'

'Yes, and my cook has a grave complaint to lay at your feet,' added the commodore. 'He was telling me that the local fisherman have become somewhat shy of our approach since the *Titan* surprised those two boats. He is in despair as to where he will be able to obtain a new source of fresh lobsters.'

'Pity,' said Warburton, sipping at his wine. 'Still, I daresay the desire for some of your specie will bring them back soon enough. But stationing a frigate in the bay certainly shows how provoking for the Frogs your attack was, Clay, even if they are rather bolting the stable door after the dashed horse has gone, what?'

'Quite,' agreed Pellew. 'I hold it to be very satisfactory that Captain Clay has obliged them to take such measures. The more we can bring them out of the shelter of Brest, the more opportunities we shall have to fight and defeat them.'

'Hear him,' said Warburton, drumming the flat of his hand on the table top in appreciation of the sentiment.

'Gentlemen, a toast to the *Titan*'s splendid victory, if you please,' said the commodore, raising his glass. His two guests followed his lead and drained their wine.

'Ah, that is a lovely drop of bishop, Sir Edward,' enthused

Warburton. 'I would dearly love to know how you are able to source such excellent claret. Pray tell, what is your secret?'

'Oh, that is simple enough,' said Pellew. 'Anything can be obtained, even during wartime, for a price. Being from Cornwall, some of my people know where to find those with the diligence to source the odd case that has slipped across the channel on a moonlit night, while the revenue cutter was in port. I use my connections, and the weight of my purse does the rest.' He chuckled to himself for a moment, and then turned towards his other guest.

'Do not attend overly to my swaggering, Captain Clay, I pray you,' he said. 'I like to play at being a man of breeding like Warburton here. The fact is that all this, the knighthood, my estate, all the luxury that surrounds you, the whole lot is paid for with the newest of money. Much like you, I came into this world with little more than my wits. My people were barely above tradesman. I ran away to sea at fourteen to escape a fresh beating at the hands of my headmaster at Truro Grammar School. Every promotion I received, every ship I was given was as a reward for some act of gallantry or minor success. You of all people will understand how hard it is to make your way in the service without any preferment.'

'Quite so, Sir Edward,' said Clay. 'I cannot count the times I have had to watch those with connections be promoted ahead of me.'

'Steady there, you two,' protested Warburton. 'You have both made post now, haven't you? I may have a father who was an admiral, but I was still required to pass the same examination as you two to become a lieutenant, don't you know?'

'Examined by a kindly godfather who overlooked that he had three years too little sea time, I'll warrant,' said Pellew to Clay in a stage whisper. They all laughed at this, although it was noticeable that the captain of the *Concord* made no attempt to deny the accusation.

Clay sat back in his chair and sighed with contentment. He made a mental note that should he ever be as wealthy as Pellew, he too would spend at least some of his money on the very best of cabin stores and the finest of cooks to prepare them. The food and drink were far better than anything he had tasted on board a ship before. He smiled at his host and fellow guest. They were very different from each other, the aristocratic Warburton and the down to earth commodore. He had half-expected that two such veteran captains would look down on him as a junior with no connections, but he could not have been made to feel more welcome. He was contently full, in convivial company, with a glass of Pellew's smuggled wine in front of him. The capture of the brig would net him a further generous slice of prize money; the victory would help to cement the positive work he was doing with his mutinous crew. He was young, in command of his own frigate, and was well regarded by his superiors. All was going splendidly, he told himself.

'Now, gentlemen,' said Pellew, setting down his glass. 'Pleasant as our dinner together has been, I have had some disturbing news that I must appraise you of. Where do you suppose the Channel Fleet to be?'

'Thirty leagues due west of Ushant, Sir Edward, ready to support us,' said Clay. 'Unless the wind should blow above a topsail gale, that is, in which case the fleet will withdraw to the shelter of Torbay.'

'Bravo, captain,' said the Cornishman. 'I see you have committed my sailing instructions to memory, and can recall them in spite of the five bottles of claret we have drunk already.' He turned to his steward and waved forward a sixth bottle. 'You can clear away the dead marines, Weaver,' he added, pointing at the empty bottles, 'and then kindly retire and see we are not disturbed.'

'Aye aye, Sir Edward,' murmured the steward as he clanked out of the cabin and closed the door behind him.

'Unfortunately, gentlemen, Captain Clay has informed us as to where the Channel Fleet *should* be,' continued Pellew, his face becoming grave. 'I must inform you that at this moment the fleet is actually at anchor in Spithead, with all of the ships' crews in open revolt. I have just this morning received the news from Lord Bridport. He himself has been put ashore from his flagship, as have all of the ships' captains, together with some of the more unpopular officers. The men say they will not sail until their demands are met.'

'Good God,' exclaimed Warburton. 'The whole damned fleet have mutinied! It quite beggars belief. What are their demands, then?'

'Actually they are not so unreasonable,' replied the commodore. 'Better pay, better vittles, a Royal Pardon for the mutineers, more shore leave and the removal of certain officers. How long all this will take the Admiralty to resolve is anyone's guess, but I live in hope it shall be tolerably soon. Admiral Bridport believes the government is in a mood to be conciliatory, given that with no Channel Fleet there is little to stop the French from invading. But even with goodwill on the

Government's part it shall still take some time. An increase in the men's rate of pay will require an Act of Parliament, for example.'

'What must we do, Sir Edward?' asked Clay.

'First of all, you must breathe no word of this to anybody,' said Pellew. 'If the hands find out what is afoot, they may all seek to join the revolt.'

'Agreed,' said Warburton. 'My crew has been petitioning me over pay for months now.'

'Secondly, no hint of this must get to the French,' continued their host. 'They must see that the Inshore Squadron is carrying on as if nothing were amiss. If once they realise that there is no fleet over the horizon, and that all that stands between them and control of the Channel is our four little frigates, the game will well and truly be up.'

*****

The orlop deck of the *Titan* was below the waterline. Tucked between the hold beneath and the lower deck above, it had only five feet of head room, which was quite inadequate for any of the six sailors who had gathered there. On the other hand it was one of the few places on board the frigate where they could meet even for a short while in anything approaching privacy. The six were grouped in a circle around the single lantern they had taken from its place by the main hatch way and brought in to this normally dark space. They had crawled their way into the centre of the cable tier, where there was a small area of empty deck. The flickering orange light turned their hunched forms into the shadows of giants that stretched and flowed over the coils of cable that occupied the tier around them.

'Here is the paper what I was given when we took Pipe across for his shindig with the commodore,' said Thomas Rodgers. 'Like I promised, Able, I am showin' it to you first, but I got to give it to Sexton. He's expecting it and he will bloody kill me if I don't get it to him soon.' He glanced up as the sound of footsteps sounded on the lower deck just above their heads. 'Be quick, lads, for Christ sake.'

'All right, Tom,' said Sedgwick. 'Calm down. None of us want to pass more time down here than needs be.' He passed the paper across to Rosso. 'I can make most of it out, but you are better at reading than me, Rosie.' Rosso flattened the paper onto the deck in front of the lamp and read the note out loud.

'Friends onboard the Titan,

Now is the time to make the ship your own. Intelligence on which total reliance may be placed has reached us that the Channel Fleet has risen at last. The crews have taken control of their ships, set their captains ashore and cast out their more wicked officers. A list of fair and just demands has been given to the Admiralty.

Our gallant shipmates aboard are steady in their resolve, and more ships join them every day. The ships of the Inshore Squadron must follow their brave lead. The time has come for us all to throw off

our yokes and join our brothers at Spithead.
Huzza for the Red Flag of liberty!

The Delegates of the Indefatigable.'

'That can't be right, can it?' queried Trevan. 'The fleet is just off Ushant in the Soundings.'

'Are you fecking sure of that?' asked O'Malley. 'When did you last set eyes on the buggers?'

'Jesus,' said Evans. 'The whole fleet in mutiny? What is that all about?'

'Pay mainly,' said Rosso. 'We have all done alright in the matter of prize money, thanks to sticking with Pipe these last two years, but for those sailors in ships of the line who must rely only on their basic pay, it has been right bad.'

'That's right,' agreed Rodgers. 'An' the fucking soldiers got their pay put up too. What fighting do they do, I ask you? They just have to set upon rioting mill workers and round up rick burning peasants. What about us in the navy, out in all weathers actually fighting this bleeding war! Aren't we the true bulwark of England?' The others looked at him in silence for a moment. 'N... not that I'm a mutineer or nothing,' he added, looking a little sheepish.

'So what should we do?' asked Sedgwick. 'Shall we warn the Grunters?'

'They probably know already, Able,' said Rosso. 'And they are keeping it real quiet like. I know I would. Pipe will not want news like that spreading on a ship as has just had a mutiny of its own.'

'Aye,' agreed Evans. 'And it don't seem quite right to grass up a shipmate to the Grunters, even if it is that bastard Sexton.'

'Since when did you start watching out for him, Sam?' asked Rosso. 'I have not heard you pipe that tune before.'

'I am just saying, till the ship rises he is still a shipmate, like,' muttered Evans.

'Do we reckon the ship will rise?' asked Trevan. 'Seems to me to be a happier place of late, especially since we got that prize an' all.' The others looked at Rodgers, who shifted uneasily on the deck.

'There is no doubt the lads are a lot happier with Pipe than with that bastard Sheridan,' he said. 'But they are still right sore about their pay an' all. Some are saying the last mutiny served to get rid of a bad captain, so maybes that's what you got to do to get the Admiralty to listen to you.'

'He's right, you know,' said Sedgwick. 'I have known tension like this back on the plantation, before a slave rising. The atmosphere on the lower deck is bad. There are plenty enough as might rise if things start to go wrong.'

The others were quiet for a moment. From the forecastle far above them came the sound of eight muffled bell strokes, and the deck over their heads exploded with noise as the watch was called.

'Oh, Christ!' yelled Rodgers, snatching up the paper. 'If I don't get this to Sexton, I am going to be in a world of trouble.' He hurried off towards the main hatch, followed by the other sailors, all of whose faces bore grim expressions in the guttering light.

On the Lee Shore

*****

The frigate spent much of the next afternoon beating out to sea into a strengthening westerly gale. The cliffs and reefs of the Brittany coast now showed their true character after several days of mild weather. The rushing wind conjured up huge waves that sped across the ocean and thundered into the land, sending towering white columns of spray that rose ever higher up the cliffs before cascading back down again. The quiet reefs that Clay had observed in the spring sunshine with Henry Warwick now foamed and spat like the boiling cauldrons of sea hags.

But the ship was relatively safe. The coast was a black-notched saw edge on the horizon stretched between the dark green sea and the heavy grey clouds overhead. The *Titan* had swayed down her upper masts, and set enough fore and aft sails to allow her to beat forward into the wind at about the same rate as the long Atlantic rollers were pushing her back towards the coast. The motion of the ship had become a long series of corkscrew rolls as she passed diagonally across the flow of waves, making life uncomfortable for the ship's officers in the wardroom of the frigate, tucked down on the water line just behind the rudder.

'He's a queer one, our new captain,' said Lieutenant Morton, his voice forceful to make himself heard above the loud creak of the timbers by the other officers gathered around the wardroom table. They were all waiting for the arrival of their evening meal. With each fresh roll of the ship their sets of cutlery started to move across the cloth, and each officer at his place instinctively halted the motion with the palms of his hands, without the need to look down.

'Why do you say that, Edmund?' asked John Blake, the frigate's third lieutenant, who was seated next to Morton. He was a thin young man of medium height with sandy coloured hair.

'Well, taking that prize was all very well,' said the second lieutenant. 'But the way that he made use of those fishing boats to sneak into the bay like a thief in the night was rather a base trick. Not the sort of thing a gentleman would do at all. Still, I suppose if you stand in need of the prize money.' He brushed away some imagined dirt from the sleeve of his immaculate uniform coat, and smiled at his fellow officers.

'So how do you believe a gentleman should have approached the problem, Edmund?' asked Macpherson.

'If he was prepared to hazard a King's ship to achieve the capture of a merchantman at all, which is doubtful,' said Morton, 'he would certainly have been more straightforward about the whole enterprise. Up and at 'em, that's what I say.'

'Hear him,' said Blake. 'Up and at them, that's the way!' He was about to thump the table in appreciation with his fist when a further roller forced him to turn the movement into a quick grab to prevent the escape of his fork. 'I hope Mr Warwick is contriving to make himself understood on deck. I do wonder how he manages when it blows above a cap full of wind.'

'You have taken part in plenty of cutting out expeditions I collect then, Mr Blake?' asked Macpherson. 'To have such firm views on how they should proceed?'

'Eh no, not actually taken part in any as such,' replied the young lieutenant, a little flustered. 'My comment was more in the way of general approval of Mr Morton's sentiments.'

'Mr Blake was one of our young midshipmen until Captain Sheridan was able to arrange for him to pass for lieutenant late last year,' explained Taylor. 'He has only ever served on the *Titan*, and Captain Sheridan was rather less industrious then Captain Clay. We saw little direct action with the enemy these last few years.'

'Ha, you can say that again,' snorted Haywood, the purser, turning towards the wardroom door. 'What can be keeping the food?'

'Ah, I see,' replied the marine, returning his attention to Morton. 'I am still unclear as to which of the gentlemanly virtues would have served to get our cutting out expedition through the cross fire of a pair of forty-two pounder gun batteries as efficiently as the method we actually employed, Edmund?'

'Perhaps that's just it, Macpherson,' he replied. 'A gentleman might not have been motivated to try in the first place. He would have saved his men and powder for a more worthy opponent.'

'But surely then a valuable ship with a considerable cargo of military stores would now be at the disposal of the enemy, rather than on its way in to Plymouth?' persisted Macpherson. 'Unlike Mr Blake here, I have participated in numerous cutting out expeditions, both of the blunder straight in variety and those involving a degree of stealth and deception. I am quite clear as to which method answers the best.'

'So are we to expect more such distasteful assaults on trade from our new captain?' asked Morton.

'I believe we shall,' said the Scotsman. He turned towards Blake. 'And I am sure they will involve your participation, John, if only to complete your education in the art of war. I was thinking that we should invite the captain to join us at one of our dinners in order to celebrate our recent victory. It might also permit an opportunity for him to share with us some of his future plans?'

'That's a very worthwhile suggestion, Tom,' enthused Taylor. 'Does anyone object?' Most of the officers nodded their assent, even John Blake, until he realised that Morton was glaring at the marine officer rather than responding.

'Excellent,' said Taylor with an awkward glance towards the second lieutenant. 'I will get an invitation arranged. Ah! Here comes our dinner at last. Mr Morton, Mr Macpherson, a glass of wine with you both.' All three drained their drinks. Morton's face was more flushed then it should have been after one drink. He placed his glass down and leant across to wipe the table cloth in front of Taylor with his napkin.

'Your pardon sir,' he said. 'I believe I may have seen some coal dust.'

*****

Forward of the wardroom, on the lower deck, the violent motion of the ship filled the space with a chorus of groans and cracks as the frames twisted with each fresh roller that ran under the keel. But in spite of the noise and the violence of the motion, the watch that was off duty tried their best to relax. At some of the mess tables men worked on pieces of scrimshaw, adding little cuts and blowing away the dust from their elaborate carvings, and reaching out without looking to catch their open clasp knifes as the motion of the ship rolled them off the edge of the tables. In the middle of the deck O'Malley was playing a duet with Fraser, the *Titan*'s Scottish sail maker's mate, and a fiddle player of some repute in his own right. The tune sawed backwards and forwards between the two rivals, while a party of sailors danced in front of them, the elegance of their whirling hornpipe punctuated by volleys of rapid steps as the performers tried to combat the sudden pitching of the ship. In a quieter space towards the aft end of the deck sat two figures, apparently trying to read out loud in spite of the fury of the gale, the cascade of music from the fiddlers, and the uncertain light. After a stumbling hour of work, the task was completed at last.

'I must say your letters is coming on right well there, Able,' said Rosso, looking up from the dog-eared pamphlet that lay on the mess table between the two friends and reaching with his arm to thump his pupil on the back. 'You do still have to spell out some of them long words, mind, but we got there in the end.' The captain's coxswain smiled in return.

'You've been so patient teaching me, Rosie,' he said. 'I don't know how to thank you. I have wanted to understand all those little squiggles, ever since I first saw slave traders use them. You may laugh to hear me say it, but back then I used to hold that they were the secret to a sort of evil magic, and that in some way it was that which gave them their power over us.'

'That so?' said Rosso. 'I suppose that may not be so far from the truth, in a way. Ain't it learning and the like that gives civilised folk all the guns and ships and money?'

'You're right there, Rosie,' smiled Sedgwick. 'You had best watch out, then, now that at least one savage has the secret to your magic!' Rosso snorted at that and picked up the pamphlet from the table. He read out the title, putting on an aristocratic voice.

'*An Essay on the Treatment and Conversion of African Slaves in the British Sugar Colonies by the Reverend James Ramsay,*' he intoned, before reverting to his usual Bristol accent. 'Not sure that will supply any magic as will change the world any time soon, Able. How did you come by this?'

'Do you remember Mr Linfield, the surgeon on the *Rush* who left the ship and married that planter's daughter back in Barbados?' said Sedgwick.

'Oh, aye. He was right hot on abolition as I recall. Did he give it to you, then?'

'He did,' said the coxswain. 'And you are wrong about these pamphlets, you know. I believe they may change the world for some of us. When I can write well enough I shall publish one myself.' Rosso looked across in surprise. There was a look of determination that was new to him in the face of his friend, a glint of zeal in his eye.

'I do declare you will,' he said. 'There's a strength in you, Able, that is right good to behold. Mind, if it's all the same with you, can we read something a little less worthy next time?'

'Sure we can, Rosie,' said Sedgwick, folding up the

pamphlet and slipping it into his pocket. 'So how did you come by your letters?'

'I learned them as a nipper,' said Rosso. 'They were thrashed into me by Mr Samways with the help of his cane when I was in school. Only good thing my Pa ever did for me, paying for me to attend. I didn't think it at the time, mind. I learnt my figures there, too.'

'If you can read and count, how come you're on the lower deck, and not a Grunter?' asked his friend. Rosso shrugged.

'Ah, that is because I still needs to lie a little low, and not draw too much attention to myself, Able,' he looked around him and saw that they were being watched from another mess table. 'I will tell you about it some time, when we are off the ship, like.'

Farther down the deck the pair of keen blue eyes that Rosso had spotted continued to watch the pair of sailors with naked hostility.

'That black monkey has been reading my letters from the *Indy*, I bleeding know it,' growled Sexton.

'Don't be bloody daft,' said Page. 'He's only a Negro. Who ever heard of one of them as could read?'

'If it ain't him, he will be passing it to one of his civilised mates as bleeding well can,' insisted the big sailor. 'He's got to that sniveling shit Rodgers in the barge crew somehow, I know he has.'

'Do you reckon he will go to the Grunters then, Dick?' asked his friend.

'Aye, maybe he will,' mused Sexton. 'Which means we need to find some way to stop his bleeding interfering. We need to sort him out and that great big sod he hangs around with, too. I think I can see how it might be done. I will need your help, Morris, and Shane and some of his paddies, an' all. Leave it to me. I believe I might have a plan as will answer.'

*****

The gale lasted for two days and nights, but before dawn on the third night the wind began to moderate and back towards the north. When Clay awoke at dawn he immediately felt the change in the ship's motion. He hurried over to the barometer mounted on the cabin bulkhead and examined the long column of mercury. The level had risen since yesterday. Good, he thought, the weather is moderating at last. He called out for Yates, his servant, and began to undress. As soon as he was shaved and in uniform he went up on deck.

'Good morning, sir,' said the officer of the watch. 'Did you pass a restful night?'

'Very comfortable, thank you, Mr Blake, now that the gale has past,' replied Clay. 'How has your watch been? Is there anything to report?'

'The wind has been moderating steadily since I came on deck, sir,' said the young lieutenant. 'Otherwise it has been quiet. From the look of the sky I believe we may have seen the last of that gale.'

'Yes,' said Clay, looking around him. The wind was still strong, but had become gusty as it lost its strength and the sea was calmer. Above his head the early morning sky was much brighter than it had been for days. 'Any sign of the rest of the squadron?'

'No, sir,' he replied. 'Perhaps they stood farther out to sea to avoid the worst of the weather.'

'Hmm, perhaps they did,' said the captain. 'You will be coming off watch shortly, I collect?'

'Yes, sir, very soon,' he replied.

'Are you hungry, Mr Blake?'

'Famished, actually, sir,' he replied with a grin.

'I well remember the morning watch being particularly trying when I was your age,' said Clay. 'Would you care to join me for breakfast? It will give us the opportunity to spend a little time together.'

'Why, I should like that above all things, sir.'

'Good, let us make it so,' said his captain, turning towards the midshipman. 'Mr Russell! Can you pass the word to my steward? Tell him I shall have a guest for breakfast this morning at eight bells, if you please.'

'Now, Mr Blake, while our breakfast is preparing, let us put her on the other tack and take her back towards the land,' ordered the captain. 'I want to see what the French have been about while we have been absent.'

'Aye aye, sir,' replied the lieutenant. 'Shall I have the upper masts set back up?'

'Not immediately,' said Clay. 'It can wait till after the men have broken their fast, too.'

'Oh, really?' said the lieutenant. 'Of course, as you wish, sir,'

'You seem surprised, Mr Blake,' said his captain.

'It is only that Captain Sheridan would never have let the hands' breakfast stand in the way of such a task, sir.'

'I do not doubt it,' replied Clay. 'But consider what consequences flowed from his lack of attention to the needs of the men, Mr Blake. Those on watch will be every bit as hungry as you and I. Expecting them to perform several hours of hard work swaying up the top gallant masts on an empty stomach while we have gone below to gorge ourselves would be decidedly poor leadership.'

'Aye aye, sir,' said Blake. 'I understand.'

*****

Eight clear strokes from the ship's bell rang out from the forecastle, and with a thunder of noise the watch was changed. A torrent of seaman swept up the ladder ways from the lower deck, each man carrying a warm hammock he had recently been sleeping in, tucked into a neat canvas package. As they arrived on deck the flow of humanity spread out in a fan as the hands ran to deposit their bundle in its numbered spot in the netting troughs. Then there followed the ritual dance of change as each member of one watch was replaced by his successor. Lieutenant Morton, who arrived to replace Blake, was still working on the last mouthful of his breakfast while he listened as the younger man handed over the ship. Clay watched his jaw grind with bovine regularity, which served to remind him how hungry he was.

'I will see you shortly, Mr Blake,' he said as he hurried below.

'I hope Mr Blake will not be over long, sir,' said Hart, as

he settled his captain at his place at the table. 'The bacon will keep well enough in the pewter dish, but these here eggs is starting to congeal.'

'He was just behind me, Hart,' said Clay. 'In fact that may be him knocking now. Come in!' Blake hurried through the cabin door that the marine sentry held open for him, and took his place opposite his captain.

'I do apologise for keeping you waiting, sir,' said the young man, glancing round at the loud sniff that came from the steward. 'But I was explaining to Mr Morton the need to wait till the hands below had had breakfast before sending the upper masts up. I am not sure he quite followed the advantages of delaying the operation.'

'No matter, I am sure he knows how to follow an order,' said Clay. 'Let us at least delay no longer. We have salt bacon, eggs, some fried pieces of ship's biscuit, and more biscuit in the basket there with butter and jam. Hart, hot plates if you please, and can you pour the coffee now.'

The start of the meal was spent in companionable quiet as the two men ate their way through what was on the table. The clink of flatware on china and the scrape of spoon on pewter was punctuated with requests to pass the jam, or to Hart for more coffee. Eventually Clay pushed himself back from the table, dropped his napkin onto the cloth and drew his coffee nearer.

'So tell me, Mr Blake, how did you come to be in the service?' he asked.

'In a rather curious fashion, sir,' explained his guest. 'My father is a grain merchant in the northern part of Wiltshire.

He is a reasonably prosperous man, and was able to fund a fair education for myself and my older brother with a view to our joining his business when we were of an age. All had gone to plan as far as my brother was concerned, and might have done for me too had it not been for an encounter I had when I was but twelve.'

'This sounds most intriguing,' said Clay. 'Another pot of coffee please, Hart. Pray continue, Mr Blake.'

'You see, sir, my home town is far enough from the sea, yet one day a sailor came to our door who I had not set eyes on before. He was a cousin of my mother's who had gone to sea as a boy and had been away for many a long year. He chanced to be in the area and had decided to renew his acquaintance with her. He stayed with us for a week, and then returned to his ship.'

'What manner of sailor was he?' asked the captain.

'For an impressionable boy of twelve, the worst as far as my father's plans for me was concerned, sir,' laughed Blake. 'My mother's cousin was a true man-of-war man, a tall powerful fellow, with a pigtail to his waist, rings in his ears and tattoos up his arms. He had a rich fund of tales to tell of storms, battles and voyages he had made to the most exotic of places. He filled my head with cutting out expeditions under the stars and of fights with Malay pirates in the East Indies. When I reflect back on what he said now I make no doubt that the yarns he spun had all the exaggeration to which sailors' tales can be prone. I daresay in reality he spent much of his time in the Channel Fleet at anchor, but back then I knew little different. By the time he left to rejoin his ship, my head was quite turned.'

'As you are here, I suppose your father acceded to your boyish notions of going to sea?' asked Clay.

'Only with enormous reluctance, sir,' said the lieutenant. 'I doubt he would have done so at all if my brother had not already been established in the business. It took two years of pleading for him to eventually concede that my mind was so full of the sea, that there would never be any room for talk of bushels of wheat and bags of grain. He did a considerable amount of business as corn factor to the Morton family estate, and so was able to get me my place here aboard the *Titan* as a midshipman, thanks to an application from Lieutenant Morton on my behalf to Captain Sheridan.'

'Ah, I think I see how matters rest,' said the captain. 'You must feel a strong sense of obligation to Mr Morton, I collect?'

'Oh yes, sir,' enthused Blake. 'The family have preferred me both in finding me a place as a midshipman, and then helping with my step to become a lieutenant.'

'And that is all very proper,' said Clay. 'But you must also remember that you are an officer in your own right now, able to hold your own opinions. What, for example, do you think of the mutiny that occurred against Captain Sheridan?'

'I find the actions of the Admiralty to be very ill judged, sir,' stated the young lieutenant. 'Why, it is much as Mr Morton says, those among the crew of a rebellious character believe that they have succeeded in overthrowing the natural order on board. Surely it will only serve to encourage them to further disobedience?'

'Perhaps it shall,' said Clay, 'unless we can win over the

majority of the people to our side of the divide. To the side of obedience and duty. In my experience a crew really have only two requirements of their officers to be truly content. They want to be led with competence and to be treated with fairness. If they perceive those virtues in their officers, it is quite remarkable what they can be persuaded to accomplish in the service of their country. Come in!'

'Mr Morton's compliments, and the ship is two miles west of the Goulet, sir,' said the midshipman.

'Thank you, Mr Butler,' replied Clay. 'Please tell Mr Morton that I will be up directly.'

'Aye aye, sir,' replied the departing teenager.

'Thank you for a most interesting breakfast, Mr Blake,' said his captain, standing up from the table. 'I look forward to renewing our conversation. One last question, though. Do you enjoy being at sea, now you have experienced the reality, or do you regret not joining your father's business?'

'I like it above all things, sir,' smiled the young man. 'I would not trade this life for any other, in spite of its many privations.'

The morning was well advanced when Clay came on deck. The *Titan*'s upper masts rose up, massive once more, into the heavens. Looking up he could see Harrison, the Titan's boatswain working high above his head as he and his mates checked that all was as it should be aloft. The ship was under steady way, sliding back up the Iroise channel once more towards Brest. Although it was calm overhead now, the effect of the gale could still be guessed at from the choppy waves that flowed in from the open ocean, striking the reefs on either side of her to send up the occasional spout of white water as if from surfacing whales.

'Up you go with your glasses, gentlemen,' said Clay to the two midshipmen as they reached the end of the channel. 'Can you bring her into the wind please, Mr Morton.'

'Aye aye, sir,' replied the second lieutenant. He gave the string of orders that brought the frigate to a halt, and then joined his captain by the rail.

'I see Bertheaume Bay is full once more, sir,' he said, looking to the south at the scene of their cutting out expedition.

'Yes,' said Clay. He pointed to where a set of lofty masts towered over the shipping around it. 'It also still contains a rather large French frigate at anchor to put a stop to any more attacks. I wonder how we might tempt her out into the channel here, away from all these cursed shore batteries. Mr Taylor has not quite got the gun crews up to my three broadsides every two minutes, but they are close.'

'It would be good to lock horns with a worthy opponent, if you are sure that the hands will fight, sir?' said Morton.

'They fought tolerably enough to take that brig,' said Clay.

'They did, sir,' conceded Morton. 'But a single ship action against another frigate would be an altogether more brutal affair.'

'All rather speculative, unless she should come out to fight us,' said Clay. Morton thought about this for a moment.

'She might come out if she thought we were an easy victim, sir,' he said. Clay looked at him with surprise.

'She might indeed. How would you endeavour to achieve

that, Mr Morton?' he asked.

'I am not sure,' he replied. 'But would you like it if I might give it some thought? Your pardon, sir, but the midshipmen are back from aloft with their observations of the French fleet.'

Clay turned to receive the report from the two young men, and then ordered the *Titan* to sail back down the channel once again. After half an hour they drew level with the Pierres Noires reef where they had surprised the fishing boats and where the channel opened up to join the wide sea beyond. Clay exchanged glances with Morton. He had been expecting a hail from the masthead lookout as they cleared the land. The captain picked up a speaking trumpet and looked up towards the figure who sat on the foretop royal yard, holding on with a single hand that rested on the foretopgallant mast beside him.

'Masthead there,' he yelled. 'Any sign of the *Indefatigable*?' The lookout swept the horizon with his free hand shading his eyes. He cupped his hand and yelled down.

'No sign of the *Indy* at all, sir,' he replied.

'How about the *Concord*, towards Ushant, or the *Argos* to the south?' called Clay.

'No sign of any of the squadron, begging your pardon, sir,' he replied. 'Just a few fishing boats and the usual Frog coasting trade.'

Clay thought for a moment, then turned to the signal midshipman. 'Mr Butler, can you send this signal. "*Titan* to flag. Enemy fleet in Brest unchanged from last report." Then I want you to count slowly to one hundred and replace the signal with an acknowledgement.'

'Eh, I beg your pardon, sir?' asked the midshipman.

'I am quite sure you heard me, Mr Butler,' said Clay. 'Kindly carry out my orders.'

'I believe Mr Butler is unclear to whom he is signalling, sir,' explained Morton. 'There being no ships in sight.' In answer Clay pointed towards the sea cliffs behind them.

'His signal is for the benefit of the many French observers who are all around us, Mr Morton,' he replied. 'Or would you have them deduce that we are all alone out here and that at present only a thirty-six gun frigate guards the entrance to Brest?'

Chapter 7
Portsmouth

'Aunt Mary, you must come up on deck directly,' urged Miss Lydia Browning. 'We are within sight of England! Mr Jones says that we have now past the Isle of Wight, and that the ship will soon be approaching Portsmouth. We are almost home!' Lady Mary Ashton looked up from her chair at her niece and ward. Her face creased into a frown of annoyance.

'Lydia, please tell me that you have not been on deck again without your damask wrap,' she said, in spite of the proof of her own eyes. 'After the heat of Bengal, you must be more careful not to take a chill, especially in such a state of agitation. We have already lost your poor uncle.'

'But he died of the cholera,' she said. 'I am not sure that wearing more clothes would have answered.'

'No, we should never have gone to India in the first place,' said Lady Ashton. 'An Ashton as Collector of Bengal? Why, it is barely a step up from being a tradesman! I warned him this would happen, but could I make him see beyond all the wealth that would flow his way? Well, we have been made to pay a heavy price for his folly, and I have no intention of increasing my loss.' Lydia rolled her eyes in despair.

'Oh, Aunt, we left Bombay nearly four months ago,' she exclaimed. 'And it is not as if we passed any great time there. Look at my countenance. Do I seem unwell?' Lady Ashton regarded her niece for a moment, and had to admit that she did look the picture of health. The wisps of her dark hair that had been worked free by the wind from beneath her hat were thick and glossy and her blue eyes sparkled with excitement. Her skin glowed from all the sea air and sunshine they had encountered on the voyage.

'Your complexion is all together too ruddy for my liking,' sniffed her aunt. 'Not at all the pallor to be expected of a young lady of your position, but I will concede that you do appear to be in good health. Very well, if you will agree to wear your wrap, I will happily accompany you on deck. I must say that I do long to feel solid ground beneath my feet. I have not left the ship since the Cape, however many weeks ago that was.'

The *Somerset* was a large East Indiaman, almost the size of a small ship of the line, and from her high poop deck there were excellent views to be had. One of the male passengers gave up his place at the rail for the new arrivals with a polite touch of his hat.

'Thank you, Mr Jones, you are too kind,' smiled Lydia, and she and her aunt gazed across the water towards the approaching mainland. The turf of the South Downs rose up in a wall of green a little way inland, while nearer at hand they could see smoke rising from the iron foundries and mills of the Royal Dockyard at Portsmouth.

'My goodness, what a huge armada of shipping has been gathered here,' remarked Lydia, pointing towards the long lines of warships that swung at their moorings close to the shore.

'This is Spithead, Miss Browning,' said Mr Jones. 'There is often a deal of Royal Navy vessels at anchor here, although I have seldom seen so many. One would think with the war with France still raging they might be deployed on station.' Lydia stared towards the ships and felt her heart beat faster. Her beloved Alexander Clay now commanded such a ship. Could it be possible that it might be one of those gathered here? She remembered from his letters that his ship was called the *Rush*, and that it was a sloop of war, whatever that was.

'Tell me, what manner of ships are these, Mr Jones?' she asked.

'Chiefly line of battle ships, Miss Browning,' replied the man. 'There are also some frigates, too. Those are the ones over there with but a single gun deck.'

'Are there any of the ships that they call sloops of war?' Lydia asked.

'Really, Lydia,' said her aunt. 'You are engaging in such a curious discourse, what must Mr Jones think? Surely a lady can have no possible interest in such matters.' Lydia said nothing, and after a pause Mr Jones continued.

'A sloop has a single gun deck and three masts like a frigate, but is considerably smaller,' he explained. 'If you direct your gaze towards the other side of the harbour entrance I believe there are a few moored over there, Miss Browning.'

Lydia looked to where he pointed. The East Indiaman was tracking towards the row of little ships that lay stern on to their approach. She shaded her eyes with one gloved hand and tried to read the names painted in gold letters on the counters below their windows. She could not quite read them, but the distance was reducing all the time. They sailed a little closer, and she realised with disappointment that the nearest sloop had a name with far too many letters to be the *Rush*. She moved her attention on to the one beyond it. Now was that a four letter name, she wondered?

'Tell me, Mr Jones,' she heard her aunt ask. 'Why do so many of the ships have red flags flying? Should they not have naval ensigns?'

'Red flags, Lady Ashton?' queried the passenger. 'Upon my word, you're right! I declare that is strange indeed. A red flag is certainly not normal. It generally denotes revolt and rejection of authority, but surely that cannot be the case here.'

Lydia only half listened to what they said as she watched the next sloop approach. It at least bore no red flag, and definitely had a four letter name, but was the first letter a P or an R?

'I say, Lieutenant,' she heard Mr Jones call. 'Why do all of those men of war fly red flags?'

'It is curious, sir,' mussed the officer. 'The anchor watch on that last ship we past did appear surly, and I could see no officer directing matters. I do wonder what can have happened.'

Lydia's whole attention was focussed now on the stern of the second sloop. Her vision seemed to narrow into a corridor. The rest of the ships slipped from view and the conversation around her faded. She could feel her heart race, the blood banging in her ears as she read the name. The letters were large and obvious now. The sloop was indeed the *Rush*.

'Lydia, my dear, are you quite well?' asked her aunt. 'Your face has a very ill look, and you are gripping the rail as if we were in a storm.'

She closed her eyes for a moment, breathed deeply, and turned towards her aunt. 'Sorry if I alarmed you, Aunt,' she replied. 'I did feel a little odd, but I have regained my composure now.'

'Would you like me to summon the surgeon, Miss Browning?' asked Mr Jones.

'Thank you but no,' said Lydia, as calmly as she could. 'I am quite myself again. What was it you were saying about the ships?'

'Mr Jones believes that the fleet may have been convulsed by some form of revolt,' said Lady Ashton, before he could answer. 'The sooner we are safely ashore, my dear, the better, I say.'

*****

'Are there always such a lot of soldiers in Portsmouth?' asked Lydia. She was stood looking out of the bay window of her private parlour at the Dolphin Inn. The road below was filled with a column of redcoats marching in step, followed at a short distance by several local urchins and a stray dog.

'No, miss,' replied the maid, looking up from the trunk. 'It is all on account of these wicked mutineers. Why, the whole of the town is in uproar. They have put all of the ships' captains ashore, and many of the officers too. Even poor old Admiral Bridport has been turned off his flagship. I don't know how it will all end. What shall we do if the base French should come to murder us in our beds?'

'All the captains are ashore, you say?' said Lydia. 'What of the captain of the *Rush*, is he presently in the town? His name is Alexander Clay.'

'I have not heard of that ship, miss,' said the maid. 'Shall I ask Tom, our pot man? He is an old tar who knows about the comings and goings of the ships.'

'If you please,' said Lydia, forcing herself to sound calm, in spite of the churn of emotions inside her. As soon as the maid left the room she began to pace up and down. Oh, he must be here, she thought, if only I can find where. After over a year apart, a year on opposite sides of the world, the thought that they might both be in the same town was almost too much for her to bear. She spun round at the end of the room once more and had taken a few steps back down the parlour when she stopped. A strange thumping sound was approaching up the corridor outside her room. It stopped at her door, and there was a polite knock. She forced herself to stand still, smoothed down the front of her dress and turned to face the door.

'Come in,' she said. The maid entered, followed by a heavy-built man in his fifties with the long grey pigtail of a sailor. As he advanced into the room the leather covered end of his wooden leg thumped down on the floor boards every other pace.

'The battle of the Chesapeake Bay, back in eighty-one, miss,' he said, following her look. 'I was a quartermaster on the old *Royal Oak*.'

'Oh, you poor man,' said Lydia, 'to have to endure such an injury. It must be a sore trial and inconvenience for you.'

'Not really, miss,' he replied. 'I can't say as it slows me up over much. I am not able to run, of course, but then I was never much inclined to do that before, and now when folk are all impatient and shouting for their drinks to be brought, they do tend to stow their noise once they catch a sight of it.'

'Yes, I am sure they do,' smiled Lydia. 'I would never really have thought of such an injury as having any advantages.'

'Oh, plenty, miss,' enthused the pot man. 'Only one foot to wash. Never more than five toe nails as need cutting. New shoes and stockings for half the price. I am that used to my jury leg now that I hardly recall what it was like to have two feet. The curious thing about it is how I still wants to scratch my toes even after all these years, if you will credit it. But look at me a jabbering on, and you all anxious to find this friend of yours. Tell me now, what was the name of that ship?'

'The *Rush*,' said Lydia. 'Her captain is a particular acquaintance of mine.'

'*Rush*, *Rush*,' mussed Tom, stroking his chin. 'She'll be one of those little Swan class sloops of war, ain't she? Deptford built and sixteen guns if I am not mistaken. Now let me consider. Ah, I think I have her. Might she have come in from Barbados a month back?' Lydia nodded, unable to trust herself to speak. 'Now she is one of the few ships in the fleet as has stayed loyal to the King, so her captain, like as not, will still be aboard her.'

'Oh,' said Lydia, struggling not to show her disappointment. 'Not ashore, then? I suppose it is good that his people have not joined in the revolt.' Tom saw the moisture that was welling up in Lydia's eyes, and exchanged glances with the maid.

'Begging your pardon, but is the captain someone special to you, miss?' asked the maid, her expression kind.

'Yes, very much so,' whispered Lydia.

'Well now, I shall be going off duty shortly,' said Tom. 'If you might want to take the air, miss, before your dinner, that would be a natural enough thing for you to do. Then perhaps I could step out along with you, it not being proper with all these soldiers about for you to go on your own. Our route would probably take us down by the hard where I know most of the boatmen. Be passing strange if we couldn't find us a wherry as would take us out to the *Rush*, if that would serve, miss?'

'Oh, you are so kind,' exclaimed Lydia. Then she stopped as a thought came to her. 'What of my aunt?'

'She is resting in her room, miss,' replied the maid. 'Would you like her to come too, or would you rather she was left here?'

'It might be better if she did not know,' replied Lydia.

'I see no obligation for her to be told,' replied the pot

man. 'If she should ask after you, you're taking the air with old Tom. And if we was to be away a little longer than we should, why, we can always blame it on me being a bit slow on my missing peg, or yarning away for too long, which is like enough to be the truth of it. We need say no more to her Ladyship than that.'

*****

'A lady you say? To see me?' asked Commander John Sutton of the *Rush*, looking up from his desk.

'Yes, sir,' replied Midshipman Croft. 'She is in a boat alongside, with an older man. He is a disabled sailor, but she looks to be a lady of some quality. She says her name is Miss Lydia Browning.'

'Miss Browning!' exclaimed Sutton. 'By Jove, what can she be doing here? She is meant to be in India. Let her come aboard and show her down here, Mr Croft, if you please.'

What on earth is Alex's intended doing in Portsmouth? he thought to himself as he waited for Lydia. He stood and buttoned up his shirt. Then he retrieved his coat from where it hung behind the door and looked around for his neck cloth. Once he was properly dressed he ran a hand through his thick, dark hair and glanced around the tiny cabin for inspiration. After a moment's thought he yelled for his steward.

'Ah, Chapman,' he said. 'What refreshment do we have that would be suitable to offer a lady?'

'We have rum, gin, wine or coffee, sir,' replied the steward.

'Hmm, is that all?' mused Sutton. 'We had best make it coffee, then. Anything resembling cake to serve with it?'

'I could tap the weevils from some ship's biscuit and cover one side with molasses, sir?'

'Ah, I think maybe not,' concluded his captain. 'Just the coffee then, please.'

Chapman disappeared and shortly afterwards there was a knock at the cabin door.

'Come in,' called Sutton, sitting back down behind the desk so that he could rise politely to his feet. 'Miss Browning, what a wholly unexpected pleas... ' His greeting tailed away as he saw the beautiful face of his guest, radiant with joy as it came through the door, crumple at the sight of him.

'Oh, Mr Sutton,' she said. 'I thought... that is to say... I was really....'

'Miss Browning!' he cried, taking both her hands and leading her to a chair. 'How foolish of me! You were expecting to see Alex. Oh, what an intolerable disappointment I must be for you.' Lydia looked at Sutton's anxious face and laughed aloud in spite of her tears.

'I am so very sorry, Mr Sutton,' she said. 'How rude you must think me. Today has been very emotional, but I shall regain my composure presently. I am of course delighted to see you again. Are you well?'

'Very well, I thank you,' he replied, passing across his handkerchief. 'Beneath your current confusion you seem to be in good health, too,' he added. This made Lydia smile again, and she wiped away the last of her tears.

'I am fine, thank you, Mr Sutton,' she said. 'I have arrived in England this very day from India. My uncle succumbed to cholera in Bengal and my aunt and I decided to return home.'

'I am sorry to hear that,' said the commander of the *Rush*. 'I had wondered at your wearing a black dress. My sincere condolences to you and Lady Ashton. I know how close you were to your uncle.' Chapman came in with the coffee at that moment, and placed it on the desk.

'Would you care for some coffee?' he asked. 'Or perhaps something stronger, after the shock of my not being Alexander?'

'A cup of coffee would be most welcome, Mr Sutton,' smiled Lydia. 'As would be some intelligence of your friend. The last letter I had from Alex he was the commander of the *Rush*, and was blockading St Lucia. That is why, when I saw this ship as we came into Portsmouth, I had hoped to find him onboard.'

'Oh my, so much has happened since then, Miss Browning,' he said. 'I hardly know where to begin. Shortly after the time that letter would have been written, we played our part in the capture of St Lucia from the French. We had barely defeated them when the *Rush* was involved in an action with a Spanish seventy-four, together with our old ship the *Agrius*. Alex was quite the hero of the hour, and earned his promotion to post captain as a result. I was promoted to command the *Rush* in his place, and he was sent home to convalesce.'

'To convalesce?' cried Lydia, spilling a little of her coffee into the saucer. 'What is the matter with him?' Into her mind came the image of Tom the pot man, stumping along the wharf beside her.

'Calm yourself, Miss Browning,' said Sutton, resting his hand on hers. 'He is quite restored. He took a bullet in the shoulder, and was very bad for a while, but has since recovered. In fact he is but recently returned to active service. He has command of a very fine thirty-six gun frigate called *Titan*, and is now serving as part of Sir Edward Pellew's Inshore Squadron off Brest, or at least that is where he should be. I am afraid it is hard to say with any degree of certainty in these strange times. If his people have succumbed to this wretched mutiny, God knows where he may be. I had heard that the disorder had spread to Plymouth and was affecting ships there, too.'

'I so long to see him again, Mr Sutton,' she said. 'How can I best do that?'

'The *Titan* will have to come back to Plymouth at some stage, if only to resupply,' said Sutton. 'You might write to him there, or at sea if mail is still being delivered to ships on station. Oh, or you could try to contact him through Betsey, his sister. She should know where he is. I know how deeply he regards you, Miss Browning. I am quite sure he will come and find you the moment he knows that you are back home.'

*****

'There he is,' hissed Sexton to the others. 'That interfering black bastard.' The group of men were crouched down out of sight behind the main mast where the huge column of oak passed through the lower deck on its way to the keel.

'Are you sure about this, Dick?' asked Morris Page. 'He's a

dangerous looking brute, and the other one is bloody massive.'

'Which is why we need them out of the way,' said Sexton. 'No need for you to worry. It will be me, Shane and the lads as will be running the risk here, Morris. You just have to slip away and get the Grunters.'

'Why don't we just stick the feckers ourselves?' muttered Shane Kenny. 'Toss their bodies over the side an' all. It would be a lot easier.'

'Because it is very doubtful the crew will rise with us if they think we've been killing fellow shipmates ourselves,' explained Sexton. 'This way is much tidier. Let the Grunters sign their own death warrant. Now you boys get into position, and I will lead them down into the trap.'

Kenny and his fellow Irishmen slipped down the main ladder way and disappeared into the gloom of the orlop deck under their feet. Sexton gave them a few minutes to get settled, and then left Page in hiding. He strode along the lower deck towards where Sedgwick and Evans stood deep in conversation.

'Out of my way, you fucking ape,' he spat towards the coxswain, as he barged past the two men.

'Hey! Don't you talk to my mate like that,' shouted Evans towards the retreating back. Sexton held up an abusive finger as he clumped down the ladder way towards the hold. Evans started to follow but Sedgwick held him back.

'It's alright, Sam,' he replied. 'I have been called much worse than that. I am more interested in what our friend is about down on the orlop deck. He will up to no good, you can be certain of that. Come on, let's follow him.'

As the two sailors made their way towards the hatch, Morris Page emerged from hiding. He smiled as he watched the head of Evans disappear from sight, then composed his face into one of distress and hurried away in the direction of the quarterdeck.

Down in the gloom of the orlop deck the two sailors searched for Sexton. Sedgwick had to stoop beneath the low beams, while poor Evans was almost bent double. They had passed the dank cable tier where Rosso had read Sexton's note, and ahead of them stretched a corridor with locked doors on either side.

'Where has he bleeding gone, then,' whispered Evans. He pointed towards the corridor. 'Down there is only the sail room and the boatswain's store. Doubt if we will find him there.'

'Would you be looking for me, lads?' came a voice from off to one side. Sedgwick turned towards it just in time to receive a crashing blow to the side of his head. He reeled into Evans, knocking him off balance. The moment the two men were down they were set on from all sides. A flurry of kicks from out of the dark winded Sedgwick as he tried to get back up.

'Get to a bulkhead,' yelled Evans. He crawled forward through the rain of blows, dragging Sedgwick with him until he felt the solid timber of a store room wall rising up in front of him. He pulled himself upright and turned around, placing his back against the bulkhead. Reaching down he hauled his friend up and pushed him into place next to him. A shadowy figure loomed up close by him. He threw a crunching left hook towards the shape and felt the man's head rock back as he collapsed into the other assailants. In the short interval of breathing space won by this blow, both men whipped out their clasp knives, and at the sight of their faint glitter in the gloom, their attackers backed away.

'Nobody move!' said a commanding voice. Evans and Sedgwick froze as Lieutenant Morton opened the shutters on his lantern and the dark space was suddenly light. Behind him stood a group of men, including Page.

'Thank God for that, sir,' bleated Sexton. 'Those two were up to no good down here, and when I challenged them they attacked me. Look!' He held up his arm. A long shallow cut ran across the mass of tattoos.

'Me too, sir,' whined one of the Irish seaman, holding out his left hand, which also dripped blood from another cut.

'Why, you lying fuckers,' roared Evans, stepping forwards. His former assailants all cowered away from him in fear.

'I said nobody move, Evans,' ordered Morton.

'Sir, if I can explain what happened here… ' began Sedgwick.

'What explanation can you possibly offer?' interrupted the lieutenant. 'Knives drawn? Fellow shipmates injured? I have always thought it a mistake to promote your kind into positions of authority. Your savage instincts always come to the surface in time. It is in your nature.'

'But sir… ' persisted the coxswain.

'Silence, I say!' roared Morton. 'I have heard all I want to from you. Master at arms! Disarm these two and place them in custody. Then take statements from everyone involved and bring them to Mr Taylor. Sexton, Murphy, you had best go and see the surgeon and get those cuts attended to.'

*****

Sexton was careful to maintain the pained expression that would be expected of a man who was fighting to suppress the agony of a nasty looking knife wound while he watched the two sailors being led away. As they disappeared from view it melted into a broad smile of triumph.

'Well done, boys, that went about as sweet as it could have,' he said. 'I thought we was in trouble when that great ox punched you, Shane. I reckoned him to be a bit more tame after the kicking we gave them. He is a tough bastard to still have a shot like that, and no mistake.'

'I am telling yous, I was nearly out cold,' said Kenny, working his jaw from side to side. 'I saw fecking stars when it landed.'

'It was right lucky old Beaky Morton arrived when he did,' continued Sexton. 'You did alright there, Morris. What did you say to make him come?'

'Oh, Mr Morton, sir, please come *quick*!' playacted Page in a high-pitched voice. 'Two of them new recruits are up to no good in the hold. I think they are planning to break into the spirit room. Some of the loyal hands are trying to stop them, but they have pulled out their knives and attacked them!' The group all burst out laughing at this.

'Ah, thank Christ for stupid fecking Grunters,' chuckled Kenny. 'So now we have those two out the way, what now?'

'We act soon, lads,' said Sexton, throwing his long arms around both men's shoulders. 'The rest of the fleet has risen, and we must join them. Now is our time.'

'Are you sure that the fleet has mutinied, Dick?' asked Page.

'Yes, Morris, I know it for certain,' answered Sexton. 'Pipe knows it too, I reckon. That is why he stays on station and doesn't go hunting for the rest of the squadron. The tinder is dry as bone, my friends. All we need now is a spark.'

Chapter 8
Revolting

'Now are all the places set just right,' muttered Taylor to himself as he walked around the wardroom and eyed the table with unease. 'Britton, can you move the captain's place a little aft, if you please.'

'Aye aye, sir,' said the wardroom steward, 'Back aft again, was it?' He rattled the cutlery down on the table with unnecessary force as he moved the setting three inches to one side.

'This is what comes of not having your own servants at home, John,' said Morton in a stage whisper to his neighbour. 'Let us hope he will not start polishing the silver next.' Blake smiled at the second lieutenant's joke.

'George, do please stop your fretting,' said Macpherson, shooting a withering glance towards Morton. 'It will make no difference if the place setting is a wee bit this way or that. Come and take your chair, I pray, and have a glass with me. Britton, some wine for Mr Taylor, if you please. I have known Captain Clay longer than any of you. I can assure you that he is very natural in his manner. He is certainly no stickler on matters of ceremony and precedence, so I am sure that place there will answer well enough for him.'

'It does still look very ill,' sighed Taylor as he sat down at last. 'The wardroom table is just a little too small for our numbers.'

'It will not be the first time he has had to dine in a confined manner,' said the marine. 'Why, the wardroom on the *Rush* was barely half the size of this one.'

'So do you know the captain well, Tom?' asked Morton. 'What sort of people are his family?'

'I know a little of them, Edmund, but I cannot say I am closely acquainted with the Clays,' replied the marine. 'I know he has a mother and a younger sister, and I believe an uncle who may be employed by the Navy Board. But I think that you may ask him yourself, for if I am not deceived that is him now at the door.'

'Really, do you think so?' said Taylor, jumping up. 'Oh, but the surgeon is not yet here. Why is that damned man never on time! Britton, will you pass the word for Mr Corbett, if you please, and ask him to make haste.'

'My apologies, gentlemen, for being a little late,' said Clay as he ducked under the low frame of the wardroom door. 'I was visiting some of the hands in the sick bay, and was detained by Mr Corbett here, who was sharing a most interesting theory with me.' The slight figure of the surgeon bobbed through the door behind his captain and slid along the row of officers' cabin doors that lined the sides of the wardroom towards his place at the table. There was a considerable scraping of chairs as the officers who had been sitting down rose to their feet.

'You are most welcome, sir,' said Taylor as he stepped forward to grip his captain's hand. 'Your place is over there.'

'Thank you, Mr Taylor,' said Clay, as he squeezed with difficulty past the line of standing officers and their chairs. 'Perhaps it might be easier if you gentlemen were to resume your places,' he suggested. 'I had forgotten how snug a wardroom can be, even on an eighteen-pounder frigate like ours. Ah, here we are at last,' he exclaimed, as he squeezed into his chair and smiled around him.

'What was the theory that detained you, sir?' asked Taylor. 'A glass of wine for the captain, if you please, Britton.'

'Thank you,' said Clay, accepting the drink. 'It is really Mr Corbett's theory, so perhaps he should expound on it, but it is certainly interesting. It concerns those two hands that you caught fighting, Mr Morton.' All eyes looked towards the little surgeon, who blushed in consequence.

'Eh, you see I was explaining to the captain that I had just finished dressing the knife wounds inflicted on Sexton and Murphy earlier this evening, and that in my opinion they did not look genuine.'

'Why so?' asked Morton, bridling a little. 'Because I can assure you that the altercation that generated them was very much in earnest.'

'It was the nature of the wounds that seemed wrong,' explained the surgeon. 'In my experience a man who uses a knife in anger will stab with it in fury. The wound that such a blow produces is a relatively small but deep puncture in his victim, and it is the depth of its penetration that is so often fatal. The wounds I dressed were impressively bloody at first sight, but when I washed them they proved to be quite superficial.'

'How might they have been produced?' asked Taylor.

'I should say they were closer to what I would expect if a sharp blade had been drawn lightly across the skin,' said Corbett.

'Might the wounds not have been inflicted in a glancing fashion?' persisted the second lieutenant. 'Evans or Sedgwick may have caught their victims as they sprung back from the fray.'

'No, I don't believe that explanation will answer, Mr Morton,' said the surgeon. 'Wounds generated in such a tumult as you describe might indeed be shallow, but they would also be rather jagged and irregular,' said Corbett. 'These wounds are quite straight. Self inflicted harm is something a naval surgeon must be prepared to detect. They are an obvious device that a seaman might use to avoid an unpleasant or hazardous duty. In my opinion what I treated today were two such wounds.'

'Did you see the knife blows fall, Mr Morton, or just the aftermath?' asked Clay.

'I did not observe the actually blows being struck as such, sir,' conceded the lieutenant. 'I arrived just after that moment.'

'Did either man's blade appear to be bloody?' asked Macpherson. 'Or were their clothes marked by the blood of their victims?

'In truth, I did not notice one way or the other,' said Morton, after a pause. 'I am sure the Master at Arms would have made a record of such particulars. Shall I have him sent for, sir?'

'Not now, Mr Morton. Let us not turn the fine meal you have invited me to into an inquest,' said Clay. 'We can resolve such matters latter. What I will say is that I do have firsthand experience of the character of both Evans and Sedgwick. You gentlemen have direct experience of the mutinous behaviour that Sexton and his associates are capable of. Should it come down to a matter as to whose version of events we should give credence to, I believe it is clear where we must place our trust.' There was a rumble of assent from the officers around the table. Morton looked as if he was about to say something further, but then thought better of it.

'Before you joined us tonight, sir,' said Taylor, wanting to move the conversation on, 'Mr Morton had asked Mr Macpherson if he knew any particulars concerning your background, which in truth he knows little enough of. If it is not an impertinence, might you tell us a little of your origins... sorry, one moment please. What is it, Britton?' The steward bent down to whisper into the first lieutenant's ear. 'Really? Can it not wait? Oh very well. Mr Haywood, Cook would like a word with you. He is waiting outside. Apparently it is urgent.'

'Apologies, gentlemen,' said the purser as he rose from his seat and hastened to the door. As he left the room he heard Clay begin to speak.

'To answer you, Mr Morton, my late father had the living

in the village of Lower Staverton, where I was brought up, and where my widowed mother and younger sister still live. My father died when I was but eleven years old, and I left home shortly after to go to sea... ' The door then shut behind him, cutting off the captain's voice.

'This is rather provoking, Walker,' he moaned. 'What on earth is there that can be so urgent?'

'Sorry to disturb you at the table, Mr Haywood,' said the cook. His face looked anxious and he was balling his apron between his fists. 'I just don't know what to do, sir. I am about to start cooking the hands' dinner, and my assistants have brought up the first tub from that batch of pork we took on in Plymouth. It smells really bad, much worse than is usual. Charnel houses ain't in it.'

'Ah yes,' said the purser. 'Well, that cannot be helped. Vinegar and mustard is what you need, Mr Walker. Cook it up with plenty of those and it will be tolerable enough.'

'I am not sure as that will answer, sir', said the cook. 'You need to come and see this meat. I am most uncertain as it is fit to be eaten at all.'

'And where exactly do you expect me to get replacement flesh, Walker?' asked Haywood. 'Sail into Brest and ask the Frogs for some? Now go along and do as I have said, and all will be well.'

*****

'What the fecking hell is this?' said O'Malley, staring down at the large square wooden plate that had been placed in front of him. He prodded at the hunk of salt pork and it fell limply open. 'Sweet Mother of God!' he exclaimed. 'Is that a fecking maggot?' Trevan looked over his shoulder and nodded.

'That it is, Sean, mate,' he said. 'Actually, yours is looking a bit better than what mine does. I've just got this here stinking puddle.' He sniffed at the meal and then wrinkled his nose in disgust. 'Oh! That is real bad, and the bastards have soaked it in vinegar to try and mask the taste.'

'Hey, lads,' said Rosso, nudging his messmates. 'Watch yourselves. Matters look as if they might get lively.'

The lower deck around them was in uproar as the tubs of pork were distributed out from the galley and placed at the end of each mess table. Everywhere they looked they could see sailors recoiling from their meals and turning to their neighbours in protest. An angry crowd had gathered at the foot of the main ladder way around the forlorn figure of Walker.

'What the bleeding hell is this?' demanded one burly young top man, thrusting his plate under the cook's nose. 'I wouldn't feed a dog on this shit.'

'Now easy there, Peter Hobbs,' said Walker. 'I did question if we should be serving this meat with Mr Haywood, and he said if we cooked it up in a made dish with mustard and vinegar it would come out fine.'

'Come out fine! I bet he fucking did!' shouted Hobbs. 'What will *he* be eating tonight, eh? Not this pork, I'll warrant.'

In all the uproar, there was only one mess table where the evening meal had been received calmly.

'Breathe deep lads,' said Sexton as he held his steaming plate up to his nose and closed his eyes. 'Tell me what you can smell?'

'Bloody hell, Dick,' exclaimed Page. 'I smell something that died several years ago and has lain in a muddy ditch ever since.' Sexton opened his eyes wide, and smiled at his messmates.

'No, Morris,' he said. 'That is because you ain't breathing deeply enough. Coz if you did, you would be able to sense something altogether much sweeter. What I can smell on this here plate is trouble, lots of trouble.' He pulled something metal from deep in his pocket and passed it over to Page. 'This is the key I spoke of before, the one that Stephenson made for me. Go and slip away with Shane and his mates to the arms chest and bring back weapons. Muskets, pistols, cutlasses, handy stuff like that.'

'Alright, Dick,' said his friend, slipping the key into his pocket. 'What are you going to do?'

'What I do best, Morris,' he replied. 'I am going to talk to the hands.' He stood up from the table, picked up his heaped plate, stepped out into the middle of the lower deck where all could see him and roared aloud for silence.

'Enough is enough, my fellow shipmates,' he said, once he had everyone's attention. 'Have we not laboured bleeding hard this day? Have we not stood our watches, four hours on and four hours off, through the wind and the rain? Have we not come a running when the Grunters called for all hands, in all weather, at all times of day and night? Have the brave top men among us not risked their lives battling the elements?'

'That's right, Dick,' called a voice.

'And what is our reward, shipmates, after our long day of labour?' asked Sexton. 'Do we get a rate of pay as is fair, settled regular at the end of our commission?'

'No, we bleeding don't!' shouted several voices.

'Do we get shore leave when in port, to visit our loved ones?' he asked.

'No, no!' came back the answers.

'But we loyally serve our King and Country,' he said. 'We are the Hearts of Oak that those arses on shore like to sing their ballads about. Surely the very least we can expect is a hot meal fit to eat at the end of a hard day of work?' He held his plate out in front of him and turned in a slow circle so everyone on deck could see him. As he rotated he tilted his plate so that the food on it splattered down onto the deck in a ring, the noise clear in the spellbound silence. He looked at the faces that crowded the deck, although he knew already he had everyone's attention. He paused for a moment and filled his lungs with the heady atmosphere. This is power, he thought. Real power. So much better than being a stupid petty officer.

'Shipmates, we are not alone,' he resumed. 'Have you questioned why the captain makes his signal to the empty horizon each day? Why does he not go and seek for the rest of the squadron, eh? Or why does he not sail out to sea to join the fleet? He doesn't seek to find the fleet, because he knows that they are not there to be found.' The men looked at each other and a buzz of chatter broke out.

'No, but I know where they are,' said Sexton. In the resulting quiet he drew out the paper that Rodgers had brought him from the *Indefatigable.*

'I need to halt him right now,' said Rosso to the others. 'We must stop him before he has the whole ship in open revolt.' He started to rise to his feet, but froze when he felt the barrel of a pistol pushed against his back.

'Sit your arse back down on that stool, Rosso,' hissed Page in his ear. 'You keep your trap shut, and you others do the same. This is our moment. Ain't no need for you to cause no ruckus.' He nodded to a couple of his accomplices who crouched down and pressed pistols against Trevan and O'Malley. The two seamen had begun to get up from the table to help their friend, but now sat back down. Rosso looked back towards where Sexton was unfolding his sheet of paper. You have to admire the bastard, he though. God, he knows how to rouse up a mob.

'The Grunters think we are just dumb animals to be bullied and flogged and fed on shit, but what little do they really know. I have been communicating with like-minded friends on every ship in the fleet these last few months,' said Sexton, holding aloft the letter 'This comes from the elected delegates of the squadron's flagship,' he said. 'They write to tell us that they have seized their ship, as has every crew in the Channel Fleet, and all have sailed for Spithead. In this letter they urge us to join them in their hour of need. What will our answer be to our brother shipmates? Shall we rise too?'

Cries broke out across the deck of 'Yes!' and 'Let's fucking do it!', but other men looked around more nervously.

'I am not so sure, Dick,' said one voice. 'I was with you all the way when we rose against that bastard Sheridan, but this new captain be different. Can't we just go and complain to him about the pork, like?' Other voices rose in agreement.

'That's right!' called another. 'We ain't had no floggings since he took over, except for Adams, and the thieving bleeder deserved it. Don't seem right to act all uncivil like.'

'I thought matters had been mended, too,' said Sexton. 'I was ready to be obedient. To hold that maybe this captain was different, for once. But what power does he truly have? Can he increase our pay? Will he give us more shore leave? And what changes has he made? While we are here being served rotten meat, where is he? I shall tell you where. He is dining with the Grunters in the wardroom, and let me tell you this, my shipmates,' he paused to sweep the deck with his gaze. 'They ain't eating no rotten fucking pork!'

'That's right,' shouted O'Malley, pushing aside the pistol held against his back to stand with the other Irish sailors around their table.

'Sean, what are you doing?' asked Rosso.

'I am sorry, lads, but I have got to fecking join this,' he said. 'Hey, Shane,' he called across the deck. 'I am with yous all! Ireland shall be free, brother, Ireland shall be free!' Kenny smiled back and applauded him.

'O'Malley, you treacherous bastard,' snarled Trevan. 'Four years you've been my tie mate, but now you're dead to me.'

*****

'So though this prize bull was admired by most of the county, it was my uncle that acquired it,' explained a flushed

Morton as he held court in the wardroom. 'But he had barely paid the exorbitant price and brought the beast home, when the damned creature dropped down dead.'

'How much had he paid?' asked Haywood.

'Thirty guineas, all in coin,' replied the lieutenant.

'Thirty in gold! For an ox! And then it just died on him?' The purser cackled with glee.

'So what did he do then?' said Blake, swaying a little in his chair.

'He let it be known that he would offer the bull as a prize by lottery, sixty tickets only, at one guinea each,' continued the second lieutenant. 'Well, naturally they sold in a flash among all those that he had beaten in the race to buy the animal.'

'But what happened when the unfortunate winner presented himself to collect his price?' asked Macpherson, sipping at his wine.

'Why, he told him the bull had recently perished, offered him the carcass and refunded him his guinea.' The company all roared with laughter, none more so than the purser. He cleared a path through the empty wine bottles that littered the table, and was extending his hand across the cloth to shake that of the second lieutenant when the door to the wardroom burst open.

'Stay in your places please, gentlemen,' shouted Sexton, covering the table with a pair of cocked pistols. 'Anyone who is not an officer can fuck off.' A group of hands armed with muskets trooped in behind their leader.

'What is the meaning of this?' demanded Clay, pushing himself up from his chair.

'I said remain in your place,' snarled Sexton. 'Unless you're after a bullet in the guts? And I will thank you to keep your damned hands where I can see them, Macpherson.' Clay sat back down and Britton and the servants filed out.

'That's better,' smiled the mutineer's leader. 'O'Brien, Murphy. Would you oblige me and search these nice gentlemen's cabins. Take all their weapons away.' While the men searched the little rooms off the wardroom, he turned back towards the officers sat around the table.

'I have taken command of this ship on behalf of the crew,' he explained. 'The lobsters have been disarmed and those among the hands who did not wish to take part in the mutiny are confined to the hold. As you can see, there is little point you gentlemen making any trial to recover the situation. If none of you does anything desperate, nobody shall come to harm.'

'What have you done with Mr Warwick, you mutinous dog?' asked Clay, remembering that the ship's master had been on watch.

'Calm yourself, captain,' urged Sexton. 'There's no call for such intemperate language. He is still on the quarterdeck, under guard. We will have need of him to navigate the ship back to Spithead, where we will join with the general mutiny of the Channel Fleet. You shall all be put ashore when we get there, along with all the other officer scum.'

'The Channel Fleet has mutinied?' exclaimed Taylor. 'Surely this is some ill jest! How can that possibly be the case?'

'Ask your captain, if you don't believe me.'

'I am afraid what he says is correct,' said Clay. 'Sir Edward swore me to secrecy, although how this blackguard got to hear of it, I have no idea.'

'Perhaps I am not as bleeding simple as you seem to think, Pipe,' said the mutineer.

'Show some respect to your captain,' barked Macpherson, but Clay held up a restraining hand.

'Look, Sexton,' he said. 'I understand there to be resentment in the fleet at present. I also know that the Admiralty are working tirelessly to address those wrongs. In the meanwhile your country is still at war. This ship is all that stands between the French and control of the Channel. If they should be able to descend on England and land an army, all will be lost. No more King, no more Parliament, a guillotine set up in Whitehall, and a regime in place that I doubt will be much to your taste. I urge you, please, to think about what you are doing.'

'Ah, doesn't that all sounds very fine,' sneered Sexton. 'Strange how accommodating you captains can be when you find the whip is in the other hand. That Sheridan became very obliging too, when he saw I had a loaded pistol aimed at his fat belly. Perhaps you should have thought about all of that a bit sooner.' He called over his shoulder to one of his men. 'Let's have that bucket up here.' A sailor pushed his way into the room, and banged a steaming wooden tub down on the table.

'What the hell is this disgusting mess?' asked the captain.

'While you gentlemen were dining on the best of the wardroom stores, this is what was being served to us.'

'You had this food served to the men?' said Clay, turning to the purser.

'I... I didn't realise it was so bad, sir,' stuttered Haywood.

'Don't you give me the lie to my face, damn you!' shouted Clay. 'This is why the cook came to see you earlier! Yet you took no action. And why do we have such poor quality stores on board anyway?'

'Well, this is all very diverting, I am sure, but please do not reprimand poor Mr Haywood on my account, Pipe,' interrupted Sexton. 'I am very pleased with him. Few things serve to rouse a crew quicker than a corrupt purser who serves up rotten vittles to hungry men. But charming as I have found you gentlemen's company, I do now have what I came for.' He moved aside to allow the two seaman to pass, their arms full of the officers swords and pistols.

'That was my father's blade!' shouted the marine. 'If it is not returned in perfect order I will hunt you down, Sexton, if it is my last act on earth.'

'Which it may prove to be if you don't stow your noise, Macpherson,' said the mutineer. 'This door will be blocked and guarded. If anyone tries to leave the wardroom, my men will kill them out of hand. Do sleep soundly, won't you? If you should feel hungry in the night, there is always the pork.'

Chapter 9
Redemption

After Sexton left the wardroom the officers were quick to sober up, in spite of the large amount of alcohol they had consumed. Clay rounded on Haywood, his face white with fury.

'I will trouble you for a proper explanation as to how this rancid meat came to be on board my ship, Mr Haywood,' he said.

'It must have been slipped past me by the victualling yard, sir,' whined the purser. 'You recall how we were in such a perishing hurry to leave Plymouth?'

'Slipped past you?' repeated Clay. 'Perhaps in a similar manner to the inferior clothes Mr Taylor tells me you were issuing to the hands before I joined? Did they slip past you too, or have you been taking bribes, Mr Haywood?'

'Sir, that's a dreadful accusation!' he protested.

'Yes, and it is one I am resolved to get to the bottom of, I promise you that,' he said. 'I believe you will find that when I complain to the Victualling Board and tell them this meat provoked a mutiny, your accomplices at the Plymouth yard will give you up quick enough, if only to save their own miserable hides. What were you thinking of, man? Serving such filth to a crew but recently restored to obedience.' He stared at the tub of pork congealing in the centre of the table. 'Well, gentlemen, that is all for the future. Does anyone have a suggestion to offer to get us out of our current predicament?'

'Are there any other ways out of the room?' asked Macpherson. 'Apart from through the guarded door?'

Taylor shook his head. 'We are at the very back of the ship, Tom. Behind us is the rudder, and then the sea. Above us is the Captain's cabin, and below our feet the bread room and aft magazine,' he said. 'All of which we are separated from by three inches of seasoned oak planking.'

Macpherson stood up and banged his fist against the deck over his head. 'No opportunity to pierce it, then?' he muttered.

'What with?' scoffed Morton. 'Our finger nails? Or the cutlery?'

'I am merely considering all the options, Edmund,' said the marine. 'I am not in the habit of just capitulating at the first hint of any set back.'

'Gentlemen, please,' said Clay. 'Let us not add to our woes by falling out among ourselves. Mr Morton is correct when he says that we cannot pass through the decks. We have the sea on three sides and oak above and below. Therefore we perforce must exit by the door. Could we attempt to overwhelm the men who guard us? Do we know how many we have to deal with?'

'No, but they are speaking freely enough,' said Blake, who sat at that end of the table. 'I could sit with my ear to the door and try to deduce how many distinct voices there are.'

'Might I suggest you use a wine glass?' said Corbett. 'I believe that is said to aid such endeavours.'

'Upon my word, how on earth does a gentlemen get to learn of such things?' said Morton. 'The preferred manner for listening at doors, for goodness sake!'

'It is a technique well known to philosophy, Mr Morton,' snapped the surgeon. 'I will have you know that I have used a wine glass on occasion to aid me in listening to my patients' chests.'

'Mr Morton,' said his captain, 'can you kindly refrain from vexing your fellow officers at every occasion? Thank you for your valuable suggestion, Mr Corbett, I am sure Mr Blake will put it into effect. We will stay quiet while you listen.'

The junior lieutenant wiped a glass clean with a napkin, and pulled his chair close to the door. He placed the glass with care against the wood, then pressed his ear to the base. The minutes dragged by in the silent wardroom as the officers waited for him to come to a conclusion. Haywood stared straight in front of him, dread knotting in his stomach, and tugged at his sparse hair. Whichever way I examine the future it all looks bleak, he thought. What am I to do if this mutiny should succeed? God, the men hate me! Why, some of the rougher ones might even take the opportunity to quietly kill me off. Of course, the mutiny may be defeated, he told himself. He glanced up the table at the brooding figure of the captain. He is right; I am finished if that happens. That bastard of a superintendent will give me up in a flash if it comes down to a simple choice between his job or mine. Oh, how I crowed over those stupid twelve guineas. They may as well be the thirty silver coins that Judas was paid for all the good they will do me. Why, oh why did I let my greed get the better of me?

Lieutenant Morton sat with folded arms and stared at Macpherson. Why is it that I hate that man so? he asked himself. He looked around the wardroom, with its four cabin doors on each side and its table with the trunk of the mizzen mast plunging down through it from the deck above. This space was all mine three months ago, he reminded himself. I was the one who was really in charge. Blake is just a puppy, yapping whenever I condescend to stroke him. Taylor is far too weak to stand up to me, and that previous marine lieutenant was nothing but a drunken fool – what was his name? Well, no matter. Captain Sheridan was always happy to share a bottle with the only other genuine gentlemen aboard. And now Sheridan has gone, and Lieutenant Bloody Enthusiastic of His Majesty's Royal Marines has joined, complete with his father's blade. Doubtless it was last used in Bonny Prince Charlie's name by some half naked barbarian back in forty-five. Look at him, just itching to play the hero of the hour for his beloved captain. Well, I will show him. He has no monopoly on courage. I can fight bravely too. I am more than capable of standing up to these damned mutinous dogs.

Clay appeared to the others to be sitting still and watching Blake as he crouched by the door. In reality his mind was an active whirlpool as he ran through the events of the last few weeks, searching for the error he had made. Where did I go wrong? he wondered. What was it that I should have foreseen or could have done to prevent the mutiny? Was I too indulgent with the men? Should I have had Sexton marched off the ship back at Plymouth the moment I saw his arrogant face? He shifted about in his chair. God, this is humiliating. I am a captain in the Royal Navy in command of a powerful warship and have been granted such authority by my country. Power to chose when to fight and when to run. Power over every aspect of the lives of the two hundred and forty odd souls aboard, yet here I sit, confined unlawfully in my own damned ship. I am not even in my bloody cabin! He felt his face burn red with shame.

'Five men, I should say, sir,' reported Blake at last. 'One of whom is much closer than the rest. I believe he may be seated on something that has been placed against the door.'

'That would seem to be similar to last time, sir,' explained Morton. 'The wardroom door opens outward. They placed a pair of sea chests across the entrance to prevent us from rushing them.'

'Five armed and desperate men that we are unable to take unawares,' said Clay. 'And we are but seven, all unarmed. Those are not good odds, gentlemen. Not good at all.'

'We are not wholly unarmed sir,' said Macpherson, indicating the mass of empty wine bottles on the table. 'They could be useful in a melee.'

'Even assuming we can persuade Mr Morton to use such an un-gentlemanly weapon as a broken bottle, the odds are still unrealistic, Tom,' said Clay, smiling at the marine. 'Keep them to hand in the hope that an opportunity may present itself. Until then I suggest we set watches, while the rest of us get some sleep. I shall take the first watch with Mr Blake. I fear we may be in for a long night.'

*****

Four bells in the mid watch had just rung out from the forecastle. Sean O'Malley counted the strokes, and as the last one faded away he raised himself up and peeked out of his hammock. The occasional lantern cast orange circles of light down onto a strangely deserted lower deck. The Irishman peered around him. He was used to seeing the space packed with a dense carpet of swaying hammocks, all moving together with the gentle roll of the ship. That was in normal times. None of the marines or petty officers who shared the space with the men had chosen to join the mutiny, he reminded himself, nor indeed had many of the crew. They were all confined in the hold, together with his friends. He thought of the look of horror and disgust on Rosso's face when he had joined the mutiny. But what had hurt him the most had been his best friend Trevan's reaction. He had never seen the Cornishman so angry. Normally he was the mildest of men, and his fury had cut O'Malley with its unexpectedness. Still, it had to be endured in a good cause, he reminded himself.

He checked his fellow mutineers in the hammocks that hung around him with care. Those nearest to him all seemed to be sound asleep; those farther away could be detected from their snores. That will be the extra tot Sexton had had issued to his men, thought O'Malley. He had wisely (and regretfully), poured his away, knowing he would need to be alert later in the night. He slipped from his hammock and dropped to the deck. He stayed still for a moment while he checked again that no one had been disturbed. Satisfied, he stooped to picked up the pistol he had been issued with from the deck beneath his hammock. He checked the priming, slipped it into the waistband of his trousers and then, after a moment's thought, he took his neighbour's pistol too. He then reached for where his cutlass hung at the foot of his hammock. The blade rattled in its ill-fitting scabbard as he draped the strap across his chest, and the man whose pistol he had taken muttered in his sleep. O'Malley remained still, his heart thumping against his ribs, as the sailor rolled over towards him. His eyes opened wide and seemed to look straight into the Irishman's from a range of a few inches. He frowned for a moment, and then his eyes slid closed again. Once he was snoring, O'Malley let out a huge breath and tiptoed across the dimly lit deck to where Stephenson, the armourer's mate, lay in his hammock. He looked up as O'Malley approached.

'I ain't sure about this at all, Sean,' he murmured. 'That Sexton can be a right bastard when he set's his mind on it.'

'Look, it will all be fine,' whispered O'Malley. 'Just you be after keeping quiet. Let me do the talking, and make sure you bring your tools with you.'

'I got them here,' breathed Stephenson, patting his pockets. 'So if I help you now, you're going to put a good word in for me with the captain, like?'

'That I will, feller,' said the Irishman. 'You'll be quite the hero of the hour. But first you need to get your arse out of that there hammock.'

'Cause this is all wrong, us rising against Pipe like what we done,' continued the armourer's mate, as he swung himself down onto the deck. 'He don't deserve it at all.'

'So why did you fecking mutiny then, you daft fool?' hissed O'Malley, his exasperation getting the better of his caution.

'It's that bloody Sexton! When you listen to him you can't help yourself. He gets you all hot and angry like. It all makes such sense, when he is a rattling away. It's only afterwards that you get to thinking, and then you says to yourself, "Tom Stephenson, you ain't no bleeding mutineer! What the hell is you doing mixed up in all of this nonsense?" But by then it's too late.'

'Well, Tom Stephenson, I am after thinking it's never too late to right a wrong,' whispered the Irishman. 'Get your weapons, and come with me.' The two men crept along the deck to the fore ladder way, which they ascended in silence onto the main deck above them. It was dark outside, and the ship sailed through the night under easy sail with a skeleton crew of mutineers on watch. As O'Malley's head came above the level of the deck, he forced himself to move normally.

'Greetings, lads,' he called out as he strode up to a group of men. 'Have any of yous seen your man Morris? Is he still up on the quarterdeck?'

'No, mate, he's in Pipe's cabin with Dick and Shane,' said one of Sexton's messmates. 'What you after him for?'

'He wants Tom here for something,' replied O'Malley. 'Probably another fecking lock as needs opening. I'll be seeing yous later.' He walked on down the deck with Stephenson beside him. O'Malley could sense suspicious eyes as they bored into his back. His neck prickled, but he forced himself to walk on as normal as he could and not look round. As soon as they were out of sight, he changed direction and clattered down the main ladder way back to the lower deck, then continued down to the orlop deck below it. As he had expected, a party of armed mutineers sat at the bottom guarding the hatchway that led down to the hold. They were each armed with one of the marine's muskets, and the hatchway itself was covered by a heavy grating to keep the loyal members of the crew in the hold.

'Evening, lads,' said O'Malley, ducking his head under the low beams. 'Any sign of trouble from the prisoners?'

'No, mate,' said one of the mutineers. 'There was a deal of grumbling and plenty of bleeding abuse from them earlier, but no trouble since. I reckon they must be asleep.'

'You can hardly blame them being a bit fierce like,' said another one of the guards. 'How would you fancy spending the night trying to kip down in the hold among all the rats?'

'So the bleeders should have joined with us, then,' said the first mutineer, who seemed to be the leader.

'I am not so sure, Bryson,' said a third guard. 'It does bother me that so few of them has bleeding joined us. Why ain't they? We was all in on the rising against Sheridan, but this time it's barely one in three. If Sexton hadn't had all them weapons to hand out, we wouldn't of had no mutiny at all.'

'They will be after coming round when we gets to Spithead,' said O'Malley, 'once they realise how the whole fleet is with them.'

'I don't know,' muttered the last guard. 'I've killed a few Frogs in my time, but it don't seem natural somehow, pointing a gun at one of your own kind. I mean another shipmate, like.'

'What are you down here for, anyway?' asked Bryson.

'Dick is after Tom here checking on them two in the lockup,' said O'Malley. 'He is worried about their irons coming loose.'

'They looked fine to me,' grumbled the mutineer.

'He is probably troubling himself over nothing,' said O'Malley as he walked towards the door. 'Shouldn't take us long.'

'Sean!' exclaimed Sedgwick, as the Irishman came through the door of the lockup. 'What are you doing here?'

'Easy now, lads,' whispered their friend, holding up a restraining hand. 'Keep the noise down. We got four of Sexton's men just over by the main hatchway keeping guard on the hold. Tom here is going to get those irons off you.'

'What do you mean, Sexton's men?' asked Evans as he sat up to let Stephenson come at his leg irons. 'We've heard a deal of shouting and stuff, but no one has told as bleeding anything.'

'That bastard's taken command of the fecking ship, that's what,' said O'Malley. 'He managed to get hold of a key to the arms chest somehow, so him and his boys was able to overpower the lobsters.'

'What of the captain?' asked Sedgwick. 'Is he still alive?'

'Sure he is well enough,' said the Irishman. 'Last I heard he was after being trapped in the wardroom with the Grunters. Few enough of the lads have joined in with Sexton, but them as have are all armed, and they have the rest of the crew locked tight in the hold, including Rosie and Adam. Come on, Tom, can't you get them fecking locks picked at all?'

'Almost there,' said the armourer's mate. 'Try and hold still you two.'

'So how come you are armed, Sean?' asked Sedgwick.

'I played along as how I was with them,' he said. 'First time that being Irish has been some use since I joined the fecking navy. Mind yous, I don't know as if Adam will ever let me tie his pigtail again. I never seen the man so angry like.' There was a smooth click from the lock, and Stephenson sat back on his haunches.

'Got it,' he announced. Evans rubbed his chaffed ankles and Sedgwick rose to his feet.

'I want to go and rescue the captain,' he said.

'One thing at a time,' said O'Malley. 'First we got to get past these four clowns outside.'

'Leave 'em to me,' said Evans. 'I've been spoiling for a fight since those bastards set on us yesterday.'

'Steady, Sam,' cautioned the Irishman. 'These boys have got muskets and will use them if we try and rush the buggers. This needs a bit of blarney rather than muscle. I am after thinking we may not need to fight them at all. They were starting to talk real shy about the whole mutiny earlier.'

'What should we do, Sean?' asked Sedgwick.

'Let Tom and myself get them in here. It's too snug for muskets to be much use. You can speak to them, being Pipe's coxswain an' all, and if that don't answer, Sam here can whack them.'

'Hold on, Sean,' protested Stephenson. 'I only agreed to pick a bleeding lock. We never said nothing about no fighting with any mutineers.' Evans reached across the small room and grabbed the collar of the armourer's mate with one hand while he drew back his other and balled it into a huge fist. 'See, I am going to fight with mutineers, maybe kill a couple. So if you ain't with us I am thinking maybe you must be with them?'

'N..n..no!' stuttered Stephenson. 'I am with you, Big Sam. I was just saying what we agreed, like. If he had asked me to join you properly, of course I would have.' Evans released his collar, and pulled his shirt straight again for him.

'Good. Glad we got that nice and clear before anyone got hurt,' he said.

'Hey!' came a shout from outside. 'What's going on in there? You two have been bleeding ages.' O'Malley ducked out through the door.

'Bryson, I tell you, it's a fecking miracle these two haven't escaped,' he exclaimed. 'Will you come and have a look at this?'

Two of the mutineers exchanged glances, and came over to the cell. The Irishman stood aside and they entered the tiny room. Evans and Sedgwick were seated against the wall once more, their ankles hidden behind the crouched figure of the armourer's mate.

'Not a word,' hissed O'Malley, whipping out his two pistols and pressing them into the men's backs. Sedgwick sprang up and grabbed the muskets from their unresisting hands. He handed them to Evans without taking his eyes off the men.

'Sean says that you two are having second thoughts about the mutiny,' said the coxswain. 'Is that right?'

'Maybe,' conceded Bryson. 'But we're committed to it now. We got no choice but to carry on.'

'Sure you have,' said Sedgwick. 'Nothing is fixed yet. Join us now. Just like Stephenson here has. I will make sure the captain knows that you did the right thing.'

'I don't know,' said the other. 'If Sexton was to get to hear about it....'

'Sexton is finished!' exclaimed Sedgwick. 'The mutiny is over. Most of your shipmates have stayed loyal. Sexton has tricked you, just like he did Evans and me. Now, in a moment we shall rush out of here with these arms of yours, overpower the other two, and release the rest of the crew. Then how long do you think this rising will last?'

'Come on, Bryson,' urged his mate. 'He is right, you know. This ain't never going to work without the whole crew behind it.'

'And you're both smart lads,' said the coxswain. 'You know how failed mutinies end. There will be pardons for them as did the right thing and chose to return to obedience and loyalty to their captain. Or there will be a reckoning, and a long drop from a short rope for those that fought on. Now it is time for you both to choose, shipmates. Are you with us, or do you plan to be strung up by the neck between Sexton and Kenny?'

The two mutineers exchanged glances, and Bryson nodded to the other.

'We'll join you,' he said, and then grinned. 'Christ, that's a relief. What do we do now?'

'Can you persuade the other two to join us?' asked Sedgwick.

'Aye, that we can,' said the other. 'If we can say you will speak up for them with the captain.'

'Here is my hand on it,' said the coxswain. 'Once you have them on side, let the hands out of the hold nice and quiet like, and tell them to wait for us on the orlop deck. The rest of us will go and get the Grunters released. Evans, give them back their muskets.' The Londoner hesitated for a moment, then flipped open the priming pans and raised each musket to his mouth in turn. He spat expertly onto the pinches of dry powder. Then he handed them back.

'Not that I don't trust you, lads,' he said. 'But the bayonets will still work just fine, should you need them.'

*****

Macpherson looked up with a start as there was a heavy thump against the wardroom door.

'What the devil was that?' whispered Morton from the other side of the table.

'I am not sure,' said the marine. 'But something is unfolding. You had best go and wake the others.' He reached for the neck of the nearest empty wine bottle and smashed it down against the edge of the wardroom table. Shards of glass rained down onto the deck. The marine hefted the remaining half of the bottle in his hand and moved till he stood to one side of the door, the broken bottle raised. From beyond the thick wood he heard another thump, as of a heavy body falling to the deck, followed by the clear double click of pistols being cocked.

'Pass over them fecking muskets, or I'll shoot the pair of yous,' came a hiss, full of growling menace. Macpherson paused for a moment, trying to place the familiar voice. He heard a double crash from behind him, and turned to see Taylor and the captain, both now armed like him.

'What's going on, Tom?' asked Clay.

'It sounds like the guards are being overpowered, sir,' said the marine. 'I believe I may have heard O'Malley's voice. His language is always rather laden with profanity.' They all looked down at the base of the door as something heavy was dragged aside along the deck, and then the door cautiously swung open.

'Be ready,' warned Macpherson, as Evans' huge shape filled the door frame.

'Bloody hell, steady with that, sir,' said the Londoner as he pushed Macpherson's broken bottle to one side with a careful hand. 'Have you gentlemen had a falling out in here?' He turned to speak to those behind him. 'Careful, lads,' he warned. 'There's broken glass everywhere. It's worse than chucking out time at my Uncle Bob's gin shop.'

'Is the captain there?' asked an anxious voice, and a figure pushed his way forward.

'I am here, Sedgwick,' said Clay. 'Tell me swiftly, what is afoot?'

'Sexton, Page and Kenny are in your cabin, sir,' he replied. 'I am not sure who else is with them. Much of the crew have stayed loyal, and we have been able to release them from the hold. They are assembling on the orlop deck. The mutiny is weak, sir. If Sexton had not been able to arm his followers and overwhelm the marines I doubt if he would have taken the ship at all.'

'Did any of my men join the revolt?' asked Macpherson.

'No lobsters involved that I have seen, sir,' said O'Malley.

'How many men do you have with you?' asked the captain.

'O'Malley, Evans and Stephenson, sir,' replied Sedgwick. 'It was O'Malley and Stephenson that broke us out of the lock up.'

'And you were able to overcome the five guards stationed here?' asked Clay.

'To be honest they were not too game, sir,' replied the coxswain. 'Once Evans floored the first two, the others gave in pretty easily.'

'We never wanted to rise in the first place, sir,' said an anxious voice.

'That's right, yer honour,' supplemented another. 'Might we be permitted to join with you?'

'I will deal with you later,' said Clay, glaring at the disarmed mutineers. 'Mr Taylor and Mr Blake, go and take command of the loyal people on the orlop deck, if you please. Arm them as you can improvise, and take control of the lower deck. The rest of you follow me.'

'Sir, we found your swords in a heap over here,' said Sedgwick. 'You may wish to trade those bottles for something more regular.' With a cry Macpherson sprung forward and picked up his sword. He pulled it out and let the empty scabbard fall to the deck.

'Shall we go and cut off this revolt by the head, sir?' he said.

*****

'I must say I would have expected a bleeding sight more of Pipe,' slurred Sexton. He waved his glass in an unsteady circuit around the great cabin. Rum sloshed out and pattered down onto the surface of the table. 'The last time we were enjoying the delights of this fine establishment it was crammed with old Sheridan's best furniture. Look at it now! A tiny little desk over there, this here table and a few chairs in the whole place. He hasn't even got anything to cover the floor.' Shane Kenny focused with difficulty on the interior of Clay's quarters.

'I have heard of hermit's cells with more in them,' he offered. The cabin was brightly lit, which only served to emphasise how empty the space was. Page raised his head briefly from his folded arms to look about him.

'He's not even bothered to try and cover up the bleeding guns,' he contributed.

'But far worse than that, we have barely managed to find a decent drop of grog in the whole place,' added Sexton. He held his glass up towards the light and regarded the dark brown service rum with distaste.

'Aye, that Sheridan may have been a vicious bastard, but he was after having some proper quantities of fecking knock-me-down for us to sample,' said the Irish mutineer, smiling at the recollection. 'French brandy, Hollander Gin, Madeira, fine wines, bottles and bottles of the stuff.'

'Still, let us toast our triumph in what we have,' replied their leader. He nudged Page awake and rose to his feet. More rum fell to the deck as he raised his glass. 'To the new Lords of the *Titan*!' he bellowed.

'And a free Ireland,' added Kenny.

'And a good night's sleep,' muttered Page, his head dropping towards the table top once more.

'And an accurate piss,' concluded Sexton. 'God, I am fit to burst.' He thumped his glass back on Clay's dining table, made his unsteady way over to the quarter galley and disappeared into the captain's privy.

'How long will it be till we get's to Spithead?' asked the Irishman.

'We need to ask that old fart Warwick,' answered Page. 'Shall I have him fetched?'

'No, the morning will be soon enough,' said Kenny after a pause. 'If he was to tell me now, I doubt I would fecking recall it at all tomorrow. But we need to watch him, Morris. See he doesn't play us false and put the barky on the rocks.'

'Why would he do that?' asked Page. 'That would send far more loyal crew to their deaths than mutineers, on top of all the Grunters. Any road, he's a bleeding sailing master. Doubt if he could find it in his heart to harm a ship on purpose if he tried. What's the matter, Shane?'

'Ssshh!' said Kenny, holding up a hand. He reached across the table for his cutlass. 'Were you after hearing anything outside? A cry maybe?' Page picked up his pistol, suddenly awake, and put his head on one side to listen. He heard a thump, some scuffling and a few muffled shouts come from the far side of the door.

'Do you reckon some bugger has jumped the bleeding lads guarding the cabin?' he asked. From the far side of the door came a voice. Even through an inch of oak both men could recognise the sound of their captain.

'Put up your weapons!' ordered Clay. 'This mutiny is over. I will have no blood of shipmates shed here. Put up your weapons, I say! That's better. Stephenson disarm those men, you others follow me.' The door to the day cabin burst open and Clay led the party of officers and men surging forward.

'Stay back, all of you!' shouted Page. He jumped to his feet and swung his pistol from side to side in an attempt to cover the whole group as they fanned out in the broad space of the great cabin. Kenny lurched to his feet too, knocking over his chair as he did so. He held his cutlass out in front of him, the edge glittering in the lamp light.

'Come now, Page,' said Clay. He advanced in small steps towards the mutineer. 'One shot, if you're lucky, against all of us. I call those decidedly poor odds. Your mutiny is finished, put up your weapon, man. Let us keep this a bloodless affair.' Clay held his sword low and unthreatening as he edged forward, while he extended out his left hand, palm open to receive the gun.

'Stay back!' shouted Page again, the pistol settling its unsteady aim on Clay's stomach. The captain came to a halt, his left hand still held out. 'One shot, you say? Plenty enough to send you to hell, Pipe.'

'Have a care, sir,' cautioned Macpherson by his side.

'Why are there only the two of them?' muttered O'Malley to Sedgwick, his own two pistols both covering Kenny. 'Where is your man Sexton?'

Lieutenant Morton was off to one side of the group. He was watching Page and Kenny so intently that at first he didn't notice the door of the quarter galley beside him as it inched open. A single bloodshot eye appeared in the gap, focused on the captain and narrowed with anger. It was only as the door opened a little wider to allow the barrel of a pistol to slide through that he realised what was about to happen.

'Oh no you don't!' he yelled, leaping across the cabin towards the door, his sword raised. His sudden movement broke the spell of the standoff, and the other poised figures burst into life.

Page swung his pistol towards the moving Morton and Macpherson seized his chance. He darted forward and slashed with his sword, his blade a glittering scythe in the lamp light. With a howl of pain Page dropped the gun and clasped his bloody hand to his chest. The tip of Macpherson's sword then whipped back up like a snake and came to rest close to the mutineer's throat.

'Breathe and I'll skewer you to the bulkhead,' he hissed, his Scottish accent much more obvious than usual.

Kenny was the next to react. With a shout of fury he swung his cutlass towards Morton. O'Malley pulled the triggers of both of his pistols in quick succession. He was standing a bare five feet away from his target. The first heavy lead ball spun the mutineer around and the second sent him crashing to the deck. The deafening sound of the two explosions in the confined space of the cabin was stunning. Everyone stopped for a moment to try and shake their heads clear of the ringing. The upper half of the cabin filled with thick, acrid powder smoke that veiled the lanterns like clouds around the sun. It was only slowly that they realised that beneath the grey fog, two men were locked in a vicious struggle on the deck.

When O'Malley had fired his pistols, Morton had already ripped open the door of the quarter galley and had thrown himself at Sexton. Both men crashed to the ground at much the same time as Kenny fell. They thrashed and rolled together as they struggled on the deck. Morton's sword had clattered from his grasp when his arm had struck the planking. He was desperate to wrestle his opponent's grasp from the pistol that was caught between their two bodies. Sexton was struggling to free himself from the lieutenant's clinging embrace so that he could take a shot. He lashed his head into the officer's face in a series of heavy butts. Evans was the first of the group to react. He rushed across to help Morton, but before he could pull the mutineer off him there was a flash between their struggling bodies as the pistol went off.

*****

'Come in!' called Clay from deep within his sleeping cabin. He continued to adjust his silk neck cloth, pressing the folds into place and tweaking the front of his full dress coat, until he saw the bulky shape of Midshipman Butler appeared in the mirror just above his right shoulder. With a final pat, he turned towards the cabin door.

'The first lieutenant sends his respects, and wishes you to know that all the preparations are now complete, sir,' he said.

'Thank you, Mr Butler,' replied his captain. He reached out with his arms as if about to embrace the officer, and his servant, Yates, stooped down to buckle his sword belt around his waist. Butler's eyes flicked towards his captain's left arm, trailing a little lower than his right. 'Please tell Mr Taylor I will be with him directly.' Once the midshipman had gone, he settled the sword belt into place, adjusted the single gold epaulet on his right shoulder that showed him to be a post captain with less than three years seniority, and strode out into the great cabin.

Through the sweep of glass at the back of the space he could see the cliffs and little islands of the Brittany coast, orange and pink in the light of the setting sun. The restless sea glowed amber under the ship's counter, while farther away he could see the first few lights as they started to glow in the fishermen's cottages and farmers' crofts ashore. He walked to his desk and picked up his service book. Then he flipped open the small leather volume to where a slip of paper marked the page he would need and checked the words he would have to say. He looked out of the stern window for a moment, and then closed the book once more and turned his back on the coast. He strode out of his cabin, collecting his hat from Yates by the door, and ducked through under the low door frame. The marine sentry that once more stood guard outside clicked to attention. Clay touched his hat in acknowledgement, feeling pleased at this sign that the ship was once more under control.

Even before he came out on deck he was able to tell from the unusual motion beneath his feet that the ship was as near to stationary as Taylor had been able to achieve. She rose and fell in rhythm with the waves, each movement accompanied by a chorus of rattles and bangs. He paused for a moment to place the sound. Then he smiled. Of course: it came from the hundreds of blocks and miles of rope that made up her running rigging as they slapped against the spars and masts high above his head. Normally at sea they would all be under tension, but not today. He looked up towards the top of the main mast as he emerged from under the quarterdeck and noted the single black ensign that flew there.

Stood next to the ship's side were eight members of the crew in their best shore-going clothes. Clay saw that they had been chosen with care by Taylor. Four had been drawn from among the loyal members of the crew, including the bulky figure of Sedgwick, and the other four were former mutineers. Between them and borne on their shoulders was the solid top of a mess table, one end of which rested on the rail of the ship. On that platform lay the flag-shrouded shape of a body.

'Carry on, please, Mr Hutchinson,' said Clay to the grizzled boatswain of the *Titan*, who stood waiting for him beside the party of seamen.

'Aye aye, sir,' he said in return. He brought his silver call up to his mouth, inflated his lungs and blew into it. The callused fingers of one hand fluttered over the silver cylinder to produce a trilling note. The call was taken up by his mates on the deck below, and their cries rang through the ship. 'All hands! All hands to witness burial.'

With a thunder of bare feet those crew not already on deck rushed up from below and arranged themselves into their divisions in an open sided box around the mess table. Here were not just the men of the two watches, but all the specialist warrant officers and their mates, who made the little world of their ship function. The cooks and carpenters, the sail makers and coopers, the gunners and armourers. From behind him Clay heard the stamp and clatter of the marines as they formed up on the quarterdeck. He gave the crew a moment to settle, and when they were quiet he took the time to look at the faces all around him in their long lines, illuminated in the warm glow of the evening light. He thought back to the first time he had seen them in Plymouth. They had been a nameless crew then, sullen, resentful and angry. He remembered how most had met his inspection with hostile stares of defiance. Now as his gaze moved from one man to the next he found he could remember a good third of their names easily enough, and all the rest after only a brief struggle. Their expressions had changed too. Very few were angry now. Most could not meet his gaze at all. Their eyes slipped away from his towards the deck. They are ashamed of themselves, he concluded. Ashamed of what they have done. That is a good start. I can work with shame, he thought. I can build it back up to what I want to see in their eyes. Pride.

'Off hats, if you please, Mr Hutchinson,' he said.

'Ship's company, off hats,' roared the boatswain. When the crew were bareheaded, Clay went to open his service book. Out of the corner of his eye he saw the boatswain remove the shiny leather hat of his office with the royal arms painted on the front, reminding him just in time to remove his own hat and place it under his arm. Then he read out the short, simple service.

'For as much as it hath pleased Almighty God of His great mercy to take unto Himself the soul of our dear brother, Edmund James Morton here departed, we therefore commit his body to the deep. Amen.'

The burial party raised the end of the mess table. The angle became progressively steeper, until with a slithering rush the canvas wrapped body of the *Titan*'s second lieutenant shot out from under the flag and splashed down into the darkening sea.

Chapter 10
Reunion

The morning after the burial found Clay sharing a pot of coffee once more with his first lieutenant in his great cabin. With all the vagaries of a Brittany spring, the delightful weather of the previous evening had vanished. Through the sweep of glass behind the captain's back a vast plain of choppy green sea surged about under a low sky of boiling grey cloud. They were together for their regular daily meeting, but for once the smaller concerns of boatswain's stores and the carpenter's ongoing complaint at the state of the frigate's knees had been set to one side. Today they had more pressing matters to address.

'How are the prisoners this morning?' asked Clay as he stirred his drink.

'Mr Corbett holds out little hope that Shane Kenny will pull through, but he believes that Morris Page will survive,' said Taylor. 'He is at least a little penitent. The doctor has attended to his wounded hand, although he will never regain the use of several of his fingers.'

'Macpherson's sword must be devilish sharp,' said the

Captain. 'Still, it may serve to remind him of the perils of mutiny. Where is he now?'

'I have placed him back in the custody of the Master at Arms, sir. He is down in the lock up alongside Sexton. That man shows no remorse at all, and seems quite resigned to his fate. As you instructed I have allowed the other hands involved in the mutiny to resume their duties.'

'And how has that been?'

'To be frank, sir, very ill,' sighed the first lieutenant. 'The mutiny may be over but it has left the people quite beset by division. When they rose against Captain Sheridan their actions were of course quite wrong, but at least they were of a united purpose. This time was quite different. Force was used to coerce the reluctant. Most messes were split between mutineers and loyal seamen. It has left much resentment and bitterness amongst the crew. The Master at Arms can barely keep up with all the disorder and fighting.'

'Is it the damned mutineers who are causing the trouble?' demanded Clay. 'Because they should regard themselves as very lucky I have not had them all clapped in irons for what they have done.'

'Not for the most part, no' explained Taylor. 'To be sure there has been a little of that, with those who mutinied naming those that did not cowards and traitors. But chiefly it is the men that stayed loyal who are at fault. They look to pay back those who forced them at gun point to spend an uncomfortable night in the hold. Then some blame the Irish, who were very prominent in the mutiny, and yet ignore all those Irish hands who did not join their compatriots. Even the volunteers who followed you aboard when you first took command are not immune from some resentment. Adam Trevan took a great deal of persuasion that when Sean O'Malley joined the mutineers it was all a ruse, and that he was loyal the whole time.'

'Can the petty officers not help to control such disorder?' asked Clay.

'They are some of the worst offenders,' exclaimed the lieutenant. 'None of them joined the mutiny I am pleased to say, but they would scarce be human if they did not seek to use their authority over the hands to pay back the many slights they have been made to endure.'

'Then we must act to bring them back together,' said Clay, his voice passionate. 'How can we expect to defeat an enemy, when we are at war amongst ourselves?' He pointed to the two dark patches on the deck behind him. Both were still wet from hours of scrubbing to remove the stains that had marked where Shane Kenny had been wounded and Lieutenant Morton had bled to death. 'We need not look very far to see where such divisions can lead. I am quite resolved not to witness such a misfortune onboard this ship again.'

'Amen to that,' said Taylor. 'I am not sure what council I can offer you, sir. Captain Sheridan would have met such uncivil behaviour with savage punishment for all, but I do not believe that will answer. If truth be told I hold that your approach when you first took over the ship was working well with all but the worst of the men. You were firm, but you also showed some delicacy towards the ills that the men had suffered in the past. I tried to show a similar approach yesterday when we committed poor Mr Morton's body to the deep.'

'Yes, I did notice your choice of crewmen to bear the body,' said his captain. 'I, too, thought that my way would answer, but let us face the world as it is, not as we would have it. The men still rose against us.'

'By no means all did, sir,' said Taylor. 'Most stayed loyal. Had it not been for the encouragement of the news of the Channel Fleet mutiny, combined with Mr Haywood's wretched pork, there might have been no mutiny at all.'

I shall deal with Mr Haywood in time,' said Clay. 'But a settled crew would not have risen purely over vittles. To be frank with you, George, I am still very angry at what happened. To be removed from my position in such an undeserved manner, and to be compelled to yield to their demands, it beggars belief! No, I have been altogether too lenient with the men.' He rose from his chair and paced up and down the width of the cabin, his head bowed forward, partly in thought, and partly because he was a good two inches too tall to walk upright beneath the deck.

'Sir, may I ask if you detected any change in the men's demeanour yesterday evening during Lieutenant Morton's funeral?' asked Taylor. Clay stopped midstride.

'You noticed it too?' he said. 'The want of the belligerence that was so evident back in Plymouth when I first joined the ship? I found them to be much more quiet and subdued. I sensed shame in their actions and a little obligation towards me. We must use that to our advantage.'

'How might we do that, sir?' asked the lieutenant.

'I have gone lightly with them up till now,' said Clay. 'I do not mean as far as discipline is concerned, that must always be administered in the same manner, but in how hard I have pushed them in training. Principally I was reluctant to add fresh causes for resentment on an already troubled crew, but I believe that can change now. We shall drive them very hard, Mr Taylor, till they forget completely who it was that was a mutineer and who was loyal. By the time the squadron returns, whenever that will be, I want us to have them well in hand. Let us resolve to turn them into a crack crew together. Make them into a body of men who are all *Titan*s first and proud to be named so.'

*****

'Christ, I am bleeding knackered!' exclaimed Evans, rolling his head around on his shoulders to try and ease the stiffness in them. 'What the hell is Pipe about? Whoever heard of having races between the watches to see which one can sway down and set up the upper masts the quickest?'

'It was a strange piece of work, I grant you, Sam,' said Trevan from the other side of the mess table. 'Mind you, we did beat them starboard watch buggers good an' proper like. We was near as damn it five minutes faster, according to my mate Noah.'

'I can't see what you has to fecking moan about, Sam Evans,' added O'Malley, leaning with his back against the ship's side, his face still flushed red with the afternoon's labour. 'Weren't you having it right soft, down on deck just hauling away with the other waisters, like? Spare a thought for top men like Adam and me, working a hundred fecking feet up having to rig the buggers.'

'It's been four bleeding weeks of this,' moaned the big Londoner. 'Every day he's got us doing something different. I mean all that gun drill at the end of each day I get, but what about last week? When he had us pretending there's was a battery on one of them little empty islands near Ushant and we had to man the boats and make like we was storming it. What was that all about, then?'

'Or the week before that,' added Trevan. 'When we was after anchoring in that little bay down the coast. We had to make believe we was cutting out the barky every bloody night till we done it the way he wanted us to. That was a proper pain in the arse. I am all for Pipe in most things, but I don't get it at all.'

'Come on, lads, isn't it obvious?' said Rosso. 'Have you really not smoked what he's about yet? He's decided he is going to sweat any trouble right out of this crew.'

'How you figure that then, Rosie?' asked Trevan.

'Remember how many fights there was, right after the mutiny?' he said. 'We were scrapping like ferrets in a sack. When was the last time you saw a proper fight?'

'Well that's 'cause we're all too bleeding knackered to mill!' exclaimed Evans. 'Any road, there were a scap during the afternoon watch day before yesterday. Duplain said Fatty Carr had spilt his grog, and Fatty took a swing at him.'

'That's right, Sam, two days ago,' smiled Rosso. 'And it wasn't anything to do with the mutiny then, was it? In fact as I recall Duplain and Fatty both stayed loyal.'

'That ain't right, Rosie,' said Evans. 'I think they was both mutineers.'

'No, you wrong there, Sam,' said Trevan. 'Leastways about Fatty Carr. He was definitely down in the hold near me that night. We both slept leant up against the same hogshead. I tell you, I am right happy I don't have to swing my hammock near to his. His snores are a thing to behold. Louder than a pissed bishop after evening song, he was.'

'You see?' said Rosso, looking around the group. 'Now do you follow? Four weeks of driving us hard, and even we are no longer sensible as to who rose or not. He's a right deep one, that Pipe. All this training may be a pain in the arse, but have you noticed how much better we are? There's a few less bellies around the place – even your Fatty Carr is hardly fat anymore. And we're getting proper quick at doing stuff. We might be five minutes faster than the other watch at striking down the upper masts, but both watches will be a good twenty minutes faster than they used to be.'

'Do you know, you have the truth of it there, Rosie,' said Evans. 'I hadn't thought of it before, but it feels just like all the graft my Pa used to get me to do before a big mill. Hours of work that don't seem to be about prize fighting at all, but served to make me quicker and stronger, and to give me more bottom so as I could stay longer than the other sod. What a crafty bugger!'

'Well that's all very fine an' all, but I am still knackered,' said O'Malley. 'An' don't yous go a-thinking he's about to ease up any. Hart was after telling me that Pipe has been locked in his cabin this past hour with the other Grunters, so you can be sure they'll be plotting another load of fecking training for us for the morning.'

*****

In addition to her captain's punishing schedule of training, the *Titan* still had one further duty to perform. Each day, when wind and tide served, they would stand in up the Iroise Channel towards Brest to observe the French fleet. All aboard now understood that their mission here was a sham, a conjuring trick to deceive their enemy. The approach of the bold frigate was the obvious flourish of the magician's hand that drew attention away from what he wanted to conceal. Watch the warship, not the wide empty sea beyond it. The crew on deck would gather, waiting to hear the news from the masthead, hoping that the French would still be at anchor in their neat lines with their masts struck down on deck. All of them feared that today might be the day on which the news of the Channel Fleet mutiny had reached Brest at last, and those long lines of warships would be sailing down the Goulet to brush them aside. Some days the frigate arrived just as a fresh spring shower had drawn itself like a veil across the harbour mouth, soaking the midshipman at the mastheads, and forcing them to squint into the curtain of water in a futile attempt to see through it. But on all days when they were able to make a sighting, the news had been the same. The French fleet was still in port, and their country was safe for another day. Then they turned their stern to the land and sailed back out to sea to share the happy news in lines of fluttering signal flags with the empty horizon, and to search the lonely sea for a sign that their solitary vigil on this lee shore might be over at last.

Five weeks had passed since the mutiny had ended, and

another long hard day of training was coming to its conclusion with the usual two hours of gunnery drill. Spring had slipped almost unnoticed into summer on the Brittany coast. The afternoon sun had real heat in it now as it twinkled off the wave crests and made solid squares of light on the deck where it shone through the open gun ports.

'That will do, Mr Blake, the crews have rested long enough,' said Clay. He snapped closed his pocket watch and slid it back into his waistcoat. 'Let us see what progress today's training has made.'

'Aye aye, sir,' said Blake. 'Gun crews, man your pieces!'

'I want three aimed broadsides, Mr Blake, not the men just blazing away as quick as quick,' added his captain. Clay ducked his head down to look out of the gun port next to him. The main spine of Les Pierres Noires was drifting past the ship a hundred yards away, the black rocks wet with kelp and marked with startling patches of brilliant white bird excrement. 'There is your mark. Those rocks over there. Let every ball strike home.'

'Aye aye, sir,' said the lieutenant. 'Gun captains, the reef is to be the target. Quoins in a quarter inch. Run up your guns. Mr Russell, are you ready?'

'Yes sir,' said the midshipman, the two-minute sand glass in his hand.

'Open fire when you wish, Mr Blake,' said Clay. He stepped back and admired the long line of big eighteen pounder cannon that stretched away in a gentle curve up to the bow. The crews crouched around their pieces like sprinters, most stripped to the waist, ready for the off.

'Fire!' ordered the lieutenant, and Russell flipped over the sand glass. All along the line the linstocks came down as one. There was a heartbeat of time when all Clay could hear was the splutter of burning powder, and then came the colossal fury of all the canons roaring out as one. A wall of smoke gushed up and the frigate heeled over with the force of the broadside. At each port a gun thundered back into the ship till halted by its gun tackles, and the crew threw themselves into the process of reloading. Stop the vent, sponge out, charge in, ram home, ball in, ram home, then wad, run up, prick the charge and then a pause. That's good, thought Clay, the gun captains are making certain of their aim. As the captain of the slowest gun raised his hand to signal that he too was ready, Blake gave the order to fire again, and the guns blasted out once more. Clay ducked down to look through the nearest gun port. In the instant before his view was obscured by smoke, he saw the broadside tearing up the water all around the reef. Several balls had struck the rock, sending up puffs of shattered stone and dust. He glanced across at the sand running out of the two minute glass. It was going to be close. Here came the final broadside. The ship was engulfed in smoke once more and a distinct few seconds later the last grains of sand fell in the timer.

Blake spun around and looked first at the midshipman, then back at Clay.

'That was it, sir!' he shouted. 'By Jove, we have done it at last! Three broadsides in two minutes!'

'Was it, Mr Russell?' asked Clay. He knew the answer, but wanted to draw the moment out. Up and down the gun deck he could see the panting gun crews as they listened to their officers, many with arms draped around each other.

'Yes, sir, by a good couple of seconds too,' replied the time keeper. The rest of what he said was lost in the storm of cheers that erupted as the men celebrated with each other. Clay smiled on, noticing the togetherness the achievement had produced, and at last some of the pride he had been waiting to see.

'A very creditable exercise, Mr Blake,' he said. He was about to add something further when a hail came from high above them.

'Deck there! Sail ho!' yelled the lookout.

'A Frenchman, I hope, with the people firing so brisk,' said Clay to general laughter from the nearest men. 'Secure the guns, if you please, Mr Blake,' and he hurried off towards the quarterdeck.

'Where away?' the first lieutenant yelled towards the foremast as Clay ran up the companion ladder from the main deck.

'Just rounded Ushant and heading towards us, sir,' came the hail from above. 'Man of war by the look of her.'

'Warship, eh!' said Taylor, rubbing his hands. 'She is certain to be one of ours on that course, sir.'

'Let us hope so, Mr Taylor,' replied Clay. He turned his head towards the masthead and bellowed 'What do you make of her?'

'Large frigate, sir,' came the reply. 'I can see another ship behind her now, and some mastheads beyond that.' Clay turned towards the young midshipman of the watch.

'Up you go with a glass, Mr Butler,' he ordered. 'Tell us

what you make of them.'

'Deck there,' came Butler's excited cry. 'She looks like the old *Indy*! I can see the commodore's broad pennant now, sir. Ship behind could be the *Argos*.' All the gun crews were listening on the main deck as they secured their guns. They gave a collective cheer at this news, until reprimanded by their petty officers for such indiscipline. With a grin their captain shook his first lieutenant by the hand.

'I declare we are about to be relieved at long last,' he said. 'Thank God for that, Mr Taylor, thank God for that.'

*****

Sir Edward Pellew's barge was a beautiful craft. The hull was painted in primrose yellow which contrasted pleasantly with her glossy black gunwales. The oars that swung forward in a neat fan of motion were a perfect match with their pale yellow shafts and black tips to their blades. Inside the boat the crew all sported matching yellow shirts decorated with black ribbon, while on their heads they wore black tarpaulin hats with yellow ribbons around their crowns. Able Sedgwick looked on with covetous eyes as the boat swept alongside the *Titan*. He decided that once the ceremony of the commodore coming aboard was over, he would slip down into the barge to have a word with the coxswain and try and find out where he had obtained his batch of coloured shirts. It would be hard to outdo the commodore's transport with the limited resources available to him here on the Brittany coast, but perhaps when they were back in Plymouth he might come by some bolts of green linen. As the boat came to a halt, Sir

Edward rose from his place in the stern and ran up the side.

He was a magnificent sight in his full dress uniform, complete with the broad red ribbon and badge of the Order of the Bath. The sunlight glittered off his gold lace as he stood to attention in the entry port. Before him was a corridor of white-gloved ship's boys backed by lines of more solid looking boatswain's mates who twittered away with their calls, while off to one side Macpherson ordered his marines to present arms. As the last warbling note faded away, he strode forward and grasped the *Titan*'s captain by the hand.

'Where are the French, Clay?' he asked, his face grave.

'Safely at anchor in the Rade de Brest, Sir Edward,' he replied. 'Or at least they were at three bells in the forenoon watch when we last observed them.' The commodore closed his eyes for a moment, his face wreathed in smiles.

'Bless my soul, but that is good news!' he exclaimed. 'How the Frogs have not smoked that something was up with the fleet, I shall never understand. God must be an Englishman. There can be no other explanation.' Pellew laughed aloud for a moment in the sunshine, and Clay smiled with him.

'Would you care to come below, Sir Edward?' he asked, and the two men disappeared to the privacy of Clay's quarters.

'I can certainly see why it takes you so much less time to clear your cabin for action than it does mine in the *Indefatigable*,' said the commodore. He settled himself down in the wooden chair that stood in front of the little desk and looked around him at the bare scrubbed deck and empty bulkheads. 'Do you not find your furniture to be inconveniently small?'

'My previous command was only a sloop of war, Sir Edward,' explained Clay. 'The Admiralty wanted me to take command of the *Titan* directly, which left me no time to order anything more extensive. Can I offer you a glass of sherry?'

'With pleasure,' the commodore said, taking a drink from the battered tray that Hart held beside him. He sipped at his drink and his eyebrows rose for a brief moment. 'Very eh... nice,' he commented.

'I was not able to complete my cabin stores before departure either, Sir Edward,' explained Clay.

'Well, no matter. I have some excellent sherry wine onboard the *Indy*,' said Pellew. 'Will you permit me to send you across a couple of cases? It is the least I can do to apologise for my absence these last several weeks. Believe me when I say I had no control over events, but was compelled under duress by my crew to abandon you here.'

'I had assumed that must be the case, Sir Edward,' replied Clay. 'But I have been quite starved of any intelligence this last month or more. Might I trouble you to tell me what on earth has been going on?'

'The day after that gale, the whole damned squadron mutinied, that's what,' replied Sir Edward. 'The people must have learnt that the Channel Fleet had risen, how I cannot begin to fathom, for I shared that intelligence with no one other than my four captains. But the fact that four ships of the squadron all revolted as one suggests a well laid plot amongst the men had been afoot for some time. The only mystery is how the *Titan* came to stay loyal.'

'We did not escape the mischief wholly, Sir Edward,' replied Clay. 'Some of the men did mutiny, shortly after the rest of the squadron withdrew, but thanks to the intervention of a body of loyal hands I was able to regain control of the ship. I have the chief ringleader in irons below, and of his main accomplices one is now dead and the other injured. The rest of the crew members are obedient to their duty. Regrettably Lieutenant Morton was killed by the mutineers, and I shall need my purser to be relieved of his duties, but apart from a generally deficiency in water and stores, particularly pork, we are in good shape.'

'That is excellent news,' smiled the commodore. 'For my part we were all forced to sail to join the Channel Fleet at Spithead. When we got there it was a truly dreadful sight. There were red flags at every masthead. Unpopular officers were being roughly manhandled off the ships. Lord Bridport had been cast ashore together with all his captains, myself included, while delegates from the ships negotiated with the Lords of the Admiralty as if they were their damned equals. I tell you, Clay, I have never seen the like, and hope I never shall again. Fortunately it is all now resolved, and the fleet is obedient once more, although I hear there is some fresh mischief that may have started at the Nore. But what of you Clay? What have you been about for all these weeks?'

'I have been keeping the men busy, pushing them hard so they are unable to dwell on thoughts of mutiny, Sir Edward' he replied. 'We have patrolled the approaches to Brest as normal, but I have avoided any action with the enemy, not wanting to hazard the ship with no other vessels at hand to take our place.'

'Very wise,' said Pellew. 'And what of the French?'

'They have been quiet, Sir Edward,' replied Clay. 'We have carried on as if the fleet were still in place, just beyond the horizon. We have reconnoitred when we could and signalled to the empty sea for the benefit of the French watching us from the shore.'

'Have you, by George?' chuckled Pellew. 'That was cleverly done. Remind me never to play you at whist. You certainly know how to act when you are dealt a deuced poor hand.' He regarded Clay for a moment, his look kind.

'Are you not curious to know how the mutiny in the Fleet was brought to a successful resolution?' he asked.

'Yes, of course, Sir Edward,' replied Clay. Pellew returned his glass, still half full, to Hart and rose to his feet.

'I thought so,' he said, with a mischievous twinkle in his eye. 'If you would be good enough to have your crew summoned for me to address them, I will reveal all. Shall we return to the quarterdeck?'

'All hands!' went out the call. 'All hands to assemble by divisions!' In a disciplined rush the watch below flooded up the ladder ways till the main deck was thronged with a jostle of figures all making their way to their places. Every man aboard was present, except for the ringleaders of the mutiny and their marine guards. When the blocks and lines of upturned faces were quiet and settled, Pellew strode forward to the quarterdeck rail, and took out a sheet of paper from the inside pocket of his coat. As he unfolded it the corners fluttered a little in the breeze that flowed across the ship from the open ocean. In a loud voice that was pitched to reach the furthest man, the commodore began to read aloud.

'The Lord Commissioners of the Admiralty have ordered that the following notice is to be read aboard every ship of the Channel Fleet,' he began. 'In light of the recent disorder that has afflicted the fleet of His Majesty the King, the actions listed below have been executed.' Pellew paused to run his eye over the assembled crew to confirm that he had all of their hushed attention. He then returned to the paper.

'His Majesty the King has this day, at the Court of St James, signed into law an Act of Parliament that shall provide for an increase in the rate of pay for the loyal seaman of His Majesty's Navy. All seamen rated able shall have their pay increased by five shillings and six pence per month, and all other ratings shall receive an increase of four shillings and six pence.' Pellew paused till the excited hubbub that had broken out among the crew was silenced by the petty officers. When it was quiet again he resumed reading.

'His Majesty's Government shall form a commission of enquiry to investigate the quality of all manner of provisions supplied to His Majesty's ships by the Victualling Board with a view to their immediate improvement. The Lord Commissioners of the Admiralty have further issued new instructions to the officers commanding His Majesty's ships requiring them to grant any reasonable requests for shore leave that do not imperil the efficient running of said vessels.' He again paused while the men turned to one another, many of the faces now openly smiling.

'Furthermore, His Majesty has graciously issued a Royal

Pardon to any seaman charged with mutiny following the recent disturbances that have taken place aboard His ships, on condition that the said individuals return to dutiful obedience of their lawful officers without delay. Any further incidents of revolt will be dealt with under the full rigor of the Articles of War and the Mutiny Act.' Pellew refolded the sheet of paper with care and returned it to his coat pocket, before facing the men once more. 'Three cheers for the King!' he bellowed. 'Hip hip!' After a moment of hesitation the men began cheering, and he turned back towards Clay.

'You can dismiss the men now,' he said. Clay looked across at Taylor, who gave the order, and the life of the ship returned to normal as the men went back to their duties, many still discussing the news.

'You have my thanks, Clay,' said Pellew. 'You have done your duty this last few weeks. It only saddens me that you had to do it alone. The *Argos* will relieve you now so that you can return to Plymouth to resupply, and I will send you instructions with regard to a new purser and lieutenant to replace poor Mr Morton. Let the men have some shore leave, and take some yourself. I shall expect you to rejoin the squadron by mid June. We should be able to keep an eye on the French without you till then.'

'Thank you, sir,' said Clay. He touched his hat in salute as they walked back to the entry port together. As they reached the ship's side a number of small sacks were being swung up from Pellew's barge.

'Ah, I almost forgot,' he said. 'What with all this nonsense going on in the fleet there has been a decided build up in undelivered mail. I brought it all out with me. There is a considerable amount for you, including a lot forwarded from your previous ship the *Rush*. Goodbye for now, Clay, and well done again.' He waved a hand in farewell and disappeared down over the side to the further squeal of boatswain's pipes. Clay waved back at him, and then turned towards his first lieutenant.

'Do I understand that this Royal Pardon is to apply to our mutineers too, sir?' Taylor asked.

'You heard of the Lord Commissioners instructions on that point as clear as I did, Mr Taylor,' said Clay. 'I do not believe that we have very much of a choice upon the matter.'

'I can just about stomach that rogue Page and those who followed him escaping justice, sir, but surely it cannot apply to that blackguard Sexton,' he said. 'Where is the justice in that?'

'What would you have me do?' asked his captain. 'Go against an order from the King?'

'No, of course not, sir,' conceded Taylor. His hands worked in front of him for a moment, and then hung limp by his side. 'So must I order his release?'

'Yes,' said Clay, his grey eyes stern. 'And then you may have him confined in irons once more.' The first lieutenant looked at his captain in surprise.

'He has been pardoned for the crime of mutiny, Mr Taylor, but I heard no mention of any Royal Pardon for murder. I am quite resolved to see that he swings for the death of Lieutenant Morton.'

Chapter 11
Ashore

His Majesty's frigate *Titan* swung at anchor once more, safe within Plymouth harbour. She was turning around her mooring with the flow of the tide, so that the view from Clay's great cabin had changed from the sunlit fields above Cremyll point via the naval dockyard to the grey stone town itself. He looked up from the gunner's indent he had just signed as his first lieutenant came into the cabin for their regular morning meeting.

'Goodness, sir,' exclaimed Taylor. 'What an extensive correspondence you have.' Clay glanced across the cabin at the large piles of opened letters that were heaped on top of his sea chest.

'Yes, I do,' he smiled. 'Some are from my mother and sister, but the chief part are from a passenger who I met aboard an East Indiaman last year. I was the first lieutenant of the *Agrius* then, and we were convoying her ship as far as Madeira. Then we sailed for the Caribbean while the convoy carried on to India.'

'Ah, I see,' said Taylor. 'A lady, then, I collect?'

'I do not believe I mentioned my acquaintance's sex?' said Clay.

'I beg your pardon, sir, but you did indirectly. You described the vessel you were convoying as "her ship".'

'Oh, did I?' said his captain. He looked so crestfallen at this lapse that Taylor found himself forced to laugh.

'I am sorry, sir,' he apologised. 'It is very impertinent of me to pry. I would have guessed that your correspondence was from a lady even if you had not let slip. I have rarely seen you in such good humour since you joined the *Titan*, and I must say I am delighted for it. These last few months have been so trying that it is a miracle you have not acquired some of my many grey hairs. But perhaps we can now look forward to some calmer waters ahead?' Clay looked at the older man with surprise, and then he too started to laugh.

'Let us hope so, George,' he said. 'I have been writing letters to this person for over a year now, with never a reply to sustain me. At times it has felt just as it did when we signalled to that empty horizon. The reason was that I was chiefly writing from the West Indies, and she from Bengal. It would take a ship four months just to sail from Barbados to Bengal, and a letter must travel by a much more circuitous route. What with my change of ship and this mutiny, it is small wonder I have had to wait. And here is the reward for my patience, at long last.' The two men looked at the stacks of letters.

'I can see her correspondence has been extensive, but has it been, eh... satisfactory?' asked Taylor.

'Very much so, George,' grinned Clay. 'It seems she has been every bit as diligent in writing to me, including the excellent news in her last letter that she is recently returned to England. Which brings me on to the vexing subject of shore leave.'

'Ah, yes, sir,' said Taylor, the smile draining from his face. 'Sir Edward's pronouncement on that subject has resulted in every man jack of them putting in a request, sure that they will all be granted.'

'Which in most cases we must accede to,' said his captain. 'I have the new regulations here, they are quite specific. We can only deny leave to those that we know will desert.'

'But most of them shall!' protested the lieutenant. 'They always have, given the opportunity, sir.'

'You must consider that this time will be different,' said Clay. 'Apart from our vessel being a rather happier ship, matters have changed in other ways. What do you believe stops a man from deserting?'

'Well, by rights it should be the fear of a flogging when they are caught, sir,' said Taylor. 'But that has never really answered. We catch too few of them.'

'Indeed so,' agreed his captain. 'The main discouragement has always been the back pay that the Navy holds back. If they run, they lose the lot. Except that their pay had become much too low to serve as any true deterrent. Most of our people could make up any lost pay in a few months aboard a merchantman. But not anymore; the case is altered.'

'So you hold that the pay rise will keep them from

deserting, sir?' said Taylor. He shook his head in disbelief. 'I hope you are proved right.'

'We are sure to lose a few ne'er do wells,' said Clay. 'I would be surprised if Page does not take this opportunity to run, but for most it will answer. Give the men two weeks of liberty, the officers too. That will still give us time to prepare the ship for our return to the squadron by the middle of June.'

'Two weeks, sir!' protested Taylor.

'Two weeks, you and I included, George,' repeated Clay. 'If the men are quite resolved to desert, they will do so whether we grant them two hours or two weeks. If we are certain to be hanged, it may as well be for a sheep as for a lamb.'

'Aye aye, sir,' grumbled Taylor.

'Now, I have been giving some thought to our new officers,' continued Clay. He searched for a letter on his desk, and produced it from under the ship's log. 'What are your feelings about us giving an opportunity to an excellent young man who has just been promoted to lieutenant?'

'How young is the gentleman you have in mind?' asked Taylor.

'He is eighteen years old,' replied the captain.

'Oh, that is very young,' said the first lieutenant. 'And of course Mr Blake is quite inexperienced too, sir.'

'I can confirm that this gentlemen certainly does have the advantages that comes with youth,' smiled Clay, 'while each day he is being cured of its shortcomings.' Taylor failed to smile at his captain's joke.

'I was more concerned with his want of experience, sir,' he said.

'Have no fears on that score,' said the captain. 'He has done his six years of sea time as a midshipman, all in the Navy, and much of it with me. His record is good. He has experienced several actions at sea firsthand and was commended by General Abercromby for his part in the defense of some siege guns during his last commission. I can vouch for his character, which is very amiable and open.'

'What is the young man's name?' asked the first lieutenant.

'Edward Preston,' said Clay. 'He was one of my midshipmen on the *Rush*, and now he has made lieutenant. My particular friend Captain Sutton has no role to offer him aboard his current ship, so he wrote to me to see if I might oblige him with a position. We could move Mr Blake up to second lieutenant and make Mr Preston our new third. As you say he will have much still to learn, but I can think of no better mentor for the young man than yourself, George.'

'That is very good of you to say, sir,' said Taylor, smiling a little. 'If he comes with your recommendation I am sure he will make a very valuable addition to the wardroom.'

'Good, that is settled,' said Clay. He wondered for a moment if Sir Charles Middleton had found him as malleable as Taylor, when he had flattered him into accepting command of the troubled *Titan*. He returned to the letter from the commander of the *Rush*. 'Captain Sutton goes on to say that his purser, Mr Charles Faulkner, very much misses his close friend Lieutenant Macpherson, and if we have need of such an officer he would be interested in a transfer.' Clay looked across at his first lieutenant. 'This could hardly have worked out better,' he said. 'Not only is Mr Faulkner a capital fellow in his own right, he has the unusual trait among pursers of being an honest man. After all the trouble that Mr Haywood has caused, that would seem to be just what we require. Shall I write to Captain Sutton and say we will take both officers?'

'Yes, please do, sir,' replied the first lieutenant. 'I look forward to meeting them.'

*****

The motion of the cart was doing little to help Adam Trevan recover from his hangover. The unmade road was narrow and winding, with steep banks topped with stone walls that hemmed them in to such an extent that the carter had no option but to lurch from one deep rut to the next. As the vehicle swayed and bumped along, even the cast iron stomach of the seasoned mariner began to protest.

'What was I thinking?' he groaned. He held his hand up to his mouth for a moment, and then retched over the wooden side. 'Why did I let that sod O'Malley lead me on to that damned gin cellar? I should have returned to the ship with Rosso and Sedgwick when we left the tavern, or I could have gone off along with Evans when he went to find a whore.' He closed his eyes as the cart heaved first to one side and then the other, and like countless men before him suffering from the aftereffects of drink, he wondered if death might be a preferable outcome to the way he felt now.

At last the cart creaked to a halt and Trevan opened his

eyes. He blinked for a moment at the tall chimney that belched a thick smear of black smoke across the otherwise clear blue sky. He sat up and as the angle changed he recognised the grey spoil heap of the tin mine that loomed above the road. He grabbed his canvas bag of possessions and jumped down, feeling a little better as soon as his feet touched solid ground.

'Thanks, mate,' he croaked. The carter waved to him in friendly fashion, laid his whip on the horse's back, and the cart wallowed back into motion. Trevan watched him go for a moment, and then set off down the side track that led towards the coast.

As he walked his spirits lifted. The May sun warmed him as it shone down, and the fresh breeze that blew in from the sea helped to clear his head. His mouth was still thick and furred with the excesses of the previous night, but even though he was now very thirsty, he knew better than to drink from the first stream he came to. The water was discoloured and smelt foul, flowing down from the mine at the head of the valley. A few hundred yards farther was a spring, clear and bubbling as it spilt down the moss covered stone wall. He drank greedily for a while, cupping his hands against the wet stone till they brimmed and then raising them to his mouth. When he had at last quenched his thirst, he dashed water over his head and let it soak into the thick blond pigtail that ran like a rope down his back. Finally he wetted his neck cloth and tied it back into place. The water cooled him as he walked, trickling down his chest under his shirt.

The track started to become more and more familiar as he neared home. The stone walls on either side were almost lost under a heavy pelt of tufted grass. Wild flowers studded the turf banks, and the occasional small trees grew up on either side, gnarled and bent over like old crones by the constant wind from the west. He rounded a corner, and saw the sea at last. The Channel spread out before him, blue and tranquil under the caress of the sun. The slope of the path grew steeper now as it plunged down towards the little fishing village. To his left a flock of sheep was scattered over the hillside. He could hear the tinkle of their bells amongst the flowering gorse bushes. He waved at the shepherd girl, who waved back uncertainly. Can that truly be Farmer Werrin's youngest daughter, he thought to himself, old enough to tend the flock now?

A little farther down the track he came to a break in the wall. He glanced up and down the path, but he was alone. With a smile of recognition he passed through the gap and into the sloping field beyond. Near the centre was a collection of larger gorse bushes, and in among them a patch of short, scented grass, warm beneath his hand as he sat down. He was sheltered now, both from the wind and from prying eyes, just as he had been all those years before when he would meet Molly here on sunny days like this. He leant back with his hands behind his head and closed his eyes. He remembered how she would lean over him, her red hair cascading down like molten copper, her skin pale and her eyes green as a cat's.

A little while later he walked into the village. The track had widened into a cobbled thoroughfare that led down past the houses to the little harbour. To left and right were small stone cottages, their windows shuttered against the sun. It was mid-afternoon, and the street was quiet. That will be the war, thought Trevan to himself. The young men have all been pressed into the navy like me, and the old have had to take their places in the fishing boats while the women work in the fields. From somewhere farther down the path he thought he heard the sound of a child crying, and he wondered if it might be his son. Too young, he concluded. His Sam was a sturdy five year old now; the child he could hear was no more than a baby.

The prospect of seeing his little boy again put a smile back on to Trevan's face once more. He reached into his pocket to check that the carved model boat he had promised to make for the lad when he saw him during the winter was still there. Satisfied, he carried on down the road. He arrived at the opening of one of the many narrow alleys that led back up the hillside towards the church and caught a flash of movement. He turned to see the figure of a women disappear around a corner. He paused for a moment. Something in the gait of the lithe figure had been familiar.

'Molly?' he called, but she did not return. He wondered what to do. Should he carry on the hundred yards to her mother's cottage, or follow the figure? He made his choice, and plunged into the cool shade between the houses.

The alleyway was narrow and unmade. It rose up in a series of short slopes punctuated by occasional flights of rough stone step. Halfway up he turned around the corner the woman had taken, but could see no sign of her. He carried on, passing openings to left and right into walled courtyards and buildings. At one point he had to squeeze past a line of old lobster pots, still pungent with the sea, until at the top of the rise he came back out into sunshine. He was above the village now, on a shelf of land that overlooked the harbour. Beside him was the little church. He looked towards it, and saw a white mop cap among the grave stones.

He strode along the churchyard wall and through the gate. The figure kneeling by a small pile of fresh turned earth was unmistakable now. He recognised the curve of her neck, the line of her heaving shoulders and the wisps of copper hair that had escaped from the confines of her cap.

'Molly, my love,' he called to his wife. 'I don't understand. What are you doing here?' She looked around, her tear-stained face turning from grief to wonder at the sight of him.

'Adam! You're back.' She stood up and in two strides had flung herself into his arms. He closed his eyes in joy as he held her tight to him. When he opened them again the little grave was still there. He did not have the skill to read most of the words on the headstone, but he could make out the shape of his surname, and could read the dates below it.

1792 – 1797.

*****

Although Captain Alexander Clay's journey home had been rather longer than Trevan's, it had been done in a lot more comfort. Not only had he not been suffering from a hangover when he left Plymouth, but he had spent the journey in well sprung carriages seated on plush upholstery, and had travelled for the most part on made turnpike roads. As a result he was able to jump down from the carriage when it pulled into the driveway of Rosehill Cottage still relatively fresh. He left Sedgwick to deal with their luggage and dashed up the familiar steps to the front door.

'Why, sir!' exclaimed the maid as she let him in. 'You have returned from the sea.'

'Indeed so, Nancy, for two whole weeks of leave,' smiled Clay. 'Is my mother at home?'

'No, sir,' replied the girl. 'She is away visiting some of the village sick with the parson's wife. Miss Clay is here, mind. She is taking a turn in the garden with a friend of hers what is staying with us for a few days.'

'A visitor?' he said. 'How unusual, I wonder who that might be?'

'It is a very elegant lady who they say has been to India, if you can believe that, sir,' said Nancy. 'Miss Browning is her name.'

'Miss Browning? She is here, right now?' he exclaimed.

'Yes, sir, that's right,' said the maid. 'Are you quite well, sir? You have gone all pale like.'

'I am fine, thank you, Nancy,' he replied. He pushed on past her and strode towards the back of the house. 'Did you say they were in the garden?'

In fact the two friends were no longer in the garden. They had strolled down past the cottage's formal beds packed with flowers, had paused to admire the progress of the plants in the vegetable plot, and had now moved through into the little walled orchard. The blossom of spring was long gone, and they walked amongst the gnarled tree trunks with their arms linked and their heads close together as they talked. It was cool and shady under the canopy of apple leaves. Only the odd ray of sun penetrated the foliage to cast spots of light like brilliant coins scattered across the grass. Lydia Browning was dressed all in black satin, while Betsey Clay wore a pale lemon dress with a pattern of tiny flowers on it. The cut of the two dresses differed too. Lydia's dress was cut modestly, as befitted one in mourning. In contrast that of her companion was in the latest fashion. Its short sleeves were puffed and round and the dress was gathered into a high waist with a contrasting bronze coloured ribbon that matched that which held her straw hat in place.

Betsey was the first to see him as he swept through from the garden and into the orchard searching about him. She felt a rush of pleasure at the sight of her brother, but she resisted the urge to run over and greet him. She knew this was Lydia's moment. She gently disentangled her arm from that of her friend and stepped away from her side. Her companion looked at her in surprise, and Betsey smiled to reassure her.

'I shall return to the house now,' she said, looking past her towards the brick arch from where Clay had appeared. Lydia followed her friend's gaze and let out a small cry.

'We shall speak later, Alex,' whispered Betsey as they passed. She trailed her hand against his and felt him squeeze it for a moment as they crossed.

'Oh, Lydia,' he cried as he came rushing across the grass. 'Can it truly be you at last, my darling?' He threw wide his arms and she came into them, her face wet with tears. The long remembered smell of her perfume filled his nostrils and he felt joy surge within him. He turned her face up towards his with a single gentle finger under her chin and they kissed, nervous at first but soon with growing confidence and passion.

'Alexander, I have missed you so much,' she murmured and he crushed her to him once more. When they parted he looked at her, and smiled at her flushed face and tousled hair.

'I... ah, fear I may have allowed my emotions when we first embraced to get the better of me,' he said gravely. 'Your bonnet is sadly crumpled.'

'Is it indeed?' she grinned. 'Then I shall take it off directly.' She undid the bow beneath her chin and shook her hair free. It cascaded down in a glossy dark river that complimented the satin of her dress.

'How very shocking, Miss Browning!' he laughed. 'I have no idea what my mother or your aunt would say if they could see you in such an immoral state of undress.'

'Have a care, Captain Clay,' she said in her turn. 'Your emotions have quite disordered your attire too, you know.' She reached up to pull his uniform coat straight and placed a firm hand on his left shoulder. Pain troubled his face for a moment.

'Alexander, how careless of me,' she exclaimed. 'I quite forgot you have been but recently a wounded there. Does it still trouble you?'

'A little,' he said. 'Chiefly when the weather is wet.'

'It troubles you in the wet?' she asked, the mischievous twinkle he had so admired when they first met once more in her clear blue eyes. 'Is that not rather inconvenient for a sailor?'

'Yes, I suppose it is,' he laughed. 'I have so missed your humour, Lydia. May I share a confidence with you regarding my injury?'

'Of course,' she replied.

'Thanks to my shoulder I am no longer able to ascend the rigging, which might be thought of as an even worse inconvenience for a sailor,' he explained. 'But I am exceedingly grateful for it because I have had a guilty secret.'

'Really, do tell me more,' she said, moving close. 'If the nature of this secret is suitable for a lady to hear, that is.' Clay looked around the empty orchard, as if he feared to be overheard.

'I am morbidly afraid of heights,' he whispered. 'For years I dreaded going aloft, but somehow I managed to master my fears. I have had to fain indifference to the terrifying void beneath me. But now I have my wound climbing is an impossibility, which suits me very well indeed.' She nodded at this, her face grave.

'I shall endeavour to be discreet when I next find myself being interrogated by the Board of Admiralty on the climbing abilities of their officers.'

They walked on a little, she still close beside him, his right arm forming a protective arc about her shoulders. He could feel her warmth through the light cloth beneath his fingers, and her hair lay softly over the skin of his wrist.

'When did you return from India?' he asked, finding it hard to think how to make polite conversation while his senses were so loaded with her closeness.

'Several weeks ago,' she replied. 'We returned to a

Portsmouth convulsed by this extraordinary mutiny. It was there that I met with dear Mr Sutton, poor man.'

'Why do you call him poor man?' he asked. 'I had heard that his was one of the few ships in Portsmouth whose crew remained obedient. He has gained much credit with the Admiralty in consequence.'

'Because I had seen his ship on our way in to Portsmouth,' she explained. 'I saw it was called *Rush*, and in the last of your letters, you had informed me that was the name of your ship. So naturally I hastened on board asking to see the captain. I was so sure that I was about to meet you that when I was presented to poor Mr Sutton it was all too much for me. I burst into tears of frustration the moment I laid eyes on him!'

'Did you, by Jove!' he chuckled. 'John does like to regard himself as something of a beau where the ladies are concerned. It will have done him no ill to have found himself so utterly rejected, for once.'

'Naturally when I had calmed down a little he was able to give me some welcome news of you,' continued Lydia. 'He was unsure if your ship had been caught up in the mutiny. Did your men rebel too?'

'No, I am pleased to say that they did ultimately remain loyal, but it was touch and go for a while,' he replied. 'The *Titan* had been a troubled ship, so a part of the crew did rise. Of all things they were chiefly provoked by my fool of a purser deciding to feed them on pork that was over three years old.'

'Meat that was three years old!' exclaimed Lydia. 'Surely

it would have long since become rotten?'

'It had, hence their uncivil reaction,' he said. 'Although at sea we do quite often feed on salt meat that was slaughtered over a year ago, without any apparent ill effects.'

'Bless my soul, do you really?' she said, 'Is it pleasant to eat?'

'Not especially, no,' he conceded. 'The men call it Irish horse, being unwilling to believe it can ever have once been pig meat. They maintain that the best way to cook particularly venerable salt pork is to boil it in a pot with an iron nail. When the nail is soft, the meat will be tender.' Lydia laughed aloud at this. Her neat white teeth contrasted with her sombre clothing. Clay enjoyed the moment a little, and then he frowned as he thought about the implications of the black dress.

'How insensitive of me,' he exclaimed. 'What was I thinking of going on in such a fashion, letting you ask after my foolish shoulder when I had not yet enquired about your much more grave injury. How have you and your aunt endured the loss of your poor uncle?'

'I will not say that it has been easy,' she replied. 'Oh, Alex, I feel such a curious mixture of emotions! It seems strange to speak of so painful a matter when I am overjoyed to be with you at long last. In truth I feel the loss very keenly. Over the years he had quite taken the place of the father who died when I was but a little girl, and since he and my aunt were without issue of their own, he had become very much as close as any parent could.'

'It is terrible to lose a father,' he said, 'but I suppose in that regard you were fortunate to have been able to replace that paternal love with his, at least for a while.'

'That is true, but the cholera took him so swiftly that I find myself quite cheated,' she said. 'There was such a lot I still wanted to do with him and say to him which I shall not now be able to. Of course, for my dear aunt it is even worse.' She felt Clay hold her a little tighter.

'I understand a little of what you speak of,' he said. 'As you know I too lost my father as a boy. I cannot say that I miss him now for himself, I have so much else in my life, not least you and my dear mother and sister. But there are yet matters I would have wanted to share with him, about my life in the navy, my ideas and my ambitions. If I had had an uncle like yours, he might have taken that role. In consequence I find myself drawn towards the council of older men that I encounter in the service. I have that very situation on board my current ship. My first lieutenant is much older than I, and as a result I am obliged to be careful that I am not tempted to confide overly in him. It could end very ill, if our relationship should no longer remain appropriate to one between a superior and inferior officer.'

'Perhaps I could be of help?' suggested Lydia. 'I would be happy for you to share with me those ideas and ambitions that you would have engaged your father with. And in return you might take the place of my uncle when I wish to share my own considerations?'

'Lydia, my darling,' he said, taking both of her hands in his and bringing her to a halt in front of him. 'There is nothing that I would rather do, from now and forever. I will happily commit myself to your future happiness in all things.' Then he dropped to one knee in the grass beneath the apple trees. 'You must know by now how much I love and admire you. Our long months apart have done nothing to lessen the regard I have for you. Will you consent to be my wife?'

She looked down into his calm grey eyes. There was something different in them now. The boyish good humour she had so liked when they first met was still there, but now they had a gravity and depth to them. They were eyes that had seen much in the time they had been apart, both of good and bad. She could see little lines that radiated out on the skin around them that had not been there before. That will be all the pain he suffered from his injury, she thought. He had made light of it, but his sister Betsey had been more frank, sharing with her the horror she and her mother had felt at the pale, thin invalid who had returned last winter from the Caribbean. She sensed that tears were welling up in her own eyes again, partly at that thought, but mostly at the feeling of utter joy that this long delayed moment had come at last.

'Yes, my darling Alexander,' she said, stroking the side of his face. 'I will marry you.'

Chapter 12
Tents

Edward Preston shrugged his cavernous uniform coat back up onto his shoulders for the umpteenth time and silently cursed once more the man who had sold it to him. His elevation from senior midshipman on the *Rush* to his appointment as third lieutenant of the *Titan* had only given him a few days to acquire all the new clothing and equipment he needed. He was not a wealthy man, and once he had bought his full dress uniform, his sword, telescope and sextant, he had been running very low on funds. So when he had spotted the coat in the window of a Plymouth pawn brokers it had seemed to be the answer to his prayers. The coat's former owner had been of a similar height to him, but what was obvious to him now was that he had also been a much larger man than the slim eighteen-year-old. This had been concealed from him at the time of purchase by the shop keeper. He must have gripped a fist full of broad cloth in the hand he held behind my back when he was presenting me to the mirror, thought the *Titan*'s newest officer, shrugging at the garment once more.

On the Lee Shore

If he had had a better fitting coat to wear, Preston would have cut a good figure. He was an attractive young man of medium height, whose friendly adolescent face was filling quickly into that of an adult. His dark hair and brown eyes had combined well with the tan he had gained serving in the Caribbean last year to give him a dashing, Mediterranean look. It was only when he spoke that his broad Yorkshire accent became apparent.

The *Titan* had sailed back up the Iroise channel towards the Goulet in order to look into Brest once more, and now lay with her topsails backed close to the entrance to the Rade de Brest. The last of the thick early morning fog that had hampered her progress at first had drifted off in the gentle breeze revealing a fine clear blue sky. There was good visibility now for the two midshipmen at her mastheads to be able to observe the French fleet at anchor as they looked over the intervening low peninsular. Although Preston was the lieutenant whose watch it was, the quarterdeck was full of his fellow officers, which was perhaps why he was so self conscious about the coat. Some, like Macpherson and Corbett the surgeon, were just taking the air before the wardroom's lunch was served. But others, he felt, were making little attempt to conceal that they were watching him. Warwick the ship's master was stood near the wheel in a banal conversation with Taylor that did little to conceal either man's true purpose.

'I am sure you will have noted how the tide is taking us towards that reef off the larboard beam, Mr Preston,' called the ship's master. For once he spoke loud enough to be heard in spite of the volleys of noise that came from the backed topsails.

'I have the rocks in view, Mr Warwick, but thank you for your concern,' replied the officer of the watch.

'Of course the Titan will be much slower to manoeuvre than that handy little sloop you have come from,' added the first lieutenant. He looked pointedly towards the distant forecastle, over a hundred feet from where they stood.

'Yes, sir,' said Preston. 'I did note as much on the half dozen or so watches I have stood since I joined.' He looked at the two concerned faces and relented a little. 'I will put her about just as soon as Mr Butler and Mr Russell have completed their observations.'

'Ah now, when you do that, you will need to stand to the southward,' said Warwick. 'Which shall bring us down towards...'

'The Courbin reef and the Trepieds,' completed the young man, 'Which bear southwest by west two and half miles distant. Rest assured that I did make a thorough study of the chart before I came on duty, Mr Warwick.'

'Did you indeed, Mr Preston?' said Clay as he came across from the weather rail where he had been pacing the deck. 'That was very diligent. And here come our midshipman to report. Kindly put the ship about, if you please.'

Under the gaze of his two nursemaids, Preston picked up his speaking trumpet and gave the sequence of orders to the crew that brought the ship back to the wind and swung her away from the dangers of the lee shore. When he was certain the ship was on the right course, with all her sails drawing correctly, he wandered over to listen to the tail end of the two midshipmen's reports.

'Tents, Mr Butler?' queried Clay. 'What manner of tents?'

'Sort of bell shaped ones, sir,' said the midshipman. 'There are plenty of them, all set out in rows. They are just out of sight from here, on the other side of the headland from Kerviniou, but you can see them clearly enough from the masthead.'

'With soldiers moving about too,' supplemented Midshipman Russell. 'The smoke from their cooking fires is visible from here, sir.'

Clay looked where he pointed. The long headland of Quelern lay like a low wall between him and the French fleet on the far side. To the north was the gate in that wall, the narrow Goulet with Les Fillettes rocks plumb in the centre of the freeway, and to the south he could see Bertheaume Bay, where they had used fishing boats to cut out the brig in the spring. As usual there was plenty of shipping gathered in the bay waiting for the tide to turn, but it was still being guarded by a large French frigate moored in among them. In front of him a little hamlet of grey buildings lay by the shore, flanked on either side by large gun batteries. Behind the buildings the land rose up towards the crest of some low hills, above which the grey sky was streaked with lines of smoke.

'Are there many of these tents?' he asked. Butler consulted his notes.

'I counted twelve rows, with about twenty tents in each one sir,' he replied.

'Any idea how big the tents are?' asked Clay. Butler shook his head, but Russell was more positive.

'They were bigger than the men stood near to them,' he supplemented. 'Perhaps as much as eight or nine feet high, sir?' Clay was digesting all this when he spotted Macpherson's red coat as he strolled past still talking to the surgeon.

'Mr Macpherson!' he called. 'Might I have the benefit of your military knowledge?' The marine came over and Clay asked the two midshipman to repeat what they had seen.

'I am familiar with that type of tent, sir,' Macpherson said. 'You may recall the Shropshire regiment used similar ones when we were involved in the attack on St Lucia last year. They have a central pole, and a file of eight to ten men will sleep around that, laying on the ground like the spokes of a wheel.' Clay made a swift calculation.

'Two hundred and forty tents would shelter between two to two and a half thousand men,' he said.

'Aye, sir,' confirmed Macpherson. 'That would be a single infantry brigade. They will probably also have an artillery battery.'

'That's right, sir,' said Butler. 'There was a row of little field guns with horses.'

'Why in tents?' mused the captain. 'All the other troops deployed here about are in huts, or other buildings.'

'I should say much the same reason that the Shropshires used them in St Lucia, sir,' said Macpherson. 'They are temporary. Whatever brigade this may be, I would say that they do not plan to be here over long.'

'Yes I see, that makes sense. Well, no matter,' concluded Clay. 'They are probably little concern of ours then, but I will add them to our report on the French fleet's strength. You gentlemen can keep an eye on them when you are next observing the fleet.'

'That will not be for a few days, sir,' said Warwick, who had been listening from his place by the wheel. 'With the wind as light as it is we shall have the same fog tomorrow as today, but the tide will be a good forty-five minutes earlier.'

'Is that fog certain, Mr Warwick?' queried Clay.

'Yes sir, or I am no Channel pilot,' replied the ship's master. 'We shall have fog at first light each morning until this wind should strengthen or revert back to a westerly, sir.'

Clay looked at all the coasters hastening from shore battery to shore battery along the coast as they hurried to catch the rising tide.

'Tell me, gentlemen, am I imagining it or is the costal trade rather more plentiful than of late?' he asked.

'I don't think so, sir,' replied Warwick. 'I imagine that some of them have been held back by the fog this morning, and are now hurrying to catch the last of the tide so that it will sweep them up the Goulet and in to Brest. It is that that makes them seem more numerous.'

'They don't generally like to move in the fog, then?' asked Clay.

'Not if they can avoid it, sir,' said Warwick. 'But if these early morning fogs persist they shall be forced to for fear of missing their tide.' Clay paused for a moment, tapping a hand on the rail, deep in thought.

'Will they indeed?' he said, 'Mr Warwick, will you kindly join me in my cabin for a pot of coffee? You as well, Mr

Taylor. I would be obliged if you could also bring the chart and tide table for the next few days with you. I believe you have given me an idea.'

*****

'Edward,' said Blake to the wardroom's newest recruit later that day, 'may I make an observation?'

'Of course, John,' smiled Preston.

'I truly mean no disrespect, but I could not help but notice that your coat seems a little ill fitting,' he said. To his relief Preston smiled at him.

'Is it that obvious?' he said. 'That is very provoking. I had hoped that it might have gone unnoticed. I fear its previous owner was the size of an ox. I had intended to have it altered before we left Plymouth, but I ran short of time.'

'Then I may have a solution for you,' said his fellow lieutenant. 'My servant Marway started life as a tailor's apprentice. Would it answer if I was to ask him to adjust it?'

'That is very obliging of you,' said Preston. 'But what would I wear in the meantime? I only have my full dress uniform, which I can hardly wear for everyday.' In answer Blake stood up and slipped off his own coat.

'Try on this one,' he said. 'We must be of a similar size, and I have several. I could lend you one with perfect convenience while yours is altered.'

The two men were alone in the wardroom, waiting for their fellow officers to join them for dinner, but as luck would have it Tom Macpherson strode through the door at that moment.

'Goodness, I could eat a horse,' he exclaimed, and then stopped in surprise. 'Pardon my intrusion, but why are you gentlemen exchanging coats?'

'It is no great matter, Tom,' said Blake. 'We are making trial to see if we are the same size. If so I shall lend Edward here my coat while one of his is being worked on by Marway.'

'I see,' said the Scot. 'Would that be the rather large garment you were sporting earlier, Edward? But perhaps you would rather borrow my coat than John's? It would match the shade of scarlet that your face has turned admirably.' There was a pause, and then the three young men all roared with laughter.

'What is it that is so amusing?' asked the elegantly dressed new purser Charles Faulkner, as he too arrived in the cabin. He was an aristocratic man with coiffed auburn hair. Macpherson explained the joke to his friend, who nodded in approval.

'Thank goodness you are having that sack taken in at last, Edward,' he exclaimed, brushing at the sleeve of his own garment, which was perfectly tailored. 'It has been annoying me for days now.'

'Well bless my soul,' said Preston as he flopped down into his chair. 'So has everyone noticed the size of my coat, then?'

'I did hear the sail maker mention that it might be of use should the main course be in need of replacing,' said Corbett the surgeon, emerging from his cabin to renewed laughter.

'Goodness, you gentlemen are in good cheer,' beamed Taylor as he too came into the wardroom. 'What has occasioned such mirth?'

'Mr Preston's coat, sir,' said Blake.

'Oh yes? Would that be the rather voluminous one?' asked the first lieutenant.

Once the laughter had subsided and the officers had taken their places, the wardroom steward brought in the evening meal. Soon cheerful conversation ebbed and flowed around the table. Lieutenant Taylor let his food cool a little on his plate, and looked around at his fellow officers with obvious pleasure.

'You seem in good spirits tonight, Mr Taylor,' said Corbett, who sat beside him. 'Has anything in particular occasioned that?'

'I was just observing to myself what an agreeable young man Mr Blake is,' he replied. 'He is making Mr Preston most welcome in the wardroom. It is strange, but I had not really noticed that amiability in his character before.' The surgeon looked at him and raised an eyebrow.

'Strange, sir?' he queried. 'I believe the reason is quite plain. If you want to understand why our wardroom is so much more pleasant you must consider who is absent, rather than who is present. I do not wish to speak ill of the dead, but it is since Mr Morton's departure that we are at last beginning to see Mr Blake's true character.'

'Do you know, I believe you may have the truth of it,' said the first lieutenant.

'Indeed,' said Corbett. 'And when you add to that the change in purser, where we have exchanged the sneering Mr Haywood for the thoroughly amiable Mr Faulkner, it is small wonder we are a distinctly happier band.'

'It is not just the wardroom either, sir,' said Macpherson, who had been listening from the first lieutenant's other side. 'Have you not noted how much more pleasant the atmosphere has become onboard, compared with when I first joined? The removal of most of the men's grievances, combined with a good long run ashore, has been most advantageous.'

'Not to the men's health,' grumbled the surgeon. 'The more notorious fornicators amongst them have returned with the inevitable range of maladies for me to treat.'

'And yet I was quite set against so much liberty,' said Taylor. 'Not for the reasons that you allude to, Mr Corbett, grave as they must be, but because I was fully resigned that we should lose one man in three.'

'How many did run?' asked Faulkner from across the table.

'We lost six, all former messmates of either Sexton or Kenny who I am quite content to see the back of,' he replied. 'And we gained twelve good hands from the receiving ship in exchange.'

'Sexton and Kenny? Would they be the two notorious mutineers I have heard of?' asked Faulkner.

'Indeed,' said the first lieutenant. 'Kenny died of wounds acquired during the suppression of the mutiny, and Sexton is back in Plymouth now, awaiting court martial for the murder of Edmund Morton.'

'Am I the only one to note that the captain too seems to have been infected by this general lifting of spirits?' added Corbett. 'Yes, I will have a little more of the pie, please.'

'Only a surgeon could classify happiness as a sickness,' said Faulkner in a stage aside to Macpherson.

'I believe that is right,' said Taylor. 'I hope I am not being indiscrete when I say that he has met with a lady of his acquaintance that he has long been separated from.'

'If the lady in question is the same who came looking for him aboard the *Rush* in Portsmouth it is small wonder he is in good spirits,' said the purser. 'She was deuced handsome. What did Sutton say her name was, Edward?'

'Miss Lydia Browning,' said Preston. 'He met her when he was the first lieutenant on the *Agrius* back in ninety-five.'

'Has a formal understanding been reached between them then, sir?' asked Macpherson. 'Should we be offering the captain our felicitations?'

'That would be a little premature, Tom,' said the first lieutenant. 'The lady in question has accepted him, but I believe that when he met her aunt in London she did not immediately endorse the proposed match. She is withholding her blessing till she has had the leisure to make some further enquiries into his character.'

'Really?' said the marine. 'Surely there can be no objection to him in that regard?'

'You might think not, Tom, but the captain is setting his sights very high,' said Taylor. 'This Miss Browning comes from an exceptionally well connected family, I believe.'

'If it is the Miss Browning who is a ward of the Ashtons then they are a very patrician lot,' said Faulkner. 'She will come with quite a fortune. I expect her guardians are concerned to ensure she has not fallen prey to a fortune hunter, in which case there can be no real objection to Captain Clay. With all the prize money he has earned of late he must be tolerably solvent in his own right.'

'Well, gentlemen,' said Macpherson, raising his glass. 'Let us wish him every good fortune in his ambitions with this Miss Browning, with a bumper too, if you please.' The wardroom rose as one to toast the success of their captain with a roar of approval that echoed through the ship.

*****

'The Grunters are having a proper fecking roister,' said O'Malley, as he sat on the forecastle next to his friend Trevan. Most of the hands on watch had looked round when the noisy cheer had echoed up from the wardroom, responding with a buzz of comment, much of it uncomplimentary, but the Cornishman had not been amongst them. Instead he continued to stare out to sea. The *Titan* was back at the entrance to the Iroise Channel. She whispered along under easy sail in the dying light of the day. Off the starboard bow was the long jagged line of the Pierres Noires reef. The occasional wave slapped up a plume of spray, the foam pink in the light of the setting sun.

'It's a grand fecking sight,' said the Irishman, indicating the reef. 'None the worse for us having seen it most days this commission. I likes it best of an evening, just as she is now.'

'It looks well enough,' murmured his companion. The two men watched as the reef slid by in silence, O'Malley waiting for his friend to say more.

'Listen, Adam,' he said at last. 'You know I'm no good

with me words. That'll be why I am always after fecking cursing. Rosie and even Able do all that much better than me, so I'm just going to go ahead and say it. Would it be your boy you're thinking on at all?'

'Aye, it is Sean,' replied Trevan. 'I miss him real bad. By rights I shouldn't, for I barely knew the lad at all. So why I does I can't rightly fathom, but when he was alive, somehow just knowing he was there, away over yonder horizon with my Molly, was a comfort to me. I could tell myself all the things I would show him one day. Ways how I would make it up to the nipper for all the time I was away, like. Simple stuff that I did served to make him seem closer. Working on a bit of scrimshaw for him of an evening, like that little boat I carved.'

'Sure you're after pining for the lad,' said his friend. 'It don't signify any how much time you spent with him. He was still your blood, like.'

'Aye, that's right. He was still mine.'

'How did it happen, with your boy?' asked O'Malley.

'My Molly is not rightly sure,' the Cornishman said. 'Young Sam came in from running with some other lads in the yard one day saying he felt sickly. She stripped his clothes off him, and he had these red spots, all over him like a flounder. So she put him to bed with a hot brick to sweat it out of him. Next day it had turned into some manner of brain fever, and she couldn't raise him or make him sensible. The sawbones came and bled him an' all, but it wouldn't answer. Following day he was... ' His voice caught and died. O'Malley reached out with his arm and patted his friend's shoulders.

'That's proper cruel, Adam,' he said. 'Poor Molly.'

'Cruel is the word, Sean,' said Trevan. 'I was away whaling down beyond the Cape when he was born, then I was pressed into the navy soon as I got back home. I was taken off the ship within sight of the Lizard, if you can believe it. A few miles farther I could have seen my village. Then what with us being sent to the West Indies an' all, I had only been with the lad twice in his little life. So when we got our two week's liberty I was thinking how at last I might get to know him a bit, like. But he was already cold in the ground.'

'It's a hard lot ours, Adam,' said his friend. 'Who would be a sailor in time of war? But you know how easy children can slip away, especially the young ones. My mother buried as many nippers as she ever saw old enough to leave by the door.'

'That's true,' replied the Cornishman. 'It don't answer to dull the pain any, though. Maybe one day you may understand when you have some of your own.'

'Reckon I might have a few now,' smiled O'Malley. 'The amount of whoring I've been after doing. Could easily be a couple of little black Irishmen back in Bridgetown.'

'That may be true,' smiled Trevan. 'Ain't the same, mind you. Have you never had no one special then, Sean?'

'I did have once,' he replied. 'I had a colleen back home in Drumgallon, before the fecking war an' all.' Trevan looked at his friend in surprise.

'That so?' he said. 'You never mention no sweetheart before, Sean.' O'Malley shrugged at this.

'I doubt if she will have waited any,' he said. 'It's near

three years now since I've been home. Why would she, without any encouragement?'

'Haven't you written to her?' asked the Cornishman.

'How would that be after working?' protested O'Malley. 'I can't fecking write, and she can't read.'

'Doesn't stop me and my Molly,' said Trevan. 'Rosie sets down what I wants to say, and when Molly gets the letter she goes to see the parson, who reads it back to her. It do mean I has to keep it proper, with no saucy talk like, but it seems to answer well enough.'

'What would I be after saying?' said the Irishman gloomily. 'Sorry you've not heard from me for three winters, and I can't say when I will be fecking back home, but wouldn't you mind waiting at all?'

'Do you have feelings for this girl?' asked his friend.

'Maybe I do,' said O'Malley. 'I been after thinking upon her of late, which must mean something.'

'Why not start by telling her that?' said Trevan. 'How you miss her, and that you been thinking about her. Get Rosie to set it down a bit poetical like, and see what comes back. I can help you with the words, if you want.'

The two friends returned to looking over the sea. It was dark as wine now that the sun had gone. High above them the first few stars had appeared as tiny points of silver in the deep blue dome of the sky. After a while O'Malley began to shift uncomfortably on the deck.

'There may be a fecking problem with Rosie writing the letter, Adam,' he said. 'Did I say that she can only speak the Irish at all?'

Chapter 13
Fog

Two days later Clay was awoken from deep sleep by the sound of flowing water. He frowned for a moment as he tried to fathom how the smiling face of Lydia Browning had managed to turn so quickly into a blank wall of painted wood a few inches from his nose. After a moment he rolled over in his cot till he faced away from the bulkhead of his sleeping cabin and towards the muted light. He watched while his young servant poured the last of the steaming water he had brought from the galley into his wash basin. He then hung the lamp he carried on its hook, adjusted the wick and turned to face his captain.

'Seven bells in the mid watch has just sounded, sir,' he said. 'There are light airs from the south east and Mr Warwick says it will be sunrise in two hours.' Clay took all this in slowly, and then remembered the most important piece of information of all.

'Is there any fog, Yates?' he asked.

'Thick as porridge, from what I can tell, sir,' replied the boy.

'That will answer very well,' said Clay, rubbing his hands as he swung himself out of the cot. He slipped his nightshirt over his head and stepped across to the washstand. Yates caught the nightshirt and handed Clay his razor.

'I will just get your clothes sorted, sir,' he said as he retreated back into the main cabin.

Thick fog again, just as Warwick had predicted on the day they saw the tents, Clay told the face in the mirror as he drew his razor across it in short precise strokes. Perfect.

Ten minutes later he had washed and dressed and was running up the ladder way and out onto the quarterdeck. It was still black night, but the fog was apparent as a halo of silver in the air around the lights of the binnacle. Clay shrugged his coat a little closer in the chill, moist dark and approached the group of grey figures around the wheel.

'Good morning, gentlemen,' he said. The nearest figure touched his hat and the voice of the first lieutenant returned his greeting. 'Now, Mr Taylor, have all the preparations been made for our little adventure?'

'Yes, sir,' replied Taylor. 'All navigation lights are doused and the ship's bell will not be sounded again. I have posted lookouts in the bow, and a good man to heave the lead with a chain of reliable hands posted up the starboard gangway for communication, ending with Mr Russell here.' He indicated the small figure of the midshipman just visible in the gloom, before continuing. 'Also Mr Hutchinson has the best bower anchor hanging from the cat's head, ready to be dropped when required.'

'Very good,' said Clay. 'What of the boat crews?'

'Told off, armed, and waiting in the waist,' replied the first lieutenant. 'They have all had a hot breakfast. Mr Blake has the pinnace, Mr Preston the launch and Mr Butler the cutter. The boats themselves are in the water being towed behind us.'

'Excellent, Mr Taylor,' said Clay, before turning to the figure of the ship's master. 'Let us begin then, Mr Warwick. Are you certain of our position? Good, then kindly navigate us to the mouth of the Goulet.'

'Aye aye, sir,' he said. 'Mr Russell, I will have that lead going in the bow if you please. Helmsman, steer east by north half east.'

'East by north half east it be, sir,' said the man. He spun the wheel over and then reversed the movement a little till the compass needle settled on the right course. Clay looked about him in the dark. He could see almost nothing of the world around him, so thick was the air with fog, but his other senses told him a little of what the ship was doing. He could feel a faint breath of wind on one side of his face, and the occasional tendril of thicker fog seemed to flow across the deck, a finger of greater darkness in the night. From over his head came a constant drip from the rigging as the fog soaked into the invisible masses of hemp and canvas that crammed the space above him. He felt the gentle heel of the deck under his feet as the ship rolled to the last dying surge of an Atlantic wave that had penetrated this deep up the channel.

'What speed are we doing?' asked Clay.

'Barely a knot through the water, but the water itself is moving at two knots with the tide, sir,' murmured Warwick, angling his pocket watch towards the light of the binnacle. 'I would like us to be up with some rocks soon, so I can fix our location properly.'

The figure of the Russell appeared to double for a moment in the gloom as a message was passed back from the bow, and then the midshipman walked over.

'Leadsman reports twelve fathoms and grey shell sir,' he said, before returning to his station.

'You are using a tallow lead I collect,' said Clay.

'Yes sir,' explained Warwick. 'In this fog I must rely on the man casting the lead in the bow much as a blind man does his stick. The nature of the bottom is as useful to me as its depth. Grey shell is what I would expect on the north side of the channel.'

'Lookout says he can hear breakers two points off the larboard bow sir,' reported Russell.

'That will be the Vieux Moines sir,' said the master. 'East south east now helmsman.'

'Aye aye, sir,' replied the quartermaster, turning the wheel once more. 'That's east south east.'

'We need to draw to the southward for the next half mile to avoid the council rocks ahead, sir,' explained Warwick.

'Very good,' said Clay. 'I will leave you to your navigation then without the distraction of my constant interrogation.'

Clay walked away from Warwick and joined the figure of the first lieutenant, hunched in his pea coat and looking forward over the quarterdeck rail. From ahead of them came the quiet shifting murmur and clink of weapons of the boat crews assembled in the dark well of the main deck.

'The master knows what he is about,' Clay commented.

'Were I faced with such a game of Blind Man's Buff amongst all these shoals and reefs, I am quite sure it would end with us upon the rocks. And yet when I suggested this operation to him, he accepted the task with remarkable calm.'

'He is an exceedingly capable pilot, sir,' agreed Taylor. 'I know a little of this coast, and it is quite hazardous enough in God's honest daylight for me.'

Both men turned as a flurry of sightings of breaking surf heard in the fog came in from the bow. Russell was rushing to report them to the master, who received each piece of information calmly, translating them into quiet instructions to the men at the wheel, and the *Titan* glided on into the impenetrable night.

'Dawn soon, sir,' said Taylor, as he sniffed at the cold air.

'Still blacker than the Earl of Hell's hat,' muttered the captain.

But it was Taylor who was right. With infinite stealth the night began to lighten to a faint shade of dark grey, as if the ship sailed through deep shadow. Now dim faces began to resolve themselves into recognisable people, and the main mast of the frigate grew like the trunk of some huge tree, a darker mass soaring up into the thick canopy of fog.

'Breakers dead ahead now,' said Russell, his voice urgent.

'That will be Les Fillettes,' said Warwick. 'Bring her up into the wind, helmsmen. 'My compliments to the boatswain, and he can let go the anchor and get in the sail.' Taylor and his captain heard the splash of the anchor from forward and the ship swung around in the flowing tide as the anchor bit into the shallow sea bed beneath them. When he was satisfied that the anchor held firm, Warwick came over and touched his hat to Clay.

'Ship at anchor, two cables west of Les Fillettes with one hour of the flood tide to go, sir,' he reported. Clay held out his hand in reply, and after a hesitation Warwick took it.

'That was a notable feat of navigation, Henry,' he said. 'Congratulations to you.'

'Why thank you, sir,' replied the sailing master with a smile. 'I must confess I am rather proud of it.'

'Strange to think we are at anchor right in the centre of a most murderous crossfire,' said Clay to the others. He indicated the walls of fog, now pearl as the light grew. 'There must be any number of French guns trained on the entrance to the Goulet, and yet we can remain at anchor here in the centre of the freeway into Brest with perfect convenience.'

'But only while the fog serves to cloak us,' cautioned the first lieutenant. 'These summer fogs never endure. The sun will be thinning it from above even as we speak.'

'Quite so, Mr Taylor,' said Clay. 'Kindly have the boats manned, as quietly as possible.'

'Do you think we shall catch any coasters, sir?' asked the lieutenant, a few minutes later, when the inevitable slight noise made from the boat crews had faded into the billowing fog around them.

'I hold it very likely, Mr Taylor,' said his captain. 'We are in position at the point where the routes they must take to enter the Goulet from both the north and the south converge. We are sure to intercept some trade.'

'But why are you so decided that they will hazard such a

journey in this fog, sir?' asked Taylor. 'Surely it serves to make them blind, and robs them of the protection of the batteries?'

'Think of all those French coasters in the bays around us who have missed their tide these last few days because of the fog,' said Clay. 'All with deck hands to pay, whether they sail or not, or contracted to deliver their cargo by a certain day. Might you not say to yourself, what is the chance that you will encounter an enemy ship in the fog, right in the middle of the freeway into Brest?'

'Sir!' hissed Midshipman Russell. 'There is a coaster on the starboard bow.' Clay exchanged glances with Taylor, and both men hurried to the rail. It was light enough now to see a stretch of green flowing water and then a wall of unbroken fog. They heard a faint splash and the sound of a voice shouting an order.

'There, sir,' said Taylor, pointing into the gloom. 'I can see the lugsail of a boat.' Faintly showing in the fog was a square of something more substantial.

'Mr Blake,' Clay called quietly down to the boat below him. 'See that coaster passing us on the starboard beam? Kindly capture it, put a prize crew onboard, and then return to the ship. Cold steel only, if you please. I do not want to raise the alarm.'

'Aye aye, sir,' replied the lieutenant, and the pinnace pushed out into the flow and then darted away from the ship's side to disappear into the gloom.

*****

'When's our fecking chance going to come?' muttered O'Malley in the bow of the launch, as he watched the pinnace disappear. A few moments later came the sound of a startled cry, abruptly cut off.

'Sounds as if they caught the bleeder,' replied Evans through the side of his mouth, his whisper a little too loud. Lieutenant Preston looked up from his place in the stern sheets.

'Silence in the boat there!' he hissed. 'Don't you men like the chink of prize money in your pockets?' Several of the crew turned around to glare at Evans, and the big Londoner dropped his head in shame.

'Mr Preston,' came the sound of Clay's voice from just above their heads. 'There is some manner of two masted chasse-maree approaching to larboard. Once you have taken her, leave a prize crew aboard to bring her out, and return to the ship. Be swift now, for this fog is starting to lift.'

'Aye aye, sir,' replied Preston. 'Shove off in the bow there, O'Malley. Give way all.'

Evans swung backwards and forwards with the rest of the crew, pleased to be on the move at last. The air was still chill and the fog had soaked into his shirt and hair. Grateful warmth began to spread down his arms as he rowed. Behind Preston's back the looming shape of the big frigate dissolved into the fog, leaving the launch at the centre of a disc of deep green water, apparently alone and lost in its own grey world. Evans glanced over his shoulder, but could see nothing ahead.

'Eyes in the boat!' ordered Preston.

'He's bleeding changed,' muttered Evans. 'I remember when he was a right little pip squeak.'

'Steady, lads,' muttered Preston. 'Starboard side! Be ready to board when I say, and remember, use your pistols to threaten, but no firing. Cold steel if you need to kill.'

'Ah, here she comes,' whispered O'Malley to his friend. 'She's a right big fecker, an' all.'

Evans heard a cry of warning from just behind him, and the side of a large boat loomed up next to him.

'Easy all!' ordered the lieutenant. 'Oars in. Hook on there, O'Malley. Borders away!' Evans pulled his oar inboard just in time, stood up in the rocking boat and pulled himself over the side of the chasse-maree. He was the first to drop onto the deck and heard a shout of anger from behind him. He turned to see a crowd of French sailors dashing towards him, armed with an assortment of belay pins and clubs, and one with a heavy looking sword. The sight of the sword reminded him that he had still not drawn his own cutlass from its scabbard.

'No time now for any of that now,' he muttered to himself. Instead he bunched his hands into fists and turned side on in a prize fighter's stance. The sailors stopped in amazement at the sight. Evans's left fist flew out in a quick jab, and the leading Frenchman in the group dropped stunned to the deck, his club clattering away into the scuppers.

'Rende-toi!' called Preston from behind Evans, at the head of a more orthodox armed party of seaman. The remaining French hands laid down their weapons with a clatter, most of them still eyeing the huge Englishman.

'An impressive punch you have there,' said the lieutenant, 'but do please use your cutlass next time.'

'Aye aye, sir,' replied Evans. 'I sort of forgot, like.'

'Mr Griggs,' said Preston to one of the *Titan*'s compliment of young master's mates. 'Take command of the prize, if you please. I can leave you with eight men. Secure the prisoners and then head south east. You need to be clear of this coastline when the fog lifts. The tide will start to flow in your favour soon, but I suggest you anchor for now while you get the boat fully under control.'

'Aye aye, sir,' said Griggs, a thin, uncertain man barely older than Preston. The lieutenant reeled off a list of names for the prize crew, and the rest of the men returned to the launch.

'Good luck, Griggs,' said Preston. 'I shall return to the frigate now to see if we can catch another prize.'

*****

'Right, secure the prisoners,' Griggs reminded himself. He clapped his hands together with decision as the launch vanished back into the fog.

'Would you like Evans and me to see about that anchor at all, Mr Griggs?' prompted O'Malley. 'The Fillets reef will be getting awful close now, and I can't swim at all.'

'Oh God yes, the reef,' said the master's mate, moving both of his hands up to his face in horror. 'A very worthy suggestion, O'Malley. Carry on then, you two.' Evans and O'Malley needed no prompting, and disappeared towards the bow. The boom of breakers crashing against the notorious rocks was very close now as the last of the tide swept them onwards towards the Goulet. They dropped anchor just in time, and the big cargo boat swung round in the tide. She pulled and fretted at her anchor cable like a dog trying to break free.

'This fog is after lifting fecking soon,' said the Irishman, indicating the tendrils of cloud that drifted by in the freshening air. Off to one side they saw a flash of white spray from another reef, before the fog closed in once more.

'We had best go and bleeding remind our new captain what he needs to do next, before he kills the lot of us,' said Evans.

Back at the stern of the boat the prisoners had been locked away below deck, and the other hands stood around waiting for the next order. Griggs seemed content to look at the fog while he gathered his thoughts.

'That anchor is holding, Mr Griggs,' announced the big Londoner.

'Thank you, Evans,' said the warrant officer, still peering into the fog. The circle of sea visible from the boat was much larger now, and when Evans glanced up a patch of blue sky was briefly visible.

'Would you like me to take the helm at all, Mr Griggs?' suggested O'Malley. 'The lads could sheet home these two lug sails, Big Sam here can slip the anchor cable, and we will be on our way before the Frog gunners in all of those batteries are any the wiser.'

'Batteries?' said Griggs. He looked round towards the

land. A break in the fog showed a small patch of rocky shore no more than five hundred yards away, easy range for a cannon.

'Shall I get ready to slip that cable then, Mr Griggs?' prompted the Londoner. 'Like what Sean just said?'

'Yes please, Evans,' decided the master's mate at last. 'I will take the helm, O'Malley, you get those sails sheeted home.'

Once they were underway it was slow work for the chasse-maree to beat against both wind and tide, in spite of her two tall masts and huge brick-red sails, for she was laden with cargo and the wind was light. Once the anchor had been slipped she clawed her way forward away from the land behind her, while all the time the fog continued to lift.

'Tide is easing, Mr Griggs,' reported Evans after twenty minutes, looking over the side. 'We should be able to make a bit better progress once it is slack water.'

'Oh, look,' said several excited voices at once, as a wide gap was torn in the fog ahead of them. Through it they could see the frigate as she beat out to sea a few miles away. Scattered behind her were five captured coasters of various sizes.

'It's the fecking old *Titan* herself,' said O'Malley with a smile, 'Ain't that a princely sight.'

Moments later a chain of huge splashes skipped past the boat, followed by the sound of a heavy calibre cannon. The men all looked round at the shore behind them. Another gap in the fog had opened to reveal the solid grey stone wall of a battery perhaps a thousand yards away. It promptly disappeared behind a cloud of dirty white smoke, and the air was full of the sound of shot tearing past them. A large hole appeared in one of the sails, and Evans was splashed as a near miss ripped into the sea close over the side.

'How the fuck do they know we ain't one of their bleeding coasters?' he spluttered, dashing water from his eyes.

'Might be because we're after sailing in the wrong fecking direction, Sam,' replied O'Malley.

An age seemed to pass for the sailors as they waited for the battery to reload its guns. Meanwhile O'Malley scanned the water around them for a solution. He looked to the north and his face cleared.

'Mr Griggs,' he yelled. 'We're a sitting duck out here moving so slow in the open. Can't we head for the remains of the fog over there?' The warrant officer paused for a moment, and then threw over the tiller, steering the boat towards the last clump of the vanishing fog. They had almost reached it when the air once more filled with the shriek of passing shot. There was a loud crack from the foremast of the chasse-maree. For an instant all seemed well to the watching sailors, but then the tall spar began to topple forward. It gathered pace as it fell with a crash into the sea alongside, amongst a welter of clattering blocks and falling rigging. The boat flew up into the wind and came to a rocking halt.

The men picked themselves back up from the deck and turned towards the helm for orders to find that Griggs was no more. While his little crew had been crouched down to avoid the shower of falling debris, they had not noticed the ball that had dashed him into an unrecognisable bloody pulp on the deck.

'Come on, lads,' said O'Malley, becoming their leader by dint of being the first to emerge from shock. 'Let's clear away that wreckage. Ain't we still got one mast as works? Use knives, cutlasses, whatever you can find.'

They fell on the wreckage with the fury of the desperate. Cutlasses flashed in the early morning sun, and gradually they cleared away the wreck of the foremast. Another salvo splashed all around them as they worked, but mercifully did no further damage. With a final heave the last of the mast slid over the side, the hull of the chasse-maree rolled back up again, and the men looked about them once more for direction.

'Right then,' panted O'Malley. 'Sam, you take the helm. Rest of yous man the sheets on the main mast.'

With only the one sail now the boat was very slow, even when the tide began to pull them towards the open sea. The green fields and grey cliffs of the Brittany coast were visible around them on three sides, with the open sea away to the west. O'Malley searched for any remaining fog to hide them, but the warm sun had burnt it all off. Now the light glittered on the surface of water that was turning from green to blue in the morning light. The battery that was firing at them disappeared in smoke once more, and moments later the sea foamed into white all around them as the cannon balls ploughed into it. Out in the channel the *Titan* waited for them, hove to amid a cluster of little prizes. A fresh battery joined the first one, and struck lucky with its first salvo. Evans saw a line of splashes flash up off the surface of the sea as a cannon ball sped towards the boat. It seemed to be coming straight for him. For a brief moment he thought of the pitiful remains of Griggs that lay bleeding at his feet. Then he heard a massive crash underneath where he stood, and the whole boat slewed round as if it had been hit by a monstrous hammer.

O'Malley rushed to the ship's side and peered down at the spot where the shot had struck. He bobbed back up and pulled a face at the others.

'Barky's gone, lads,' he announced. 'Fecking great hole right between wind and water.'

'An' she's settling fast,' said Evans, the sluggish motion of the stricken boat obvious to him through the tiller he still held.

'What shall we do now, Sean?' asked Brown, a thin, tall seaman with a prominent scar on his neck.

'Go and find the fecking tender!' shouted the Irishman. 'Every coaster has one. Unless you fancy a swim.'

'It was stowed by the foremast,' said another of the hands, an older seaman with a blue skin of tattoos up one arm.

'Mother of God!' exclaimed O'Malley as he led a general charge forward. 'Was it damaged when the mast fell at all?'

They found the tender lashed down beneath its canvas cover. It was a little rowing boat with only four oars, but mercifully it was undamaged.

'Christ, it's bleeding small,' exclaimed one of the men. 'Why, it's even smaller than the *Titan*'s jolly boat.'

'It will be tight, lads, but the sea is calm enough,' said the older seaman. 'She should get us as far as the old *Titan*. Let's get her over the side.'

Getting the boat afloat was an easy task. The tender seemed to weigh little to the eight desperate men, and the chasse-maree had now settled so low that the sea was almost lapping over the side. Another salvo ploughed into the water all around them and one ball bounced across the deck. It sent a shower of splinters flying up, but did no damage to the precious little tender. As the ball struck the deck they heard the sound of furious hammering and cries for help from near to the stern.

'Shit! The prisoners!' exclaimed O'Malley. 'They will be up to their arses in water.'

'Ah, leave them,' said Brown. 'They're only bleeding Frogs. We ain't got no room for passengers.'

'You shut your mouth,' snarled Evans. 'We ain't leaving them to drown. Go and let them out, Sean.' The Irishman sloshed along a deck now awash with sea. When he was out of sight, there was a general push forward towards the tender.

'You may want to drown with them Frenchies, Sam Evans,' said the old seaman with the blue arm. 'But I ain't going to hang around to watch.'

'Back off, all of you!' yelled Evans. He picked up one of the tender's sculls in a single huge fist and waved it in front of him like a cudgel. The others stepped away from the furious Londoner. 'That's better. No bleeders going to drown, unless they try and make off in this here tender, in which case it'll be me as will be doing the fucking drowning.'

O'Malley returned with the original ten man crew of the chasse-maree at his heels just as the latest salvo from the shore swept away their vessel's one remaining mast. Every one ducked for cover once more as fresh wreckage poured down from above.

'At least the bastards may leave us alone now,' said Evans, the first to regain his feet. The others stood up too, and contemplated the little tender as it bobbed on the oily water beside the stricken coaster.

'Ten of them and eight of us,' counted Brown. 'That's way too many for that little boat. It's only got four benches.'

'Two in the stern sheets, four on each bench,' said O'Malley. 'Come on, lads, let's give it a go.' The men began to gingerly step across. The coaster had settled so low in the water now that they had to step up a little to get into the boat. Those left on board stood knee deep in sea, while the occasional wave washed over the gunwales.

'It's a fecking miracle it hasn't sunk on us yet,' said O'Malley. He turned to the chasse-maree's former owner. 'Monsieur Captain, why le boat he not sink?' The Irishman made a diving motion with the flat of one hand, and accompanied the gesture with a look of enquiry. The Frenchman pointed towards the flooded hold.

'Chanvre,' he said, and then seeing the incomprehension on the faces around him he picked up a trailing line and mimicked pulling it apart. 'Chanvre,' he repeated.

'Hemp!' said Evans, realising what the man was trying to say. 'They must be carrying a cargo of hemp for rope making. Does rope float, then?'

'It does for a bit, until it gets waterlogged like,' said O'Malley.

The little boat was packed full now, and there were still four men left on the coaster, including both Evans and O'Malley.

'You lads wait here while we row over to the barky,' suggested Brown. 'Once we unload we can come back for you.'

'Why the fecking hell is it not you as is going to do the waiting?' questioned O'Malley.

'That's right,' said the seaman stood next to him. 'How do we know you are going to come back? Five minutes ago you was all for leaving the Frogs to drown.'

'Look, the sooner we go, the sooner we can return,' said one of the other sailors. 'Why would we leave you?'

'Hey, weren't you one of the mutineers?' said Evans. 'I remember cracking your skull. You're John Waite, one of Sexton's mates. Why the fuck should I trust you?'

'You go and suit your bloody self, Sam Evans,' said Waite. He pushed the tender away from the side of the coaster. Evans grabbed the end of his oar and pulled the crowded boat violently back. There were cries of dismay as it heeled to one side and water sloshed into it. Several of the occupants reached for their weapons.

'Just you let go there, Evans,' snarled Waite, pulling a pistol out from the back of his waistband.

'What is the meaning of this!' shouted a voice behind them that came from low on the water. Evans spun round to see the angry face of Lieutenant Preston in the stern sheets of the *Titan*'s launch. The boat had slid unnoticed up to the side of the coaster behind them. 'You men, put up those cutlasses there. Waite, away with that pistol! Disgraceful! Royal Navy sailors squabbling like Spanish Bumboatmen! You should all be ashamed of yourselves.'

'Sorry, sir,' muttered a few of the men.

'Very well,' continued Preston. 'Now, get out of that little boat at once. It is far too over burdened. Let those Frenchmen use it to return to the mainland if they so wish, and the rest of you climb aboard the launch before that wreck settles under you.'

Chapter 14
Storm

'There is barely a milliner in Piccadilly we haven't visited this morning, Kitty,' said Lady Mary Ashton to her maid as she undid her bonnet in the hall. 'I am quite exhausted, but I must confess to being rather pleased with my new hats. What is a little fatigue compared with the jealousy the blue one with the spray of feathers will cause Lady Catherine tomorrow. What is it, Hilton?'

'Sir Charles Middleton has arrived to see your ladyship,' announced the butler. 'I have shown him into the Orangery as you instructed.'

'Has he now?' said Lady Mary, looking at the magnificent figure of her servant in his embroidered coat and powdered wig for a moment. She returned her attention to the hall mirror and examined her reflection, angling her face first one way and then the other before patting at her hair. Once she was satisfied with what she saw, she crossed the hall towards her drawing room. The butler scrambled ahead of her to throw open the double doors, and she swept through. She settled down at one end of the chaise-longue and arranged the folds of her pale green dress into a pleasing fan. 'You may show him in now, Hilton,' she ordered. Her butler bobbed his head in acknowledgement, and stalked out of the room.

'Lady Mary, my dear,' said Sir Charles as he came through the door. He bent over her proffered hand and lightly touched it with his lips. 'It is so very good to see you. And out of those dreadful widow's weeds at long last. Black is such an ill match for your character. There are few ladies of my acquaintance more disposed to be cheerful.'

'Sir Charles, my dear friend, you are such an inveterate flatterer,' she smiled. 'Thank you so much for coming to see me in my time of need. Please do take a seat.' She patted the seat next to her in invitation, and he parted the tails of his admiral's coat and sat down.

'How are you coping Lady Mary, without the protection of Sir Francis?' he asked.

'Oh, very ill, Charles,' she said, dabbing at the corner of a dry eye with her lace handkerchief. 'I have barely been able to leave the house.'

'How very odd, Lady Mary,' he remarked. 'I could have sworn that your butler said you had been out most of the morning.'

'Only in an attempt to restore my fragile constitution with a little air,' she insisted. 'When Francis died, I must confess that I was quite persuaded out of my senses. Were it not for the support of my dear niece Lydia, I do not know what I would have done.'

'She is a most agreeable young lady, to be sure,' he said.

'How old is your ward?'

'She is three and twenty.'

'Is that so?' mused the admiral. 'And still not wed, I collect?'

'With all the trying events that have happened of late, I have hardly been at leisure to address such matters,' said Lady Mary. 'But you are right. She really should be married by now. Francis and I had hoped to find a suitable match in India, but he succumbed to the cholera before we were able.'

'It must have been difficult to make progress under such circumstances, Lady Mary,' said the admiral. 'Do you miss him greatly?'

'Oh indeed, Sir Charles, you have no idea!' she exclaimed. 'I find myself having to engage in all manner of activities that as a lady I am wholly unprepared for. Not only is there my niece's future happiness to plan for, but there are matters of property and business that need to be resolved. It is his guidance and council in such affairs that I truly miss.'

'I do sympathise, my dear,' he said. 'It is fully five years now since I lost my own dear Margaret, and I declare there is hardly a day that passes when I do not miss her advice on matters that fall within a women's nature.'

'Five years! Has it been so long, Sir Charles?' she said. 'Have you never considered remarriage?'

'Frequently,' said the admiral. 'But a suitable candidate has yet to appear.'

'Not yet, perhaps,' she said, rolling a languid eye in his direction. 'But one never knows when the opportunity may present itself.'

'That is very true, Lady Mary,' he said, smiling at her. 'Shall we address the substance of my visit? Your note mentioned seeking my advice on a matter of some delicacy.'

'I was interested to learn what your opinion was of Captain Alexander Clay?' she asked.

'Clay?' he queried, surprised by the shift in the conversation. 'The commander of the *Titan*?'

'I suppose so, Sir Charles,' she said. 'Does the navy have more than one Captain Clay?'

'No, of course I know of whom you speak,' said the admiral. 'I have only met with him on the one occasion. He is newly promoted, and therefore quite a junior captain. That said, he does possess a growing reputation in the service. He performed very well last year when he was in the Windward Islands with Admiral Caldwell, and his current commander, Sir Edward Pellew seems very content with the manner in which he has discharged his duties. I set him a delicate and difficult task when I persuaded him to take command of the *Titan*, which at the time was a most unhappy ship. It is a duty which he seems to have performed with some distinction.'

'Well, that all sounds very fine,' she said. 'What about his more important qualities? Is he rich, for example?'

'I doubt his family is wealthy,' replied the admiral. 'His father was a clergyman who passed away when he was but a boy.'

'When I met him recently he informed me that he had several thousand invested in the Funds, and would soon touch more prize money that was due to him. Would that be an accurate summary of his holdings?' said Lady Mary.

'I dare say that may be the case,' he said. 'He has certainly done tolerably in the matter of prizes. But I am all agog, Lady Mary. Money due to him? Investments in the Funds? I cannot conceive under what circumstances you might have had such a peculiar conversation with him.'

'Captain Clay came to see me recently to ask for my niece's hand in marriage,' said Lady Mary.

'Did he, by Jove!' exclaimed Sir Charles. 'I knew he was a plucky cove, but you do surprise me. I wonder at him having the opportunity to be introduced to Miss Browning? He doesn't seem the type of person who would naturally mix in the society of ladies of her standing. How did they chance to meet?'

'Oh, as for that I hold myself to be very much to blame,' she said. 'It was over a year ago. Back then he was a mere lieutenant aboard the warship that was protecting our convoy on the first part of our journey to India.'

'Ah, I see,' he said. 'Matters are often rather less formal onboard ship.'

'So I learnt to my cost, Sir Charles,' she continued. 'Had I attended properly to Lydia, I might have been aware how close their acquaintance was becoming before it was too late. Once my suspicions had become firm, I made my husband aware of his approaches to her, and he naturally forbade any further contact with such an unsuitable match.'

'Yet that was not an end of the affair, I gather?' he asked.

'Regrettably not,' she replied. 'You must know how wilfull young ladies can be when they imagine themselves to be in love. Apparently Lydia was able to accept him in an informal way just before the ships parted at Madeira. Now I learn that his declaration has been repeated the day before Captain Clay came to see me. What am I to do, Sir Charles, left all alone, with such decisions to make?'

'There there, Lady Mary,' he said, taking up the hand that she had left within easy reach beside her. 'I can see that these matters must be very vexing, but you are not without friends in the world.'

'Oh, Charles,' she murmured. 'You do so fill me with hope.'

'I believe that the solution to your problem does indeed lie in forming a marriage alliance to another suitable family, one that may supply the male guidance you stand so much in want of.'

'Do you truly, Charles?' she asked.

'I do, Lady Mary,' he replied, still holding her hand. 'You need someone who is able to take the burden of such weighty decisions from your slight shoulders.' She glided a little closer across the smooth satin of the chasse-longue.

'Did you have a particular gentleman in mind?' she asked.

'Would you consider me to be suitable?' he replied.

'I might, once I had heard a suitable declaration of your admiration for me,' she purred, smiling up into his eyes.

'Ah... yes, Lady Mary,' he said. 'I believe I may have been guilty of a failure to communicate with adequate clarity. It is your niece, Miss Browning who was the object of my interest.'

'My niece?' she exclaimed, pulling her hand back. 'Lydia? But how can that be? Surely it was to me that your remarks tended.'

'As the one in need of masculine council, yes,' said the admiral. 'I would propose to furnish such advice from the position of your son in law.'

'My son in law!' she repeated, her face flushing. 'But Sir Charles, you are older than I am! No, there must be some mistake.'

'No, madam, no mistake,' he said. 'I urge you to consider for a moment the advantages of such a match.'

'But this is quite absurd,' she said. She rose to her feet, her eyes ablaze with fury. 'I have been led on in a most cruel and insupportable fashion! You were clearly referring to me earlier. How can you now switch you attention to Lydia? You are quite old enough to have sired her yourself. In fact you could almost serve as a grandparent to her.'

'Steady now, Lady Mary,' he said. 'I am still a man in the full vigour of life. Consider the superior merits of my connections, my status and my ability to confer preferment when compared with the slender advantages available to Alexander Clay, fine man though he is. I offer an alliance with one of Scotland's chief families as against an association with the son of a rural parson's widow. I beg you to think of all this before you reject my handsome proposal out of hand.'

'Ha!' yelled Lady Mary. 'And how do you suppose my niece will react when she finds that the young, dashing officer she has set her heart on has been replaced by an elderly Caledonian satyr?'

'A Caledonian satyr!' roared Middleton. He in his turn stood up, his face red with rage. 'I have never been so insulted in all my days! If you were not a lady, I should call for my horse whip! Am I to stand here and have my sincere and well meaning proposal tossed back in my face! It is not to be borne! Very well, I will remove the pollution of my presence, since you now seem to find it to be so revolting.'

'At least we can agree on one thing, Sir Charles. Hilton!' she called.

'Yes, Lady Mary?' said the butler as he glided into the room, the only oasis of calm between the two indignant protagonists.

'Sir Charles is leaving,' she spat. 'At once!'

'Before I depart, I will observe that it is passing strange how welcoming you were earlier when you thought that my attentions were intended for yourself, eh? There was no shortage of interest in me then, with your "come sit next to me" and your pawing at my hand! Good day to you, madam.'

'For my part, you have my eternal thanks, Sir Charles,' she said, her voice now calm as ice. 'You have rendered me a singular service.'

'How so?' he said, pausing mid-way to the door.

'You have quite made my mind up for me,' she replied. 'I am now resolved that I must see my niece wed, if only so she will no longer be prey to every lecherous old widower who has a fancy to bed a young maiden.'

*****

'Here they are again, sir,' reported Lieutenant Blake. 'Like a pair of eels they come sliding out from their cave amongst the rocks.' Clay followed the line of the lieutenant's pointing arm, towards the two powerful French warships that were standing out of Bertheaume Bay. The first was the big French frigate that had been anchored there ever since they had cut out the brig back in April. Behind her came a companion ship that had recently joined her. It was a similar sized frigate to the first. They both had long sleek hulls, decorated by a broad white stripe that ran the length of their gun decks. The ships looked to be fresh from the dockyard, to judge from how clean the white paint was and how bright their new canvas sails. They slid out across the Iroise Channel like a curtain, blocking the *Titan*'s approach to reconnoitre Brest.

'Is the second ship not a touch superior in size?' asked Clay, trying to count the number of lids in the row of gun ports.

'Perhaps sir, yes,' replied Blake. He frowned with concentration as he too counted. 'Her masts do look to be a little taller. She might be one of their new forty-four gun frigates, sir.'

'One such ship we might challenge, but two is a perhaps too much for us to handle, especially with so many hostile gun batteries here about,' said his captain. He tilted his head back and called up to the masthead. 'Mr Butler, Mr Russell! Are you able to see anything in the Rade de Brest?'

'No sir,' replied one of the midshipmen. 'I can only see a jumble of masts at this range.'

'The enemy is closing quickly with us, sir,' urged the officer of the watch beside him. 'Shall I have the ship cleared for action?'

'Not today, Mr Blake,' he replied. 'Put the ship about, and let us stand back out to sea.'

'Aye aye, sir,' replied the lieutenant. He reached forward to take the speaking trumpet from its becket and ordered the ship to turn around.

Clay watched the men at work as the ship swung up into the wind and then fell away onto the other tack. The crew all knew their places now and moved with purpose and efficiency from rope to rope as the manoeuvre progressed. He smiled to himself at what he saw. Each mass of seamen arrived at a point together, coalescing into a line as they took their places along the length of the rope. Then they hauled and pulled in time, secured the rope, and dissolved back into a mass as they ran to the next task with barely a second lost. He could sense the much better atmosphere on board now, the gentle skylarking among the men, the shared laughter and jokes that drifted up from the main deck as the watch returned below once the ship was on her new course.

'One might almost mistake them for an efficient crew, sir,' said Blake. He had replaced the speaking trumpet in its place and joined his captain once more.

'You might indeed, John,' agreed the captain. 'They are certainly better natured, to judge by how thin Mr Taylor's punishment list has grown. Pumping the bilges and cleaning the heads may need to become a normal part of the men's duties if we cannot find enough ne'er do wells to perform the task.'

'Why should they not be happy, sir?' replied the

lieutenant. 'Two weeks shore leave just enjoyed, a pay rise in place and a good slice of prize money to come from all those coasters.'

'They shoot tolerably, too,' said Clay. He looked round behind them at the two French frigates. They had hauled their wind as soon as it was clear that the *Titan* was retreating, and now they too were turning about. 'I almost wish we might take on those two. Fresh out of dock, their crews barely worked up after years blockaded in Brest, while we are close to a peak of efficiency. Who do you suppose would win?'

'Why, we would of course, sir,' grinned Blake. 'But alas, we shall not find out today. The eels have slithered back into their cave. It's been the same story for a week now. Why do you think they are so keen to block our approach?'

'I live in hope that the French have simply grown weary of our regular trips to peer into their naval base, and have decided to put a stop to our antics,' said Clay. 'But I am not at all certain that that is the true explanation.'

'What is it that you fear they may be up to, sir?' asked the lieutenant.

'Why do they do this now?' replied his captain. 'Our frigates have been reconnoitering these waters since the start of the war.'

'New orders from above?' speculated Blake.

'Maybe,' said Clay. 'Or perhaps the enemy is up to something that they would rather we did not see.'

'If Mr Warwick is to be believed, it will be a few days before we can try and look in again, sir,' said Blake. 'He holds we may be in for some heavy weather.'

'With the glass falling like a stone, and the wind strengthening from the west, one doesn't need to be an expert pilot to make a prediction like that,' replied Clay. He looked beyond the frigate's long elegant bowsprit. Out towards the horizon was a wall of towering grey cloud, the sea dark and angry beneath them. 'Signal the commodore when the flagship is in sight, if you please, Mr Blake. *Titan* to flag. Unable to observe enemy fleet. Then you had best strike down the topgallants and get some sea room between us and the shore before this storm arrives.'

'Aye aye, sir,' replied the lieutenant.

*****

By the time that four bells struck in the dog watch later that day, the storm that the ship's master had predicted was about to reach its climax. The wind that howled in from the Atlantic had had almost three thousand miles of open ocean to gather speed. All that lay between the driving wind and the colossal waves on one hand and the iron hard reefs and granite cliffs of the Brittany coast on the other were the fragile little ships of the Inshore Squadron. Aboard the *Titan* every preparation that could have been made for the storm had been. Her upper masts had been brought down on deck and secured. Every gun or other piece of heavy equipment that might work loose had been double lashed into place, and her most competent quartermasters manned her wheel. The frigate battled her way from the summit of one huge Atlantic roller to the next via the deep trough in between. First the bow was forced up the slope of the onrushing wave, tilting the frigate steeply backwards. Then the ship rolled over first to port and then to starboard as the wave travelled diagonally down the length of her keel. Then to finish it was the bow's turn to descend into the trough between waves, while the stern climbed ever higher.

Four bells in the dog watch was also the time when dinner was taken by the crew of the *Titan*. It was the main hot meal of the day, and was served to the men as they sat at their mess tables on the lower deck of the ship, a windowless space down on the waterline. In the narrow confines between the deck below them and the one above, most of the crew of the *Titan* struggled just to stay seated at their wildly swaying places. Each time the frigate pitched, anything on the tables not held in place by its owner was sent cascading to the deck. Conversation had to be pitched above the constant groan and creak of the ship's timbers all around them. The lanterns that provided the only lighting for the crew circled in wild loops, making the demented shadows of the men surge and retreat across the wooden walls of their ship. Over all there was a constant wetness. Water dripped down from above as the seams in the planking of the main deck worked above their heads. It wept in silver beads through the ship's sides and ran down the painted walls. It sloshed down the ladder ways whenever a freak wave surged across the deck outside. Most of all it steamed into the dank air in a fetid vapour from the sodden clothes of all the men packed into the space.

'Well, I'll be damned,' exclaimed Evans, as he loomed up in his dripping oilskins and thumped himself down on an empty mess stool. 'I've just been collared by that John Waite as was on the coaster we captured – you know, Sean, the bleeder as wanted to leave us behind.'

How could I fecking forget?' growled O'Malley. 'I was after running the fecker through with me cutlass, if Preston hadn't turned up when he did. What did that shite want, Sam?'

'What do you make of this?' said Evans. 'He has just come up to me all civil like, asked me how I was doing, and then said how he wanted to say he was sorry about what happened. He told me how he was right scared then, him being no swimmer, and no hard feelings like.'

'That's very big of him to say that to you,' enthused Trevan. 'Proper shipmately like.'

'Easy for the shite to say that now,' muttered O'Malley. 'Let's see how sorry he is the next time we're on a sinking ship and he's after fecking drowning.'

'What's it like up top, Sam?' asked Sedgwick.

'It'll be worse before it gets better, Able mate,' said Evans. 'I reckon we are in for a long night. The *Indy*'s put up the signal for us to take up our storm positions, which means the rest of the Channel Fleet boys will be scarpering for the shelter of Torbay as quick as quick, the bastards.'

'It'll not blow over long though,' said Trevan. 'These summer storms never last. Not like back in my whaling days in the Southern Ocean. You boys should try forty degrees south. You get a proper storm blasting away on eight days from ten.'

'Your summer storm is like to a whore,' declared O'Malley. 'Wet, fierce and fecking over before you knows it.'

'Have a care with the vittles, lads,' said Rosso, as he appeared at the head of the mess table, and banged down the kid of hot food he had brought from the galley in front of him. 'Cook says they'll be dousing the galley fire after this. It'll be cold provender for us till this gale blows itself out.'

'Let's be having it while we fecking can then,' said O'Malley, holding his plate up. 'I am starving.' Like hungry nestlings the men pressed forward with their empty plates, just as the piercing sound of whistles reverberated through the air.

'All hands, all hands on deck!' The boatswain's mates hurried along the deck from table to table, urging the sailors to their feet and plying their ropes ends around them to drive the men on. A collective groan of disappointment sounded around the deck, accompanied by the noisy clatter of mess stools as the men rose from their tables.

'All hands there!' yelled Powell, quite the fiercest of the boatswain's mates as he came level with the table. He was second only to Evans in height amongst the crew, a dark haired brute with a savage red cutlass scar on his face that lay across one eye. 'Stow that grub, Rosso, and show a leg! Rest of you can run now!'

Rosso stared around him in desperation for somewhere safe to wedge the container of hot food on the heaving deck. Eventually he hung the rope handle over a hook on the beam above the table and ran to join the throng of men who poured up the ladder way, with Powell close at his heels.

The lower deck was deserted now. From the deck above came the shout of orders and the collective cries of men heaving in unison. Beneath one of the beams the wooden bucket with its solid lid steamed in the air as it swung freely with the motion of the ship. The rope handle of the bucket moved jerkily up and down the hook as the ship was battered by the sea. Then the bow of the frigate crashed into a particularly large wave, tilting the ship to its steepest angle yet and the handle slithered along till it reached the end of the hook. It held for a moment on the very tip of the curve of iron, and then slipped free. With a crash the heavy kid hit the planking below. It now began a rolling journey across the deck. With each surge of the ship it swept first one way, and then another. The lines of its progress were marked by arcs of food that dribbled out until there was nothing left inside for the cold, wet and weary messmates when they should return from battling the storm above.

Chapter 15

Escape

'If I had a farthing for every time we have proceeded down the Iroise Channel this commission, I should no longer be obliged to make my living as a King's officer,' said Lieutenant Blake to Lieutenant Preston as they stood together on the quarterdeck of the *Titan*. Blake was officer of the watch, and so compelled to be there, but his friend had joined him merely to enjoy the early morning light and to keep him company. The strong wind that pressed the frigate forward still had a little of the gale's residual chill, but it was backing towards the south with every moment and was losing its sting. The blue sky above them was dotted with white domes of cloud that hinted at calmer weather ahead. Preston looked at the patterns of cloud shadow and bright sunlight that dappled the coast and sea for a moment.

'So what occupation might you follow, John?' he asked. 'If your torrent of farthings was ever paid to you and you no longer had to serve as a lieutenant.'

'I might try my hand as an artist,' said the young man,

after a few moments of thought. 'I have always enjoyed drawing and I showed a modest ability at painting when I was a child.'

'Really?' said Preston. 'You do surprise me. So why don't you?'

'What, give up my career and paint?' laughed his friend. 'I have not actually been paid those farthings for our frequent visits to this stretch of sea, you know, Edward.'

'Granted,' said Preston. 'But I meant that you could still pursue your interest in art without having to stop being a naval officer. Does our time off duty not give you the leisure to pursue other interests? Many of the men use their time below deck to do scrimshaw and the like. My friend Croft once served onboard a ship with a lieutenant who had a passion for marine life. He had half the gunroom fishing over the side for all manner of creatures for him when they were off duty. I believe he was quite an accomplished cove, with learned papers read at the Royal Society and such like. I don't see why you might not do a little sketching, if you feel so inclined.' He pointed towards the fabulous view that had opened up all around them. 'You have plenty of agreeable subjects.'

In response Blake turned his back on the coastline. 'Mr Butler,' he said, 'my compliments to the captain, and we will shortly be in a position to start our observations of Brest.' While he waited for Clay to appear, he ran a quick eye over the ship to make sure that nothing was out of place. Once he was satisfied he looked back at his friend and laughed out loud. Preston had pushed his hat to the back of his head in a rakish manner and had pulled out his neck cloth into a ballooning cravat. In one hand he held the slate that normally hung by the wheel for recording course directions, while in the other he held a stick of chalk at arm's length as if he was measuring perspective.

'I am pleased to hear my officers are enjoying themselves this morning,' said Clay as he approached the pair. Preston began to stuff his neck cloth back into his shirt while Blake returned the slate and chalk to their place beside the wheel.

'Your pardon, sir,' replied Preston, catching at his hat just in time to prevent it from falling to the deck.

'No matter, Mr Preston,' he said. 'I am sure the jest was worth it.' He then looked around to find the two midshipman waiting to one side, both grinning at the discomfort of the lieutenants. 'Mr Russell, Mr Butler, do you have your spy glasses and note books? Excellent, aloft you go now.'

'Any sign of those eels of yours, Mr Blake?' asked the captain as he watched the two young midshipmen scamper up the shrouds.

'No, sir,' replied the officer of the watch. 'I had a good look into Bertheaume Bay earlier and saw no ships of war at all. Perhaps they have returned to the shelter of Brest to avoid the storm.'

'Let us hope that is the case,' said Clay. 'We are close enough in shore now. Kindly bring her to the wind, and let us see what our two little spies have to report.'

'Twenty ships of the line, same as last time, sir,' said Butler, once the two midshipman had returned to the deck and consulted together. 'But only five frigates now, sir. There were ten last time, two of which were stationed in that bay.'

'Now, are you sure of what your saw?' asked Clay. 'Take your time and think. It is most important that you are certain in your view.'

'Quite sure, sir,' supplemented Russell. 'You could see the gaps in the line of moored ships where they had been.'

'Did you look for them elsewhere in the harbour?' persisted their captain. 'Might they not have been amongst the smaller shipping, or returned back into the inner harbour? If you want to return aloft to check, I shall not be angry.'

'That will not be necessary, sir,' said Butler. 'They have definitely gone.'

'Very well, gentlemen,' said Clay. 'So we have as many as five frigates that have slipped out to sea.' He thought for a moment, and then something else occurred to him. 'What has become of all those tents you saw a few weeks back? The ones just on the other side of the headland?'

'Oh, no need to worry about those,' said Butler. 'They have all disappeared too, sir.'

'What!' exclaimed Clay. 'The soldiers and guns as well?'

'Yes, sir,' said Russell. 'You can still see the marks on the ground where the tents once stood.'

'Thank you, gentlemen,' said the captain. 'That has been most illuminating.' He spun on his heel and called across to the officer of the watch. 'Mr Blake, kindly lay us on a course that will most directly take us back out to sea. I want you to close with the flagship as soon as may be convenient. Signal to the commodore that I wish to come onboard, and that it is urgent.'

*****

'Captain Clay, my dear fellow,' said Sir Edward Pellew, as the last twitter of the boatswain's pipes squealed into nothingness, and his visitor's hand descended from the side of his hat where it had been held in salute. He grasped that hand, shook it and smiled at his subordinate. 'Delighted to see you again. I take it that the *Titan* came through our recent blow unscathed?'

'Tolerably well, sir,' replied Clay. 'We did have a stay sail blown out while the hands were at dinner, and a little of our rigging was wounded, but I have a good boatswain in Mr Hutchinson who has put all to rights once more.'

'That is good news. We shipped rather a lot of water, but endured nothing worse. Will you please come this way?' The commodore led him under the quarterdeck and past the marine sentry who stood to attention outside his cabin door. Inside was the familiar luxury he remembered from before. The same thick Persian rugs under his feet, and he still found himself scrutinised by the gilt framed portraits that looked down from the bulkheads. I shall have a picture of Lydia commissioned to hang on my cabin wall, once we are married, he told himself. After a moment he reached forward to lightly touch the cherry wood of Pellew's desk. If we are married, he corrected himself, remembering how noncommittal Lady Mary Aston had been when they had met.

'Do please take a seat, Captain Clay,' said Pellew.

'A glass of sherry, sir,' murmured a steward at his elbow,

and Clay accepted the proffered glass from the tray.

'Now what has happened to bring you out to see me?' asked the commodore. 'Pleasant as your visit is, I take it this is not just a social call. Are the French out?'

'I believe they are, sir, but only in part,' he replied. 'The twenty ships of the main battle fleet are still at anchor, but five of their frigates have gone.'

'Yes, I did fear they might avail themselves of the opportunity of this storm to slip a few of their more weatherly ships out,' said Pellew. 'They often do this after a blow, knowing our heavy units will have fled back to Torbay, and we will have been driven from our proper station. Generally they are sent out on a cruise to attack our commerce. Very vexing, to be sure.'

'Sir, if it were but one or two ships, that might be the case,' said Clay. 'But five frigates on the same night? Does that not strike you as more like a squadron, despatched with the object of creating some particular mischief?'

'Perhaps,' said the commodore, sipping at his drink. 'Do you have any other intelligence to support your view?'

'I do, sir,' he replied. 'For a week now I have suspected the French of having in preparation some design they wished to conceal from us, hence those two frigates stationed in Bertheaume Bay to intercept our approach. Now their object has been achieved both ships have gone. The *Titan* was able to make her observations with perfect ease this morning.'

'That is certainly suggestive,' agreed Pellew, 'but hardly conclusive.'

'No sir, I agree,' he replied. 'Do you recall the brigade of troops in a tented encampment I informed you of? They too have disappeared. I surmise the troops have been taken onboard the five frigates. It is this accumulation of detail that makes me fear the worse.'

Pellew waved forward his steward to refill the glasses, and then he looked out of the stern window, deep in thought. Outside the blue Atlantic stretched to the silver horizon, with only a few little islands close at hand to break the seascape.

'I believe you may have the truth of it. Five frigates, and let us say two thousand troops, somewhere out there,' he said, pointing at the empty ocean. 'Where are they going, Clay?'

'They will not be bound for the West Indies, sir,' offered his visitor. 'Now that we have deprived the enemy of their sugar islands, there are no garrisons for them to reinforce, and a single brigade is too small a force to attempt any conquests.'

'Agreed,' said the admiral. 'I would add that we can rule out the Mediterranean for a somewhat different reason. If they were bent on forcing their way past our forces at Gibraltar they would have sent ships of the line, not just frigates. Very well, not west across the ocean to the Caribbean, and not south to enter the Med. Are they headed north then?' Both men looked at each other as the same thought came to them.

'Ireland,' said Clay. 'Isn't the militia struggling to contain the rebellion there?'

'That's right,' said Pellew. He put down his glass with decision. 'That damned rebel Wolfe Tone is still proving troublesome, together with all those United Irishman. Two thousand trained French troops coming to assist them would be an infernal problem. Doubtless they will be carrying arms and supplies for the rebels too. The Munster coast is no more than three hundred miles away.' He got up from behind his desk, and began to pace up and down the cabin.

'Very well, we must go after them then,' he said. 'Yet I cannot leave Brest unguarded. The *Argo* can take your place in the Iroise Channel to keep an eye on the French. The *Phoebe* is the swiftest of my five frigates, so I shall send her with word of all this to Admiral Bridport. He should be on his way back from Torbay with the fleet. So that leaves you, me and Captain Warburton in the *Concord* to go after them. Three of ours against five of theirs. They are not the kindest of odds.'

'I have faced worse, sir,' said Clay. Inside he felt rising excitement at the prospect of action.

'So you have,' smiled Pellew, and then his face changed. 'But I was forgetting. Are not a good number of your people Irish? Can they be relied on in such a fight?'

'Absolutely,' said Clay. 'I would stake my life on the conduct of my men.'

'Have a care what you say,' cautioned the commodore. 'That may prove to be exactly what you will be doing.'

*****

'A seven again!' exclaimed Faulkner, glaring at the board. He stroked one of his auburn sideburns with the edge of a spare playing counter and stared at the impossible position he seemed to have got himself into.

'With two dice a seven is quite the most probable result, Charles,' said Macpherson, with an assurance that came from the certainty of victory. 'The philosophers calculate the odds as one in six. The trick in Backgammon is to accept such inevitability and factor it into your play.'

'Hmm,' grunted the purser. He eventually moved a counter and sat back.

'There, you see?' said the marine. 'I too have a thrown a seven. Which will permit me to do this.' He moved his counters with practiced ease, and removed another of his opponent's from the board. 'Ah, Henry,' he said as the ship's master came into the wardroom. 'So do you know where we are bound? You have been closeted away with the captain and Mr Taylor for some time now.'

Warwick began his reply just as the tiller above their head swung across the wardroom ceiling with a groan of rudder lines and a squeal from one of the blocks.

'Your pardon, Henry,' said the marine. He cupped a hand to his ear. 'I missed what you said. Will you not come a little closer, I pray.'

'I said that we are bound for Ireland,' he repeated, taking a chair next to the Scotsman, and putting a slim leather bound volume he was carrying on the table. 'I have just given the captain our course. We are in company with the *Indefatigable* and the *Concord*, spread in a line abreast with twelve miles between each ship.'

'Curious formation,' said Faulkner. 'What may its purpose be?'

'It will serve to maximise the area of sea we can cover as we advance, Charles,' replied Warwick. 'We do not know which path the French will have taken. We are to follow the direct path, but they may have stood farther out to sea in order to avoid our cruisers who patrol the mouth of the Channel.'

'Yet we are certain they are bound for Ireland, I collect?' said Preston as he looked up from the letter he was writing.

'The captain is quite resolved that is the case,' said the master. 'Where in Ireland is more uncertain. A remote and sheltered bay where they can land their troops and supplies unmolested, you may be sure. Which on the coast of Ireland will mean somewhere in the far west.'

'In my experience the captain's instinct is generally to be relied on in such matters,' smiled Preston. 'Some action at last! Capturing a few scrubby little coasters in the fog is all very well, but it will be good to cross swords with a ship that is our equal.'

'You sound like the late Lieutenant Morton,' said Warwick. 'He too was rather contemptuous about making war on merchantmen.'

'Oh, I am content to receive a bit of easy prize money, you may be sure,' said Preston. 'Are not all naval officers part pirate when you scratch them a little? But there is so much more honour to be had from besting another warship.'

'Well then, Edward,' said the master, 'I give you joy of your battle. Let us hope the French are just below the horizon, and that we are closing on them fast.'

'What is that volume there, Henry?' asked the purser. 'Is

it some sort of sailing directions for the Munster coast?

'This here?' he said picking up the slim green book. 'We are like to be thrown ashore if this is all we have to navigate by.' He flicked through the large pages so they could see that every one of them was empty. 'I am going to give this to Mr Blake. He asked me earlier if I had any blank paper he might have, and I remembered this. I had been keeping it with thoughts of writing a journal, but I never did start. I have no notion what he intends to do with the book.'

'I think I may know,' said Preston. 'He may be considering using it to sketch in.'

'Oh really?' said Faulkner, taking the book from the master. 'I had not thought of him as being an artist?'

'I do not think he has practiced the skill much of late, Charles,' said Preston. The new purser twisted the book in his hands for a moment.

'Useful things books, are they not, Tom?' he said with a smile. He slapped Macpherson on the shoulder and turned back to the master. 'We almost lost our bold marine last commission. Macpherson here was reading a novel when he was called into action to repel a French attack on a redoubt that Preston was commanding. He deposited the book into his tunic, and thought no more about it till a base Frenchman shot him in the chest. The book stopped the bullet dead, leaving him with no more than a cracked rib and a generous bruise. Damnedest thing I ever saw.'

'Bless my soul, Tom,' said Warwick shaking the marine officer by the hand. 'A bullet stopped by a novel, perhaps the pen may truly be superior to the sword. What a tale! I do hope your prodigious good fortune may have followed you across into the *Titan*.'

'Let us hope that it has,' Macpherson replied. He sat back in his seat for a moment while the others continued to discuss the remarkable incident. What the hell do they really know, he thought to himself. Faulkner's jolly account was accurate in as far as it went, but it left out so much. He had not mentioned the slow moment of rising horror that had rooted him to the spot as he had watched the soldier train his musket round and select him as his target. Where was the long terror as time froze while he waited for the gun to fire? What about the massive impact of the bullet on his chest when it struck, spinning him around? Or the hard ground as it raced up towards him. He felt a prickle of sweat on his forehead and went to pull out his handkerchief from his coat pocket. His hand was trembling so much that when he drew it out he found it had dropped on to the deck. As he bent down to pick it up he heard Preston cry out.

'Have a care for the board,' he shouted. The ship had heeled over and settled at a more pronounced angle. With a despairing lunge Preston just managed to stop the board from slipping to the floor, but the counters had all collected in a black and white drift along one side. 'Ah, I fear your game may have come to an abrupt close, gentlemen.'

'Thank God for that,' said Faulkner. 'You did have me soundly beaten, Tom.'

'The captain is certainly cracking on,' mused the master. 'I believe he must have added topgallants over topsails for the ship to heel at such an angle. We may catch these Frenchmen yet.'

*****

'Deck there!' yelled the lookout the following morning. 'Sail ho!'

Preston tilted his head back and yelled towards the distant little figure who sat on the royal yard high up on the foremast. 'Where away?' he asked.

'A point off the starboard bow, sir,' came the reply. 'Topsails just lifting over the horizon.'

'Mr Russell!' said the lieutenant. 'My compliments to the captain, and please inform him that a ship is in sight, bearing north by east.'

'Aye aye, sir,' replied the midshipman, and he ran for the companionway ladder.

'Good morning, Mr Preston,' said Clay, as he arrived on deck a little later. 'Where is this ship of yours then?'

'Not visible from the deck yet, sir,' he replied. 'The lookout can just see the topsails.' Clay looked around him and spotted Blake seated at the very stern of the ship with Warwick's book on his knees.

'Kindly have Russell sent aloft to see what he makes of this sail,' he ordered. 'And signal the commodore. "*Titan* to Flag. Ship in sight bearing ten degrees. Am investigating." '

'Aye aye, sir,' replied Preston. Clay walked back along the length of the quarterdeck to join Blake, who rose to his feet at his captain's approach.

'Good morning, sir,' he said. 'I trust this sail may be the French.'

'Good morning, Mr Blake,' replied his captain. 'That might be the case, although like as not it will prove to be one of our merchantmen. We are presently crossing the mouth of the English Channel, so we are sure to encounter some shipping. You have chosen a nice spot for your reading.'

'It is pleasant here for sure, but I am not reading, sir,' replied Blake. 'I am trying my hand at capturing Nancy's likeness.'

'Nancy?' queried Clay. The lieutenant showed him his sketch book. The pages fluttered beneath his grasp in the keen breeze. His captain angled his head a little, and his face cleared. 'Oh, I see. You are drawing the wardroom goat. May I?' He took the book and looked at the collection of drawings on the page. In the centre was the animal, lying on a section of deck with her neat hooves tucked in beside her. She held her head high and alert, caught in a moment as if startled by some noise. Around the main sketch were smaller drawings that captured some of the detail. One just showed the goat's head, a single liquid eye looking back out of the page at Clay. As he looked he could almost feel the animal regarding him. He glanced across to where Nancy was tethered to one of the aft carronades munching on some ship's biscuit, and back at the page.

'This is really very good,' he said admiringly. 'I have always thought that goats have eyes like the devil, which you have captured very well. I had no idea what talent lurked down in the wardroom.'

'Thank you, sir,' said Blake as he took back his book. 'I am obliged to Lieutenant Preston for suggesting to me that I might try my hand at a little drawing. I must confess I had forgotten how engaging a pursuit it can be. In time I may progress from goats to some more challenging subjects about the ship.'

'That will be very interesting,' said the captain. 'Shipboard life is so ill recorded in general. And should you ever find yourself progressing onto portraits I may have a commission for you. Yes, Mr Butler?'

'Mr Preston's compliments, and Mr Russell reports that the sail is a merchant brig flying British colours,' he said.

'Thank you,' said Clay. 'Kindly ask Mr Preston to lay us on a course to intercept the brig. I wish to pass them within hailing distance.' Once the midshipman had saluted and left them, Clay turned back to Blake. 'As I feared, it is not the French, but at least with no prospect of immediate action you will have the leisure to complete your drawing of Nancy.'

Carrying all the sail she could manage in the gusty wind, the *Titan* sped down towards the little ship. Her sharp bow plunged into each fresh wave with gusto and threw a fan of spray downwind. An occasional rainbow flashed into existence in the sunlight as she tore on. The ships converged quickly, till the brig was hull up from the quarterdeck. She had not altered her course at all since they had first seen her, in spite of the large frigate that loomed ever closer. As soon as she was within range, Clay had a signal sent up that ordered her to haul her wind.

'Why is she ignoring my signal?' he fumed as the brig continued on her way.

'She probably fears we plan to press some of her hands, sir,' said Taylor.

'Which I damned well might if she doesn't stop soon,' said Clay. 'Mr Preston! Have the bow chaser cleared away and send a ball across her bow.'

'Aye aye, sir,' replied the lieutenant.

A few minutes later a gush of dirty white smoke erupted from the forecastle, followed by the deep boom of the long nine pounder firing.

'Ah, that's better, sir,' reported the first lieutenant.

'About time too,' muttered his captain.

'Why did I ignore your direction to stop, sir?' repeated the brig's master in response to Clay's hail. 'We did see your flags, but my ship's mate who understood what all these damned signals mean was pressed off my ship last voyage. Still, no harm done. How is it that I can help you?'

'I am seeking a French naval squadron that has escaped from Brest,' explained Clay. 'Five warships, all frigates, probably bound for Ireland. Have you seen them at all?'

'Five warships, you say?' said the brig's master. He was a large man, unused to being hurried. After a few moments of staring towards the horizon, lost in thought he returned his speaking trumpet to his mouth. 'Yes, I believe I might have seen them, sir. There was a mass of navigation lights on the horizon, around dusk yesterday night. We thought it was like to be a convoy of some sort, but it might very well have been these Frogs you are after.'

'Perhaps so,' said Clay. 'Do you recall where it was you saw them, captain?'

'Well now, let me think,' he replied. He returned his gaze to where sea and sky met for a further moment of contemplation. Clay shifted from one foot to the other while he waited.

'Maybe twenty-five or thirty miles north west of here,' he eventually replied. 'Would you like me to go below and consult the log?'

'No, no, captain, I pray,' hailed Clay. 'I have detained you quite long enough. You have been most helpful. I trust you have a prosperous voyage.'

'You too, sir,' came the reply.

'Mr Preston, kindly bear away and let us make all speed to close with the flagship so I can signal to them,' he ordered. 'I fear the French are still far ahead, but they may suffer some mishap that will serve to slow their progress.'

'You believe we may catch them before they reach Ireland, sir?' asked the lieutenant.

'Probably not, but we can but try,' he replied.

*****

'Ah, the hills of County Kerry in all of their fecking glory!' enthused O'Malley. He stood up against the bow rail of the frigate and threw wide his arms. 'Did you ever hear tell of such a beautiful green at all?'

'What about them forests we saw back in Saint Lucia?' asked Evans as he coiled the middle staysail halliard with care and hung it over its belay pin. 'They was about as green as it comes.'

'But that was in the fecking tropics!' protested the Irishman. 'That don't signify. Where have you seen green like over there in any proper Christian land like?'

'Cornwall is very green,' said Trevan. 'In the spring it can be proper lush in the fields near my village. Easily as green as these hills here of yours.'

'Cornwall!' spluttered O'Malley. 'Don't tell me you're after comparing fecking Cornwall with them mountains over there?'

His shipmates all paused in their work to contemplate the view. The *Titan* had rounded Bray Head and was standing into Dingle Bay, while the other two frigates pressed on to search the next inlet up the coast. The north side of the bay was a majestic sweep of green mountains tumbling down into the blue water at their feet. Just near them the land had been sheared off as if by a blow from some monstrous cleaver which had left towering cliffs of grey stone, streaked with white from the clouds of sea birds that flew in drifts of smoke across them. At their base Atlantic rollers thudded in from the open sea and sent white water foaming up the rock. Above the cliff tops the hills were indeed lush and green in the sunshine, fading to blue in the distance as the land rose again to form a broken spine of mountains.

'Tis a mighty fine land, our Sean,' said Trevan, patting his friend on the shoulder. 'You know we be only jesting with you. Must seem strange for you, mind, to be so near to home like?'

'Oh Christ, this isn't home, Adam!' exclaimed O'Malley. 'No, I don't come from round here at all. Your folk from Kerry are fecking peculiar sods. Mad savages the lot of them, barely human at all. But they do have nice green hills.'

'Look alive,' hissed Rosso from the base of the foremast. 'Grunters are coming.'

The men hastened to carry on their work as the tall figure of their captain strode up the portside gangway with Lieutenant Taylor by his side. Both men were carrying telescopes in their hands. The sailors stepped aside as the officers passed them, knuckling their foreheads in salute.

'Carry on, you men,' said Taylor, and the friends continued to coil and tidy the ropes on the forecastle while trying their best to overhear what the two officers were saying.

'Any sign of the French?' asked Clay. He scanned the far shore of the bay as it opened up before them.

'Nothing yet, sir,' replied Taylor. 'This inlet does go a long way inland, so they may be farther up it.' His captain shook his head.

'I doubt it,' said Clay. 'No French commander would take his ship so far from the open sea. In a westerly he could be trapped in here for weeks. No, Mr Taylor, I fear we have drawn another dud, as we have been doing all day. No French in Kenmare, or in Dunmanus Bay.'

'I thought we might have found them in Bantry Bay, sir,' replied the first lieutenant. 'That is where they attempted to land troops last year.'

'There are such a multitude of inlets on this blasted coast,' muttered Clay. 'Where can the damned French be?'

'Begging your honours' pardon,' said O'Malley, 'but do we know what these Frog ships are planning to do here abouts, sir?'

'O'Malley!' bristled Taylor. 'You speak when spoken to! If you have something to say, you know you must ask permission to speak first.'

'Sorry, sir,' replied the Irishman. 'Can I have your permission to speak at all?'

'Yes, you can,' said Clay. 'To answer your question, we believe that the French plan to effect a landing on this coast. Perhaps of as many as two thousand soldiers, some guns and a lot of supplies. Do you have anything to suggest, O'Malley?'

'I do sir,' he said. 'I was thinking that you might want to asked some of the Kerry men amongst the crew where they would go to land such a body of men. Murphy in the afterguard would be best. He's a fisherman from Tralee. I doubt if there's a soul aboard as knows this coast better.'

'Murphy was one of the mutineers wasn't he, O'Malley?' asked Taylor.

'Aye, sir, but that was only because them arses Kenny and Sexton filled his head with all sorts of stuff, pardon my language,' replied the Irishman. 'He's steady enough now.'

'Just a minute,' said Taylor. 'I recall you were reported to me for fighting with Murphy by the Master at Arms.' O'Malley looked a little sheepish at this.

'Well sir, Murphy was one of them what tricked Beak..., I mean Mr Morton into having Evans and Sedgwick put in irons,' he said. 'I was angry with your man, for setting on my messmates. Murphy's not what you might call quick on the uptake. He takes more note of fists than words like, but we are fine with each other now.'

'Very well, O'Malley,' said Clay, trying hard not to crack a smile. 'Can you give my compliments to the captain of the afterguard, and let him know I would like to have a word with your fellow countryman.'

When he appeared on the forecastle, Murphy was a pleasant looking young sailor with dark hair and eyes, and a thin, angular frame. He shifted from one foot to the other in the presence of both his captain and his first lieutenant.

'Stand still, man,' ordered Taylor. 'You're not in any trouble.'

'O'Malley here told us that you are familiar with this coastline,' said Clay. 'Is that the case?'

'Why yes, sir,' replied the sailor. He pointed towards the shore. 'My family come from the other side of that peninsular over there. I've been after fishing these waters with my father and uncles since I was first able to totter down to their boat.' Clay smiled in encouragement.

'Very good, Murphy,' he said. 'I want you to imagine that you had come to this coast with five warships, all much the size of the *Titan,* with the object of landing a large body of men, together with some cannon and a good quantity of warlike stores. Where might you choose to go to accomplish such a thing?' Murphy looked around for a moment, took in the natural beauty all about him and shook his head.

'If it was troops and guns an' all you was after putting ashore, I would not be doing it here, sir,' he said. 'Dingle Bay is awful pretty like, but it has no shelter to speak off if it was to blow above a cap full of wind out of the west like, which it pretty well does all of the time hereabouts.'

'Very well,' said Clay. 'Let us discount this bay then. So where might you go instead?'

'Once I had put these troops an' all that other stuff

ashore, would I be thinking of heading inland like?' asked the Kerry man.

'Most likely that will be their intention,' confirmed his captain. Murphy's face cleared at this.

'Then I would go a bit farther up the coast. Just round the next headland is Ballyheige Bay. She's a fine wide inlet, nice and deep like. That's where I would be fetching up, for certain,' he said.

'You seem most decided in your view, Murphy,' said Clay. 'Would you share your reasoning with us?'

'For a start there is plenty of shelter from the west, sir,' he explained. 'I have taken refuge from a blow behind Rough Point many a time with my Da and Uncle Niall. Good holding ground to anchor a ship in, and plenty of sandy beaches to land them stores and men. Open to the north, so I wouldn't be trapped with the wind in the west. Perfect for what them Frogs is about.'

'It does sound promising, sir,' said Taylor.

'I agree,' said Clay, considering the sailor. 'And what of the French troops moving inland from there?'

'Which they could do as easy as kiss my hand, sir,' said Murphy. 'Doesn't the mighty Shannon River empty into that very bay? She cuts right through these mountains. You could land at dawn and be beating on the gates of Limerick itself before nightfall.'

'Very good, Murphy,' said the captain with decision. 'We shall try this Ballyheige Bay of yours. Mr Taylor, have the ship put about on the other tack and see if we can weather that headland.'

'Aye aye, sir,' said the first lieutenant. He hurried off towards the quarterdeck. Clay turned back towards the two seaman. 'Thank you for your help, Murphy, your advice has been most useful. And to you too, O'Malley, for your valuable suggestion that we avail ourselves of Murphy's local knowledge.' The two sailors muttered something unintelligible, and Murphy's pale skin flushed red with embarrassment. Clay spared them any fresh agony by looking out into Dingle Bay.

'Tell me, Murphy, does the surf always sound as loud when it beats against the cliffs over there?' he asked. The sailor glanced across to the far side of the inlet, a puzzled look on his face.

'Not really, sir,' he replied. 'It can boom a bit like, but I have never heard it like this.' They all looked at the far headland for a moment and the realisation came slowly that the rhythm of the sound they could hear was quite out of time with the crashing waves.

'That's not surf we are after hearing, sir,' said O'Malley. 'That's the sound of gunfire.'

Chapter 16

Ballyheige

As the *Titan* sailed back out of Dingle Bay, her crew were busy clearing their ship for action. They were encouraged in their efforts both by the increasing sound of distant gunfire from somewhere ahead, and by the roar of noise produced by their marine drummer as he beat to quarters. He was positioned at the centre of the main deck and his drumsticks were a blur of motion. Men swirled around him as they ran to their places, or paused to deliver and receive hasty hand-slaps from friends as they passed each other. From behind him came the sound of the carpenter and his mates knocking loose the wedges that held the bulkheads on the main deck in place. Soon the captain's suite of cabins, already stripped of their furniture, would vanish completely. That would leave the gun deck as a single uninterrupted space from the very apex of the bow to the glass window lights at the back of the stern.

Some of the drummer's fellow marines hung in the air above him as they made their way up the shrouds, hauling their muskets and extra pouches of ammunition behind them. These were the better shots among the men who would act as sharpshooters, sniping down on an enemy ship alongside to add their puny musket fire to the massive eighteen pounder cannon that formed the *Titan*'s main armament.

The drummer had a good view of the guns. They ran down both sides of the main deck, and around each one he could see their crews as they prepared for action. Most of them had stripped to the waist, ready for the furnace heat and hard physical labour to come. Many wound their neck clothes into bandanas which they pulled tight around their heads to protect their ears from the deafening roar of each broadside. Some checked over the rammers and hand spikes that they would use to point and load the cannon. Others cast loose their pieces and pulled experimentally on the rope tackles that they would need to run the loaded guns back out through the ship's side. The drummer found his view had become hazy and vague with smoke as each gun captain lit his spluttering linstock and whirled it into glowing life. Then the ship's boys came running up in an excited pack from below with the first of the charges. They spread out across the deck, each one carrying his heavy bag of powder in a leather case to his allotted gun.

Down below the drummer's feet the officers in the wardroom were busy with their own preparations for battle.

'Has anyone laid eyes on my pistol?' shouted Preston, poking his head out of his cabin door.

'How can you mislay a pistol in such a tiny space, Edward?' asked Macpherson, checking the priming on his own weapon, then thrusting it into the red marine officer's sash that was wound around his waist.

'It should be in the top draw of my desk, but Dray must have moved it,' explained the lieutenant. 'And he will be busy bringing up the first charge to number eight gun now. My, you do look quite the buccaneer, Tom,' he added, indicating where the butt of the marine's pistol stuck out from the sash.

'Here, take mine,' said Blake, passing it across on his way out of the cabin. 'I doubt I shall have occasion to need one down on the main deck with the guns. Good luck to you all.'

'You too, John,' said Preston, placing the pistol in his coat pocket and buckling on his sword. On the other side of the wardroom table Macpherson was doing the same with his.

'Is that what they call a claymore, Tom?' he asked, pointing to the unusual brass basket guard that surrounded the hilt.

'Aye, that's right,' said the marine, drawing the glittering blade a few inches from its scabbard. 'It's a wee bit too long to be handy onboard ship, but it has an edge like a razor. It's been used in my family for generations.'

'Has it now?' smiled Preston. 'I will not ask you in whose cause they bore it.'

'Best not,' grinned Macpherson. He took the hand that the teenage lieutenant held out to him.

'You look after yourself now, laddie,' he said. Preston glanced down at the marine's hand in surprise.

'Are you unwell, Tom,' he asked. 'Your hand, it's trembling quite violently.'

'Oh, 'tis nothing,' replied the Scotsman. He pulled his

hand back and gripping it with the other. 'I often feel nervous excitement before action. Now away with you.'

Preston looked at the marine and noticed for the first time how pale he was. Beads of sweat lay in tiny pearls on his forehead.

'No really, you do look quite ill,' he said. 'Can I not get you something for your present relief? A tot of rum perhaps? I have some in my sea chest.' He disappeared back into his cabin, and the sound of rummaging came from inside. Macpherson closed his eyes for a moment. In an instant the image was back in his mind's eye again. The fury and roar of battle all around him. The French soldier who swung his musket around, knee deep in gun smoke as if he were wading through water. The barrel foreshortened till it became a black hole pointing straight at him. The endless pause as he waited for the shot, and all the time the dreadful figure swelling till he filled his whole vision. Then came the release, the gush of smoke followed a fraction of a heartbeat later by the impact of the bullet, and after that only cold, black night.

'Here, drink this, Tom,' said Preston as he returned and placed a glass into the marine's hand. Macpherson took the drink. Droplets of rum dripped from it as his unsteady hand approached his mouth. He drank deeply and then choked and spluttered as the fiery spirit snatched at his throat.

'My thanks, Edward,' he coughed. 'I shall be fine now.' He returned the glass to his fellow officer and noticed the concern on his young face. 'It is just a stupid wee thing that has come on to trouble me of late. It started the other day when Faulkner was telling Warwick that damned story about me and the book. I found myself dwelling again on that time

I was shot in St Lucia last year, saving your skin as I recall.'

'But surely you were only lightly wounded that day?' said Preston.

'Oh aye, so I was,' said the marine, rolling his eyes. 'That most amusing of tales which has made its way around the service. The marine saved by the intervention of a romantic novel. I sometimes wish the ball had struck me fairly, as happened to the captain. Perhaps it might then have been easier for me now.'

'Tom, I am not sure I follow you at all,' said the young lieutenant. 'How can you wish to have been injured? The captain almost died of his wound.'

'Because the anguish in the mind is the same!' said Macpherson. 'To my brother officers it is just an amusing tale, but for me it is different. I was certain that I would die that day, book or no book. I still retain the vision of the moment before the bullet struck. I can feel the horror of it even now.' He twisted away from Preston. 'Oh, the shame of it!'

'No, Tom, not shame,' urged the lieutenant. 'We all have our fears, you know. Think how bravely you dealt with the mutineers.'

'Aye, I did,' he conceded. 'I was fine then, and I will doubtless make a passing imitation of a brave man today too,' he said. 'But what if that does not happen? What if today I should fail in my duty? What if I let down my men? How will I ever face all those past generations of Macphersons, highland warriors to a man, as they shake their heads at me and look away?'

'Come, Tom, we must put aside such melancholy thoughts,' said Preston. 'You and I should have been at our posts long ago now. I know you, Thomas, and I have every confidence that you will do your duty this day. You may not know it yet, but I do.' He embraced the marine officer, and after a moment he felt the pressure returned. 'Do you have all you need? I could fetch Blake's sketch book if required, for you to place within your tunic?' Macpherson broke off to smile at this.

'Get away with you, puppy,' he replied. 'Truly you have my thanks, Edward. I shall be fine now.'

*****

The *Titan* had left Dingle Bay and was once more out in the Atlantic, sailing north parallel with the coast that lay a mile off her starboard beam. The landscape that slid past them was dramatic in its rocky splendour. The sea cliffs here were even taller. They rose straight up out of the water and soared to the height of the ship's topmasts before they softened into a sloped wall of grass and scree that rose higher still towards a mountainous summit. The Atlantic thundered against the base of the cliffs, the sound counterpointed by the deep roar of heavy guns being fired somewhere close at hand.

'I beg your pardon, Mr Warwick,' said Clay. 'Would you say that again?' He moved closer to the ship's master.

'I said that yonder peak is named Mount Brandon on the chart, sir,' he repeated. 'The bay that Murphy spoke of is on the far side of this peninsular. We should be able to round the point that lies ahead there and enter it shortly.'

'Thank you, Mr Warwick,' said Clay. 'Any navigational hazards I should be aware of?'

'None marked on the chart, sir,' he replied. 'The water is plenty deep enough for us, with good holding ground should we need to anchor. There is a beach at the bottom of the bay and a little settlement named Cloghane, if that is the proper manner to pronounce it.'

'Let us hope we shall arrive in time to make some difference,' said the captain.

'What do you believe we shall find, sir?' asked Warwick. Clay smiled at the older man.

'I expect to find five enemy frigates attempting to land troops and supplies, and the *Indefatigable* and the *Concord* doing their damnedest to thwart them. I hope that we may arrive in time to aid them in their endeavour. My fear is that they will have been overwhelmed by the numbers that oppose them, and that we shall be too late.'

'The ship is cleared for action, sir,' reported Taylor as he appeared on his other side. He touched his hat to his captain, and Clay returned the compliment.

'Thank you, Mr Taylor,' he said. He looked around the crowded quarterdeck as if noticing the change that had occurred there for the first time. The space was now packed with humanity. The quarterdeck thirty-two pounder carronades were all manned. They had short but very broad barrels which gave them an odd, squat appearance when compared with the more elegant cannon with their eight feet of gently tapered barrel on the main deck. Between the gun crews stood groups of scarlet coated marines, muskets by their sides, while clustered around the wheel were his officers. The first lieutenant and master had been joined by young Preston and Macpherson, looking pale but determined as he stared towards the land.

'Does it remind you of home, Tom?' asked Clay.

'Aye, sir,' replied the marine. 'It does a wee bit. But you would need to add a coat of rich purple heather to the mountainside if you truly wished to compete with the majesty of the glens.'

'And perhaps some mist and rain to mask the view?' added his captain.

'That too, sir,' agreed Macpherson with a brief smile.

'We can make our turn about the headland now, sir,' said the ship's master.

'Take us around it then, Mr Warwick,' ordered Clay. 'Once we have made the turn reduce our sail to fighting trim.'

'Aye aye, sir,' he replied. Clay picked up his telescope and turned towards the first lieutenant.

'Mr Taylor, would you accompany me to the forecastle?' he said. 'Let us see what manner of battle is raging beyond the headland.' The two officers walked forward up the gangway towards the bow. The sound of gun fire was loud now, and wisps of powder smoke trailed across the water. Taylor began to hurry, conscious that the ship was already beginning to turn around the point and into the bay.

'Steady there, George,' muttered Clay out of the side of his mouth. 'The people are watching us.' Taylor glanced down onto the main deck. A sea of faces looked back at him, grouped in clusters around each gun, while little wisps of smoke rose like steam from the gun captain's linstocks.

On the forecastle it was a little less crowded than the quarterdeck. The boatswain stood at the head of a party of the *Titan*'s more competent seamen, ready to deal with any shot damage his precious rigging might suffer. He lifted his hat to the officers, revealing his thick grey hair scraped into its usual pigtail.

'Good day to you, Mr Hutchinson,' said Clay.

'It will be, sir, once we get to grips with them Frogs,' he replied. The crews of the forecastle's pair of thirty-two pounder carronades growled at this, and their captain smiled in response before he continued forward to the rail and opened his telescope.

The frigate was turning quickly now, swinging around the rocky headland with increased speed as the wind settled onto her quarter. The point of the cape slipped away behind them, and a moment later the whole battle was laid out before them. Perhaps a little over a mile away was a blazing volcano of fire and thick gun smoke that swirled up in a column above a cluster of three ships. Clay looked here first. He settled the disc of his telescope on the heart of the inferno, where he could read the gold letters that spelt out *Indefatigable* across the stern of the centre ship. Pellew was locked in battle with a French frigate on each side effectively sandwiching his ship between them. Tongues of flame spat out from the big British frigate in both directions, while the French ships thundered away at their opponent.

A little farther on, in the centre of the bay was the smaller *Concord*. She was closely engaged by a single French opponent. This battle seemed to be going Warburton's way. The French ship had lost its mizzen mast and much of its main one too. The wreck of spars and canvas that drooped down across her stern had pulled the French frigate around so that most of her guns could to no longer bear on the *Concord.*

'I only count three French frigates,' said Clay.

'The other two are anchored at the end of the bay, sir,' replied Taylor. 'They carry no sail, which makes them harder to observe. Just off that beach that lies beyond the *Concord.* They seem to be unloading troops with their boats. See, there are more soldiers assembled ashore.' Clay looked in the direction his first lieutenant had indicated and saw the two black and white hulls. They swung at anchor with their bare spars blending against the hills behind them. The wind that was blowing the *Titan* on into the bay had pushed them around till they were bow on to him.

'Yes I have them now,' he said. As he watched a fresh boat left the side of one of them, packed with men. It made its insect-like progress towards the shore where he could just see some blocks of soldiers formed up on the sand alongside piles of supplies.

'I wish the French would wear scarlet like our troops,' he grumbled. 'Till you drew my attention to them I had quite lost their dark blue coats against the green of the land.'

'That might make for a deal of confusion when the armies come to fight each other, sir,' commented the first lieutenant.

'Perhaps you are right, Mr Taylor,' grunted Clay, and then closed his telescope. 'So what do you make of what you see?'

The older man looked at the scene ahead of him and rubbed a hand over his chin.

'I should say that the French were busy unloading their men when the commodore rounded the headland, much as we did, sir,' he said. 'He tried to intervene, but those two ships he is engaging stood out to head him off.' Clay nodded at him.

'I agree,' he said. 'Then Captain Warburton would have been ordered to skirt around that fight to try and stop the landings, but was intercepted in his turn. Meanwhile the other two French ships are continuing to land their men.'

'So what should we do, sir?' asked Taylor. Clay took a final look at the scene.

'Those two French frigates will join the fight as soon as they have completed what they are about,' he said. 'That will turn matters decisively in the enemy's favour. What we must do is ensure that we have defeated the other three before that can happen. The *Concord* has her opponent almost beat. Let us come to the aid of the *Indefatigable*.'

*****

'I reckon they likes the look of your green hills almost as much as what you does, Sean,' said Trevan, indicating the captain and first lieutenant as they walked back along the gangway above his head towards the quarterdeck once more. 'They've been staring out at the bay for ages, like.'

'I can't see what needs so much puzzling over,' grumbled Evans. He peered forward through the open gun port and pointed. 'It's bleeding obvious. Them two Frog ships ahead are giving the old *Indy* a right seeing too. Let's get stuck into them.'

'Fecking right,' agreed O'Malley, crouching down so he could see too. 'Look! She's just after losing her foretopmast. Mind, she's dishing out plenty with them fecking great twenty-four pounders.' He rubbed his hands at the prospect of action. 'Come on! Let it be our side of the ship that faces towards the enemy.'

'Amen to that,' said Rosso. He gave the linstock he carried a fierce whirl above his head till the end glowed angry red in the rushing air. 'Remember the scrap with that *Couraguese* when we was back on the *Agrius*, and all the fighting was happening on the other side of the ship?'

'God, yes,' said Evans. 'We had nought to bleeding well do for hours, except get picked off one by one like pigs at the slaughter house. Remember poor old Drinkwater?' The others fell quiet at the recollection of their former gun captain. He had been crouched over the barrel of their gun fussing away one moment and killed in an instant by a cannon ball the next.

'Larboard side!' yelled Lieutenant Blake from his place beside the main mast. 'Run out the guns!'

'That's us!' crowed Rosso. 'Man the tackles there, lads. Run out!' The deck vibrated beneath the men's bare feet as they strained to send the huge canon rumbling forward till the brick red gun carriage thumped against the ship's side.

'Gun captains! Have your quoins fully in!' ordered the lieutenant. Rosso stepped to one side and looked down at the wedge under the back of the barrel to check that it was in place, holding the gun level at minimum elevation.

'No messing around with fancy shooting at range, then,' said O'Malley, rubbing his hands together once more. 'Wade straight into the middle of the fecking brawl, lads, that's the way.'

The frigate sailed onwards, and as she did the roar of the battle between the three ships ahead became ever louder. Evans tried to crane his neck to peer forward but could see nothing but lapping water and distant mountains out of the square gun port. On and on the *Titan* came. The thunder of heavy guns had grown to be almost deafening now. Trevan pulled his bandana on a little more securely. Evans was passing the gun's rammer from one hand to the other. O'Malley went to spit on his hands, only to find that his mouth was too dry.

'Fecking hell,' he muttered to himself. Rosso stood upright and sniffed the air, his nose held high.

'Can you smell that?' he asked. The others tested the air too.

'Oh aye, Rosie,' said Trevan. 'That's gun smoke, or I ain't never smelt it. We must be close.'

'I always think it smells of eggs as have gone off,' added Evans.

'Back home Father O'Connell used to tell us that the Devil smelt that way,' said O'Malley. 'And how we would all find the truth of it firsthand unless we confessed our sins regular like.'

'Bloody Hell, Sean!' exclaimed Evans. 'Just how long had this O'Connell bloke got? It would take at least a week for you to confess all your fights, two more for fornication, three for drunkenness and God knows how bleeding long for foul language!' The others were still laughing at this when a volley of orders was shouted from behind them and the ship began to turn. The figure of Clay appeared at the quarterdeck rail behind them.

'You may open fire as your guns bear, Mr Blake,' he shouted down. 'Then keep hammering away as fast as ever you can.'

The friends crouched back down around their cannon. Rosso held one arm aloft to show that they were ready to fire. He glanced along the sweep of the deck and saw a line of other raised hands. He knocked the ash from the slow match of his linstock and blew hard on the glowing end. Then he returned his attention to the square of sea in front of him. He could see tendrils of smoke that clung to the water as they passed through them. Then the colour of the sea changed as a dark shadow fell across it and finally the back of a frigate appeared not thirty yards away. It was painted in bright blue with beautiful gilded decorations swirling across it. Sunlight light sparkled back at him from the gold leaf. On each side of the stern was a large carved figure of bulging muscles and draped cloth that seemed to be straining to hold up the rail that ran across the back of the ship. Right in front of him was a curved line of seven glass window lights, beneath which was painted the name of the ship in capital letters. The *Titan* drifted to a halt, giving him plenty of time to see the name. *Immortalite*. Rosso read the name out loud for the benefit of the others. He had just time to think how beautiful their opponent looked when Blake shouted the order.

'Open fire!' roared the lieutenant.

'Stand clear!' warned Rosso. He stepped to one side out of the path of the recoil and dabbed the linstock down on the touchhole. It spluttered for a moment and then the gun leapt backwards and the French frigate disappeared as a curtain of thick smoke towered up over the ship. Now their long hours of training bore fruit in a swirl of well drilled movement around the smoking gun. The moment the cannon came to a halt with a groan of protest from the breaching, Evans thrust the wet sponge end of his rammer down the barrel. There was a hiss of steam as the few glowing fragments from the last round were extinguished. The moment the sponge was clear O'Malley thrust the bulky charge bag into the barrel, while Evans spun the rammer round and with the dry end drove the charge home. Ball followed charge and wad followed ball, each stage accompanied by Evans working the rammer to push the item home. The gun was run out again with a thump against the side and Rosso stepped forward with his metal spike. He pushed it down the touch hole till he felt the sharp barb at its end pierce the canvas of the charge bag. Then he pulled the spike free and pushed a quill of fine powder down the touch hole in its place.

'Stand clear!' he yelled, and a bare forty seconds after the first broadside they sent another huge ball into their helpless opponent.

*****

'Glorious, simply glorious,' spluttered Taylor as the second broadside smashed into the stern of the *Immortalite*. A brief gap in the wall of gun smoke revealed the back of the

French frigate, the beautiful gilded figures smashed, the deep blue paintwork riddled with jagged holes. By some fluke one of the windows had survived intact. Of the other six, not a trace of glass remained. 'Did you ever see such a raking?' he continued. 'I swear that every ball will have travelled down her entire length, and with not a shot in reply!'

'Glorious indeed, Mr Taylor,' said Clay, who was stood next to him. 'She must have been so intent on her battle with the *Indefatigable* she cannot have seen our approach. A few more minutes of such rough handling and she is sure to strike her colours.'

He looked across at his opponent and noted that she still had a little fight left in her. Her large tricolour may have had a portion of its red fly ripped away, but it still flapped from her rigging. Along her side he could see the occasional orange flash in the smoke as the few of her cannon that were still firing continued to batter the commodore's flagship. For their part, the crew of the *Indefatigable* seemed to have hit a second wind at the unexpected turn of events. They had abandoned the guns facing the *Immortalite* and were now concentrating on their other foe. A cliff of smoke and fire reared up on that side of the big frigate.

Next to him on the quarterdeck one of the big carronades shot back down its slide, grey smoke pouring from its gaping mouth. The hull of their opponent disappeared once more behind clouds of gun smoke, but he could still see the tops of her masts as they soared up proud of the reek. Then the silhouette began to shift. The central main mast moved a little to one side. The movement checked for a moment, still held up by the other masts, but then the fore topmast gave way too and with a rush the whole mass crashed down across the *Indefatigable* in a welter of torn canvas and broken spars. Another broadside roared out from the *Titan.* Clay noticed that the timing had become a little ragged as the quicker crews outpaced the slower, but the effect on their crippled opponent was much the same. When the smoke cleared a little Clay saw the French tricolour was making its jerky way down towards the quarterdeck. Clay glanced across at Taylor, who pulled out his whistle to order the ceasefire.

A storm of cheers erupted across the main deck of the *Titan.* Joy mingled freely with relief at the ease of their victory. Men slapped each other's backs and leant across the smoking barrels of their guns to touch knuckles. Clay ignored the men and watched as the gentle wind tore at the banks of gun smoke and rolled them farther down the bay. Gradually the wrecks of the three frigates, all locked together under masses of fallen masts, emerged from the grey fog. Clay was about to order the *Titan* to bear down on the second French frigate when he realised that the firing there had ceased too. The cheers from his crew were being faintly echoed by the crew of the *Indefatigable.* Then the initial exuberance of the crew faded away as they contemplated the carnage before them.

None of the three ships had more than one mast left standing. On the second French frigate some of the wreckage had caught fire. He could see members of her crew as they hacked away at the blazing mass, their axe blades points of silver that flashed in the watery sun. All of the ships' hulls were blackened with gun smoke and had holes torn in them. The stern of the *Immortalite* had been beaten open into a cavern out of which drifted the cries of the French wounded.

The figure of the commodore appeared at the stern rail of the *Indefatigable*. His hat was missing, replaced by a swath of white cloth tied around his head, but he seemed otherwise unharmed. He leveled a speaking trumpet across the strip of water that separated the ships.

'Captain Clay?' he asked, with his distinctive Cornish accent.

'Sir Edward,' replied the *Titan*'s captain through his own speaking trumpet, 'I give you joy of your victory.' The figure of Pellew waved a dismissive hand.

'We shall have plenty of time for crowing when the battle is truly over,' he hailed. 'What state is your ship in?'

'Quite untouched, Sir Edward,' replied Clay. 'How does the *Indefatigable* fare?'

'Sore wounded, I fear,' he said. 'Several guns dismounted, two foot of water in the well and rising, and until we can clear all this wreckage and set up some jury masts there is no prospect of us playing any further part in the action. I shall secure these two prizes here, but I will be able to contribute little further. You must tackle those other two frigates with what help you can obtain from Captain Warburton.'

'Aye aye, sir,' he replied. 'Do you require any assistance? I could send across my boatswain with some hands.'

'My thanks for that handsome offer, but we shall do very well,' he replied. 'Besides, I fancy you may need the services of every man before this day is done. Good luck to you, Clay.'

Chapter 17

Titan

Clay watched from the front of the quarterdeck as the excitement of the crew was replaced by the calm return of discipline. Just below him on the main deck Blake had called all the portside gun captains over and had them gathered in a ring around him.

'Now pay attention, men,' he said. 'You have done well so far. I never witnessed eighteen pounders handled so brisk, but this battle is far from over. We have perhaps ten minutes before we shall be back in action, and we must use that time as profitably as we are able. Chiefly you must all reload your guns with care, for it will be passing strange if a step was not missed in the heat of the action. Then look over your crew's equipment as if it were a fresh battle to see all is still as it should be.'

'My gun's rammer has sprung, sir,' said one of the men. 'I have lashed it together, but it has a crack as runs right down the side of it.'

'Mr Butler!' said Blake. 'Go and find Mr Rudgewick. Give

the gunner my compliments and can he issue you with a new rammer for number eleven gun.'

'Aye aye, sir,' said the midshipman, and he hurried off below.

'Any other problems?' asked the lieutenant, looking around him. 'Good. Once that is done you can let your crews get a drink from the scuttle butts. Off back to your guns, now.'

'Mr Blake starts to become a valuable officer, does he not, sir?' said a voice from beside him.

'Yes he does, Mr Taylor,' agreed Clay. 'I was just musing to myself how strange it is that I had not noticed his true character and abilities until after the mutiny.'

'I had a similar thought in the wardroom a few days ago,' replied the first lieutenant. 'It was Mr Corbett who pointed out to me what had truly changed.' Clay looked at him in surprise.

'Really?' he said. 'What observations did the surgeon have to offer?'

'That I should consider who was absent rather than present sir,' said Taylor. 'It is only with Mr Morton's unfortunate departure that young Blake has been able to emerge from under his rather domineering shadow.'

'Yes, I believe you may have the truth of it,' said Clay. 'What a sad thought. Still, let us not be distracted by any such philosophical diversions. For now it is enough for us to know that the command of the great guns is in sound hands. Let us consider how the next part of this battle will proceed.'

The *Titan* had pushed on into the heart of the bay now,

with the mountainous green hills in a wide loop around them. Long fingers of gun smoke advanced across the water with her, driven by the same gentle breeze that pushed her on. Ahead of them, at the end of the bay, the two unengaged French warships still lay at anchor. He could see their boats were busy as they continued to ferry soldiers to the beach. Off to one side the fight between the *Concord* and her opponent was over. The French ship had struck her colours and looked to be in a similar battered state to the three ships behind them, while the British frigate had come through the fight with all her masts intact.

'Mr Russell,' he said. 'Can you send this signal to the *Concord* if you please. "Am engaging the remaining enemy. Are you able to assist?"'

'Aye aye, sir,' said the midshipman. He wrote down the signal on his slate, his tongue pink and prominent in the corner of his mouth as he concentrated. Clay watched Warburton's ship, looking for signs that she was making sail to join him. A long stream of coloured signal flags rose up her mizzen mast in response.

'That is strange,' said Taylor. 'I was expecting a simple "yes".'

'Signal from *Concord* to *Titan* sir. "Am repairing damage and securing prize. Will assist when able",' translated Russell.

'Fat bloody use that is, sir,' grumbled the first lieutenant. 'How long will all that take him?'

'Her rigging may be cut up worse than is apparent at this range, Mr Taylor,' said Clay. 'Meanwhile let us see how we may best engage those two ahead of us. We shall at least have the weather gauge whilst this wind continues to blow from us towards them.'

'One of the Frogs is signalling, sir,' said Preston. Clay turned his attention back to the two ships ahead. The frigate on the right had a line of what looked like bunting flying from her, the flags barely visible with the wind blowing them away from him. He turned his attention to the other ship. A lone flag rose up from her quarterdeck in response from her consort.

'So the bigger one on the right is in command, sir,' said Taylor. 'A month's pay says that signal was an order to get underway, and the single flag is an acknowledgement.'

'No takers, Mr Taylor,' said his captain. 'The real question is whether they mean to come out and fight us, or will they try to cut and run?'

'Right hand one is making sail now, sir,' said Preston.

The two enemy ships were still bow on to them. On board the leader the clean lines of her shrouds thickened as a rush of men poured up them and made their way out along the yards, spaced like beads on a string. From beneath the topsail yard a slip of white appeared, swelling as the canvas sail was unfurled, till it dropped like a curtain into a large square of white against the green fields behind.

'Ship on the right is in a perishing hurry, sir,' said Taylor. 'Did you see that splash? They have cut their anchor loose rather than pull it home. The other ship has not even sent anyone aloft yet.'

Freed of its anchor, the larger French frigate swung

around and the shape of the bow lengthened into her long hull. The other two masts appeared from behind the foremast, with topsails set on them too, all braced around as she beat against the wind. She gathered speed and began to claw her way out towards the *Titan*.

'I think I recognise that frigate, sir,' said Preston. 'See how the main mast is stepped a little aft of where one might expect? Is it not the one that was stationed in Bertheaume Bay after we cut out the brig?'

'Yes, perhaps you are right,' said Clay, moving his glass from one ship to the other. 'One of Mr Blake's eels. He is certainly eager to come at us. The other ship is only now starting to make sail. Any sign of the *Concord* coming to our aid, Mr Preston?' The young lieutenant strode over to the rear of the quarterdeck and looked across the growing length of water between them and Captain Warburton's ship. He returned to join the others.

'Still locked yard arm to yard arm with her prize, sir,' he reported. 'I can't imagine what will be taking them so long.'

'Can't you, Mr Preston?' asked Taylor, one eye brow raised.

'No matter, gentlemen,' said Clay. 'We shall do very well, even if we have to shift for ourselves.'

'Against two untouched frigates, sir?' queried Taylor. 'One of which is much superior to us in size?'

'The *Indefatigable* has just defeated two such opponents,' said Preston.

'The *Indefatigable* is much larger than us and has the advantage of twenty-four pounders on her main deck, Mr

Preston,' said Taylor.

'We have already defeated one Frenchman today,' said the young lieutenant. The older man raised both of his eye brows at this.

'Mr Preston,' he protested. 'We despatched a badly damaged opponent who was unable to fire back! It was done ably, I grant you, but that is hardly the same as...'

'Gentlemen, please,' said Clay lowering his telescope. 'Diverting as all this is, can you kindly attend to what our enemy is about?' The two lieutenants muttered an apology, reopened their telescopes and focussed them back towards the approaching ships.

'The lead ship is still coming on very bold, sir,' said Preston. 'Look at that. A tricolour flying from every mast. Fair spoiling for a fight, I should say.'

'Her consort seems a little more shy, sir,' reported Taylor. 'She means to recover her anchor properly before coming against us. Do you suppose her captain might be a distant relative of Captain Warburton?' Clay snorted back a laugh, before looking with care around the bay.

'So how shall we fashion a victory from the elements of this messy battle, gentlemen?' asked Clay. He pointed back towards where the stricken *Indefatigable* still lay between the two prizes. A haze of dispersing gun smoke masked the cluster of damaged ships. 'The commodore we can ignore. Even at this distance we can see that they have made little progress with cutting themselves free.' The two officers nodded at this.

'What about the *Concord,* sir?' asked Preston. Taylor

snorted at this.

'Still drifting around hopelessly locked to her opponent,' he said. 'We shall have precious little help from that quarter.'

'Agreed, so we must shape to fight this battle alone,' said the captain, returning his attention to their opponents. 'We have at least forced them to abandon their troop landings.'

'That bold leader is close now, sir,' said Preston. 'Why, the other has yet to raise her anchor. Look at the gap that has opened up between them now.'

'So it has,' said Clay. 'That gap will serve us very handsomely. Mr Taylor is right. Two opponents together will be too hot for us. So we shall take our fences one after the other. Let us close with and defeat the first ship before then turning on her consort.'

'How long do you suppose we have to achieve that, sir?' said Taylor, eyeing the two ships.

'The second is only now winning her anchor, sir,' said Preston. 'Then she must cover the distance between us, all against the wind. Twenty minutes for sure, perhaps more.'

'More like fifteen, I should say,' said Taylor.

'Fifteen minutes, you think?' repeated Clay. He snapped shut his telescope. 'The way the men have been shooting today, that is time for twenty broadsides. It will be tight, gentlemen, but it shall answer well enough. Mr Taylor!'

'Sir!' answered the first lieutenant.

'Lay us on a course to intercept the first of those Frenchmen,' he ordered. 'Take us in good and close, broadside to broadside if you please. We have no leisure for fancy manoeuvres today.'

'Aye aye, sir,' he replied. He touched his hat in salute and bustled away to lay the ship on the right course.

Clay walked forward to the quarterdeck rail and glanced down onto the packed main deck. A feeling of déjà vu made him pause. He looked around him, trying to place what had triggered it. For a moment the lines of the ship about him seemed more familiar to him than normal. He looked to his left at the solid column of the main mast, and then to the right at the line of halliards belayed onto the rail and soaring upwards in straight lines. Then he realised that he was standing in the exact same spot as he had been on that grey, cold morning in Plymouth, when he first took over the mutinous ship. Still the same beautiful lines of geometry in the rigging, but none to be seen amongst the men. They were clustered around their guns, fussing to have everything just right for the coming battle, or hauling the yards around in response to the ship's change in course. He looked over them and took in the calm unhurried efficiency with which they worked. Then faces began to turn to look back up at him. Individuals nudged their neighbours and pointed. Little by little all activity came to a halt and it dawned on Clay that they expected him to say something. He shifted from one foot to the other. He had nothing prepared. The moment stretched on, the French frigate loomed closer but still no words of inspiration came to him. He realised now that he had waited there too long, and he had to say something. For the umpteenth time in his career he wished again that he had the easy familiarity with speeches that so many other captains seemed to have. He closed his eyes for a moment, took a deep breath, and decided to just say what was in his heart.

'Shipmates,' he began, quiet at first, which made the men lean forwards to hear him properly. 'I have just been reflecting on what a long way we have come since I first took command of our ship. That day, back in Plymouth I stood here, on this very spot, and I looked out over a ship full of anger and hate and division. But what a change we have wrought to our ship. Now when I look at you, I see a fine crew of steady men all ready for action. There ahead of us is our enemy,' he pointed at the mass of masts and rigging that loomed ever closer. 'Two ships to our one, yet I have no doubt who shall triumph in this battle. For while they have been sulking in Brest these last few years, growing fatter and slower week by week, we have been out at sea, battling with storms and training hard for this day. They come against us like the lubbers they are, one rushes ahead while the other struggles even to raise an anchor. We shall destroy the first enemy before the second has time to draw near. Do your duty. Fire as fast as I know you can. Aim as true as you are able. Trust in your fellow *Titans*, and may God watch over you.'

'Three cheers for Pipe!' yelled a voice, and a storm of noise engulfed the ship.

*****

'Here we go again, Tom,' said Preston. 'Once more unto the breach, dear friends.' The young lieutenant had gone to stand next to the marine at the back of the quarterdeck. This gave them both a good view of the enemy frigates as they bore down on them. The second ship had just got under way, her anchor at last pulled free of the seabed. The first ship was much closer as she continued to claw her way up wind towards them. Taylor was conning the *Titan* in a long sweeping turn that would bring them onto the same course as their opponent in the next few minutes.

'Once more indeed, Edward,' said Macpherson, his voice quiet. 'It is good of you to come and see me like this, but I am quite restored, really. A touch of colic was all it was earlier.' Preston looked the older man up and down and saw that his hand still trembled a little by his side. The Scot noticed where his friend's eyes rested and clasped his hands together out of sight behind his back.

'You did seem a little ill earlier,' he said.

'But now I am quite fine,' said the marine. 'The captain addressed the men well, I thought. It surprised me to hear him speak with such passion. I had not thought of him as a man much given to oratory.'

'Nor is he,' said Preston. 'But it informed the men what they need to do well enough. Do you suppose we can knock down this fellow before the other ship comes up with us?'

'If the French are foolish enough to let us come at them from close range, perhaps,' said the Scot. 'My fear is they will haul off and take pot shots from range until they can both engage us together.' The two men watched their opponent as the ships' courses converged. The French frigate had grown very close now. The long broad white stripe that ran down her side changed into a checkerboard as her gun ports swung up, and a line of heavy cannon came poking out. All along her rail they could see the glitter of sunlight on weapons.

'She seems to be carrying a large crew,' commented Preston. His companion shook his head.

'That is the glitter of bayonets, or I have never seen any,' replied Macpherson. 'She must still have a good deal of those soldiers she was carrying on board. We must go and warn the captain to be wary of her trying to use them to take us.'

'But surely this is good news?' said the young lieutenant. 'If her plan is to try and board us, she will not keep her distance as you feared.'

'Perhaps so,' said Macpherson. 'But if she is carrying several hundred extra soldiers, she might overwhelm us in such an encounter. Will you go and speak with the captain? I should stay here with my men.' Once Preston had gone, Macpherson returned his attention to the French frigate. They were within easy cannon shot, and the range was dropping all the time. Then the side of the French ship lit up with tongues of orange flame, masked an instant later by a wall of smoke. Splashes leaped up all about the *Titan*, and several shots ripped over the deck of the frigate with a noise like tearing cloth. Moments later the sound of the broadside boomed across to him.

Macpherson glanced around the mizzen mast to check for damage, but could only see a few severed lines and a single ragged hole in one of the sails. From the bow came the gravelly voice of Hutchinson, the boatswain, directing his men to repair the damage to the rigging. If their opponent was as woeful in their shooting as this, he thought, there was hope for them yet. He returned to his place next to his sergeant and glanced over his men. All were alert, waiting for the order to open fire. The French frigate was much closer now. Her masts began to tower up above him. Her hull stretched across his vision. Up in her fighting tops he could see her parties of marines. He could almost feel their eyes as they looked towards him, picking him out in his brilliant red tunic, stood in his place beside his men. He felt beads of sweat forming on his brow, and his right hand began to tremble once more.

'Closer still, Mr Taylor,' he heard the captain call. 'Mr Blake! Standby to open fire.' Another broadside roared out from the Frenchman. Much of it poured into the sea behind the Titan, but some of the shot was better aimed. He heard a pair of solid crashes from somewhere forward as balls struck home and more shot flew past overhead. The ships came even closer together.

'Open fire, if you please, Mr Blake,' ordered Clay.

'Wait for the down roll,' shouted the lieutenant to his gunners. A small wave rocked the frigate, and as the ship leant towards the enemy the *Titan*'s guns roared out. The deafening noise of the broadside was followed an instant later by a storm of crashes from somewhere in the smoke as the well directed broadside thundered home.

'Marines,' yelled Macpherson, his voice cracking. 'You may open fire at any targets that may present themselves.'

Now the *Titan* and her foe disappeared into a grey world of chaos. The gun smoke of both ships intermingled to create a thick bank of fog, with only the stabbing tongues of flame from each side's cannon to show where their ship lay. Macpherson could tell that the *Titan* was firing much faster than her opponent. Her first broadside had followed close on the heels of the French ship's second, but her next seemed to draw no fire from the other ship, and it was only when she fired her third broadside that a ragged response came home from the Frenchman. He watched Taylor as he conned the ship. The first lieutenant barked an order to spill some wind from the mizzen topsail as he strove to keep the frigate level with the line of gun flashes of their opponent.

He winced as a cannon ball punched through the quarterdeck gunwale in front of him in a spray of splinters. Moments later a second ball ploughed through one of the carronade crews. Two men fell in succession like dominos. One had been killed in an instant. The other sat upright on the deck and stared in disbelief at his shattered foot. Macpherson found his eyes held by those of the stricken sailor. His gaze was wide-eyed with shock, seeking reassurance from the marine officer.

'You two there,' he called across two members of the afterguard, his voice gruff with strain. 'Take him below to the surgeon.'

Now his marines began to take casualties too as the ships drifted closer. Lines of little orange flames flashed out from the heart of the smoke. Macpherson realised that the soldiers on board the French frigate must be firing volleys of musket fire back at him. Balls whined past his head and a marine spun back from the rail, dropping his musket with a clatter. His hands clawed at a spurting wound in his neck. The Scot dropped to his knees beside the man and tried to hold back the tide of blood that ran hot through his fingers. He watched the soldier's eyes slip from desperation as he clung to life into a blank stare as he died. Macpherson let the dead man's body slip back down onto the deck. He rose to his feet and felt his whole body start to tremble. He closed his eyes for a moment and the French soldier sprang back at him again, dark and huge, swinging his musket round to settle his aim on Macpherson's heart. He jerked his eyes open before the shot could be fired. Stop this, he urged himself. He forced his legs to pace up and down the deck. Another line of little orange flashes stabbed out, much nearer this time. The ships have drifted very close, he thought. He hurried forward to warn the captain.

'Tom, are you wounded?' asked Clay. He looked with alarm at the Scotsman's pale face and blood-sodden hands.

'What?' said Macpherson. 'Oh, no, sir. This is not my blood. I have been tending to one of my men who had been shot. I wanted to warn you that the French have come very close. They have the advantage of a large number of soldiers, and I fear they mean to try and board us in the smoke.'

'Yes, Mr Preston told me of your misgivings,' said Clay. He strode across to the ship's side and stared towards their enemy. At that moment another of the *Titan*'s broadsides crashed out, the sound of it striking home almost instantaneous, the ships had drawn so near to each other. One of the balls hit a French gun barrel with a deep clang like that of a struck bell. No more than a handful of cannons fired in return from their opponent, the flashes close in the fog of smoke.

'They are certainly very close to us,' said Clay. 'Their return fire has been petering out in the last few minutes, which may show that they are bringing up their gun crews from below in order to board us. Perhaps this will give us the opportunity to deliver the final blow.' He turned back towards the marine. 'Are you sure of what you say, Tom?'

'Sure as I can be, sir.' Clay held his gaze for a moment and then called towards the midshipman of the watch who still stood by the wheel.

'Mr Russell! Tell Mr Blake to have the guns elevated to their maximum and loaded with canister. He is to await my signal to fire. Run, boy!'

'Aye aye, sir,' came the reply, and the teenager fled for the companionway ladder.

'Mr Preston!' I will have the quarterdeck carronades loaded with canister too,' ordered the captain. 'Keep her on this heading, Mr Taylor, if you please.'

'Aye aye, sir,' replied the first lieutenant.

Clay stepped away from the side and stared up towards the foremast. The gentle breeze had begun to tear away at the gun smoke, revealing the state of the frigate's rigging. Macpherson followed his captain's gaze. A large gash had been torn in the side of the mast, the splintered wood white in the weak sun, and one of the upper yards on the main mast had been shot through. He could see Harrison high up in the rigging as he lead a party of seaman to secure the damage. But apart from the numerous shot holes in the sails, and the many lines that swung free, the masts were still largely undamaged.

'Masthead there!' yelled Clay. 'Any sign of the other enemy frigate?'

'Deck there! Two points off the starboard beam sir, and beating up the bay towards us,' came the reply.

'How distant is she?' asked the captain. The little figure

high on the mast paused to consider matters before he replied.

'Maybe half a mile, sir.'

'Half a mile, gentlemen,' said Clay. 'We need to finish this first opponent quickly, before the second frigate can arrive to spoil matters. Let us hope that you are right, Mr Macpherson, and our enemy is gathering her crew with all these soldiers of yours on their gangways ready to take us. If so, they will present a fine target for a full broadside of canister.'

'Will the guns answer to stop them all, sir?' asked Macpherson. Clay indicated the nearest of the quarterdeck thirty two pounder carronades. Two of the crew struggled to slot a heavy copper cylinder down the barrel.

'That one round there contains five hundred musket balls,' he said. 'The blast will sweep all before it who are in the open, but it will have precious little effect on men that are stood behind six inches of oak. If the French are indeed intent on boarding us, it will serve very well.' At that moment Russell came running up the companionway ladder from the main deck.

'Mr Blake's compliments, and the guns are loaded and ready, sir,' he said.

'Thank you, Mr Russell,' replied the captain. 'Kindly tell him that the moment the guns have fired he is to send his gun crews up to board the enemy. Mr Macpherson, please gather your marines on the quarterdeck ready to board too. We shall give them a whiff of canister, and then pay the French back in their own coin.'

'Aye aye, sir,' replied the marine.

Clay returned his attention to their opponent. Both sides had stopped firing now, and without the regular flashes in the smoke it was hard to make out where the French ship was. He angled his head on one side to try and catch any faint sounds in the gloom. The creak of rigging from the other frigate seemed to be only yards away. Then he heard a shouted order in French. Someone close to the bow shouted back 'Oui, mon capitaine!' Overall came a continuous murmur, the accumulation of many little sounds. It was the noise generated by a restless crowd of people. The smoke thinned a little in the breeze, and shapes began to appear in the gloom. He saw one of the Frenchman's masts, strange and misshapen with its upper half hanging down in a mass of torn rigging and shattered wood. Then a portion of their opponent's hull was visible, riddled with holes where their remorseless broadsides had smashed home. At one shattered gun port a gun barrel poked out at a strange angle, its barrel pointing up towards the sky. Clay turned his head and called over his shoulder towards the wheel.

'Back the foretopsail if you please, Mr Taylor,' he said. 'I want to drift closer to her.'

'Aye aye, sir,' replied his first lieutenant.

The last of the smoke slid clear and Clay could see there was no more than forty yards of water between the two ships, the gap shrinking all the time.

'My God, we have hit her hard, sir,' exclaimed Preston from beside him. The hull of the French ship was pockmarked all over with holes torn by the *Titan*'s gunfire. In addition to having lost much of her foremast, her mizzen mast had gone too, leaving only a shattered stump to mark where it had once been. From below her deck he could hear a chorus of groans from her many wounded.

But there was still fight in their enemy. All along her side the sunlight glinted and flashed off the numerous weapons that were brandished in defiance. Some of the soldiers had placed their cockaded hats over the ends of their muskets, and waved them in the air as if they were flags. Mixed in amongst the troops were the remaining members of her crew armed with cutlasses and boarding pikes. Other sailors had climbed a short way up into her shot-torn rigging and swung grappling hooks backwards and forwards, ready to hurl them across at their opponent. The excited babble of noise that drifted over the water was in stark contrast to the silent approach of the *Titan*.

'They certainly mean to board, sir,' warned Preston.

'Indeed they do,' replied Clay. 'We have guessed right, but I almost wish we had not. What a dreadful waste of life.' He gauged the distance, now down to thirty yards. The ships were so close that Clay could pick out individual expressions amongst the packed faces opposite him. He could see bravado and excitement on some, doubt and fear on others.

'Would you call that range point blank, Mr Preston?' he asked.

'Yes, sir,' murmured the lieutenant, transfixed by how close the enemy ship was.

'Ready, Mr Blake?' shouted Clay.

'Ready, sir,' came the reply from forward.

'Fire!' shouted Clay.

With a deafening crash every gun on the starboard side of the ship fired at the same moment. For an instant the air was alive with a shrieking swarm of noise as thousands of musket balls ripped across the space between the ships. The *Titan* rolled away from her opponent with the recoil of her guns and smoke engulfed them once more. After a pause a mass of men poured up from the main deck with Blake at its head. The gun crews spilt out along the ship's side, armed with their cutlasses and pistols, just at the moment that the French frigate loomed up alongside. The hulls touched with a bump and Clay stared through the haze of smoke at their devastated opponent. Masses of severed rigging hung down from above like jungle creepers, the strands of rope sliced through a few feet above the ship's side. Mutilation and death had come randomly to the packed boarders who had waited to attack them. Where the men had been caught in line with one of the *Titan*'s cannon, they had been swept away in blocks, leaving groups of survivors, stunned but unharmed between the swaths of devastation.

'*Titans*!' yelled Clay. He drew out his sword and climbed up onto the quarterdeck rail. 'Let us finish this now! Boarders away!' With a roar of noise, the crew of his ship swept over the side and spilt down onto their enemy's deck.

*****

The moment that Lieutenant Macpherson had dreaded was at hand. He watched as Clay leapt across the gap between the two ships as easily as a man on a country walk might spring over a ditch. He was followed by Sedgwick, a naked cutlass held high, and then a surging mass of seamen.

He looked across at the other ship. Now the stunned groups of French sailors and soldiers in front of him were returning back to life after the shock of the point blank broadside. Behind him he sensed the unease of his men. He heard his sergeant clear his throat, the sound obvious to him in spite of the din of battle. Come on, he urged himself. It will be fine. How many times have you done this before?

'Marines! F... f... fix bayonets!' he ordered. Why had his voice stuttered over such a simple command? The men moved as a single unit, the double click of thirty bayonets slotting home made one noise. He drew his sword rasping out, and looked down at it for a moment. The blade shook and waved before him like a silver reed, the tremble in his hand amplified by the length of steel. He looked back at the enemy ship, took a deep breath and forced his feet into motion.

'F... follow me!' he heard himself shout, and he clambered up onto the gunwale and jumped across towards the nearest gap ripped in the line of defenders by the blast of the aft most carronade. He almost lost his footing as he landed on the enemy deck. It was choked with fallen Frenchmen, some inert while others tried to writhe away, leaving the planking slick with blood. A sailor lunged at him from one side with a boarding pike. The man thrust the tip towards him like a spear, and his instincts took over. He parried the clumsy blow to one side, and then one of his marines drove his bayonet into the man's side. He watched the sailor reel away backwards and drop his pike as he clutched at his stomach instead, and Macpherson looked around him. All across the deck was a melee of fighting men. A little farther down the ship he could see the huge figure of Evans as he swung his boarding axe about him in the centre of an open circle of reluctant enemies. Behind Evans he could see Blake as he cut and slashed with his sword at a well matched opponent. The young lieutenant thrust his hand deep into his coat pocket and a look of surprise crossed his face. Macpherson remembered the pistol that he had given to Preston because he wouldn't need it. Then the Scotsman's attention was drawn closer at hand as he saw a French soldier turn towards him, and he froze to the spot in terror.

For a moment he thought he must have closed his eyes, so similar was the vision to the one that haunted him. The man seemed to swing his musket around in slow motion and the sound of battle ebbed away. He was so close to Macpherson that he could see every detail of the soldier's thin face, small and almost lost under the dark curve of his hat. The musket was pointing right at him now, the muzzle a black tunnel that seemed to pull him towards it. He saw the man close one eye and sight along the barrel, his head resting over at an angle. The soldier's finger whitened with strain as he pulled the trigger. A spit of fire erupted from the lock and Macpherson waited an age for the shot to come. Nothing. He watched the soldier's eyes swell with disbelief as both men realised that the musket had misfired. Macpherson recognised the same look of shock as he had seen on the face of the sailor who had lost his foot. Relief poured over him as it sunk in that he was unharmed. He took a few rapid strides across the deck and then he was upon the man. He knocked the musket aside with his left arm and ran him through with a cruel thrust from his right. The soldier fell backwards down onto the deck and Macpherson stood over him. His hat had fallen to one side, to reveal lank, greasy hair, a thin line of moustache and a scrawny neck that protruded tortoise-like from the circle of his tunic's stiff collar. There is nothing to be afraid of here, thought the marine. He placed a foot on to the body, now heavy and lifeless, and pulled his sword free. He looked again at the long sharp blade, stained pink at the end. It was solid and motionless in his grasp. He flicked his eyes closed for a moment. No images turned towards him out of the dark. No musket spat fire and gushing smoke towards him. He opened his eyes again, and was once more in the centre of the struggle, but now his mind was calm.

He ignored the various fights that swirled around him on deck and looked for the centre of French resistance. That was where his duty lay, he reminded himself. He must find the point where his disciplined body of marines would have the most effect, where they could crush the enemy's will to resist. The glitter of sunlight on braid drew his attention towards a crowd of men stood close to the ship's wheel. He could see several officers who were barking noisy instructions, surrounded by a solid group of defenders.

'Marines!' he yelled, his voice firm. 'Form a two deep line here.' The men rushed up and spread into a solid block of scarlet across the strip of deck he had indicated. He pointed with his sword towards the group by the wheel, and the double line of muskets rose in a smooth wave up to their owner's shoulders.

'Single volley! Fire!' he ordered. The muskets crashed out and several of the group by the wheel spun away, or collapsed to the ground.

'Marines will advance!' shouted Macpherson and the block of scarlet stamped their way across the quarterdeck. Friend and foe cleared aside before the hedge of bayonets as they bore down on the group by the wheel. When they were within a few feet, an officer pushed his way out from behind his men and stood in front of them.

'Marines halt!' yelled the Scot, and the remorseless approach stopped. The officer came to attention with his head bowed over the sword he held in front of him, the hilt towards Macpherson. As if a spell had been broken, French defenders dropped their weapons to the deck in a clattering wave that spread out across the quarterdeck and forward through the ship. Macpherson pointed the French captain towards the figure of Clay, who accepted the sword.

'Mr Preston, choose thirty men and take command of the prize, if you please,' he ordered. 'Mr Macpherson, you and your marines are to stay on board to help Mr Preston secure the prisoners. The rest of the men shall return to the *Titan*. We still have one more foe to defeat this day.'

'You pardon, sir, but I am not sure that we do,' replied Taylor. He pointed towards the north with the bloody sword he held in his hand. 'I believe the last enemy may have seen enough.'

Clay followed where his first lieutenant pointed. The final French ship was making for the open sea with every sail set. She was already several miles away, with the *Concord* trailing along in her wake in a half-hearted attempt to pursue her. Clay looked at the *Titan*'s rigging with its many cut lines and sails full of shot holes.

'Perhaps you are right,' he conceded. 'We could never

match such a profusion of sail with so many wounds aloft. Let us secure this prize and deal with the dead and wounded.' The older man held out his hand to his captain, and after a moment Clay took it.

'Congratulations on this victory, sir,' Taylor said. 'The men fought like tigers. If I had not witnessed how you have transformed this ship and crew, I would not have believed it possible. It has been a privilege to see.'

*****

'So what has it to say about us then, Rosie?' asked O'Malley. He pushed the copy of the newspaper across the beer-stained table. A reverent hush descended amongst the illiterate sailors grouped in the corner of the tap room of the Globe Inn. The Globe was one of Plymouth's less inviting taverns. The room was roofed with low, smoke-blackened beams that had already delivered a lusty blow to the head of the unwary Evans when he rose in haste to relieve himself earlier. The floor was spread with a thin covering of reeds that struggled to conceal the beaten earth it was made from, and only a trickle of daylight penetrated through the filthy glass of its few tiny windows. But the beer was cheap, the location convenient for most of the city's brothels, and the dimness of the light at least served to make the serving wenches that worked there appear a little more comely.

Rosso angled the paper towards the glimmer of light that came from the tallow candle at the end of the table, but could still make little out.

'It's a mite too dark in here for me to read it out proper,' he said, his words a little slurred. Trevan took his pipe out of his mouth at this and smiled at the others.

'You mean you've had one mug of knock-me-down too many to be seeing quite straight, Rosie,' he laughed. 'You Bristol boys is all the same. If you was back home with me, you wouldn't last beyond a quart of my uncle Amos's cider.'

'If you wasn't filling the room with more smoke than a first rate's broadside, maybe I could read it,' he grumbled. 'Here, Able. You've got the keenest eyes; see what you can make of it.'

'Are you after reading now, Able lad?' said O'Malley. 'Thank Christ. We can stop having to go cap in hand to Rosie every time we wants a fecking letter written.' Sedgwick took the newspaper and spread it out in front of him.

'You may need to help me with some of it, Rosie, but I will try,' he said.

'Came in to Plymouth to refit this Tuesday last — His Britannic Majesty's ships *Indefatigable* 44, *Concord* 36 and *Titan* 36...' He paused for a moment while the others growled as their ship was named. '... from Sir Edward Pellew's Inshore squadron, in company with four captured French National ships – the *Immortalite* 40, the *Bellone* 36, the *Loire* 40, and the *Embuscade* 38 most handsomely captured by Sir Edward's forces off the coast of Ireland whilst in the act of landing an invasion force.' He looked up from the paper and reached across for his drink. An awkward pause followed.

'Is that bleeding it?' said Evans. 'Nothing more about us than that?'

'I am afraid not, Sam,' said Sedgwick, turning the paper over and scanning the other articles.

'Most handsomely fecking captured,' spluttered O'Malley. 'How can that be all! Didn't we have two of them fecking ships strike to us? And all done with a butcher's bill of less than thirty killed and wounded for the *Titan*, and half of them will serve again. Handsomely captured, for feck sake!'

'Calm yourself, Sean,' said Rosso. 'We have only returned to port a few days ago. I am sure there will be plenty more in the papers once the commodore has made his proper report to the Admiralty.'

'What about us saving Ireland from being fecking overrun with Frogs?' continued O'Malley. 'According to Hart half the troops and most of the stores was still on board the ships we captured. Them soldiers as was landed surrendered easy to the militia. Meek as lambs, so they were. Is Ireland remaining part of the fecking country covered by your man's "handsomely captured" too then?'

'Hang on, Sean,' said Evans. 'I thought you bleeding hated the English?'

'And so I do,' replied the Irishman. 'Present company excused, mind. But I hate the Frogs a damn sight more.'

'Cheer up, my beauties,' said Trevan. 'Who gives a damn about what is in the papers? I've never been able to read them anyways. We all knows that whenever our battle gets covered proper, it'll still be the Grunters as will have all of the honour from the action, not us as did the fighting, like. But what we will be getting is a right nice fat bit of prize money from them frigates, and at least four month of shore leave while the old *Titan* has all that battle damaged fixed.'

'Too fecking right!' said O'Malley. 'Ahoy! More of that ale over here!' One of the serving women came over with a large foaming jug of beer, and bent forward to place it down on the centre of the table. The Irishman took the opportunity to smack her on the bottom. Instead of rounding on him in fury she held her position and favoured him with a smile. Several of her teeth were absent, and those that remained were large, stained and crooked.

'Like to meet me round the back, my lover?' she purred. 'We got a right snug alley that barely gets no rain at all.' Her face drew close to his now, her breath foul.

'Ah, sorry, my dear,' muttered O'Malley, avoiding her knowing stare. 'I was after thinking you was someone else.' His friends all roared with laughter, while the women drew herself back up, shrugged her shoulders and sashayed away across the room.

'Oh dear me,' sighed Rosso, wiping a tear from his eye, and patting O'Malley on the shoulder. 'She was older than my mother!'

'Well, it's so fecking dark in here,' he muttered, pulling at his drink.

'What will you be doing with your leave then, Adam?' asked Sedgwick, once they had all stopped laughing. 'Are you going back home?'

'That I shall, Able,' said the Cornishman. 'It will be right strange without the little nipper an' all, but I can't wait to see my Molly. Perhaps we may be blessed again, in time.'

'How about you, Sean?' asked Evans. 'You heading back

home too, if you can drag yourself away from the wenches here at the Globe, that is?' O'Malley waited for the chuckles to subside before replying.

'I will be going home, yes,' he said. 'It will be awful queer; I have been away that fecking long. But seeing those green hills on the Kerry coast has reminded me of what I have been a missing. Besides, you never know. I may have a colleen myself back there as has missed me too.' He exchanged glances with Trevan, who smiled in encouragement back at him.

'Don't you go and slap her arse as soon as you lay eyes on her, will you?' said Rosso, to further laughter.

'That does all sounds fine,' sighed Evans. 'At least you boys can go home. I thought of trying to go back to London, but it will still be too hot for me. Do you know that bastard Sexton knew who I was? He threatened to tell the traps where I was to be found. No, Rosie and I will find a nice boarding house here in Plymouth and lay low together.'

'That's right,' said Rosso sadly. 'There's no prospect of my returning to Bristol any time soon.'

'Why is that, Rosie?' asked Sedgwick. 'Is it what you started to tell me about? When we were reading that pamphlet on slavery?'

'That's right, Able,' he replied. 'I thieved from the shipping office I used to be clerk at, and then ran away to sea. Not my proudest moment. I never got a farthing from the crime. I did it to save my fool of a father from the debtor's prison, else my family would have been turned out into the street, but that don't signify any. If I should be caught I will still either swing for it or get transported to Botany Bay. No, it's best if Sam and me stay put here till the barky is fixed.'

'What about you, Able?' asked Trevan. 'How do you reckon on spending your leave?'

'He will be going off to one of them fecking universities,' said O'Malley. 'Now he's after reading newspapers.'

'Perhaps later, Sean,' smiled the coxswain. 'No, I shall follow the captain back home to his strange little village. He tells me we have much to arrange in these next few weeks.'

Chapter 18

Tying the Knot

The flagship of the Channel Fleet, the *Royal George,* had a crew that was a few score short of nine hundred men. They filled the main deck of the first rate in solid blocks of humanity, line upon line of them. The white and blue that they predominantly wore made a pleasing contrast with the red and white of the marine company that stood formed up at the back of the quarterdeck. At the front of that deck was a line of officers, both those who served aboard and visitors who had been invited to witness the event. Here were the captains who had sat as judges at the court marshal, together with a few others interested in the outcome. They looked down on the corridor of marine guards along which the condemned man would be led.

With the waywardness of an English summer the fine sunshine of the previous week had given way to low grey cloud and the threat of rain in the air. The waters of Plymouth harbour were green and choppy enough to make even the enormous hull of the three decker roll and snub against her mooring cables. The motion of the ship made the lines of seamen sway in time together like corn in a breeze. It also forced the party of boatswains' mates that stood gathered under the main yard arm to keep a firm grip on the rope that dropped down from above so that it would not swing across the deck. A chill breeze blew in from the open sea. It flapped at the officers' coat tails and made the large plain yellow flag stream and crack at the *Royal George*'s masthead.

The weather may have been dull for those on deck, but for Richard Sexton, who had spent the last two days deep in the bowels of the flagship, it was dazzling and bright. He paused as he emerged from the gloom under the quarterdeck and tried to raise one of his tattooed arms up to shield his eyes. The gesture was awkward and angular because his wrists were bound together. As the prisoner came into sight, a marine corporal who stood nearby at attention made a slight motion of his head, and the drummers began to beat out the broken rhythm of the Rogue's March.

Sexton was given time to look around him by the two burly marine sergeants that formed his escort as he was moved along the corridor of guards. His eyes grew more accustomed to the light as he advanced. He turned around to take it all in, the masses of rigging over his head, the lines of indifferent faces among the waiting crew, and the officers who stood at the quarterdeck rail.

'All these men here, just for me,' he said with satisfaction.

'What?' muttered one of the sergeants. 'Are you pissed, mate? How much choice do you think we had?'

'But you know who I am?' he said. 'You know I am a

famous mutineer?'

'If you says so,' said the other sergeant. 'Keep him moving, Tom.' But Sexton shrugged off his hand and pushed back against his guards. He was staring at one of the officers who stood a little apart from the others. The man was dressed in the uniform of a post captain, and there was something familiar about his florid face and dark, angry eyes.

'Sheridan?' he asked. His voice gained power as he became certain of what he saw. 'Sheridan, you murdering bastard! It's you they should hang, not me!'

'Come on, you,' hissed the first guard. 'Don't make a bleeding scene.' Sexton struggled against the remorseless pressure, looking back at his former captain and shouting abuse. Sheridan smiled and made a slight gesture with his right hand, as if to wave good bye. Then the other guard struck a swift concealed blow under the ribs that winded the prisoner for a moment, and they were able to hustle him forward until he stood in the centre of the party of men gathered around the dangling rope.

The drumming stopped and the Master at Arms stepped forward. He was a large, grim-faced man who spoke in a steady bellow.

'Richard Sexton, you have been found guilty by court martial of the murder of Lieutenant Edmund Morton in violation of article twenty-seven of the Articles of War, and have been sentenced in accordance with the custom of the sea. The said article states that all murders committed by any person in the fleet, shall be punished with death.'

The words flowed past Sexton unheard. His attention was

fixed on the fingers of one of the boatswain's mates as he worked in the space a few feet in front of his face. The man's hands were large but dextrous. They pulled and twisting as they knotted the end of the rope into a noose. Once it was complete he slid the knot up and down a few times to check that it slipped without catching. The noose grew and shrank in front of Sexton's face as he did so. The man pulled the ring back open to its widest size, and passed it to his companions who stood unseen behind the mutineer. The circle of rope swung out of sight behind him, and was then pulled down over his head. Someone lifted his pigtail clear, and then he felt the rough hemp prickle against the skin of his neck. The stone-hard knot was pulled tight behind his ear, forcing his head a little out of true.

Once the rope was in place the little party of seaman stepped back, and he found himself alone. He heard a cheer from over the side and looked that way. The water of the harbour was dotted with small boats. Fishing boats, rowing boats from Plymouth Hard and ships' launches, all packed with sightseers. He caught the eye of a small boy in a nearby boat and saw him mimic being hanged with his hands around his throat and his tongue protruding. The boy's father laughed at his son's antics and then returned his attention to watching the condemned man. Sexton felt the rope tightened around his neck and his feet swing free as they lifted up off the deck. He turned through the air, the pain unbearable, and at last he was afraid. He jerked his body against the fire in his throat, and the noose narrowed with each movement. He tried to pull some air into his lungs, but his chest seemed to be locked in place. Colours around him became brighter, as if the sun had broken through at last. In his ears he could hear a growing roar, overlaid with the colossal double bump of his heartbeat. Then the sound faltered and fell away and a curtain of dark red spread across his vision. As sight and hearing failed him he was left only with touch. All he could feel now was pain, deep in his chest and the iron grip about his throat.

*****

Captain Alexander Clay hooked the finger of one hand under the linen collar of his shirt and tried to ease the pressure a little. Of all the days on which to pull my neck cloth too tight, this would be the one, he cursed. He tugged a little more firmly and at last was rewarded with some relief. He removed his hand from his collar, and brushed smooth the front of his captain's full dress coat. Beside him stood his closest friend John Sutton, similarly constrained within his own smart uniform. Sutton saw the latest nervous movement and sort to reassure him.

'Not long now, Alex,' he murmured.

Clay drew his pocket watch out from his waistcoat pocket and glanced down at the dial. The hands had hardly moved since he last looked. Time must move this slowly for a man awaiting execution, he muttered to himself.

The two men were stood together beside the altar in the Ashton family chapel. It was a cold, forbidding space. When either man moved their shoes scraped on the bare flags beneath their feet and the sound echoed off the stone walls. The two candles that guttered on the altar did little to cut through the gloom. The only natural light came from narrow little windows high in the walls. All around them were the relics of long dead ancestors. Dark square plaques, their inscriptions thin and shaky with age, lined the base of the walls. Higher up, faded banners and scraps of dusty tapestry clung like weeds to the stone. Behind them a tomb had been cut into the wall. The lid was topped by a recumbent stone Ashton who's mailed feet crushed the small dog that was placed beneath his heels.

Just as forbidding were the faces on the bride's side of the aisle, as they surveyed the two young naval officers. Lady Mary Ashton sat in the front pew, beside a severe older sister. She looked on with her face struggling to conceal her doubts.

'How the deuce did you succeed in persuading Lady Ashton to accept you?' murmured the best man. 'If she looks this sour at a wedding, I pray God I never see her at a funeral.'

'I am most uncertain,' whispered Clay. 'When I first went to visit her in London she would barely see me at all. The most commitment I could obtain was that she would consult with some friends upon my proposal. I was as surprised as you when she agreed to give Miss Browning to me.'

'Perhaps she was a little dazzled to see the caterpillar of a lieutenant she had rejected before now metamorphosed into a post captain?' suggested his friend. The groom choked back a laugh, and the sound reverberated through the chill air. It caused the congregation to swing their gaze his way again. The Ashtons' faces were dark with disapproval. In contrast the small group of guests on his side of the aisle smiled encouragement. His sister Betsey's open grin was like a beam of sunshine among the shadows, forcing her brother to respond in kind.

From the back of the chapel came the scrape of wood on stone as the door clanged open, propelled by a footman in a powdered wig. He then stood to one side to allow the chaplain to enter. This was a short man, enormously fat, with a periwig perched on top of his large head. He waddled down the aisle, his surplice swishing from side to side in time with his laboured gait till he arrived at the altar and turned to face the congregation.

'Not long now, sir,' he said to Clay. The sound of his words echoed around the space and drew fresh frowns from the bride's side of the chapel. Unperturbed, the man drew out a large silk handkerchief, mopped his brow and then blew his nose. Sutton and Clay's faces locked themselves into those of persons determined not to laugh.

'I must say, you have chosen well,' continued the priest in a conversational tone. 'Damned fine filly, that one, if I say so myself, what? Ah! Here she comes now.'

Clay turned to face the door and froze at the sight of Lydia.

'Oh my word,' he heard himself murmur as their eyes met across the dark space. She was on the arm of an elderly uncle, another Ashton, but Clay only had eyes for her. She wore a long dress of the palest ice blue silk over which was laid a net of silver lace, thin as gossamer, that caught what little light was in the chapel and shimmered as she moved. The dress was gathered to a high waist by a belt of pearls that echoed the string that were clasped around her slender white neck. Apart from a few careless locks that hung down, her rich dark hair was piled up on top of her head, making her ears and face seem small and vulnerable in comparison. Weaved into her hair was a simple crown of white and pale blue flowers, their colours echoing her ice blue eyes.

'You look utterly lovely,' he breathed as her uncle handed her across to him. She smiled up into his grey eyes, her face radiant with joy, and the chapel with its gloomy congregation and droning priest seemed to fade away, leaving the two of them, him in his dark blue broadcloth, she apparently wrapped in starlight. At that moment it was only they that mattered, lost in the pleasure of each other. It had been a long journey, but they were together at last.

The End

Note from the Author

Historical fiction is a blend of truth and the made up, and this is the case with On the Lee Shore. For readers who would like to understand where that boundary runs, the ships *Rush* and *Titan* are fictitious, as are the characters that make up their crews. I have tried my best to ensure that my descriptions of those vessels and the lives of their sailors are as close to actual ships and practices of the time as possible. Where I have failed to achieve this, any errors are my own.

The other ships mentioned in the book, such as those of the Inshore Squadron, the *Royal George* and their French opponents are historically accurate, as are characters such as Sir Edward Pellew, Lord Bridport and Sir Charles Middleton. The adventures of the *Titan* off the coast of Brittany is my own creation, although it is representative of the sort of activities that Royal Navy ships would have carried out among the extreme navigational hazards of that treacherous lee shore. There was no French attempt at landing troops in Ireland in the manner, or location I have described in my novel, but there were repeated attempts by the French to do so, most notably at Bantry Bay in 1796 with a force of 15,000 soldiers under General Lazare Hoche.

The mutiny portrayed on board the *Titan* is fictitious. That of the Channel Fleet did take place, as did the subsequent mutiny of Admiral Duncan's North Sea fleet based at the Nore. As shown in my book, no word of these extraordinary events reached Paris during the critical weeks before the mutiny of the Channel Fleet was resolved.

About The Author

Philip K. Allan

Philip K. Allan comes from Watford in the United Kingdom. He still lives in Hertfordshire with his wife and his two teenage daughters. He has spent most of his working life to date as a senior manager in the motor industry. It was only in the last few years that he has given that up to concentrate on his novels full time.

He has a good knowledge of the ships of the 18th century navy, having studied them as part of his history degree at London University, which awoke a lifelong passion for the period. He is a member of the Society for Nautical Research and a keen sailor. He believes the period has unrivalled potential for a writer, stretching from the age of piracy via the voyages of Cook to the battles and campaigns of Nelson.

From a creative point of view he finds it offers him a wonderful platform for his work. On the one hand there is the strange, claustrophobic wooden world of the period's ships; and on the other hand there is the boundless freedom to move those ships around the globe wherever the narrative takes them. All these possibilities are fully exploited in the Alexander Clay series of novels.

His inspiration for the series was to build on the works of novelists like C.S. Forester and in particular Patrick O'Brian. His prose is heavily influenced by O'Brian's immersive style. He too uses meticulously researched period language and authentic nautical detail to draw the reader into a different world. But the Alexander Clay books also bring something fresh to the genre, with a cast of fully formed lower deck characters with their own back histories and plot lines in addition to the officers. Think *Downton Abbey* on a ship, with the lower deck as the below stairs servants.

If You Enjoyed This Book Visit

PENMORE PRESS

www.penmorepress.com

All Penmore Press books are available directly through our website, amazon.com, Barnes and Noble and Nook, Sony Reader, Apple iTunes, Kobo books and via leading bookshops across the United States, Canada, the UK, Australia and Europe.

The Captain's Nephew

by

Philip K.Allan

After a century of war, revolutions, and Imperial conquests, 1790s Europe is still embroiled in a battle for control of the sea and colonies. Tall ships navigate familiar and foreign waters, and ambitious young men without rank or status seek their futures in Naval commands. First Lieutenant Alexander Clay of HMS Agrius is self-made, clever, and ready for the new age. But the old world, dominated by patronage, retains a tight hold on advancement. Though Clay has proven himself many times over, Captain Percy Follett is determined to promote his own nephew.

Before Clay finds a way to receive due credit for his exploits, he'll first need to survive them. Ill-conceived expeditions ashore, hunts for privateers in treacherous fog, and a desperate chase across the Atlantic are only some of the challenges he faces. He must endeavor to bring his ship and crew through a series of adventures stretching from the bleak coast of Flanders to the warm waters of the Caribbean. Only then might high society recognize his achievements —and allow him to ask for the hand of Lydia Browning, the woman who loves him regardless of his station.

A Sloop of War

by

Philip K.Allan

This second novel in the series of Lieutenant Alexander Clay novels takes us to the island of Barbados, where the temperature of the politics, prejudices and amorous ambitions within society are only matched by the sweltering heat of the climate. After limping into the harbor of Barbados with his crippled frigate *Agrius* and accompanied by his French prize, Clay meets with Admiral Caldwell, the Commander in Chief of the island. The admiral is impressed enough by Clay's engagement with the French man of war to give him his own command.

The *Rush* is sent first to blockade the French island of St Lucia, then to support a landing by British troops in an attempt to take the island from the French garrison. The crew and officers of the *Rush* are repeatedly threatened along the way by a singular Spanish ship, in a contest that can only end with destruction or capture. And all this time, hanging over Clay is an accusation of murder leveled against him by the nephew of his previous captain.

Philip K Allan has all the ingredients here for a gripping tale of danger, heroism, greed, and sea battles, in a story that is well researched and full of excitement from beginning to end.

BREWER'S REVENGE

BY

JAMES KEFFER

Admiral Horatio Hornblower has given Commander William Brewer captaincy of the captured pirate sloop *El Dorado.* Now under sail as the HMS *Revenge,* its new name suits Brewer's frame of mind perfectly. He lost many of his best men in the engagement that seized the ship, and his new orders are to hunt down the pirates who have been ravaging the trade routes of the Caribbean sea.

But Brewer will face more than one challenge before he can confront the pirate known as El Diabolito. His best friend and ship's surgeon, Dr. Spinelli, is taking dangerous solace in alcohol as he wrestles with demons of his own. The new purser, Mr. Allen, may need a lesson in honest accounting. Worst of all, Hornblower has requested that Brewer take on a young ne'er-do-well, Noah Simmons, to remove him from a recent scandal at home. At twenty-three, Simmons is old to be a junior midshipman, and as a wealthy man's son he is unaccustomed to working, taking orders, or suffering privations.

William Brewer will need to muster all his resources to ready his crew for their confrontation with the Caribbean's most notorious pirate. In the process, he'll discover the true price of command.

Fortune's Whelp
by
Benerson Little

Privateer, Swordsman, and Rake:

Set in the 17th century during the heyday of privateering and the decline of buccaneering, *Fortune's Whelp* is a brash, swords-out sea-going adventure. Scotsman Edward MacNaughton, a former privateer captain, twice accused and acquitted of piracy and currently seeking a commission, is ensnared in the intrigue associated with the attempt to assassinate King William III in 1696. Who plots to kill the king, who will rise in rebellion—and which of three women in his life, the dangerous smuggler, the wealthy widow with a dark past, or the former lover seeking independence—might kill to further political ends? Variously wooing and defying Fortune, Captain MacNaughton approaches life in the same way he wields a sword or commands a fighting ship: with the heart of a lion and the craft of a fox.

Midshipman Graham and the Battle of Abukir

by

James Boschert

It is midsummer of 1799 and the British Navy in the Mediterranean Theater of operations. Napoleon has brought the best soldiers and scientists from France to claim Egypt and replace the Turkish empire with one of his own making, but the debacle at Acre has caused the brilliant general to retreat to Cairo.

Commodore Sir Sidney Smith and the Turkish army land at the strategically critical fortress of Abukir, on the northern coast of Egypt. Here Smith plans to further the reversal of Napoleon's fortunes. Unfortunately, the Turks badly underestimate the speed, strength, and resolve of the French Army, and the ensuing battle becomes one of the worst defeats in Arab history.

Young Midshipman Duncan Graham is anxious to get ahead in the British Navy, but has many hurdles to overcome. Without any familial privileges to smooth his way, he can only advance through merit. The fires of war prove his mettle, but during an expedition to obtain desperately needed fresh water – and an illegal duel – a French patrol drives off the boats, and Graham is left stranded on shore. It now becomes a question of evasion and survival with the help of a British spy. Graham has to become very adaptable in order to avoid detection by the French police, and he must help the spy facilitate a daring escape by sea in order to get back to the British squadron.

"Midshipman Graham and The Battle of Abukir is both a rousing Napoleonic naval yarn and a convincing coming of age story. The battle scenes are riveting and powerful, the exotic Egyptian locales colorfully rendered." – John Danielski, author of *Capital's Punishment*

Milton Keynes UK
Ingram Content Group UK Ltd.
UKHW011415200624
444507UK00025B/113